ALL SHE EVER
WANTED

ALL SHE EVER WANTED

SARAH LIMARDO

ELEVEN ARBORS
PRESS

For the lovesick girls who never chased boys,
broke their own hearts, and bought too many books.

1

A Most Unwelcome Imagination

London, 1700

Aurelia Danby was born to be ridiculous.

It was largely due to her parents, the Duke and Duchess of Danby, who were notable fools among the aristocracy. The duke was a prince with no meaningful way to the throne, and his wife was as spoiled and lovely as he. They lived for parties and pretty things and wanted for nothing but sensibility, self-awareness, and maturity.

Naturally, with a life so full of decadence and friends who encouraged their worst faults and fantasies, the responsibility of raising a child was spectacularly lost on them.

In Aurelia's first few minutes of life, her mother announced to those attending her, "She's as lovely a babe as any other." The midwives cooed as though it were the most flattering thing they'd ever heard a mother say. Then the duchess handed the baby off and attended a party. It was the last time she ever held her daughter, but Aurelia didn't mind because her wet nurse was much warmer in both disposition and temperature.

It should be noted that fault for Aurelia's foolishness might be shared with the nursemaids the Danbys paid to keep their daughter happy, but the staff only did their best. They sang songs and offered hugs, minded her through her first steps, and taught her letters and

1

numbers as well as how to curtsy and say *thank you*. And they filled her head with love stories and fairy tales to show her that lovely things could happen to girls with no parents.

Aurelia quickly learned to love the extensive library that took up an entire wall of her nursery. Thick tomes with hand-painted illustrations provided her endless tales of lords and ladies and beautiful fairy princesses, and she clung to their stories as surely as she did her favorite toys.

If zealots and monks had scripture and prayer, Aurelia lived for games and legends. And the staff indulged her every whim because they loved and pitied her.

Despite her pretty, unproblematic life, her parents eventually decided having a child was no longer in vogue. So upon Aurelia's seventh birthday, the duke and duchess shipped her off to live with her great aunt, Lady Clara Wedderburn—a wealthy old grouch with no children of her own.

Lady Wedderburn was a large woman who wore dresses that might have suited her decades earlier, but now only gave the impression that she lived under a mound of moldy gray chiffon. It didn't matter, however, as she had no one she cared to impress. She'd inherited money instead of marrying into it and lived reclusively in a country manor dripping with vines and shadows and occupied by servants who ambled rather than rushed.

During her first days on the estate, Aurelia comforted herself with stories that proved lovely things could also happen to girls who lived with old hags. Each night, she laid awake long after the household went to bed, memorizing pictures of heroes and monsters, and she rose early every morning to do exactly the same. She only needed her books to be happy, and her only concern was that she may eventually require more.

Aunt Clara didn't mind Aurelia as long as she stayed quiet and out of the way. Aurelia didn't mind Aunt Clara either, so long as she wasn't squawking about the sorts of things old ladies squawked about—like fraying hems and tired servants.

Aurelia often escaped to the garden where her aunt would not follow, since the old woman was very much like a vampire in that she enjoyed shadows and hissed at the sun. There among trees and thorns and leafy bushes, Aurelia was an explorer seeking adventure or a soldier patrolling the plants, keeping the budding flowers safe from thieves and bandits who feared her tenacity and wit. She cracked trolls' riddles and sent them scrambling into garden sheds and overturned buckets. Though the staff never engaged with Aurelia's daydreams, she frequently caught the gardeners peeking at her over the hedges with kind smiles, and she would grin back despite her missing teeth testifying to her passing childhood.

When she tired of the gardens, she ventured into the forest behind the house. It quickly became her favorite place where she often fled with one of her fairytale books tucked under her arm. Beyond the trees was a lake, which Aurelia found exceptionally lovely on sunny days. She liked to sit on the seawall and wait for mermaids to appear from the muddy depths. Of course, she never saw any, but she held out hope that one day they would come say hello and offer her a glimmering tail so she could follow them to treasure chests and shipwrecks.

She was both damsel and knight—quiet or boisterous when it suited her—and she was always careful of her hem so Aunt Clara could have nothing to shame her for.

But as per usual in England, rain often overtook the estate and forced Aurelia inside. She didn't mind the rain, but everyone claimed she'd catch her death were she to venture into it. This inspired another fun game—chasing Death through the house so she might convince him to vanquish her enemies. And when her giggling became too much for her aunt, Aurelia found as much satisfaction returning to her books and plotting her next adventure.

As fall came, and then winter, Aurelia spent cold, dreary days wandering the empty halls. She lost herself in new, unfamiliar parts of the house, where she'd become a beautiful damsel running from invisible minotaurs or escaping a secret lair, inspired by whatever tale she'd fed her imagination the night before. She'd scamper through winding corridors to her room, her spine tingling as she hunkered in the safety of the colorless bedding and ugly furniture designed for tastes much older and finer than her own.

When she knew the house too well to get lost, she became a princess in a beautiful castle, dancing through invisible balls with imaginary knights and princes who were enraptured by her beauty. Meanwhile, books lay strewn about her room in careless, shifting piles she organized by whichever had her favorite pictures.

But gloomy weather and indifferent staff had tremendous power to occasionally dispirit a girl. Despite her lovely pictures and imaginary friends and foes, Aurelia began to acquaint herself with loneliness. On days like these—and there were many—she drifted down long halls as the only ghost in Aunt Clara's home, aching for someone to haunt.

As the years passed and her age crept above ten years old, the piles of books in her room shifted to prioritize stories of escape, and her dreaming followed suit. Suddenly, Aurelia was a fugitive, escaping through the forest behind the house to stand on the lake shore, looking for the ship on which her prince would reside, coming to take her away to new worlds full of new people and adventures.

Yearning made Aurelia reckless. Aunt Clara grew shorter in patience and was ready with harsh exclamations of *what nonsense* or *ridiculous child* every time she caught her niece chasing her imagination with her blonde hair coming undone from the fine up-dos a maid spent half an hour perfecting each day. And when Aurelia was forced into stillness by Aunt Clara's orders, she slipped her nose into a book to fill her head with more impossible things.

But devastation proved to come for rich, pretty girls as surely as it did for those who were not so fortunate as Aurelia. When she turned twelve, her books disappeared. They vanished from her room and the library as though they'd never existed.

Aurelia approached her aunt, weeping like it was her only salvation, but Aunt Clara simply declared from behind a newspaper, "Don't be ridiculous, dear. The only appropriate books for a young woman are history, philosophy, and the Bible." She flipped the paper down to study Aurelia's streaky red face and swollen gray eyes. "It's time to abandon silly pursuits. You'll be a proper young woman with the best education money can buy, and one day you'll do your family proud and marry a fine, lofty man."

Aurelia had thrown herself to the floor, wailing and flailing, her heart torn wide open as her entire world was ripped away.

After that, her hems lowered and her clothes changed to new styles fit for a young woman. Aurelia rarely ventured outside due to the endless parade of tutors and instructors for everything from math and science—which she hated—to music and dance, which she did like, while her precious tales were hidden in a trunk in a drafty attic she couldn't get into, no matter how many knives she broke in the lock.

Nevertheless, her stories lingered in the back of her mind, begging for her attention so fiercely that her toes itched in her new shoes. So desperate she became for something interesting to think about that she took to stealing the daily newspaper after Aunt Clara skimmed the headlines at breakfast and *tsk*ed at *how far England has fallen* for its politics, celebrities, fashions, and whatever else reminded her of her advancing age.

But for all the things Aunt Clara hated, Aurelia found wonder and intrigue in the latest scandals. Here she found her first silver lining, for had her books not been taken, she might never have discovered the pirates.

The papers spoke of terrible men who robbed and pillaged and terrorized on land and at sea. The crown didn't mind so much when the streets ran with pilfered Spanish gold from the Americas, but they loathed piracy in their own port cities and executed the perpetrators in grand, graphic events that made Aurelia's stomach turn.

So fascinating were they that she sought to know more about the kind of life that deserved such fierce ends. She read of all the crews dominating the Atlantic, but no one was more famous or fearsome than the dreaded Captain Robert Copson and his ship, the *Fortuna Royale*, which was said to carry at least forty cannons. Aurelia wasn't sure if forty cannons was an incredible number of guns, but the papers spoke like it was, so she responded in kind with awe.

Captain Copson was an enigma who made as much money for the papers as he did by robbing ships. He was said to have sailed for nearly ninety years, but those who reported meeting him in the Caribbean or West Indies said he was young and handsome. And those who claimed to have sailed with him said he'd drunk from the Fountain of Youth and was therefore immortal. Nestled among reports of witches and sea monsters, the story didn't seem far-fetched.

He ruled the seas, robbing the Spanish, French, and English alike, and sailing wherever and taking whatever suited him. He killed entire crews for their ships and sailed with a fleet of loyal men, striking fear into all—pirates, sailors, civilians, kings; it didn't seem to matter so long as they made him rich.

Aurelia wasn't sensible enough to be disgusted or horrified. In fact, she loved the articles so much that she'd carefully clip each story and hide them in the pages of a philosophy book she hid beneath her mattress.

All the while, she pretended to read things Aunt Clara might find more palatable, but kings and politicians never did anything so interesting as raiding ships and drinking from immortal waters, and while she skimmed the pages, she only saw colorful skies, pirate ships, and piles of gold.

Despite every attempt to correct her, Aurelia Danby was ridiculous, and everyone told her so—from her aunt to the staff to her tutors.

But if people like Captain Copson existed, she saw no good reason to stop.

2

The Lady in the Lake

By the time two years had passed, Aurelia found a number of clever ways to thwart her strict schedule. Oftentimes, she had only minutes to flee to the gardens or hide in the library where she hunted for any piece of fiction Aunt Clara might've overlooked.

On very rare occasions, she had hours to herself.

Since Aunt Clara was still a respected member of society, her summers were marked by parties, soirees, and luncheons that called her to London or other wealthy estates. Being only fourteen, Aurelia was still too young to go, so after her aunt left one spring afternoon for some monstrous affair in town, she slipped out of the house and sprinted for the forest.

She picked her way through trees and dappled sunlight until her favorite tree loomed ahead, its soaring branches easy to climb. They jutted precariously over the lake, daring her to be dangerous and free. She lifted her skirts to scramble up its trunk until she reached the best branch for sitting, and there she perched, swinging her slippered feet over the water as the sun warmed her cheeks.

Here in her tree, she could sit for a very long time and recall the most beautiful things she'd ever heard and seen—and imagine those she hadn't.

It had been two years since she last read a fairy tale or saw a picture of a handsome prince, but she clung to what she remembered, even as the memories began to wear thin. And every day, she thought of her books and wished she could once again live in their pages where she'd be surrounded with familiar friends.

For now, she sated her appetite with memories of the stories she'd loved—and reading about the villainous Captain Copson in the papers.

She closed her eyes, dreaming of a day when she might not only have her stories, but the chance to live them. Aunt Clara and her family expected her to marry, so she'd find a prince or an adventurer, or at the very least a man who sold books. If none were available, she supposed she would be a knight or a witch, or perhaps she might travel to Ireland to find the fairies, as she understood they were fond of foolish girls—

Laughter pealed over the water, clear as church bells. Aurelia opened her eyes and leaned over the branch to peer through the leaves.

Three young men drifted across the water in a small boat painted blue and silver—the colors of the Kingswood family who lived down the lane from Aunt Clara.

Though Aurelia didn't know much about many of her neighbors, Aunt Clara could talk at length about the Kingswoods and how noble and wealthy they were, and that Aurelia should be so lucky to marry one of their three sons—as though Aunt Clara knew anything about marriage.

Her high praise was surprising because Aunt Clara didn't like anybody and was very proud of it. But the Kingswoods were the one exception, such was her fondness for the earl and countess.

Of course, Aurelia had never seen them and supposed Aunt Clara might've just as easily had a pleasant dream about the neighbors and thought it real. This had once happened to Aurelia, and she'd pitched herself off a low garden wall, fancying a notion she could fly.

Nevertheless, Aurelia was curious about the family and turned her ear toward the conversation.

"...and then we ran into a Spanish merchant who thought they'd outrun us." The boy who spoke was too far away to see anything but his black hair and fine clothes, but his voice was smooth and rich. "But we caught them near Tortuga. Wouldn't you believe they were so stocked with gold that we had to take the whole ship just to sail it all back."

"So the reports are true?" one of the others asked. He had lighter features, as did the one next to him. "Copson's got a new ship."

Aurelia gaped, but she snapped her mouth shut as Aunt Clara's voice in her head swore the expression would tempt the devil to make her face eternally ugly. But surely the boy couldn't be talking about *the* Captain Copson. She scooted farther onto the limb and strained to hear against the water lapping against the seawall.

"Your father hasn't had two ships in nearly five years," said the third boy. "He must be elated."

Her jaw fell again, and this time she left it. No, surely it couldn't be Copson. Surely that couldn't be the pirate captain's *son* rowing across the lake in the Kingswood's boat.

"He doesn't show it," the first one said with a hearty laugh. "The crew from the ship we took all swore their allegiance to him so long as he wouldn't kill them. Their captain tried to swear too, but Father shot him in the head and threw him overboard."

The other two listened with awe—but neither was more awed than Aurelia.

"I captained the new ship to Nassau," the black-haired boy went on. "He said it was my first test, and I got it into port before he could bring in the *Fortuna*."

The *Fortuna Royale*. Aurelia leaned forward, so engrossed that she didn't hear the wood cracking beneath her.

"He's letting me name the ship," he said. "He told me to decide before we leave again—"

Crrrack!

Aurelia screamed as the branch gave way and dumped her into the water. Its cold, murky darkness closed over her head, and she sank.

The lake was much deeper than she realized, and as she tumbled through its frigid depths, she lost all sense of where the surface was in relation to her head. She flailed her arms, lungs burning as her dress dragged her down. Her fingers sought purchase on anything and found only gloomy nothingness.

If ever there was a mermaid in these waters, it would have been the perfect time to make itself known. Aurelia could do without the treasure and would trade almost anything in that moment for a breath of precious air. Muddy water burned her eyes, and she kicked uselessly, fighting the dress and the cold weight of death.

She would die here, and Aunt Clara would be rather vexed about it.

Then hands gripped her waist. An arm locked around her, and the lake tugged at her with a greedy current as she was pulled back to the surface. Her face broke into the open air, and she gasped and sputtered as sunlight touched her chilled skin.

"I've got you," her savior said, his deep voice smooth against her ragged coughing. "You're okay, I've got you."

He kept repeating it as he swam her along the seawall toward the bank. When she finally felt mud and sand beneath her feet, she stood and walked herself to the trees hiding them from the rest of her aunt's estate. His hand remained gently clutched around her elbow, even as sand turned to grass and Aurelia was no longer coughing.

It was the boy who'd told the story in the boat, and now that she was closer, she saw that he looked to be around nineteen years old with sharp, chiseled features drawn in concern. His dark shirt clung to his lean frame and the contours of his muscular arms, and he was tall—she had to look up to find his deep blue eyes fixed on her from beneath

11

long strands of sopping, black hair.

Mercy, she thought, wishing her eyes were such a striking color instead of their dull, unimpressive gray—and they were *owlish*, as one tutor had told her rather unkindly.

She tried to look away, to hide her flaws in front of the most beautiful person she'd ever seen, but quickly realized it would do no good. Her dress sagged around her small, shivering frame, and her braid had come undone, leaving her long, pale hair plastered to her cheeks and neck.

He bent to meet her gaze. "Are you alright?"

"Yes, sir," she said, wiping her hair away from her face.

Sunlight caught the tiny drops clinging to his lashes. "What in God's name were you doing in that tree? You could've killed yourself."

She hesitated. She didn't want to tell this boy, but his piercing gaze, those striking eyes, demanded the truth. And despite how often she'd pretended to be a lying, stealing thief, the truth was exactly what came out, because she didn't know how to lie to heroes. "I was only having fun, but then I heard you talking—and the branch—I've climbed the tree before and been fine."

She stumbled through her words as they all fought to be known by him. She wanted to tell him about the books in the attic and the lessons and newspapers—everything that would make him realize she had a perfectly reasonable excuse to eavesdrop. Perhaps then his stare would not make her feel so intimidated.

His gaze dropped to her dress before returning to her face. Then he turned and surveyed the woods. "Do you live here?"

"With my aunt."

"Lady Wedderburn?" He looked at her. "That old woman is your aunt?"

She nodded solemnly. And then, against her will, she sniffled and began to cry. "Oh please don't tell her I was in the tree! She'll ruin me for the rest of my days if she knows what I've done."

To her shock, he smirked. "She'd ruin anyone solely for her own entertainment. She's a clever devil."

Aurelia gasped. "I—Aunt Clara—" She shut her mouth, her tears suddenly forgotten. It had never occurred to her that Aunt Clara might be the devil, and after a moment, she decided it could not be possible if only for how often Aunt Clara crossed herself.

She was about to tell him this, but then one of his companions called out, "Everything alright?"

The other boys had rowed closer and lingered off the shore where she could see their features held some slight resemblance to the boy in front of her. She thought, fleetingly, that they must be cousins.

"Take the boat back," the black-haired boy said. "I'm taking her home." He looked at Aurelia. "And we'll come up with a grand story to tell old Lady Wedderburn." He offered his arm and led her into the trees.

This boy is a pirate, she thought as she stole glances at him out of the corner of her eye. She liked the way his hair curled around his ears and the mischievous spark in his eyes.

He would make a very fine storybook prince, and as soon as she realized this, she pulled her gaze away. But the damage was already done—his face would most certainly be one she would picture as her knight in shining armor. Not because she necessarily wanted him to be, but she couldn't imagine how there could be a finer face in all the world, especially when she had little else to fill the void left by her stolen books.

And the stories he could tell... Her heart did something strange in her chest. He had been places and done things—more than she could imagine.

"My name is William Kingswood," he said. "I live across the lake."

"I know," she replied dumbly. She could hear Aunt Clara's declarations about what fine gentlemen the Kingswood boys were—especially William, the eldest son who would one day be the earl.

He was also a Copson, which was far more interesting than grand titles and estates. Could she ask questions? What should she ask him first? All the rules for conversation fled her mind, leaving her only with the urge to beg him to tell her *everything*.

He chuckled. "Since there's no one to introduce us, may I ask your name?"

Color rose to her cheeks. "Aurelia Danby."

"Danby? Like the Duke and Duchess of Danby?" His brow furrowed. "I didn't know they had a child."

Though she knew her parents didn't find her enough of a fashionable accessory to liven their house, she was surprised they'd erased her existence altogether. Aunt Clara would say it was merely the way of high society, and Aurelia would understand one day when was rich and fashionable enough to forget her own child.

Remembering this, she drew herself to her full height. She was a Danby and should act like the princess she almost was. "Aunt Clara is overseeing my education until I'm old enough to return home."

"And then what?"

"I...I'm not sure. Marriage, probably, though I haven't decided." A new thought occurred to her, and she positively could not help but voice it. "Is your father really the immortal Captain Copson?"

William stopped and faced her, his voice coming low and quick. "What exactly did you hear from that tree?"

Her cheeks grew warm, and she turned her face away. "I didn't hear the details," she lied. But when she stole another glance at him out of the corner of her eye, he watched her with pointed skepticism, so she added, "I only heard he got a new ship that you captained. And that you've been on the *Fortuna Royale*."

She spotted the garden beyond the trees with its bushes trimmed into green spires and boxes. Gardeners usually bustled along the paths, analyzing every leaf and twig to avoid the nearly imperceptible flaws Aunt Clara's beady eyes would find anyway. But right now, the area was abandoned, and no one would hear Aurelia scream if this boy's charm turned out to more villainous than heroic.

"If you tell anyone," he said, his voice low and cutting, "I will know it, and so will the *immortal* captain." The edge of his mouth twitched, but his expression remained schooled. "And I'm sure you already know what he does to people who cross him. My father is Earl Kingswood, and that is all."

Despite having never stood at odds with a beautiful boy, she had practiced how to deal with enemies. She squared her shoulders and looked him in the eye, knowing very well it would be dangerous to do so. But she could also swing a stick, and there were plenty littering the ground around them.

"What will I get in return for my silence?" she asked.

He lifted an eyebrow. "Pardon?"

"I want something from you if I keep your secret."

"You keep my secret, and I won't tell your aunt what you were doing," he said, his words clipped. "That's fair."

She planted her hands on her hips with all the bravado she could muster. "Not fair. Your secret is much bigger than mine and therefore comes with a higher price. Aunt Clara may ruin me, but it's nothing compared to what might happen to you."

She was proud as she said it, because she knew it was true. There were a hundred examples of Copson's cruelty in the papers, from articles she'd clipped and saved. Aunt Clara would be hellish, yes, but surely nothing compared to the pirate.

His eyes narrowed. "What do you want?"

"Stories," she said without hesitation. "You're a pirate, and I want to know everything about it." She lifted her chin. "Like what you do

15

and the places you see. I want to know how a boat works and why it doesn't sink. I want to know how it moves with the wind and how you board other ships. And I'd like to hear about the Caribbean and North Africa."

His brows pulled together.

"And," she went on, made nervous by his silence, "I'd like a Spanish coin from the Americas. A gold one. A piece of actual pirate treasure."

He rolled his lips between his teeth and folded his arms. "Anything else?"

She shook her head.

William's gaze dropped. She'd lost her slippers, but she hid her bare toes under her dripping skirt. Finally, he sighed and peered toward the house, ducking to see more of the manor from under the crown of leaves. "What a drab little life Lady Wedderburn must force on you." He looked at her. "Fine. I'll do it, but you mustn't tell anyone what you heard today. Ever." He leaned closer, his voice turning cold. "Because I swear, Lady Danby, if you breathe a word of this to anyone, you'll have hell to pay."

She'd never been threatened before today, and it made her feel like the hero now. Of course, she had no plans to tell his family's secret, though it thrilled her to know it anyway. And to make such a fabulous bargain—she really was getting the better end of the deal. She'd have stories again, and not just from a newspaper, but from an actual pirate. "I swear I won't tell a soul."

He glanced at the house again, and something seemed to dawn on him. "You don't have a soul to tell, do you?"

"I have plenty," she countered, thinking of her imaginary friends so it wasn't technically a lie.

He studied her for a long moment, then smirked. "If you say so."

He didn't offer his arm again as they started for the gardens. They walked in silence, and when they reached the path leading to the house, he stopped and nodded at the hem of her dress. "You lost your shoes."

Aurelia looked down. "Yes, in the lake."

"Is there another way to the front door, or would you prefer to walk through the gravel?"

The garden paths were strewn with tiny white rocks with sharp edges that would surely mortify her soles. She frowned at them.

"You're turning blue," he said placidly. "I'll carry you if this is the fastest way."

Cold as she was, she assumed her face turned red enough to notice. Standing next to a handsome villain was exciting, but being carried in his arms like a distressed damsel was entirely romantic. She shouldn't want it, of course, because she didn't think Aunt Clara would find it proper...but he had a point about the rocks.

So it was *purely* for the sake of avoiding the gravel that she nodded.

Without another word, he swept her into his arms and started forward. He was warm and solid, and Aurelia prayed he wouldn't feel her heart thundering. She tried not to stare at the way his hair fell into his face, or the dark rings around his magnificently blue irises. But she dreaded missing the opportunity more than she worried about him catching her staring.

They passed the massive fountain in the middle of the garden that filled a dark green pool full of golden fish and lily pads. Still, there were no gardeners, which she supposed might actually be a good thing, since the staff were often worse gossips than Aunt Clara's sneering old lady companions who complained about London and *debutantes these days*.

"Do you read outside?" he asked as they moved around the side of the house. Once they were past the rocks, he set her on her feet. She tiptoed beside him through the grass, shivering again, which was made worse when she saw the carriage in front of the house. Due to some terrible luck, Aunt Clara had returned home early.

"Sometimes," she replied through chattering teeth as he directed their steps around stray twigs to spare her bare feet. "But they took all my books, so now I have only history or philosophy."

"Why'd they take your books?"

She wrinkled her nose. "Propriety."

"Dreadful." He glanced back at the fountain. "I'll tell her you were reading something boring in the garden, and everything else shall be my fault."

She looked up at him, but he stared ahead now. "Will she believe that? She believes me troublesome as it is."

"Are you troublesome?"

"I don't think I am."

"Silly of me to ask," he said with a roll of his eyes. "You're the one who fell out of a tree."

Panic gripped her. "Oh please don't tell—"

"I said I wouldn't," he muttered. "I'm rather troublesome myself and wouldn't dare discourage you from it." As they approached the front door, his impish grin appeared. "And I believe she thinks highly of my family and won't suspect the lie."

A family of pirates, she thought with a thrill, which only compounded at thought of hearing more about their life at sea.

William lifted the heavy brass knocker and let it drop. The crash summoned a footman whose eyes bugged at the sight of his mistress's ward soaking wet, and he beckoned them both inside. He left them in the foyer while he fetched Aunt Clara.

William's lip curled as he took in the décor and the grand staircase that curved along one wall. "I haven't been here in a decade... Somehow it's worse than I remember."

Aurelia giggled. If there had been color in any of the paintings or accents at some point, they'd been leeched of all character and personality, leaving the home in drab shades of gray and beige that made her think of caves, purgatory, and the political sections of newspapers.

They heard Aunt Clara before she appeared. She bustled through the halls, chirping and whining, "You said she *what*? With *whom*?" She turned the corner and trundled into the foyer with a tiny pair of glasses perched on her nose.

"What is the meaning of this?" she demanded in her too-airy voice that was at odds with her hulking figure. "Lord Kingswood, whatever she pulled you into—"

"The fault was entirely my own," he said with a dazzling smile that made Aurelia's heart lurch to her throat. "You see, I was spending my afternoon on the lake and fell asleep in my boat. Upon waking, I was disoriented, and the boat tipped and sank off your shore. I came to the house for assistance and found poor Lady Danby reading her philosophy by the fountain. I startled her so badly she fell in."

He lied with such impressive, emphatic confidence that Aurelia nearly believed it herself. But then Aunt Clara turned her frosty attention to her.

"Which philosopher?" Aunt Clara demanded.

"Francis Bacon," William answered with a note of pride. "I must say I was impressed by all she had to say about it, though unfortunately the book is lost to the fountain. Nevertheless, I apologize for disrupting your day. I do hope it's alright that I escorted Lady Danby to the door. My father would disown me were he to hear I left a lady in a fountain."

Aunt Clara released a heavy sigh. "It's fine, I suppose. I'd only ask for your discretion if anyone asks how you came to be acquainted."

William bowed, completely at ease despite his falsehoods. "Of course." Turning to Aurelia, he held out his hand, and she delicately set her fingers in his palm. "Lady Danby, it was a pleasure to make your acquaintance."

She nodded, rendered into silence as her thoughts tripped into one another, chanting, *pirate, gentleman, pirate, gentleman*.

He kissed the back of her hand, and as he straightened, he graced her with that same stunning smile he'd given her aunt moments earlier. It transformed him from an exciting, threatening villain into every bit a beautiful prince—the kind who would save her from a tower or an evil witch or dive into a freezing lake to pull her from a watery grave...

Now his perfect lips had touched her hand, and he'd smiled at her like she was the lovely damsel she so often pretended to be.

And he was the son of the immortal Captain Copson. A witness to all her favorite stories in the papers, a character in some of the most exciting tales she'd ever read.

It was as though he'd stepped off the page to rescue her from boredom and solitude.

Her heart flopped in her chest and nearly stopped altogether. It was that moment, as he swept out the door, that she knew—with shaky, invigorating, terrifying assurance—that she'd fallen madly, hopelessly in love with William Kingswood.

3

Her Less Dismal Existence

The first letter came three weeks later.

Aurelia had never received a letter, and upon its arrival, she marveled at her name written in looping, slightly jagged script on the envelope's face. Lying on her stomach on her bed, she kicked her feet up and traced the ink, lingering in the anticipation of its contents.

When she flipped it over, however, her heart tumbled into her stomach when she saw her family's seal pressed in red wax. She tore into it, and her eyes immediately dropped to William's signature at the bottom.

Frowning, she started from the beginning.

Lady Danby,

I've decided letters are the best way to fulfill our agreement while I'm abroad, so here is the first. Please note I've written *burn after reading* at the bottom. I would greatly appreciate you heeding this instruction, as it would put my mind much at ease knowing you don't let secrets lie around.

Also, please don't be alarmed at my use of your family's seal - it was taken long ago, and I only use it now so no one thinks they are privileged to read your correspondence.

By the time this letter reaches you, I will have returned to the Fortuna Royale (which I will call FR). We cannot dock such a vessel in England's ports since the authorities would likely arrest us all and string up our bodies along the Thames. So she (ships are referred to as 'she,' in case you didn't know) remains anchored far off shore, and we sail a less conspicuous ship between the harbor and the FR

That is not to say we can't dock the FR in other ports. We often dock where we are welcome, which is helpful for when the ship needs repairs or cleaning - you wouldn't believe how much faster the FR sails after removing a couple barnacles. We're headed for a Spanish trade route we discovered three months ago It's lucrative and dangerous, which I'm sure will make for several fine stories to sate your rapacious curiosity.

I haven't told my father of what happened weeks ago, as he'd likely throw me overboard for being so foolish. So again, I'd appreciate your discretion - for my sake.

William

Burn after reading.

Aurelia read it three times before dutifully tossing it into the hearth.

She watched William's handwriting turn to ash and pressed a hand over her pounding heart. It was real—the ocean, ships, pirates. He was really on the *Fortuna Royale*, and hearing about it made it feel so much closer—a legend come to life, the same as if Merlin or Lancelot had shown up at her door.

There would be more letters, and she could hardly contain her excitement.

It was enough to get her through the dull monotony of living in Aunt Clara's home. While her usual daydreams had turned gray and hazy with overuse, her imagination revived with thoughts of William while she sat in her lessons. She wondered where he was or what he was doing at any given moment, knowing she'd hear of it eventually.

Four weeks later, the second letter arrived, but not in the same way as the first.

One afternoon, while Aurelia was rotting in one of her many lessons with an instructor whose bulging eyes reminded her of a fish, she was summoned to the parlor. She was only too eager to escape, and upon entering the room, she found Aunt Clara sitting in her cloud of chiffon, her lips pinched and eyes squinted against the cheery sunlight streaming through a window. Though the room itself was decidedly gaudier than the rest of the home—and just as outdated—it was far livelier than her aunt's usual haunts with its yellow walls, fringed pillows, and bronze accents.

A boy stood by the unlit fireplace. He couldn't have been older than sixteen, and he bowed as she entered. His brown eyes were set in a boyish face still round with youth, and he wore a crisp blue coat that complimented his nearly golden hair.

"This is Ralph Kingswood," Aunt Clara said. "He heard of your residence here and thought to extend friendship." Her voice was oddly nasally for July. It might've been dissatisfaction, though Aurelia couldn't imagine what she could find so disagreeable about a Kingswood.

"A pleasure to make your acquaintance," Ralph said.

Aurelia nearly forgot to curtsy, surprised to meet another boy from down the lane so soon after the first. Friendship—what an unexpectedly marvelous reason to forsake her tutor.

"My brother spoke highly of your gardens," Ralph said to Aunt Clara. "I hoped I might see them."

"Aurelia will show you," Aunt Clara said with a wave of her handkerchief. "But be mindful of the staff."

They were dismissed, and Aurelia waved Ralph along to follow her out of the parlor.

Outside, the spring flowers had fully blossomed and fallen away, giving room for summer blooms and whispering leaves that played in the warm breeze. As they entered the garden, Aurelia peered at Ralph out of the corner of her eye.

Another son of Captain Copson, she realized, but she'd promised William she wouldn't breathe a word of her knowing their family's secret. This was to be her first test, she decided, so she made herself believe Ralph was *just* a Kingswood.

It wasn't hard. He had none of his brother's dangerous features or his sharpness. Ralph carried himself like a gentleman, so it would be easy to treat him as such.

"Will was right, this is a lovely garden," he said as they wandered toward the trickling fountain. He flashed a grin. "Much more agreeable than inside."

"You have good taste," Aurelia said with a small laugh, moving around one side of the fountain while Ralph rounded the other.

"Thank you for showing me," he said when they met on the other side, and the splashing water concealed his voice from the staff. "Though I must admit I'm here for more than to extend friendship."

A letter appeared in his hand with her name written across the back in familiar handwriting.

Aurelia beamed and barely kept herself from snatching it.

"My brother told me he owed you," Ralph said. "No one's ever had Will in their debt, so as someone who owes him at least three pounds at any given time, I applaud you."

She slowly took the letter. "It's not really a debt."

"He also sent this." From inside his jacket, Ralph procured a small, red velvet pouch. He untied the tiny drawstrings and dumped a single gold coin into his palm. A cross was stamped on the front, surrounded by what looked like a clover. "It's Spanish gold."

Still careful not to betray her overexcitement, she carefully lifted the coin from his palm. "It's *beautiful*," she breathed.

"As much as I'd like to have it to pay him off, he said you asked for it." He hadn't stopped grinning. "You found out about our family business, didn't you?"

She stared at the tiny piece of treasure. "I don't know what you're talking about," she said blandly, pretending Ralph was only a Kingswood and not related in any way to Captain Copson or his handsome eldest son.

"You absolutely did." He was nearly laughing now. "Was he bragging about it? He goes out in the boat with our cousins to tell them all about where he's gone, but he's been out to sea so much he forgets his voice carries over water and people on land can hear him plain as day."

Aurelia took the pouch and returned the coin to its depths before slipping both it and the letter into her dress pocket. "I heard him on the lake, but he said nothing about the family business."

They started walking again, and Ralph simply said, "Piracy. That's the family business."

Her steps faltered. "Well, he didn't say it like that."

"But he did."

Fine, so Ralph wouldn't let himself be *just* a Kingswood. But if he insisted...

She lowered her voice. "He said your father is the immortal Captain Copson, and that he sails—"

"*Immortal*?" Ralph guffawed. "No, tell me he didn't say that."

Aurelia stopped. This was the second time she'd spoken to someone closer to herself in age than her aunt, and he was breaking all the rules of decorum—what was she supposed to say to someone who spoke so openly and laughed so loud? She searched the stories she knew for a character who could inform her of how to deal with a boy who lacked any subtlety or shame, but she couldn't think of one as impetuous as Ralph.

She was half tempted to return to her tutor.

He seemed to notice her hesitancy and calmed. "Please forgive me—Will only asked me to bring you the coin and the letter, which he only sent to me because he knew it would be more secure. Then I wondered if you somehow knew about my family, and if you did, I had to take my chance to make a friend. It's hard to make friends with such a secret, and I fear I haven't got many because of it. The only people who know are my family and a couple sailors who are sworn to secrecy."

She started walking again, leading him toward the rose garden.

"And I wasn't laughing at you," Ralph said, sidestepping down the path so he could face her as he spoke. "I'm laughing at my brother. I know what the papers say about the captain and his immortality, but it's really not as interesting as that. I'll tell you, if you want."

Aurelia looked at him out of the corner of her eye. "Are you sure *I* won't tell?"

"Well...Will said you don't have any friends either."

At this, she stopped and put her hands on her hips. Heat rose to her cheeks from more than embarrassment. "And how would he know that?"

Ralph had the good sense to look guilty. "You live with an old woman no one likes or visits. And...no one's mentioned you, not even the Danbys."

"That's not my fault," she said, angry tears pricking her eyes.

"Oh—Lord, no, I didn't mean—" His hands went to his hair, and then he dropped them, his eyes wide with panic. "That isn't what I meant!"

"What did you mean? To call me lonely and forgotten?" This character she knew—the petulant, prideful one with something to prove. She puffed out her chest and spread her feet. "There's so much more to me, Mr. Kingswood."

He held out his hands, pleading. "I *meant* to give you a coin and ask for your friendship, which I realize is going abysmally. But this is what I get for not having friends. You're clearly much better adjusted than I am."

She folded her arms. "Am I?"

"Oh yes—by leaps and bounds."

Gardeners minded their business around them, but they were too far away to hear their conversation.

Aurelia huffed. "Then tell me how Captain Copson isn't immortal."

"And you'll forgive me if I do?"

"Yes."

Ralph's smile returned. "It's nothing too exciting. My great-grandfather was the first Captain Copson, and then his son took up the name after his death. My father has it now, and my brother will take it after him. People like the immortality story, so we let it perpetuate. Plus, it keeps the Spanish busy looking for the Fountain of Youth."

"Does it not exist?" she asked, surprised.

He shrugged. "Maybe it does, but we certainly haven't found it."

Across the garden, Aurelia spied Aunt Clara watching them through the window with a small pair of opera glasses. Aurelia took a step back from Ralph and continued their stroll.

"Have you forgiven me?" Ralph asked quietly. "I've bungled this, but I'm hoping you'll pity me for having no one to share secrets with."

Aurelia turned to him. "Yes, I forgive you, but I'll swear not to pity you so long as you don't pity me either."

He nodded emphatically. As they continued on, Ralph appeared as delighted as she felt to have a new friend. Since Aurelia was such a fan of pirates, and he'd been terribly awkward, he seemed eager to offer anything that might convince her she'd made the right choice in accepting his friendship. So he told her how he'd grown up on his father's pirate ship before coming to live at home with his mother when she gave birth to his younger brother. He recounted several short tales in quick succession—once, he'd adopted a rat from the brig and named him Atilius before William let the ship's resident cat loose in Ralph's quarters. He never saw the rat again. Then, for an entire month, he had a crippling fear of codfish after one of the sailors pretended one could talk. He also told her how he wasn't allowed to join raids, so while Copson's pirates set upon another ship, William, Ralph, and another pirate child stole to the helm. William declared himself captain because it was his birthright, but Ralph wanted it because William *always* got to be captain, and the other child said the position was hers because she could shoot a gun better than both of them. Consequently, none of them were good captains, and they nearly ran the ship aground.

Ralph successfully made Aurelia forget his inadvertent insults by the time he went home. Then she retired to her room, locked the door, and tore into William's letter.

Lady Danby,

I hope you received the gold piece I sent and that its inclusion might sate any ideas you may have of sharing secrets against better judgment. If you did not receive it and Ralph decided to keep it and give you only this letter, pester him until he gives it up. He's determined to be a proper gentleman, but he's not good at it yet, so feel free to shame him.

It also occurred to me shortly after writing my initial letter that you've probably never been to the open ocean. It's one of the most incredible sights you could ever behold. On sunny days, the water is blue like the sky, but dark as pitch when you look down, for it swallows all light at its deepest. As we sail, it crashes against the ship with a noise like thunder, and when you're standing on the deck, it seems like you're on some powerful beast. Sometimes I stand on the bow (the front of the ship) where it feels like flying. The wind carries the scent of brine and the sea spray stings your cheeks.

It's entirely different when we're anchored. The sea is so vast and incredible that it's hard not to pitch yourself right into it and I often do. You probably understand what that must be like, what with your recent escapade in the lake. Except the water is salty and filled with all manner of strange creatures. I'm sure you'll have the opportunity to see it one day.

William

Burn after reading.

Aurelia nearly kept this letter, but like the other, she set it in her fireplace, committing every word to memory while she watched all she knew of the ocean burn away.

The letters came almost monthly after that—give or take a week or two—usually through the mail and sometimes with Ralph who often called upon the house. Each one was sealed with the Danby crest, which assured it came to her unread and entirely her own. Aunt Clara never asked after them, ignoring that Aurelia received any letters at all.

It was the best summer she'd ever known. The boy who unknowingly had her heart sailed with it over the ocean, and she hoped he might one day bring it back to her.

4

The Ghost in the Ballroom

When Aurelia was sixteen, Aunt Clara decided to have parties again.

They'd been a usual occurrence in her aunt's younger days—which were apparently vibrant and full of exciting social affairs—and their renewal made Aurelia realize how many friends Aunt Clara actually had, and that they were not all nasty crones with sagging skin and mouths full of worn teeth and complaints.

They were society. And due to her lack of age and eligibility, Aurelia was not invited.

Two years had passed since William saved her. Two years since she'd last seen him, but she'd received twenty-five letters, most of which she could nearly recite from memory.

He told her of his travels—the Caribbean, North Africa, and exciting pirate cities run entirely by outlaws. Copson's crew sailed through storms and vengeful seas that tried to swallow them whole, and sometimes the *Fortuna Royale* hit pockets of calm air and hardly moved at all—on those days, the crew had nothing better to do than lounge around deck and pray for a gust of wind. There were raids on merchant ships, friendly sword fights among the crew, and ghost stories told by lantern light on chilly nights, though William claimed ghosts were never a worry for them.

Some letters were just about the ship—how it functioned with the different masts, sails, rigging, and everything in between—and how he managed to climb aboard other ships. He said some affixed gangplanks between the two decks, but he preferred to swing over on a rope, and she imagined this made him very dangerous and very brave.

Now she could practically map out the *Fortuna Royale* in her head, and longed to board a ship—any ship—simply to watch it work.

It's what she thought about this morning as the servants put the finishing touches on the ballroom in preparation for tonight's ball. They cleaned the bank of glass doors, polished chandeliers, and filled ornate vases with fresh carnations and roses in shades of yellow and orange that filled the room with their heady scent.

Aurelia stood in the middle of it all, imagining she was a captain and the staff were her sailors. The walls fell away and the floor began to rock, setting her in the middle of the ocean with the sea breeze fluttering the ribbons in her hair.

"Lady Wedderburn has outdone herself."

Aurelia spun to find Ralph standing at the ballroom doors, dressed in burgundy with his hands clasped behind his back as he surveyed the room.

"Hasn't she?" Aurelia plucked a yellow carnation from one of the arrangements and held the petals to her face, grounding herself in the ballroom as her mind tried to convince her she stood on a wooden deck rather than marble floors.

He lowered his voice as he approached. "I daresay it looks better than the rest of the home."

Aurelia buried her nose in the flower and inhaled deeply, smothering the urge to giggle. Now eighteen, Ralph was much taller, and he'd lost most of his roundness. He'd also started caring more about his appearance; he wore sensible colors that suited his complexion, and his golden hair was always combed back.

It made Aurelia want to ruffle her hand through his perfect locks and tease him.

But now he was a proper gentleman, and they were careful to stand far enough apart to avoid any hint of impropriety, especially as footmen and servants bustled around them. Aunt Clara warned that people might assume their friendship to be more, and Aurelia best be mindful of her attentions toward the middle Kingswood son.

Her warnings were unnecessary though, since Aurelia didn't think about Ralph like that, and she doubted he thought of her in such ways. They were comfortable friends, and the idea of something more between them felt as distant as the dry tales in her history books.

And her heart was still very far away.

"Are you coming tonight?" Aurelia asked.

"I believe so. When my father is home, he takes my mother to all the parties she wants to attend." His lips quirked, but it wasn't quite a grimace. "Only now I'm old enough to go too, and I haven't the heart to say no to her."

Aurelia tried not to let her excitement show. If the captain was in town, then that meant... "Is William back?"

"God knows. I've barely even seen my father since he returned, let alone my brother." He sidled out of the way as a maid bustled past with an armful of leaves and stems clipped from the bouquets. "Will I see you tonight?"

Aurelia scrunched her nose. "No. My aunt won't allow it until I'm out."

"Ah, how foolish of me to forget. Perhaps next year."

"I still won't be out," she said with a laugh.

"My word," he said, sounding put out even as his eyes shone with humor. "Will you ever grow up?"

"I'm sure I'll manage it one day." Aurelia shoved the flower back into the vase as a servant noticed it in her hand and looked to be preparing to scold her. "For now I am so dreadfully jealous that I can hardly stand to look at you." She glanced at him, fighting her smile as he smirked. "How dare you."

"A party without you will be no fun at all." He pulled the same carnation from the bouquet and snapped off the stem.

She waited for him to tell her to sneak into the party anyway, or meet him in the garden under cover of night so they could gorge themselves on tarts and punch he'd pilfered from the desert table. But Ralph didn't think of such things. The son of a pirate he may be, but he'd only ever encourage her to do as she was told.

With a quick movement, he stuck the flower into the end of her braid where it hung over her shoulder and shoved the broken stem into his coat.

"Good," Aurelia said, adjusting the flower to ensure it wouldn't fall. "Enjoy nothing grand without me, and we can share our miseries over tea. Then in two years I may join you for all the fun."

"Mr. Kingswood!" Aunt Clara bustled into the room, her breathing labored with the effort. "Thank the Lord you've arrived. I must know your opinion on the food. Your mother has the finest tastes, and I would be mortified to disappoint her."

Ralph bowed. "My lady, I'm sure she'll enjoy whatever you serve."

Aunt Clara tutted away his assurance and grabbed his arm. "She may say that, but *you* wouldn't dare lie to me. Come this way. You'll try the tarts first."

He offered one more grin in Aurelia's direction before he was tugged away to cater to her aunt's whims. This time, Aurelia didn't bother to muffle her laughter as she flounced along behind them.

Aunt Clara forbade Aurelia from sampling anything, claiming hers was not the opinion she wanted to hear and that a single bite wouldn't leave enough for her guests. Ralph, however, nibbled enough to be polite before passing the rest to Aurelia under the guise of clasping his hands behind his back. She popped them into her mouth and studied the walls and Aunt Clara's ugly art while Ralph offered courteous compliments about tonight's menu. He joined the ladies for lunch and set off soon after.

Aurelia lingered in the ballroom as the servants added final touches and adjusted floral arrangements, dodging Aunt Clara's critiques of perfect decorations that came at exceedingly higher pitches as the afternoon hours faded to evening.

"Be gone!" Aunt Clara finally said, shooing Aurelia toward the stairs. "Go to bed. This is no place for a child."

"Couldn't I stay for just one dance?" Aurelia asked as she mounted the steps quickly enough to avoid her aunt's swatting hand. "I'll dance with Ralph where no one will see."

Aunt Clara's face turned red as she sputtered. "I would think you too wise to suggest such a thing! You'd make a scandal of the Danby name and drag the good Kingswoods into infamy with you for all eternity. Absolutely not. I'll hear nothing of it—go to bed." She lumbered off, muttering, "You shan't even *look* at a man till marriage!"

Aurelia loitered at the top of the staircase for a moment before sprinting for her room. The first guests would arrive soon, and if there was a chance of spotting William, she'd be damned to miss it.

She grabbed some parchment, scrawled a few words across its face, and shoved it into her pocket. Wrapping a heather shawl around her shoulders, she returned to the balcony over the foyer where she crouched in the darkness behind the banister, waiting silently as revelers began wandering through the door in sparkling gowns and nice hats.

Music drifted through the air, mingling with the perfume of countless flowers in the bouquets and worn on lapels and held between carefully pinned curls. Aurelia had never heard or seen or smelled a fantasy as wonderful as the one Aunt Clara had designed on the lower floor.

An hour passed, and Aurelia was so taken with the lovely distractions below that she nearly forgot why she waited in the shadows. But then the door opened, and a handsome couple entered.

She knew, without a doubt, that these were the Kingswoods.

The earl was tall and tan, his tawny hair turning gray at the temples and his beard trimmed to accentuate a strong, sharp jaw. A scar ran through his left cheek, but it looked fierce rather than frightening with his cutting blue eyes. She tried to imagine him with a cutlass at his hip and a tricorn hat, but the gentleman in black was so distinguished that she struggled to picture him as Captain Copson.

But as surely as she was living, the king of the sea was here.

At his side, the countess was the loveliest woman Aurelia had ever seen. Her black hair curled over bare shoulders that shimmered ever so slightly above a gown in the deepest shade of purple. Her dark eyes were lined and painted with shadow that matched her dress, and she would undoubtedly be the envy of every other woman here tonight.

Behind them was Ralph, wearing black like his father. They moved through the foyer, greeting partygoers with smiles and clasped hands before disappearing into the ballroom.

Then William swept through the door.

Aurelia's breath caught. He was twenty-one now, and more devastatingly handsome than she remembered. His shoulders had grown broader, filling his fitted navy coat, and he moved with easy confidence. Strands of black hair hung nearly to his eyes, and he casually swept them away from his face, his gaze drawn to the ballroom where his family mingled.

Her memory hadn't done him justice, and once again she was struck with the painful sense that there was no prince or knight achingly lovely enough to rival him.

His eyes flicked upward.

Aurelia gasped as he caught her stare and held it. A small grin spread over his lips, and he nodded in greeting.

She scrambled for the top of the curving stairs, but stopped only a quarter of the way down, wary of anyone who might see her if she wandered too far from the shadows. Pursing her lips, she withdrew her note from her pocket, then bent forward and let it fall from her hand. It sailed down the stairs and landed on one of the lower steps.

Sparing a glance at the party, William moved toward the note. He slipped it into his pocket, then mounted the first three stairs, coming up only as many as she'd come down. From inside his coat, he produced another letter and set it on the highest step he could reach from where he stood.

The back of his hand was smooth and tan, but a bandage peeked from beneath the edge of his sleeve. She wanted to ask what it was for, but as he met her gaze again, she lost herself in his cobalt eyes, and her fingers twitched at the thought of what it might be like to touch the planes of his face.

Say something, she told herself. *Say hello.*

But before she could speak, William smiled and winked, then descended the stairs and disappeared into the ballroom, leaving her with a thundering heart.

And the letter on the step.

She snuck forward, grabbed it, and sprinted to the balcony. The letter carried a scent—like soap and salt and ink. Pausing next to the banister, she pressed the parchment to her nose and slowly inhaled.

It would be very hard to burn this one.

She remained on the balcony, unable to move toward her room despite the warm parchment begging to be read. Somewhere below her slippers was her love, whether he knew it or not, and she would be remiss if she didn't see him at least once more...

She turned back. The music covered her footsteps as she snuck down the stairs, through the foyer, and to the ballroom doors.

Aurelia hadn't glimpsed a proper fairy tale in four years, but the scene before might have been pulled straight from her dusty memories and imbued with color and magic. The air was heavy with laughter and song and springtime warmth. The doors to the garden were thrown open to let in the nightly breeze while nobles swayed and spun through intricate steps. Aunt Clara sat along one wall, smiling as though she were on a throne.

And there, in the middle of swirling, colorful gowns and handsome, tailored coats, were the Kingswoods. The earl and countess glided expertly over the floor, as did Ralph, dancing with a young woman in a pale pink dress. William held a lady dressed in light green with jewels flashing in her hair.

Aurelia wondered if she would ever be so beautiful—and by the time she was, would William notice? Or would it be too late?

She shrank against the doorjamb as a couple flew by, and she cursed the wicked schemes that left her lonely in Aunt Clara's house with only one true friend to speak of. And for the first time in her life, she despised her youth because she couldn't be like the lovely debutantes who caught the attention and flattery of young men.

Darkness passed over her. Aurelia looked up and paled.

"To bed!" Aunt Clara hissed. "Away from here. This is no place for you."

"I was only—"

"The devil will mark you as his own forever if you're seen." Aunt Clara shooed her. "Go, and pray for your soul!"

Rolling her eyes, Aurelia marched up the stairs and returned to her room where she opened the window so the strains of music from below could remind her of everything she was missing—a true, glimmering ball.

With pirates.

Oh, if only she were old enough. Someday she would be. Someday she would attend such grand affairs and be eligible for her own happy ending.

I'll be the most amazing debutante, she thought as she watched the stars. There were only two more years between now and then, and after she finally debuted, she'd dance with William, who would surely be back for at least one party.

Remembering the letter, she freed it from her dress and opened it in the moonlight.

Aurelia,

I realized the other day as we pursued a rival ship that I've not yet recounted a battle for what I imagine must be an increasingly cumbersome arsenal of tales in your head. I suppose I might've held back, fearing for a lady's sensitivities, but I found myself thinking of you in Lady Wedderburn's home - or worse, drinking tea with Ralph or whatever it is he bores you with - and decided it was very ungentlemanly of me to refrain from sharing some of the most exciting times at sea when you specifically asked me to tell you everything.

We came upon the other ship in the morning before they could outrun us. The FR has forty cannons, which was more than enough to overpower them, even with another ship at my father's command. After only four shots to their vessel   the sound of which is enough to startle even a deaf man - the crew surrendered.

This ship was overflowing with riches, and it was a marvel

our crew managed to get it all on the FR without sinking. We relieved them of their bounty, which was headed for port and the typical revelry and debauchery one finds there (I shall spare you details of that, as you are a lady). We only had to shoot a few to keep them agreeable.

Unfortunately, though, I made a mistake. As I'm sure I've told you before, I prefer the quick way to another ship as opposed to the safe way, and upon my landing, I slipped and fell onto my arm. I let out the most ghastly howl, fearing I'd broken it, and was promptly taken back to the FR in a fit. I would have stayed, had they let me, and probably hurt it worse by hauling loot. So everyone else pillaged, and I did not.

In truth, it's the worst pain I've ever felt. I couldn't hold the weight of my sword for two weeks, and my father called me a fool in any number of ways, though I fear he's right about most things he said. As much as I have my ways of doing things, self-preservation is something I ought to consider more often than I do.

Regards,

William

Please burn after reading

Music continued into the early hours of the morning, but Aurelia didn't sleep. She laid on her bed and stared at the ceiling, smelling the parchment and wallowing. As the hours turned, the voices downstairs quieted and the music fell silent. Long after everyone left, Aurelia got up, padded down the stairs, and slipped into the dark ballroom.

The scent of candle wax and fading perfume lingered in the air, and she could almost imagine dozens of fancy ghosts twirling around her in a midnight ball.

If Aurelia had ever had a fairy godmother, she'd probably gotten drunk and wandered off to find some other, more hopeful girl to turn into a fairy tale. If that were the case, and Aurelia preferred to think it was, that left a desperate girl such as herself to make her own happily ever after. But there was only so much one could do without pixie dust.

She did have money, however. And a title.

When she turned eighteen, her family would finally call her home to London where everyone would know her name. She would be presented to society, and as the Danby heiress and the daughter of a prince, she would shine brighter than the rest of the ladies. Brighter, even, than the women who came tonight.

Her perfect story came together in her head, and as it did, she joined the ghosts and began to waltz down the length of the ballroom to her memory of the music that had played so long into the night.

Only two more years, and she would be out and so lovely and desirable that all the other ladies would beg for her company, and she would be surrounded with friends. They would laugh and share secrets and stories and bat their lashes at men from behind their fans. Those women would be beautiful and wealthy and available, but none more so than Aurelia.

She would dine at the palace with her great uncle, the king, which she would proudly flaunt along with her status and education. She'd be the best, and everyone would know it, and everyone would love her for it.

Imagining herself older and lovelier, she stood on her toes and craned her neck like a swan, her back straight and her nose in the air.

And such was her imagination that she saw William spinning her in time with the string quartet.

He would return after her debut. He'd see her friends and her beauty and be so impressed at how smart and clever and lofty she was that he'd no longer want to send her letters. Instead, he'd want to speak to her in person, in private, each day and every night.

"Aurelia."

She froze at the soft voice, and her fantasy dissipated. Her aunt stood at the door, dressed in a robe with her gray hair in a cap. She held a single candle illuminating her deep eyes.

"Why are you up at this hour?"

Aurelia lowered her arms from the invisible shoulders of her imaginary William. Tears streamed down her face and dripped off her chin, and she hoped her aunt wouldn't notice.

"I'm sorry," Aurelia said. "I couldn't sleep."

Aunt Clara held out a wrinkled hand. "Come along."

Aurelia padded to her aunt's side and took her hand. Together, they walked back to Aurelia's room where Aunt Clara tucked her into bed.

"Rest," Aunt Clara said. "Don't let your mind run away with you."

Aunt Clara was not usually so tender, and Aurelia might've thought it strange had her girlish heart not found warmth in it. As her aunt left and closed the door, Aurelia's cheeks still bore tears, but she eventually fell asleep.

5

The Three Miseries of Aurelia Danby

The next years would prove to be the most difficult Aurelia had ever lived through because, as it turned out, money and titles couldn't buy a fairytale life.

Everything started well enough, with a letter on the doorstep the morning after Aunt Clara's party. Aurelia nearly squealed with delight at its delivery, but waited until she reached the privacy of her bedroom to do so.

Aurelia,

Please forgive my promptness in response to your note. I return to the FR today and thought it best to reply now rather than from somewhere I'd have to pay for postage.

Per your request, I'll tell you about the sea creatures. The ocean is home to all sorts of odd things. Strangest are the flying fish they have silver bodies and blue backs, and they jump from the water and spread translucent fins that look like wings. They glide through the air like birds before returning to the ocean. They're small, odd, delightful things.

Greatest are the whales. We see them when they come to the surface to breathe, and they are so unimaginably massive that they can rival the length of our ship. They have thick gray skin that's sometimes pocked with tiny barnacles. On a few occasions, I've seen them leap from the water and crash back in, or sometimes they seem to wave at us with giant fins.

Then there are dolphins, which breach the water as they swim in the wake of our ship — sometimes I'll see as many as twenty at a time. I wonder if perhaps you'd like them best, as there is something quite charming about them.

There are also sharks, which I've seen a number of times. They have black eyes and quick bodies, and their mouths hang open with razor-sharp teeth. Whenever we're in the water, we pray there are none nearby   one man on our crew is missing an arm, thanks to the slippery devils.

And since you asked specifically about mermaids, I am inclined to believe in their existence, though I have not yet seen one personally.

Regards,
William

Please burn after reading

Beneath his signature, he'd sketched the creatures he'd described, with exception of the mermaid, which he had not attempted to draw.

She traced their lines, memorizing their shapes and details. Her favorite was the flying fish, and because of this, she folded the letter and stuffed it into the book with her countless articles about Captain Copson.

This was the first letter she kept.

By and large, Aurelia didn't have many complaints about the majority of her seventeenth year. She threw herself into her studies and started dressing like the fashionable young ladies in London, walked with books on her head to improve her posture, and learned the subtle art of conversation. She stopped thinking about her storybooks hidden in the attic and learned about music, art, languages, and all she would ever need to know about running a household, urged on by the dream she'd concocted and chosen to want the year before.

But all the excitement of her fabulous future came to a sudden, shattering halt when the letter arrived before her eighteenth birthday.

It had only been two weeks since her last correspondence from William, so she was practically floating when she received a second letter addressed to her and stamped with the Danby seal. She only noticed the handwriting was wrong after she started reading.

Dear Lady Aurelia,

I write on behalf of the Duke and Duchess of Danby to inform you of their decision to have you remain with Lady Wedderburn through the upcoming social season and until any marriage prospects have proven fruitful.

They wish you the very best.

Richard Lanksford
Secretary to the Duke and Duchess of Danby

Aurelia stared at the words in shock. Then, once she gained her wits, she sought her aunt and showed her.

Much to Aurelia's horror, Aunt Clara was not shocked.

"Of course I knew," she said. She was seated in the yellow parlor for tea, surrounded by her dusty art and creaky furniture. "I assumed you were aware of it too, what with all your correspondence."

"What corri—" Aurelia shut her mouth. Of course her aunt would think she'd spoken with her parents. All of William's letters came with their seal. So she said, "They didn't tell me. This is the first I've heard."

Aunt Clara bade her niece to sit, and Aurelia slumped into a chair. Thankfully, her aunt didn't scold her for the lack of decorum.

"I'm sorry you're disappointed," the old woman said, not sounding sorry at all, "but it really may be for the best."

"The best!" Aurelia nearly bolted upright. "I'm a Danby! I was supposed to return home and be a princess."

Aunt Clara laughed, and the sound of it surprised Aurelia, since levity was something she rarely heard from the woman. "You wouldn't have been a princess. The king may be family, but that doesn't make you royalty."

Of course, Aurelia knew this, but she folded her arms over her chest and sulked anyway. "I was supposed to be in London for my season and be the most eligible woman in all society. But they wish me to stay here, in the middle of the country, to do what? What parties shall I go to? How shall I make friends? Who shall court me?"

"The Kingswood boy."

She nearly choked, then realized her aunt meant Ralph. She puffed out her cheeks and refrained from rolling her eyes. He would be a wonderful love match for some other girl.

"Besides," said Aunt Clara, "we can still go to London. And do not shame me so with your complaints of the country—you saw the ball I threw last year. When the other families discover I have a lovely, clever

young woman in my home, no one will care for London half as much."
She patted Aurelia's knee. "All is not lost. Refrain from dramatics,
dear, and you'll be perfectly fine."

Then she picked up her tiny glasses and needlepoint, and her niece
was as good as dismissed.

Three days passed, and she tried to see her situation from her aunt's
perspective. They could travel to London and attend parties. They
could throw their own here in the country.

But this story was different from the one she'd told herself, and
because it wasn't the same, it would surely ruin her.

Spring rains came, and she wasted away in her window, watching
the drops roll down the panes like the forlorn tears on her cheeks. She
would not be the most beautiful debutante in all of England. She'd
remain hidden away with an old maid at her side instead of a lofty duke
and duchess to ascribe her value. And because few people liked Aunt
Clara, they were sure to think little of Aurelia Danby.

She saw no other way it could go, and because of this, William
Kingswood would remain beyond her, dancing with other lovely
ladies who lived beyond the shadows of their miserly, grossly outdated
aunts.

On the third night after receiving her family's letter, Aurelia wandered the halls, her white nightgown fluttering around her ankles
while a storm raged outside. As rain pounded the windows and thunder rumbled over the manor, she navigated the shadows by candle-
light, the small, insignificant flame inviting the ghosts of her lost
dreams and childhood fears. They followed in silence, joining her in
the depths of her despair and waiting for her to fade into one of them
so they might all finally be together, joined by death and dread.

Aurelia was trapped, held hostage by a monster called Fate that held
her within labyrinthine halls she would never be permitted to leave as
her love lived free in the world beyond.

With a heavy, tearful sigh, Aurelia extinguished her candle. Its weak flame sputtered out, and she dropped it. The force of its thin body hitting the floor splattered tiny drops of melted wax over the wall, but Aurelia was already running, sprinting through the halls until she reached the dark ballroom where she threw open one of the glass doors and plunged into the night.

The stony garden path tore at her bare feet, but she welcomed the sharp pain and prayed it would be the last she'd feel. She dashed past the fountain and toward the trees, icy rain pelting her face as lightning illuminated skeletal, budding trees and her path through them before drowning her in deafening thunder.

Her nightgown clung to her skin, holding her together as she stumbled through the woods toward the lake. Her legs screamed, her lungs burned, and the wind swallowed her sobs.

She reached the water and plunged into the shallows, desperately searching for the boat she'd once seen there as a girl—as though William might appear from the storm and save her once again.

He didn't. He never would, because she was a child, alone and abandoned.

She screamed at the sky until it stole her voice. And when her tears abated and her throat had worn raw, she was left standing in a freezing lake and the slicing rain, drenched to the bone and shivering violently.

Most times, when heroines ran into storms and embraced their melodrama, they were rescued by handsome men. Since it appeared there were no handsome men awake at this hour, the next best thing was that these ladies would fall asleep and magically wake in their beds, thanks to some gardener or guard who'd found them slumbering where they shouldn't.

Aurelia was far too cold and too awake to fall asleep so easily.

The third option, though rare, was that they succumbed to the elements and died, but as Aurelia looked down at the icy black water sloshing around her legs, she didn't feel compelled to spend the time it would take to commit to the slow, painful death.

Out of ideas, Aurelia trudged back to the house. The garden path cut her feet once more, and as she slipped back into the ballroom, she left in her wake bloody, muddy footprints that were sure to frighten the maids the next morning.

She padded up the carpeted stairs and down the hall to her room where she fell onto her mattress, trembling, numb, and determined to fall asleep in her soaked, miserable state.

But even that proved too much for her. Unable to engage in these acts like a true damsel, Aurelia huffed and moved to her hearth to add a log to the fire, coaxing the flames to chase the chill from her bones. Then she padded to the wardrobe, grabbed a clean, dry nightgown, and swapped it with the ruined one. She wiped her feet with her old nightgown, hissing as debris rolled into the myriad of fresh cuts. Then she tipped herself into bed and shivered under the covers until she finally fell asleep.

She woke to frantic maids and a fever. The doctor came early that morning, drawn by Aunt Clara's hysterical report of Aurelia's deathly coughing and sneezing. She said her niece had gone mad that night, and the doctor poked and prodded and bound her cut feet, prescribing tonics and bed rest and broth. He said she would not be permitted to debut that year, for her mind and body were clearly—to him—in no condition to handle it.

So Aurelia laid in bed for two weeks, her shame keeping her silent as she stared at the wall.

Her midnight escapade through the rain was very well the dumbest thing she'd ever done, and she supposed it was for the best that her books had been locked away. Though she'd resented it for years, her aunt had been right—love and fairy tales never did make a sensible girl. Aurelia had been terribly foolish, and while she was not permitted to leave her bed for days on end, she slowly excised the parts of herself she deemed excessively childish—the silly fantasies and ridiculous dreams, the games she played, and the stories she told herself.

Among them, however, was one dream she would never be able to extinguish, for it had rooted itself deep into the recesses of her heart. William Kingswood would always linger there, smiling and kissing her hand. So instead of killing something she knew couldn't die, she wrapped it tightly and plunged it into the depths of her soul where she could shroud it in darkness and pretend—the only pretending she would do from now on—that it didn't exist.

From now on, she would be sensible, and sensible girls did not want pirates. Nor were they entitled to handsome gentlemen sweeping them off their feet, and she would no longer embarrass herself by thinking otherwise.

Thankfully, a letter did not come from him that month or the next, as though he knew she should want nothing more of him. It would be for the best, and she was relieved he'd made the decision for her.

Life would be grand, now that she expected nothing.

Shortly after her eighteenth birthday and missed debut, Ralph finally came to visit. He was the first caller she'd been allowed, but she couldn't bring herself to smile as he sat across from her in the yellow parlor.

"Are you well?" he asked, ignoring his steaming tea while he studied her pale face. He was twenty now, and his golden features and warm red coat put him at odds with her dull shades of gray. "Your aunt forbade me from coming for so long that I worried you were near death."

"It was only a cold," she said morosely. "But I conducted myself badly, so they thought it madness."

"Madness? You, mad?" He gave a lopsided smile. "Why, you're one of the most reasonable people I know."

She narrowed her eyes. "Are you making fun of me?"

"I'm trying to make you laugh," he said softly. "You look too serious, and it disturbs me. I like my friend who delights in things."

She frowned. "My parents said I shouldn't come home. I fear the news hurt worse than I thought."

"Oh." He sank back in his chair. He knew what her debut meant to her—short of her hopes for his brother—and had witnessed her hope to return home. "I'm so sorry, Aurelia."

"I suppose it's fine," she said on a sigh. "I'll debut next year, but only with Aunt Clara, and I'll have to travel to London. I suppose other ladies do it well enough." She sipped her tea and let herself dismiss the dismal topic. "But tell me about you. I've been so dreadfully bored."

William's letters—and the lack thereof—suddenly came to mind, and she kicked the thought away.

His smile turned awkward. "I actually came today to tell you... Well, I'd intended to be here for your season."

"I'm sorry I'm not having one. It would have been fun to dance with you."

His brows furrowed a bit. "Dance. Of course. It would have been terribly fun, but..." His eyes became distant until he cleared his throat. "But my father came back a few weeks ago. For good, this time. And I've been...well, not really asked or told, but maybe *expected* is the best word..."

"Ralph?"

His dark eyes had moved to the table, staring through it until she said his name again. He looked up, his expression contemplating. "I'm leaving," he finally said. Then he dropped his voice to a whisper. "To sail with the captain."

The captain. Earl Kingswood was home for good, which meant Captain Copson was now... "Your brother."

Ralph nodded.

Perhaps that's why William hadn't written—because he was the captain and no longer a mere sailor. It was good. Perfect, even. What stupendous timing.

"Do you want to go?" she asked.

He rolled his top lip between his teeth. "I never intended to. I thought I'd stay here and have a home and a wife, maybe a business of my own." He swallowed and turned his face toward the window. "No, I don't want to go. But I love my family, and I know this is best for now." With a deep breath, he looked at her again. "I must go soon, but I swear I will return next year. Even if just for a dance."

Her heart deflated, which she didn't realize it could do after all the surgery she'd done to it. But Ralph, her dearest friend...he was leaving.

"Is everything okay?" she asked, and regretted the sadness that crept into her voice.

"It is," he said, his tone lighter in response to her melancholy. "Just different than expected."

The sadness lingered a moment longer, followed by an anger that surprised her. But it wasn't anger with her friend—it was life itself. She couldn't deny him an unforeseen change of plans simply because she was still reeling with her own. The devil wasn't so benevolent to plan calamity around what was convenient for the lives he sought to destroy. It suited him better to do it all at once for maximum effect.

Perhaps he was even more melodramatic than she was.

Swallowing her feelings, she pasted on her best smile. Her last afternoon with Ralph passed too quickly, and then he was gone, and she was alone.

Three miseries had marked these weeks—her parents' rejection, her missed debut, and now losing Ralph. And not one letter from William to lift her spirits.

But it was all for the best.

6

The News That Nearly Killed Aunt Clara

The next morning, Aunt Clara read the paper at breakfast, just as she did every day. Aurelia didn't usually watch her, but today her aunt caught her attention when she *harumph*ed. Aunt Clara did not make such sounds, so when her face pinched, Aurelia worried she was having an attack of some kind.

Aurelia glanced at the butler to find him watching her paling aunt with thinly veiled apprehension.

Aunt Clara mumbled, "Oh..."

The butler looked at Aurelia, her question reflected in his eyes. *Is she okay? Should we call for a doctor?*

"Oh heavens!"

Aurelia jumped and the butler stepped forward as Aunt Clara dropped the paper and slumped in her chair, fanning herself with her napkin.

"Aunt Clara, what's the matter?"

"Oh dear! Oh Lord!" Her aunt reached for the paper and flung it toward the butler. "Burn it! Burn it now so I shall never have to read it again."

"Read what?" Aurelia watched as the butler, perplexed, fed the paper into the hearth. "What is it?"

Aunt Clara stood, her large frame shaking. "Pirates, the lot of them,

53

shall go straight to Hell for their misdeeds! Murdering, terrifying men. May the king find that awful man and string him up." She faltered as she toddled toward the door, braced herself against the door frame for a breath, then left the room.

Aurelia looked to the butler. "What was in the paper?"

"I don't know, my lady."

"Do we have another paper?"

He shook his head. "It was the only one."

"Did you see the headline before you put it out this morning?"

"I saw Copson's name, but he frequents the papers, and I thought little of it." He glanced pointedly at the door.

She gestured for him to go. "Please, make sure she's well."

"If you're sure…" He set off without another word. Aurelia slid out of her chair and knelt by the fire, but the paper had already crumbled to ash. Steeling herself, she rose and returned to her bedroom where she called for her maid and dressed in a gown suited for walking—an agreeable gray with a purple ribbon and silver buttons. Donning a matching hat, she told the staff she was going out to thank the neighbors for their well wishes while she was sick, even though no one had sent anything of the sort. They let her go without protest, fussing after her aunt who'd taken ill for the day. On her way out, Aurelia passed through the garden to pick a couple of her aunt's favorite flowers, which she tied with a ribbon before setting off down the lane.

She'd never been to the Kingswoods' home, despite Ralph being her closest friend. The walk took nearly half an hour down a winding, wooded lane, which gave her time to rehearse what she'd say when she was received. Eventually, the house rose before her, as grand as her aunt's but looking considerably less haunted. It was three stories of white marble and clear windows, with an oak front door that was easily seven feet tall.

The gilded knocker was shaped like two crossed swords. She lifted it and let it drop, and the sound echoed through the house beyond.

She tugged at her collar while she waited, sweating for fear she would be scolded for leaving Aunt Clara's unescorted or calling upon a family she'd never met.

But curiosity demanded she see the paper.

A smiling footman answered the door, dressed in a much better-fitting and more flattering uniform than Aunt Clara provided for her staff.

Aurelia cleared her throat, holding the bouquet in both hands like a bride. "I'm Lady Aurelia Danby. I wondered if you might be finished with today's paper?" She held out the flowers. "And I wanted to deliver these too. As a gift."

The footman studied her. "One moment," he said, then closed the door and left her on the step. Moments later, he returned, still smiling. "Follow me, Lady Danby."

She hadn't planned to go in, but she was too stunned to say no. So she went inside.

The Kingswoods' home was open and airy, decorated with cool, tasteful colors. As Aurelia was led through the corridors, she wondered how many of the paintings had been stolen or bought with pirated gold, or if the artifacts—and swords and tiny baubles and vases filled with flowers—were taken from other ships.

She didn't have long to wonder before she was brought to a parlor door left slightly ajar.

A woman's light voice came from inside. "Perhaps you should go back."

"He'll be fine, Cecily darling," replied a man's low, rich timbre. "Don't fret."

The footman stepped into the doorway and cleared his throat to say, "Lady Aurelia Danby." Then he moved aside.

Aurelia stared at him wide-eyed. She'd hoped to hand off the flowers, grab the paper, and go, but she couldn't shake the feeling she'd been summoned.

"I only wanted the paper," she mouthed, but he only grinned. She adjusted her sweaty hold on the flowers and entered the room.

The walls were a lovely shade of lavender, with plush, cream-colored couches and dark wooden tables furnishing the space in such a way to make it feel cozy. A mirror hung on one wall, a painting of an island on another, and sunlight streamed through tall windows that looked out onto a flourishing garden filled with stunning blooms.

The countess rose from the sofa. Dressed in a pale blue gown, she was even lovelier than Aurelia remembered, and such was her admiration for the woman that she nearly forgot her panic.

But then she remembered herself and sank into a curtsy. As she rose, she noticed the earl standing by the fireplace, watching her with steely blue eyes. His immaculate beard did nothing to soften his sharp features, and not one strand of his graying brown hair hung out of place. A scar cut through his left cheek, but dressed in a tailored, dark gray vest, he gave no other hint of being the pirate she knew him to be.

Or was. He was no longer Captain Copson.

Nevertheless, her stomach dipped at the sight of him, and she half expected to find blood staining the rug beneath his boots. He studied her intently, making her feel like a pinned butterfly.

She'd really only wanted the paper.

"It's an honor to finally meet you," the countess said as the footman left. Her skirts swished over the fine rug as she approached. "I'm Cecily, and this is my husband, Alexander."

Aurelia bobbed another curtsy to the earl, terrified to depart from proper titles like the countess did. "A pleasure, my lord."

He inclined his head. "Lady Danby."

Captain Copson knows my name. The thought flung itself through her mind and stole her breath before she could help it.

"Please, have a seat," the countess said, gesturing for Aurelia to sit on one side of the couch while she drifted toward the other. "You'll have to pardon me—our footman said you came for the paper, but when he said it was you at the door, I had to make your acquaintance."

Steeling herself, Aurelia sat. "As long as I'm not interrupting. I only intended to bother your staff."

"You're not interrupting anything. Ralph left yesterday afternoon, so Alexander and I are trying to acquaint ourselves with a quiet home." The countess laughed, but the sound came with a note of sadness. Aurelia realized then that her eyes were bloodshot and rimmed with red. "It's still strange, and we were getting eager for company."

"I know I will miss Ralph terribly," Aurelia said, her heart tugging at the thought of her friend. "I can only imagine how you must feel."

Across the room, the earl kept staring, and Aurelia worried she'd misspoken. If she had, the countess didn't let on as she said, "I know Ralph will do well—he's always been so smart. He regretted he didn't get to see you much before he left, though he was glad to know you were feeling better."

The reminder of her illness and the idiocy that had caused it brought back thoughts of William, but she pushed them aside, erasing the image of him in this very house and what it must be like to hear his laughter in the halls.

"It wasn't really so bad as my aunt feared," she said before her mind could sweep her away. "I might've seen Ralph more than I did before he left."

The earl smiled at this, and so did his wife. "You mustn't begrudge your dear aunt," the countess said with a laugh. "She is a tenacious woman, and I've always admired her for it. And don't worry for Ralph, either. You'll see him again—he's determined to return next spring for your debut."

The tension eased from Aurelia's shoulders with the countess's easy friendliness. "I hope he does. I won't know anyone else."

The countess waved her off. "You won't need to know anyone else—you're lovely, and from what Ralph tells me about you, you certainly won't have to go out of your way. They will come to you, friends and suitors both."

The assurance struck deep. Aurelia marveled at how the countess spoke with such practical boldness, as though simply declaring something made it true for everyone. It was kind, and she wanted more.

"Ralph also told us you were meant to be in London for the season," the countess ventured, "but the Danbys preferred you stay in the country with your aunt."

The earl looked at his wife, but she didn't turn to him.

Aurelia traced a leaf on the bouquet in her hands, trying to seem demure even as she longed to sink into the house and become a permanent fixture where she could always receive loving smiles like the one the countess offered her now. "They gave no reason. Not my education or my stature. I don't know what I've done to make them not want me there, but I've been disappointed and worried that it means I'm somehow lacking."

It was too much to say, but the words had come anyway. Regardless, the Kingswoods watched her with no sense of reproach. The countess's eyes were soft, though she was not the one who answered Aurelia's misgivings.

"You've done nothing wrong," the earl said, and Aurelia startled at the sound of his commanding voice. "The duke and duchess are—"

"Alexander," warned the countess, her voice light.

The earl paused, regarding Aurelia. "You don't know your parents, do you." It was a statement of fact, an educated guess that spoke of a deeper knowledge of Aurelia's family than she herself had.

"I regret that I don't," she admitted. "I haven't seen or heard from them in over a decade."

He glanced at his wife who frowned and turned her head, which must have been some kind of hesitant permission as he said, "It is nothing to regret. They are too lofty in their own eyes. Everyone was relieved when they married each other and left the rest of us in peace."

The countess winced, but didn't object.

"Don't be disappointed in their lack of welcome," he continued. "Their lives are full of charm and flattery, but it's not as true as one might think. Your aunt cares for you far better than they ever would."

"Which is not to say your family is disagreeable," the countess said.

"It is to say exactly that," said the earl. "The Danbys are—"

"Alexander, this is her *family*."

"They're not," Aurelia said. Her heart pricked at the truth, but after so many years, there was only so much pain her distant parents could inflict. "I might've wished they were my family, if only they'd wanted to be." She met the earl's gaze and held it, despite its severity. "I appreciate your honesty, even if only to save me from further disappointment." Then, with a burst of courage, she asked, "If you knew my parents, is that where you got their seal?"

"I don't know what you're talking about," he replied coolly, his expression neutral. "Nevertheless, know their ill reputation does not reflect on you. It was a benefit your aunt asked to house you when she did."

Aurelia's eyes widened, the seal forgotten. "She asked for me?"

"You didn't know?" the countess asked. Aurelia shook her head. "Lady Wedderburn is wise. You should heed her."

The footman appeared again with the newspaper in hand. As the earl moved to the door to take it, Aurelia looked at the countess and extended the bouquet. The flowers weren't as large or perfect as those beyond the window, but Cecily brightened as she accepted them.

"Ralph said the earl is home for good now," Aurelia said, folding her hands in her lap. "I suppose you're very happy."

The countess studied the petals, her eyes warm with delight. "Quite. It's been bittersweet with Ralph leaving, but Alexander's been most supportive." She looked from the flowers to Aurelia. "It never felt quite as much like home without my husband."

Aurelia melted a little. How lovely it would be to have a home with a man she loved. Again, she imagined William lounging in one of the chairs and quickly cast the thought aside.

The countess stood, and Aurelia rose too. "I hope I haven't kept you too long," the countess said. "I've quite enjoyed finally making your acquaintance, and I hope you'll come back soon, perhaps with your aunt, and we'll have tea."

Aurelia bobbed another curtsy, smiling. "I'm sure she'd love that very much."

The countess nodded. "Goodbye, Aurelia. Till next time."

The earl waited by the door with the newspaper rolled in his hand. He stood back as Aurelia passed into the hall, then fell into step beside her, his boots clicking against the stone floor as they strode down the corridor.

He was a cold, aloof presence, and even though he didn't look at her, she was sure he was somehow still watching. For what, she didn't know, but ice curled through her stomach. He didn't look like a villain, but he still *was* one—and she was alone with him. In his house.

Captain Copson, her mind chanted, as though it might make her see past the silk vest and shiny boots. *Captain Copson. Captain Copson.*

The captain she kept stories about hidden in a book under her bed. Reports of unspeakable crimes—murder and theft and sinking enemy ships aboard the *Fortuna Royale*. This man, dressed impeccably with his handsome beard, a scar on his cheek, fierce blue eyes, and the most beautiful wife in all of England, had ruled the seas with an unforgiving iron fist.

And he was walking her, a girl who'd never done anything, to the door.

"You must forgive my forwardness," he said. "I did not mean to offend when I spoke of your family."

"I'm not offended." And she wasn't, though she wouldn't admit it even if she was.

He stopped before the front door but didn't move to open it. He still held the paper, and now she saw the three large, gold rings glinting on his fingers.

Pirate gold, her thoughts whispered.

"I struggle with the duke and duchess," he said, "but that does not have to be your relationship with them. Please don't let my opinion from thirty years ago sway you when your parents may have changed."

The look in his eyes implied he didn't believe a word of what he said, but she nodded anyway. "Yes, sir."

His eyes squeezed ever so slightly. "My son inherited my penchant for speaking more than he ought." He spoke too casually, and her gaze dipped to his waist, searching for a dagger or a cutlass or a gun she hadn't yet seen. When she brought her eyes back to his, he watched her keenly, like he could search her every thought like one might fillet a fish.

But being a pirate didn't give one the ability to read minds—at least, not that she knew.

"Perhaps not my middle child," he added, "so much as my eldest. My carelessness has gotten me into trouble before, and I dread either of them doing the same."

He knew. He knew she knew their secret, somehow, though she couldn't imagine either Ralph or William would have let something like that slip. No, Alexander Kingswood had founded his suspicions simply by watching her.

The thought was mildly terrifying. Feigning innocence, she said, "I don't know William so well, and Ralph was always a gentleman." She paused, and found herself nearly smiling because she was mostly certain he'd lied about her parents' seal. In lies, they were now matched. "So I'm afraid I don't know what you're talking about."

She watched him carefully as she repeated the very thing he'd said to her, like a signal that she knew he'd concealed a truth, and she'd now done the same.

His expression revealed nothing. He flicked his wrist, extending the paper between them. "Farewell, Lady Danby. Do return soon."

She gripped the newspaper to hide her shaking hands, thanked him, and left. Her spine tingled until she had passed the bend in the road that took her out of sight of the Kingswoods' home. Only then did she dare to unfurl the paper and look at the headline.

COPSON SLAUGHTERS CREW, STEALS ENGLISH SHIP

She stopped walking, her eyes tearing over the words so quickly that she had to start over three times. Finally, she managed to slow herself even as her heart sprinted.

Earlier this week, Captain Robert Copson sailed into Portsmouth to steal the navy's largest and newest ship, the HMS *Royal Edinburgh*, with gruesome results. The captain, widely known as the most dangerous pirate in the Atlantic for nearly a century, began his theft by boarding a smaller ship, slaughtering the crew, and sailing off in the middle of the night.

When the *Royal Edinburgh* gave chase, Copson and his crew were quick to board the ship and kill all the naval officers before escaping. Reports say he's renamed the ship the *Destiny's Revenge* and has made it part of his fleet alongside the *Fortuna Royale* and the *Ophelia*. There is no word as to his whereabouts, though authorities are searching for the captain and any information that may lead to his capture. The navy is eager to retrieve the *Royal Edinburgh*, as it is reported to be the fastest ship in His Majesty's fleet, and the most heavily armed with one hundred guns.

This comes nearly a week after twenty-two men washed ashore in Plymouth, their bodies shackled together. Eighteen had died from gunshot wounds to the head, and four had their chests cut open. Miraculously, one man survived long enough to tell of how they'd been members of Copson's crew, and had been murdered by the immortal captain. The man succumbed to his condition shortly after.

However, the pirate captain's ships are not without crew members, despite the recent murders. Hundreds of sailors have reportedly signed on to Copson's crew, despite government efforts to dissuade local men from turning to piracy...

Aurelia lowered the paper and swallowed. Ralph had said his father had been home for *weeks*. This news was too recent to be about anyone but William.

William, with his charming smile and exciting letters. Who had Ralph with him now. Who'd sentenced twenty-two men to a horrific death.

Surely there was a reason. There had to be.

Aurelia sprinted home, threw the paper in her bedroom hearth, set it on fire, and stood before the grate to ensure it burned.

No wonder the countess had looked like she'd been crying. Her son had murdered so many—his own crew and so many others—and to know Ralph was there too...

"My lady," a maid said from the doorway. She held out an envelope with Aurelia's name written in familiar script.

The blood drained from Aurelia's face. *William*. He'd written *now*? After so many weeks without a word?

She paced to the maid and took the letter, waiting until the door clicked shut before tearing through her family's seal.

Aurelia,

Please accept my sincerest apologies for not writing. I do hope you've not told anyone that which you swore not to tell and accept my excuse, which is that I have been indisposed as of late.

There was recently a transfer of power aboard the FR, which is both exciting and grueling in ways too numerous and disinteresting to recount here. My busyness has made me neglect a number of things, one of which was your letters, but I am returning to them now.

Perhaps most noteworthy of all recent developments is that I've obtained a new ship It was not without effort to get, and though the price was steep, and not necessarily monetary, I know it will return my investment tenfold It's a decent size, I suppose. The sleeping arrangements are most spacious, and I believe this is the ship I shall consider my home.

I've also heard of your recent illness. I hope you're feeling better, or in good spirits at the very least. Though these last months have been trying, it's a relief to know the trials are only temporary.

I hope to have something more interesting to share next time I write. For now, please know I am not dead and can therefore still uphold my end of our deal.

William

Burn this

The letter trembled in her fingers. *Disinteresting*? His new ship was the most noteworthy...he was the captain now and said nothing about—Ralph had told him of her illness?

Indisposed.

She read it again, her eyes boring into the words to decipher his meanings and all he hadn't told her. He spoke of the *Destiny's Revenge* as though he'd simply walked onto it and sailed it away—to say nothing of the intrigue in the newspaper.

Disinteresting.

William was now the most fearsome pirate on the sea—and he was still writing to her.

The realization hit her so suddenly that she gasped, and the letter fell from her hand and spun into the fire to settle atop the burning newspaper.

"No!" Aurelia dropped to her knees, her fingers fluttering over the flames as they immediately took to the edges of his letter. The parchment curled inward, charred and crumbling, his words burning away until only one line remained.

...the trials are only temporary...

And then it was gone.

7

The Reluctant Debutante

At nineteen, Aurelia's excitement for her debut had cooled. On the day of her presentation as an eligible woman ready for marriage, she slouched in her aunt's dingy little carriage, wearing a white gown and a tasteful number of diamonds—only slightly more than the other girls would wear, but not enough to be gaudy—with her arms folded tightly over her chest.

"Can't I be a spinster like you?" she grumbled, wondering if she could count the hours until she might be free to live as she pleased.

Aunt Clara sniffed, pressing a finger under her nose because she hated the smell of London. "That's not a privilege you've earned. Court a few men, and then we may reconsider if you find no one worth your time."

"How does one tell if they're worth anything at all?"

"I wouldn't know," Aunt Clara said mildly. "I never found one."

Though Aurelia had lived seven years in London, she remembered little of it. Thus far, she'd decided she preferred her aunt's house over the city, a thought that worried her because, while she was beginning to entertain the idea of spinsterhood, she hadn't embraced the thought of becoming a recluse.

They stopped in front of the royal palace where a hundred other well-dressed ladies who were walking inside, tittering and eyeing the castle's turrets and heavy iron gates.

Aurelia stared out the opposite window. A black carriage sat on the other side of the street, its occupants shrouded in darkness. Where they going, and could she follow? Perhaps she'd run across the street and throw herself inside and beg them to take her away without a care as to who might be inside.

She considered it, but then her aunt squawked, "Time to go. We don't want to be late."

With a heavy sigh, Aurelia left the carriage and followed the others, moving at a snail's pace through the palace where they would be presented to the king before spinning their way through a royal ball and finally heading home.

"You used to be excited about this," Aunt Clara puffed as she waddled to a corner of the antechamber where they would wait until it was Aurelia's turn to meet the king. "What happened?"

Ralph. Her parents. Misery.

"I grew up," Aurelia said.

Her aunt's face scrunched. "That's very narrow of you. You used to want love."

"I was a child," Aurelia said morosely. "And I've learned life does not give you what you want just for dreaming hard enough."

Her aunt made a sound low in her throat and looked away.

Any love she might have wanted was on a ship, far from the drudgery of social games she would be forced to endure. And if he were to be a true possibility—and he wasn't—she'd be foolish.

She would not embarrass herself over a man. In fact, she'd gone an entire year without doing anything remotely ridiculous, even though her little girlish crush lingered in the back of her mind like a whisper or a shadow, or a silvery glint of spider silk that caught the light at only a certain time of day, determined to thwart even the most intent feather duster. Nothing could fix it—not even the murders a year ago, or that he continued ruling the sea in ways that made Aunt Clara burn the news more than once.

She'd known it would be this way, but she successfully pretended to ignore her heart and therefore didn't worry for any kind of resurgence of silly fantasies.

In time, Aurelia and her aunt were summoned to the throne room. It was decked in red velvet and gilded fixtures, and filled with a sea of painted faces both on canvas and flesh. Aunt Clara followed Aurelia as she approached the king and sank into a deep curtsy.

"Lady Aurelia Danby," said the courtier next to the king.

"Danby," the king mused, and when Aurelia straightened, she saw a large man in his sixties. He stroked his patchy beard. "Like my nephew."

"She is your nephew's child."

"Ah." The king nodded. "I didn't know he had a child. Very fine. Very nice."

Aurelia forced a smile even as her heart smarted. However, the king's comments were more than most girls received, and now the other young ladies watched Aurelia with jealous sneers. She ignored them and joined her aunt in the corner of the ballroom and talked to no one, glaring away suitors before they could approach.

"Go mingle," Aunt Clara commanded. "No one likes a wallflower."

"They don't want to talk to me."

Her aunt cast her an icy look. "Stop terrifying them."

"I'm doing nothing of the sort."

"You're making your face odious even to God. Go and smile."

Chastened, Aurelia prowled around the perimeter of the room, taking joy only in the way her gown swished around her ankles. It was the finest thing she'd ever worn, and now that she'd debuted, she would have more fine things to wear. The only downside was who she would wear them for. These young men with nice faces and charm, but who were boring and—

"Lady Danby, may I have this dance?"

Aurelia turned, prepared to firmly decline in such a way to assure him no other such invitation would ever be welcome. But she found herself facing a tall young man with golden, sun-bleached hair, a tan face, and dark, smiling eyes.

"Ralph!" She barely kept herself from throwing her arms around him. Instead, her sudden happiness burst from her in a loud giggle. She scanned the opulent room for any other Kingswoods, then stopped when she realized what she was doing.

Like cobwebs and shadows, she reminded herself. *I am not ridiculous*.

"I promised," he said, holding out his hand. "A year is far too long."

"I would hug you, but then you'd probably have to marry me."

"One might find it worth the price," he mused, taking her hand and leading her to the floor where other couples frolicked and spun. "You look lovely."

"You look well-traveled," she replied, eyeing his hair. "It suits you."

A year away had turned him golden in nearly every way, setting him apart from the pasty English gentlemen surrounding them. She remembered him telling her of his desire to have a home and a wife, and she thought a life like that would suit him very well as women eyed him from behind fluttering fans.

Ralph placed a hand on her waist and moved them into the steps of a waltz. "It may suit me, but it doesn't compare to being home. Being here."

"You've only written to me twice, you know," Aurelia said, teasing.

He smirked. "Does Will still write?"

"He does." She might've found a way to ask him to stop, but she couldn't bring herself to do it. A proper lady she may be, but her desire for adventure and freedom remained. So she allowed herself the letters, and enjoyed them for the few minutes she could before she turned them to ash and moved on with her day.

They were like decadent little desserts to be savored only on occasion, and she remained perfectly, utterly sensible.

"Honestly, I don't know when he has the time," Ralph said, spinning her. "But if he can manage it, I have no excuse. I swear to write more."

"Perhaps you should ask him his schedule." She dared not speak his name, because even if she was sensible, she feared his name on her lips might feel like a curse or taste like sin—and sensible girls didn't partake in such things.

"His schedule doesn't have time for questions. He exists, but only as captain."

She wondered how true that was. William's letters were short and vague, but they were still very much *him*, and that had never changed. Instead, she asked, "How long are you here?"

"Only for tonight, unfortunately." His eyes bored into hers, heavy with regret. "It's all we could manage."

A year of intention to return, and this was all the time she'd get with him. He'd hardly been here for a few minutes and already any idea of inviting him to tea or strolling through the garden dissipated.

"But," he said, pulling her close and slowing his steps, "if you swear not to marry this year, I'll return and maybe—"

Everyone stopped to applaud as the dance ended. Ralph stepped back, cleared his throat, and did the same.

"I can assure you I won't marry this year," Aurelia said as the clapping subsided. "I'm trying to convince my aunt to let me be a spinster."

"That would be a travesty," he said with a smirk. If they were anywhere else, she might pinch his cheek like she had when they were younger. Instead, she stuck out her tongue, earning a ferocious laugh from him.

Across the room, Aunt Clara glared. Aurelia took Ralph's hand

and tugged him to the edge of the room where they could snicker beyond the range of her aunt's judgment.

With Ralph's return, Aurelia's debut wasn't as dismal as she expected. She danced with him more than was appropriate, and when she returned home that night, she felt light and even a little cheerful.

Feelings that dissipated at the sight of the letter waiting on her bed.

Letters were not usually cause for alarm, but this one was different. This one did not bear her parents' seal, but another featuring two crossed swords stamped in blue wax. It bore no address on the back—only her name written in handwriting she knew as well as her own.

Suddenly fighting to breathe, she hung her head out the door and called for a maid. One came running, and Aurelia paced farther into the room, tearing off her long white gloves and demanding, "Untie me. Get me out of this dress, please, I beg you."

The maid set to work, untying as Aurelia gripped her bedpost and tried to catch her breath.

"Are you okay, miss?" the maid asked.

Aurelia gasped, "I can't breathe."

The dress pooled to the floor, leaving only her stays and chemise. Her fingers dug into the wood, and now she fully hyperventilated as the maid rushed to free her from her bindings. Once they fell away, Aurelia sucked in her first full breath and stepped aside so the maid could gather the garments and leave the room.

The letter still sat on her bed, expectant in its lack of script and its blue seal.

A letter with that seal came from down the lane.

A letter with no address…it was hand delivered.

Even with her stays and dress gone, she still struggled to breathe. She shook out her hands, and once she found her nerve, she grabbed the letter and tore the wax away.

Aurelia,

Congratulations on your debut.

You're in London tonight as I write to you, and I hope you're not forced to dance with any stuffy old gentlemen you dislike (Ralph not included).

This is a different letter than usual. Instead of the sea, I'll tell you of home. It's been three years since I was last here, and while Ralph enjoys the ball in London, I'm dining with my parents and youngest brother, who I'm not sure you know. He's fourteen and usually hides away to study books and rocks and bugs and whatever else a boy of his temperament likes. I find him amusing in the best ways.

Though I feel more at home on a ship, my childhood home holds a charm I find nowhere else. Where my life abroad is windy and loud and full of excitement, this place is quiet and secure. It makes me feel like myself without all the demands of the life I've come to know. And my mother worries, so I feel it's only kind to appear for her every now and again.

I leave again after supper, which is both a relief and a sadness. A relief because I'm returning to a life I've learned to love, but also because I leave behind a generous measure of ease and comfort.

I do hope you're well. If you ever wish to write back, you'll *find several addresses below. I can't tell you where I'll be or when, but I or someone I know might look for correspondence at these places.*

William

You don't have to burn this one.

Below his letter was a list of addresses through five port cities in different countries, along with a name—William C. Smith.

Trembling, she dropped the letter and moved to the window where she could see a single chimney above the trees.

He'd been there, just across the lake. He'd been at the door, perhaps in this very house, and she'd been too busy meeting the king and dancing with Ralph.

Spider silk and shadows, she told herself. *It's just spider silk and shadows...* She turned away and tugged at the pins in her hair, pulling down her blonde locks and leaving them a disheveled mess. With her hair in ruins and wearing a simple chemise, she couldn't possibly go out. She couldn't seek him, even if he was still home. And he wasn't going to be.

She sank to her knees, remembering the way she'd expected William to sweep her off her feet at her debut, and how foolish she'd been to think it possible. She laughed, a terrible sound that sounded more like a choke, and was grateful she'd let go of the idea before it could have followed her here, to this day, when such a disappointment would have devastated her.

How nice it is not to be devastated, she thought as she stared at the pins on the floor. *How nice it is to not be disappointed.*

The letter trembled in her hand. For a moment, she considered burning it. She even moved to the hearth and held it over the fire, watching the light shift and behind the addresses scrawled over the bottom, but her fingers would not release it.

Instead, she fished the book from beneath her mattress, its pages filled with all her old clippings of Copson's escapades. She hadn't touched or added to them in a year, but tonight she slipped William's letter among them. She'd burn it tomorrow...or next week. She'd close the door on William for good—somehow finally remove those cobwebs—and find love with someone more suitable and available.

She'd burn it eventually.

8

The Seven Sins of
Unsuitable Suitors

Despite being a rather dedicated wallflower, Aurelia was unfortunately still an heiress. Because of this, she had three suitors that first year, and all of them nearly made her write to William.

The first young man was one she heard was a catch. Reginald Cocking came to Aunt Clara's front door with a large arrangement of flowers and his nose so high she could hardly see his green eyes that gleamed with insufferable arrogance.

Reginald was remarkably tall and awfully handsome, and when he met Aurelia in the parlor, he proclaimed he was to inherit a dukedom along with a sizable fortune and an estate much finer than her aunt's. He spoke at length about his business ventures, describing his latest investments and the kinds of purchases he made with all his dividends. All throughout the conversation, his nose never came down.

When Aurelia spoke of books, he listed several he had read and hated for one reason or another. This author didn't write well, and that author was poor. When she spoke of art, he dismissed Michelangelo and da Vinci and proclaimed he listened to no music but that which he could play himself.

Having already decided to dislike him, Aurelia suggested dryly that it would be terrible to live without music and that he must be impressively proficient. He sat at the piano to prove it, and he played very well.

After he left, Aurelia told the servants he was not to be allowed back into the house, and any correspondence from him should be thrown away. She gave the flowers to the butler so he could give them to his wife.

Dear William,

Are they all like this? Am I doomed to a man who ranks as highly as I do but sees no one lower than himself? Now I wish Dante had described a circle of Hell for the proud, then I could know which one to avoid so I'd never have to see him again.

Yours,
Aurelia

She blushed so violently at the thought of him—of *Captain Copson*—actually reading her silly complaints that she crumpled the letter and threw it into the fire before the ink could dry.

The second man, Sir Victor Pyle, was opposite from the first, but also very similar. While he focused nothing on what he had, he did speak at length about possessions.

"I hear you have a dowry that could rival the king's coffers," Victor said, looking at everything her aunt possessed except for her. "I do hope you won't be dissatisfied by my lack. Even your aunt—my word, she has such fine things."

Instead of adoring her for what he could seek to gain, he looked down on her, as though having more made her less. His pride turned out to be as suffocating as Mr. Cocking's, only he seemed to dislike her because of it—though not enough, apparently, to give up trying to court her.

The second time he called upon her, Victor fell at her feet and said, "Lady Danby, I haven't stopped thinking of you since our first meeting. You are everything I could ever want, and I beg you to do me the honor of accepting my hand."

Aurelia doubted he really liked her that much. He wanted her name and fortune, so she rejected him with a simple, "I couldn't possibly," before she rose from her seat and left the room. The butler saw him out.

Dear William,

Envy is as disgusting as finding too much satisfaction in what one has. What must it be like to be so miserable in one's circumstances that one must bring down those around them to find happiness?

I have officially been proposed to. I wonder if this might be the only proposal I ever get, but my aunt assures me it is early in the season and I'm still young. I don't know if this is a relief or a warning.

Nevertheless, I think I detest this.

Yours,
Aurelia

Preaching about envy to a pirate might not make her particularly endearing, so she burned this letter too.

The third gentleman also seemed to have little interest in her, but was rather taken with her aunt's dining table. August Goring was large, which Aurelia didn't mind until he ate every morsel left over after the meal, consuming enough to feed five men while maintaining room for dessert.

Thankfully, Aunt Clara was just as horrified and ended the night an awful shade of green. He, too, was not permitted to call again.

> Dear William,
>
> If you return to England any time soon, please stop by. I'd like to speak with you about becoming a pirate.
>
> Yours,
> Aurelia

Again, she fed the fire and managed her wretchedness in silence.

Two months passed without word from William, but Aurelia didn't worry. When his letter finally did come, there were three folded together, chronicling his recent travels to the Caribbean. He described breathtaking islands with mountains that rose from white beaches and blue waters, and he told her about palm trees a sky bluer than she could imagine. There were so many kinds of people and cultures and pirates who feared Captain Copson and sought to gain his favor.

> I told them I met a witch in my youth who said the truest love of my life would only appear long after I was meant to die, so I found and drank from the Fountain of Youth so I wouldn't miss her. But in doing so, I was cursed to forget where the fountain

was, and therefore could not tell them its location.

I'm not sure if they believed it, but they certainly believe I am immortal and asked to know where the witch is. I told them she's dead because I didn't think to bring her along, and now they despair that all the best things are reserved for me.

They might have been flattering me, but it doesn't matter. We're all liars and thieves, and I certainly won't reward them for niceties. Then they would not try so hard to impress me.

Ralph wrote too, but sporadically, and he shared more of his thoughts about life and purpose rather than adventure. She wouldn't have said they were boring...to his face. But she kept them anyway as they turned out to be fantastic remedies for sleepless nights.

After Aurelia turned twenty, she noted with sadness that Ralph didn't come back as he'd promised, so she distracted herself with parties. They were awful affairs full people who laughed too loud, drank too much, and disappeared into gardens with those they fancied, only to turn up married a few days later.

At one ball, she met a young man named Lawrence Talley who was amiable enough. Aurelia supposed he was handsome—like a portrait come to life, but the artist had left out every flaw. His hair was spun gold, his gray eyes inquisitive and calm. No one had any complaints of his agreeable temperament, so she agreed to meet him again.

They courted for most of the season, and Aurelia didn't mind the speculation and scrutiny they drew for a long courtship. He was a kind man, but after several weeks, she deduced he was too perfect, and as much as she was playing the part of a perfect young woman—who absolutely did not receive letters from a pirate who filled the newspapers with blood, dread, and gold—she assumed he did the same.

She didn't know what he hid. Then one day, he showed her.

Lawrence knew her fondness for books, and teased his family's vast collection. After they enjoyed tea in his family's library under the watchful eyes of his mother and Aunt Clara, he invited her to wander the shelves with him.

She knew stories of ghosts and spirits in dusty old libraries, but since such things didn't happen in real life, she determined his ugly spirit would be the one to make an appearance. Just as she suspected, as they reached the histories, he pulled her into an alcove and attempted—very poorly—to snog her.

Surprised—but only a little—she pulled back her fist and slugged him in the face. He cried out, and the ladies still drinking their tea went silent.

Aurelia frantically grabbed a large book and tossed it at his feet. He grunted as it landed on his toe, but she was already rushing to the end of the shelves, her hands fluttering around her face.

"It was ghost!" she cried to her aunt and Lady Talley.

Lawrence limped out from between the stacks, his hand over his eye. "She hit me!"

Aurelia paced to her aunt and laid a hand on her shoulder. "I did no such thing. I don't know how." She lifted her hands, her wrists and fingers limp as though she was too delicate and too stupid to make them into fists. With a breathy sigh, she pressed them over her heart. "Oh, Aunt Clara, it gave me such a fright."

Lady Talley stood, her worried eyes moving between Aurelia and her son. "My word, Lawrence—Aurelia, are you sure?"

"It was there, I saw it. It threw a book." She threw her arm toward the shelves. "Go, look! You'll see it on the ground."

Lady Talley hurried off and came back moments later with the tome in her hand, her eyes wide, face pale.

"She hit me," Lawrence said again, gesturing wildly at Aurelia.

Executing her finest portrayal of ladylike innocence, she asked, "Why on earth would I do that?"

"I—" He lowered his hand with a huff, knowing she'd won. She had no reason to hit him unless he wanted to admit he'd kissed her.

"We must go," Aurelia said to her aunt. "You know I'm petrified of ghosts."

Once they were rolling away in the carriage, Aunt Clara studied Aurelia's smug look with narrowed eyes. "There was no ghost."

"It was terrifying," was all Aurelia would say. She had to wear gloves for a week to hide her bruised knuckles.

> Dear William,
>
> I hit a man for being daft and hurt my hand, but not badly. It's only sore with a bruise. I wonder if you might describe in your next letter how to throw a proper punch, as I don't believe my aunt will know how to instruct me.
>
> I hope you will not judge. This is my first trouble in a long while, and is not to be understood as a regular occurrence.
>
> Yours,
> Aurelia

She thought this letter was destined for the fire like the others. But if a man like Lawrence Talley could rebel against decency and get away with it, then she could commit a sin just as grievous that no one would have to know about either.

Besides, said a small whisper in her head, *that should've been William's kiss.*

A day after sending it, regret settled in. The letter had been so short, and she'd signed it *yours* as though she belonged to him. She'd thought sending it would somehow offend the expectations heaped upon her, but it would only make her look stupid because *this* was what she chose to say after seven years? She hadn't even asked after his welfare!

After spending a considerable amount of time screaming into her pillow, she prayed the Lord would somehow make the letter disappear before it reached William, and trusting God would be so kind and faithful to arrange it, she promptly put it from her mind.

The next suitor, Cornelius Price, was a gentleman with yellowing teeth and ostentatious clothes. Jewels dripped from his fingers and lapels, and every step he took glittered and jingled, despite the fact that his shoes were worn and scuffed, and he had not a penny on him.

Aunt Clara said he would probably never have more than what he wore, and encouraged Aurelia to avoid men who looked like greed, so she kindly dismissed him and attended more balls where everyone talked about the weather and the latest fashions in London and not about Captain Copson and the gold he stole from a renowned slaver the week before.

The papers were aghast, as he hadn't done it alone, but with a pirate whose name had appeared more in recent years—Davy Silver, an ex-slave who'd overthrown the crew and captain bringing him to the Americas. After the coup, Davy had enlisted his brothers to head his new crew, and for the last four years, they'd wreaked havoc among the West Indies trading routes.

Together, Copson and Silver ruined the slaver and left his company destitute. William even wrote to her about it, and these rare occasions when he vaguely acknowledged what the papers said about him made

83

his existence and his letters all the more exciting.

The sound of forty cannons discharging, one right after the other, is like the most spectacular symphony. It shakes the entire ship, splits the air, and aggravates the sea. Cannonballs rip through a ship's hull like paper, and the splinters falling into the water sound like rain.

Forty guns - which is fewer than half of what I have on the DR - can easily cripple a ship, and it gives me great satisfaction to watch it sink, knowing it was my will alone that sent it to the bottom of the ocean. I'd also like to believe I have the best gunners in all the Atlantic.

There was no contest between hearing about England's weather patterns and sinking ships. And as she was relegated to irritating, fluffy conversations with bankers and lawyers and lords, she grew more dissatisfied that her life was not exciting and not at all what she wanted, no matter how hard she tried to convince herself otherwise.

Two more letters came before the third, and this third letter is what convinced her God was punishing her. In response to his displeasure, she took a moment to regret what she'd done to Mr. Talley—but it was brief because she knew God to be understanding, or at the very least long-suffering enough to not give up on her entirely.

Aurelia,

To throw a proper fist, curl your fingers tightly into your palm. Keep your thumb on the outside, on top of your middle or fourth knuckle, to avoid breaking it. Be sure to keep your wrist stable, pull back your arm to strike, and throw your fist forward, keeping it in line with your eye. Plant your feet, and as you move, twist your body toward your opponent. This will drive more force into your hit.

Of course, they may see this coming, so be quick about it. The bruise may be unavoidable depending on which part of a person you hit, the bones that lie beneath, or how many times you wish to strike them. If you are more inclined to protect your fingers from unsightly marks, consider a swift knee to his groin. Knowing as I do that you have no brothers or a father holding your suitors accountable, I do not judge, but applaud you. I only take issue with one thing from your note, and though I don't think my advice is particularly relevant given my situation, I suggest you consider getting into some trouble slightly more frequently, if not just to keep things interesting. And then please remember to tell me about it.

William

Please keep for future reference.

After reading it, Aurelia felt an odd mix of sparkling delight and crushing embarrassment. She didn't allow herself to ponder either too closely, lest her aunt notice her giggling or crying and start to ask questions. So she stored the letter away and carried on as though nothing had happened, though it was harder now for reasons she also refused to examine, lest she start screaming and go entirely mad. As it was, William's letters were the only boon for her thinning sanity, and she would not let a cure become a poison.

At twenty-one, Aurelia wasn't fully done with courting, but she was very close to it. She only attended a handful of parties and courted one suitor who reminded her of Mr. Talley from the year before. Mr. Lucius Losh was nice enough and well liked, but she knew, as with most people, there must be a fatal flaw. It presented itself at a masquerade ball where he got violently drunk and smashed a table full of champagne flutes when Aurelia told him she thought he'd had enough to drink.

Upon turning twenty-two, most of her peers had already married, and the only ones left were either ugly or ruined. Aurelia was neither, unfortunately, so she courted her seventh and final suitor, Boric Tinsey.

Boric proposed, but only because he didn't wish to put in the effort to actually court her. They took a stroll one morning where he told her absolutely nothing of interest about his life. Not because he was withholding, but because he did absolutely nothing, had no ambitions, and was dreadfully boring, and everyone thought so, which was why he remained unmarried.

Aurelia denied him and went home, grumbling the whole way. A letter waited on her bed, and then things didn't seem so bad.

9

The Amiable Aunt

"I want to ask again about the possibility of becoming an old maid."

Aunt Clara's rickety carriage rumbled down the lane toward the Kingswoods' home, the dark, dingy interior illuminated with flickering patches of daylight cutting through the trees.

Tea with the countess had become a weekly occurrence since Aurelia's initial visit five years before. Now twenty-three, Aurelia felt the earl and his wife were more like relatives than the strangers they'd once been, even with so much left unsaid between them. They never spoke of Captain Copson or what their sons did at sea—there was only their shipping business, which was mentioned vaguely and never discussed at length.

Hidden under a pile of old blankets, Aunt Clara didn't even spare a salty look in response to her niece's statement. "You would make a fine old maid. You've developed a rather haggish disposition since your debut."

Aurelia smiled without showing her teeth. She had come to enjoy needling her aunt over the years, though now it was out of endearment rather than spite. "I learned from the best."

Her aunt squawked a single laugh. "I promised your parents I would do my best. It's no fault of mine that you've spurned every man who's come your way."

"None of them are worth anything." Aurelia smoothed her hands over her skirt. It was burgundy, the color of blood, and made her think of the latest articles scaring the public. Copson had recently dispatched several Spanish naval ships as they pursued him off the coast of Portugal, only for them to discover the captain had somehow stolen most of their cannons before they left harbor, leaving only one per ship.

"I've decided not to court this season," Aurelia said. "I'm tired of it."

"I can't force you, and I won't. But should your parents inquire, I will tell them it is you who refuses to marry."

"They don't inquire."

"They'll notice your lack of matrimony eventually. God help you if they decide to get involved." She leaned forward to peer out the window, then returned to her previous spot with a grimace after witnessing the insult that was the sun. "You talk to them, don't you?"

Aurelia raised her eyebrows. "Do you think that's what those letters are?" she asked, challenging her aunt to admit she knew better. Surely after nine years, William's letters had been noticed and thought about by someone other than herself.

"Of course not," Aunt Clara said. "Your parents don't have the minds to write that much."

"Why haven't you said anything?"

Aunt Clara smiled, and it made her look quite pretty. "Because a young lady ought to have something to occupy her thoughts."

"Do you know who it is?" Since her debut, Aurelia had gradually realized her aunt was more of an ally than a wicked witch, so her heart remained calm as the question passed her lips.

"There are so few people it could be—but don't tell me." She waved her niece into silence. "I shall figure it out on my own. Even an old spinster must have something to think about."

Aurelia regarded her aunt solemnly. A long moment passed before she quietly asked, "Why did you take my books?"

Aunt Clara sniffed and stared out the window for so long that Aurelia wondered if she'd heard the question. As they rounded a bend and the Kingswoods' home came into view, she finally answered. "You would have hidden in them and filled your mind with ridiculous notions like your mother did. And you would have married a prince with an empty head and pockets full of flattery. She wanted a fairy tale, and she was never satisfied—the story was always better than what she got." She met Aurelia's gaze. "Nevertheless, I've regretted the pain I caused you, and I love you enough to admit it."

Aurelia flushed. Her aunt had never said such a thing. To admit that it had all been to keep Aurelia from becoming like the distant mother who'd abandoned her...well, Aurelia understood, even if she could not bring herself to agree.

"But I know you've found something worthwhile in those letters," Aunt Clara said, "and they seem harmless enough. In fact, you're quite sensible, and I like you all the more for it."

Aurelia's face warmed at such high praise from her aunt, but before she could answer, the carriage rolled to a stop, and a footman opened the door.

The countess, dressed in dark purple, greeted them when they entered the foyer. She clasped Aunt Clara's hands, then took hold of Aurelia's shoulders and kissed her cheeks.

"How are you, dear?" she asked as they strolled arm in arm toward the parlor after Aunt Clara.

"Very well." Aurelia whispered it like a secret. "I am to be a spinster, and I confess I couldn't be happier."

The countess tutted, but a conspiratorial grin appeared as she leaned close and patted Aurelia's hand. "You're still so young—don't despair on love."

"Oh never," Aurelia swore in the same clever tone. They drifted into the room and toward a table set with tea and tiny sandwiches. "I've merely despaired on suitors."

The parlor hadn't changed much, but today there was a notable difference—two fencing sabers leaned against the wall in the corner of the room, perfectly framed in a patch of sun. Their blades gleamed in the light.

Aurelia glanced at the countess, imagining her fencing with the earl. It was not a difficult image to conjure. Cecily Kingswood was the finest lady Aurelia had ever met, and now she realized the countess's arms were lean and slightly muscular—just enough to make Aurelia wonder if the jewelry and manners concealed something fantastically wicked.

She supposed one would have to be to marry a pirate. William had never said anything about her, and Ralph had only ever painted his mother as the woman who'd raised him to be a gentleman. He'd told few stories of his childhood aboard the *Fortuna Royale*, in which the countess was never mentioned—as though she didn't exist beyond proper society.

Aunt Clara groaned as she sat, completely oblivious to Aurelia's contemplations. "My niece has told you she plans not to court this season."

"No," the countess said, pouring the tea as Aurelia took her seat. "Only that she plans to never court again."

"Perhaps one of your sons could convince her otherwise."

Aurelia choked on her first sip of tea and immediately began coughing. "I'm so sorry," she rasped between bouts of hacking. "Forgive me." She waved at Aunt Clara as though to say, *And her.*

"I would be delighted for her to marry one if it meant they'd be home more often," the countess said as though nothing was wrong. Then, to Aurelia's horror, she added, "If you can believe it, William will be thirty in two years, and it pains me to see him alone."

A ragged gasp offended Aurelia's efforts to purge the tea from her throat. Still, the other ladies paid her no heed as she fought for her life and fading dignity.

"Where are your sons these days?" Aunt Clara asked, not even sparing a glance in Aurelia's direction.

The countess gave a demure smile. "I'm afraid I don't know. They travel so much."

"Do they write?"

She sipped her tea. "My youngest writes most often. Will and Ralph hardly think of it."

Aurelia fanned herself, taking long, slow breaths through her mortification. She tried to stifle another cough and wheezed horribly.

"I hope they're being wise while they—are you quite fine?" Aunt Clara finally turned her disapproving gaze on Aurelia.

"Yes," Aurelia said, clearing her throat to bring her voice closer to normal. She lifted her tea. "I'm alright."

Aunt Clara turned to the countess again. "As I was saying, I hope your sons are being smart, what with all those dreadful reports of pirates."

Thankfully, Aurelia was not drinking this time, but she still hid her grin in her teacup.

"They know all they need to take care of themselves," the countess assured Aunt Clara while watching Aurelia with dark, shrewd eyes. "They're as wise as a mother could hope for."

Aunt Clara rocked back, her face drawn and fingers clutching her saucer as fervently as her prayer beads. "That Captain Copson—I read the most awful things about him. Every week, it seems, he has done something more horrible than the previous."

"He sank another slaver's ship," Aurelia said before realizing she shouldn't know of such things when her aunt had gone to such lengths to destroy the papers. She paused for a blink before adding, "A while ago... Someone mentioned it at a ball, and I thought, 'how terrifying,' but also, 'how brave' and..." Catching Aunt Clara staring, she paused. "Pirates...are so worrisome... And I hope your sons are being very careful."

The countess' eyes betrayed nothing. "The papers say so many things. I stopped reading them ages ago. My husband keeps me apprised of anything that might catch my interest."

"Probably for the best," Aurelia said, eager to agree with anything to move them toward another subject as sweat pricked the back of her neck. It was petrifying to give voice to the topic of Captain Copson in the Kingswoods' home—like walking over graves or summoning a ghost. The teacup rattled in her hand as she shivered.

The countess pulled Aunt Clara into a new topic about good help being hard to find these days. Aurelia faded into silence while her heartbeat returned to normal. The countess reached over to place her warm hand on Aurelia's without pulling her focus from Aunt Clara.

Her fingers were delicate, her nails perfectly trimmed. Aurelia's attention strayed once more to the sabers in the corner while the women discussed arbitrary things her aunt would happily pick apart for hours.

But they only stayed for an hour before they said their goodbyes and headed for the carriage. As Aunt Clara sighed and grumbled her way into her seat, Aurelia wrung her hands. When the footman turned to help her in, she stepped back.

"I forgot my glove," Aurelia said quickly. "Please excuse me." Then she rushed back into the house before her aunt could protest, and made for the parlor.

"...and I wonder how much she knows—" The countess cut off as Aurelia appeared in the doorway. The earl stood beside his wife, his gaze so heavy and direct that Aurelia's breath hitched.

"I'm terribly sorry," she said. "I don't mean to barge in."

"It's fine," the countess said, remaining seated. "Did you forget something?"

"Oh, yes, um, my glove." Aurelia looked at her bare hands. "But... I'm so sorry, I actually didn't wear gloves. I didn't leave anything. I only wanted to ask..." Her eyes moved to the sabers again. The sun had shifted, no longer illuminating their presence. "Do you spar?"

Both the earl and the countess followed Aurelia's gaze to the far side of the room. They glanced at each other before looking at Aurelia again.

"Yes," the countess said. "Do you?"

Aurelia shook her head, shy and eager all at once. Unbidden, William's words ran through her head.

I suggest you consider getting into some trouble slightly more frequently.

She wondered if he would consider this adequately troublesome. "No, but...might you be willing to teach me?"

The couple met each other's gazes again, and this time the countess smiled. The earl gave a small, nearly imperceptible nod.

"I'd be happy to," said the countess.

"Why do you wish to learn?" the earl asked.

Aurelia ducked her head, unable to help her grin. "Because my suitors were awful, and I have no brothers or a father to hold them accountable." She looked up, hoping their son's words would make them hear something of him in her excuse. "And since I refuse to partake in any more courtships, I must occupy myself with something interesting."

The Kingswoods smirked. "Can you come tomorrow morning?" the countess asked. "Tell your aunt we are having lunch."

Aurelia's smile grew. "Of course." She thanked them and left. She was nearly at the front door when she heard the earl say, "Ralph didn't tell—I'm convinced it was Will."

Upon their return home, a letter waited for Aurelia. Still in her gown, she flopped back onto her bed, uncaring for the wrinkles she was folding into the silk.

Aurelia,

Sailors are some of the grossest, ugliest people I've ever had the misfortune of knowing, and today I finally hit my limit.

It hasn't been winter for nearly a month, and certain waters are warm enough to be in for at least a few minutes. This was not temptation enough for many of my crew, and so today, we dropped anchor and I lined them up on the main deck to tell them how much they all stink and that I hate them for it. I said whoever didn't jump in the water and start scrubbing would be thrown in. Most of them jumped. Some of them I pushed when they didn't move fast enough, and I didn't let down the ladder for a good five minutes, though I really should have held out for ten. When you think this life might be exciting, you don't consider the kinds of smells I have suffered as of late.

William

Burn this now - it's an awful letter I'd like to believe I never sent to a lady.

Laughing, Aurelia read it once more before she swished to the hearth and set it gently into the flames.

10

A Handsome Prince (Or, A Letter in a Bottle)

"Mind your feet, Aurelia."

Aurelia hadn't noticed the earl looking her way, hidden as he was behind this morning's newspaper. He sat at a small table in the Kingswoods' garden, a cup of tea growing cold by his elbow as Aurelia sparred with the countess.

As Aurelia paused to look at him, the countess's saber swatted against her middle.

"That's ten," the countess said, breathless beneath the early spring sun. "I win."

Aurelia frowned at her, then the earl. "What about my feet?"

"Your stance was off," he said.

Blonde locks had worked loose from her braid, and she pushed them away as she leveled her saber at him. "I think it was fine and you just wanted the countess to win."

He grunted and lifted his tea to conceal the barest hint of a smile.

"You did," she breathed in disbelief. "You—"

"You always come through for me," the countess cooed as she slipped off her gloves and moved behind her husband to drape her arms around his shoulders. "Give her more bad advice. She's getting too good."

Aurelia flicked her saber so its point landed deep in the grass. When she pulled her hand away, it swayed and remained upright. *Pirate*, she wanted to call the gentleman dressed in a silver vest and looking every bit a fine gentleman and not a swashbuckling liar.

They still never breathed a word of the truth, though, so she laughed and said, "You couldn't even spare me on my birthday."

Another year had passed—she was twenty-four, as of today, and much happier remaining in the country and secretly learning sword-play. She certainly wasn't the best, but the Kingswoods were patient, fair instructors.

The earl turned a page and flapped his paper. "Consider it a gift of character," he said with a dry humor she'd come to appreciate once she got over her nerves at being in his presence. She smirked and earned a wink in return.

The countess slipped a hand into her dress pocket—a light frock like Aurelia's, made for movement instead of fashion—and withdrew a small box, which she handed to Aurelia. "And this is my gift."

"You didn't have to—"

"I'll hear nothing of it," she said. "I've never had a daughter to spoil with pretty things and must make do with someone else's."

Beneath the lid was a small gold pendant in the shape of a turtle. Tiny green gems sparkled in its shell. Aurelia drew in a breath.

"The turtle," said the countess, taking the necklace and moving behind Aurelia, "is a symbol of perseverance. It meant a great deal to me when I received it long ago in the Caribbean. Now I hope to give it new life through you." She fastened the clasp and pulled away, eyeing the pendant to ensure it laid flat.

The Kingswoods occasionally made vague mentions of places and times and experiences. Simple statements like these were rare and heavy with allusion, and they wrecked Aurelia's imagination with images of ships and cities she'd only read about. Though she longed to ask for more, she didn't dare. She collected every question that sprang to her lips and answered them with her own silent conjecture.

The earl stood, folding his hands behind him. "A wise choice, Cecily darling. It suits her."

"Happy birthday, dear," the countess said.

Aurelia touched the delicate shell, swallowing back tears as she said, "Thank you. You're both so kind to me, and I don't know how I'll ever repay—"

"None of that," the countess said firmly. "My home has grown quiet, and you've brought it to life again. We are even." She took Aurelia's arm and steered her toward the house. "Now go get changed. Your aunt will be expecting you, and I won't be the reason you're late."

Aurelia did as she was told, employing a maid to help her back into her dress, and returned to the foyer where the Kingswoods waited.

"Enjoy the sea," the earl said, his voice as light as she ever heard it. "I recommend sitting on the shore at sunset, if the weather permits."

As another very generous birthday gift, the Kingswoods had happily offered and arranged for her and Aunt Clara to stay the weekend at their coastal estate. Aunt Clara had required some prodding and convincing, but she'd ultimately agreed to it. It would be Aurelia's first time at the sea, and she was eager to experience it far from smelly bays and city ports.

Aunt Clara wasn't ready to leave by the time Aurelia returned. She was shut away in a parlor, grumbling and groaning, so Aurelia returned to her room. Unlocking her desk drawer, she removed a small compass.

Its silver body fit perfectly in her palm, cool to the touch and etched with swirling waves. The needle wiggled idly as she held it flat and wound its long chain through the fingers of her opposite hand.

She'd kept the letter it came with, the parchment worn from how many times she'd read it over the past month. It was a reply to a letter she'd sent nearly two months ago—one she'd carefully drafted several times before finding the courage to send it.

For all the times she'd wanted to write to him, she'd finally found an interesting-enough topic that wouldn't leave her embarrassed or regretful. Nothing about learning to wield a sword with his parents, but only that she had tea with them—and she planned to travel.

It wasn't becoming a princess or a knight, but it was conceivable and practical for a woman like Aurelia. Even Aunt Clara, surprisingly, approved. She spoke highly of travel, though she never did it, and she praised her niece for being so astute.

Aurelia,

I was surprised and pleased to hear from you. All my correspondence is usually business, and while it pays, it's nice to have something out of the ordinary.

I heartily commend your intentions to go abroad. If you ever need ideas for places to go or things to see, I'd be most happy to supply you with a list tailored to whichever corner of the world you're most inclined to see. Though I haven't yet been everywhere, I'll know people who've visited the places I've neglected, at the very least.

If you worry your aunt might not enjoy adventurous tales while you travel, you may keep me in mind as a recipient of anything you wish to share. As I said, I don't receive much mail outside the mundane, and you'd be doing me a favor to break the monotony.

Thank you for entertaining my parents while their sons fall prey to the ocean and all its inhabitants. Please continue to visit them. As they worry about me, I do for them as well. I don't know what they do to occupy themselves, but I assume they must be dreadfully bored.

Enclosed with this letter is a compass. I recently got a new one I like better and had nothing to do with this one, so enjoy it as you travel. Or use it as a paperweight it'll serve just as well.

William

PS. Do write again. I know your silence well and have often wondered if you receive my letters. I assume you've remained quiet out of guilt for challenging me so long ago in the woods, or because you've had some terrible accident that has caused difficulty in holding a pen. If it's one or the other, do let me know.

Writing to him felt dangerous and thrilling—like opening a door and feeling the welcoming warmth of hell on frostbitten cheeks. She wanted that thrill again, the likes of which she hadn't felt since she was a child when the world was entirely open to her. And now that she had left behind courtship and spent the year settling in to being free to do as she pleased, she was eager write again...once she knew what to say.

"Aurelia!" her aunt squawked from the foyer. "We must be going. Come."

Aurelia pocketed the compass and did as she was told.

Aunt Clara was in a despicable mood during the carriage ride to the sea. She huffed and hiccupped with tiny groans and sighs, worrying her hands and mumbling. Aurelia maintained silence so as to not offend her further.

However, it appeared Aunt Clara could not keep it in.

"I've had word from your parents," she said, each word a gust of frustration that left her breathless. "You are to be married."

Aurelia's blood ran cold. "Married."

"Yes, keep up," Aunt Clara snapped. "You are to be sent to France next month to Prince Pierre. He's the French king's fourth son, and I have been instructed to prepare you for your departure."

Aurelia looked to the carriage doors to make sure the handles were still there and she was not locked inside. Sweat broke over her skin. "Aunt Clara."

What about traveling and sword practice with the Kingswoods? What of her freedom? Was she really to lose everything so easily—so quickly?

"There is no arguing," she said sharply. "Your parents worried you were not courting, so they went to the king, and he arranged the marriage. It is not out of benevolence or love—it's wicked politics. It's a marriage for England. You are a pawn forging a strained alliance against the Spanish. You are meant for nothing more than diplomacy and to bear ugly French children for their smelly French palaces."

"No." Aurelia shook her head. "I won't do it. I won't go."

Aunt Clara's face drained of blood, and her eyes blackened with fury. "You think you have a choice, obstinate child?"

"I'll run away." Her voice came shrill and her vision wavered. She tried to take a breath, but there wasn't enough air. She'd only been free for a year, had only just begun to make her own choices—but she would not be allowed to have even that. "You can't make me go."

"I am making you do nothing. They are making you do it, and you will do it and be grateful. As will I, even as they tear away the most precious thing I've ever had—" Her wrinkled hand flew to her mouth as her words grew thin. Tears sprang to her eyes and rolled down her face.

Aurelia slid to her knees on the carriage floor. She'd given up on breathing, so she merely laid her head on her beloved aunt's lap as the old woman openly wept.

Aurelia did not cry. Her mind and body had gone numb. This was what she'd wanted as a child—a prince to make her a princess. Perhaps he would be handsome and kind and whisk her away to a lovely palace full of true love and wishes.

Except Aurelia wasn't a child anymore, and this was no storybook. She'd known too many prideful, lofty men to assume the prince was any better. Even if he was, she would resent him forever for taking her from her aunt, her home, and her Kingswoods.

Curled at her aunt's feet, she stared through the window until they reached the sea, but the Kingswoods' coastal estate felt like a mockery, reminding her of a boy with blue eyes and a dream of true love that still festered in a dark, forgotten corner of her heart.

The compass weighed heavy in her pocket.

She drifted through the house as her aunt hid away in an upstairs room to cry and bemoan Aurelia's stupendous luck and most fortunate arrangement. If only Aurelia were so capable of expelling her feelings as Aunt Clara, she'd cry and rage and screech at the unfairness of it all, and then maybe they'd think her crazy and wouldn't dare send her to France.

A pair of doors opened to a stone walkway leading to a stretch of beach. She followed it, hardly noticing as rocks turned to sand beneath her slippers. The sun hid behind thin clouds, offering no comfort, and gray waves crashed into the surf, drawing her near with an appealing thunder that promised to drown her every thought.

Marriage to a prince. Ballgowns and nobility and libraries full of fanciful books. She'd never be a queen, and all she'd have to do was be silent and pretty.

She should have been grateful, but even princes could be horrible.

Her own father was one, and this was the only gift he'd ever thought to give her.

Did they think this was love? Was this what they thought she wanted?

Did they care?

She thought of the earl with his stony expressions and blunt words. His sharp eyes held tales of the Captain Copson who ruled the seas and frightened every common man, pirate, and king alike. Even though he was not necessarily paternal toward her, and she wouldn't say they were close, he'd still loved her better than her own father. Better than a prince or a king. He'd let her into his home and his life, and this was the thought that finally drew the stinging tears from her eyes.

The ocean stretched before her, beautiful and welcoming. Sparing no thought to her dress, she stepped into the water. The waves sucked back into the ocean and begged her to follow. It would be so easy to keep walking and not stop until she was floating, treading water, and finally sinking.

She vividly remembered the feeling of her dress weighing her to the bottom of a lake. The one she wore now was bigger, heavier, and would kill her just as well.

Tink.

She nearly ignored the small sound, but then it came again.

Tink. Tink.

Aurelia turned, her soaked hem heavy and dragging around her ankles. Beside her was a shallow tide pool filled with tiny fish and spongy creatures sticking to the rocks. A wave crashed and flowed toward her, flushing the pool with currents that caught and rolled a small glass bottle against the sand and stones.

She bent to pluck it out of the water. It was no longer than her pinkie, and a cork shoved in the top protected a scrap of dry paper within. She peered through the curved glass to see it was a scrap of newspaper. The minuscule letters were magnified through the bottle: *Please send inquiries.*

Aurelia looked out to the ocean. *Perhaps...*

She chewed her lip, rolling an idea through her head. Perhaps she could decide she would not marry the prince. Perhaps there could be a way out, if only she had the nerve to reach for it.

She finally knew what she'd say in her reply to William.

Palming the bottle, she gripped her sodden skirts and returned to the house. This was to be her story, and she only had a month to change it.

11

A Ship Called Purgatory

As it turned out, a month was not enough to change her fate.

Aurelia stood on a dock in Dover, her hands hidden in a fur muff as a chilly breeze blew off the English Channel, teasing her brown skirts and pulling strands of pale hair from her updo. She could see France from where she stood, but preferred to stare at the weathered wood beneath her shoes as the crew hurried between dock and deck, hauling crates and trunks filled with her dowry that had arrived from London this morning onto an unassuming, little gray ship.

It was an ungodly pile of stuff. Money, jewels, trinkets—she didn't have an inkling as to what it all contained, and she didn't want to know.

She might've considered running were it not for the two French soldiers who'd been waiting for her when she' arrived. It was a sad thing to be handed off, moving from the comfort of Aunt Clara's drab little carriage to the rigid perfection of military men who said nothing to her.

Aunt Clara hadn't even said goodbye. She'd dined with Aurelia the night before, then taken to bed early with a headache. As Aurelia sat in her empty room and waited for sleep to claim her, she'd heard her aunt's cries. All night, they pealed through the house like a wretched ghost, reminding Aurelia that she was marrying a prince.

And that she'd replied to William. In perhaps her most senseless decision since the age of seventeen, she'd written to him—very nearly begged him—for help. She'd all but waited by the door for any word from him, but the weeks had passed in silence, and even his usual letter did not come.

Her hope, though waning, had warded off despair before it left altogether to leave her resigned. So as soon as she woke this morning, she'd fished the book from beneath her mattress with its collected bits of news and the few letters she'd saved. She burned the whole thing.

It was easier to let go and accept that dramatic rescues were better left to little girls in trees and fairy tales. Grown women were more interesting in tragedies anyway.

She hadn't told the Kingswoods she was leaving. They would read about her marriage in the paper, or Aunt Clara would tell them, and that would have to suffice. She'd met them once more for tea, but she could hardly meet her gaze for fear the entire truth would burst forth in a final, terrible confession encompassing the last ten years. She'd entangled herself so thoroughly into their family that leaving felt like tearing rose thorns from every inch of her flesh. She wanted them to know how much she cared for them, but it would break Aurelia to admit it aloud.

So she kept it secret until the news would break itself, and them, and spare her and her multitude of fractures.

She pulled one hand from her muff and looked at the compass in her palm. Perhaps she was torturing herself for having dared to hope. For all she'd thought she was upright and proper, she should have known better than to let herself dream.

"Ma'am."

Aurelia looked up into a boy's brown eyes. He was tall and thin as a reed, his nose spotted with freckles under a fading sunburn. A red scarf covered his hair, but dark strands poked from the edges and curled by his ears. He glanced at her compass, and she slipped her hand back into her muff.

"Are you Lady Danby?" he asked, glancing at the guards. He couldn't have been older than nineteen.

"I am."

He wiped his nose on his sleeve. "My name's Bartholomew. I've been told to accompany you."

She followed as he waved her along, flanked by her minders as they joined a dozen other well-dressed passengers on the main deck.

He glanced at the overcast sky as he headed toward the bow. "It won't be a long journey with this wind. A couple hours tops. The sun'll probably come out too, so it'll be pretty for a while."

She offered a wry smile.

"Doesn't she have a room?" one of the soldiers asked in a thick French accent.

Bartholomew stared. "What?"

"Does she—" The solider heaved a sigh and said again, in a British accent that was even harder to understand than his natural one, "Doesn't she have a room?"

"Oh. Yeah, but I figured the best view is out here." He gestured to the channel. "Unless she—" He looked at Aurelia. "Unless you'd prefer to be down below. But there aren't any windows, and it's not very nice to look at. Doesn't smell great either."

Her smile grew by a hair. "I'd like to stay out here."

Bartholomew turned back to the soldiers. "Would you like me to show you the room?"

"We must stay with Miss Danby," said the other solider, sounding offended that he had to establish this.

"I thought she was a lady, not a miss."

"I am a lady," Aurelia said.

"She's a lady," Bartholomew told the guard. "Do you not have ladies in France?"

The guards scowled. Aurelia finally smiled fully.

"Weigh anchor!" called the captain. Sailors began winding a massive chain, and the sails unfurled. Within minutes, the ship set off toward the channel.

Aurelia moved to the railing, leaving her grimacing guards closer to the bow but still within view. Bartholomew came to stand beside her.

"Ever been on a ship?" he asked.

"I haven't." She couldn't even bring herself to feel excited about it. Her fingers tightened around the compass. "Have you ever been to France?"

"Yeah." He sniffed. "I don't like it much."

Aurelia glanced over her shoulder. Ladies and gentlemen milled around the deck, watching the crew or leaning over the sides of the ship to watch the dark water flow past. Above her, the sails filled with wind. Below, the bow cut through the waves, spraying brine into the wind that flew into her face and hair.

It felt as nice as William had once told her. Her chest ached at the thought.

What more could I have done? Perhaps she should have told the Kingswoods of her plight after all. They might've helped somehow.

She leaned far over the rail and glanced at the side of the ship where *Purgatory* was written in bold red paint. "Aren't sailors superstitious?" she asked. "I'd imagine a boat called *Purgatory* wouldn't be one's first choice."

"The owner's a bit cracked in the head, I s'pose, or he's realistic since sometimes it feels like purgatory being here day in and day out. But we only cross the channel, really, so if something terrible did happen, I could swim back. There's nothing scary in these waters anyway."

"Are there pirates?"

He gave a derisive laugh. "You're one of those people, aren't you?"

Her expression shuttered. "What do you mean?"

"The kind who thinks there's a goon or a ghost around every corner." He chuckled. "Nah, there's no pirates here. The papers make it seem like they're everywhere, but I've never seen one."

"Oh."

"Awful business. I don't ever want anything to do with it."

"Probably for the best." She leaned against the rail, bracing her hands one on top of the other as she shifted her weight. "Tell me all you hate about France."

"Gladly," he said, and launched into an explanation of all he disliked about the country, from its king to the bricks that paved the streets. As they talked, the sun came out, just as he'd promised. The water changed from gray to something closer to blue, and light sparked off the ripples and waves.

Not long into the trip, the captain shouted to his crew. Bartholomew paused his lengthy description of France to look toward the commotion, his face drawn.

"What is it?" Aurelia asked. The other coast had grown, drawing nearer at a pace that stoked her dread.

"I'm not sure. Excuse me for a moment." He paced to another crew member, and as he did, the soldiers noted the changed mood and sidled a little closer. A minute later, Bartholomew returned.

"Just a ship," he said. "A big white one coming right for us. Our course might change a little."

"Will it take us longer to get there?" one of the soldiers asked, the edges of his lips tight.

"Probably," Bartholomew answered simply. "You don't mind, do you? Or I can tell the captain to sail into them and see where that gets us."

A laugh burst from Aurelia—the first in a month—and Bartholomew grinned at her. She would have to thank him later for making the journey feel less hellish.

The soldiers glared, but that didn't appear to bother Bartholomew. He took the spot next to Aurelia, his eyes on the other, much larger ship coming from their left. If neither of the ships swerved, the white one would slam right into the *Purgatory*.

A bell began ringing.

"A warning," Bartholomew said. "In case they haven't seen us yet."

The ship sped toward them, close enough now to see people on the other deck. It occurred to Aurelia that a shipwreck would be very providential, and she wondered if the soldiers would haul her to France or let her swim back to England once the boat sank.

Bartholomew licked his lips, mumbling, "Damn idiot."

The bell rang faster. The *Purgatory*'s captain began yelling, cranking the wheel and turning so sharply that Aurelia clung to the rail to keep from falling. The passengers grabbed hold of what they could—the mast, crates, rigging, each other—as the ship pitched and narrowly avoided hitting the other.

Then both were headed in the same direction, sailing side by side—and not toward France.

"You bastards!" the captain shouted. "Look up!"

A man stood on the railing of the other ship, holding on to the rigging and seeming very aware that they'd nearly collided. He wore a tricorn hat over ink-dark hair, and a long black coat snapped in the wind, hanging open to reveal a tall, strong body clad in a white shirt and black pants.

William.

Her heart lurched to her throat to avoid the torrent of hope that surged through her chest to swallow her resignation and despair.

William was here.

"My apologies for the lack of warning," he said. As he spoke, portholes opened in the side of his vessel, and pikes shot forward and sank into the side of the *Purgatory*. It lurched as William's ship tugged it forward. Aurelia stumbled into the soldiers with a gasp.

Two pirates hauled a gangplank into place, bridging the gap between the ships. William crossed and stood on the *Purgatory*'s rail, his hand curling into the lines and glinting with gold rings as he stood over the cowering passengers. Bartholomew scurried toward his crew who'd gathered in the middle of the deck, forming a wall between the pirate and the passengers. Aurelia's soldiers cautiously stepped forward, their swords raised.

"I saw a group of handsome folks and couldn't help myself," William said as, behind him, his crew brandished swords and leveled guns at the *Purgatory*. His blue eyes scanned the frightened faces, crossed over Aurelia's, then snapped back. Her stomach lurched as he looked at her for a half second longer, but that breath of time could've stretched for eternity.

He'd come for her—not as William, her neighbor, but as—

"My name is Captain Copson," he said with a wolfish grin, turning his attention back to the passengers and crew who responded with swears, groans, and gasps. The soldiers paled and lifted their swords higher while Aurelia bit her lips to keep from grinning.

"No need to fear so long as you do as I say," Copson assured them. He dropped to the deck, a gun now in his hand. "No need for screaming or death or any of that ghastly business. I'm only curious."

"We don't have anything," the *Purgatory*'s captain said. "No gold. Nothing."

"Everyone has gold," Copson said, moving toward the center of the deck. "Even if I have to pick it out of the paint or tear it from your teeth." He surveyed the passengers, noting their jewelry and tailored clothes. None of this, however, seemed to interest him. Then his gaze moved to the crew and Bartholomew hiding among them.

Copson cocked his gun and aimed it at Bartholomew's head.

"What's in cargo?"

Heat crawled up Aurelia's neck. Copson was cruel, but surely William wouldn't shoot the boy.

"Um," Bartholomew sputtered. "I—"

"Of value," Copson said. "Don't tell me it's housewares or something equally useless."

Bartholomew's gaze darted to Aurelia before settling on the pirate. "A dowry," he said quietly. "A very large dowry. Full of money and other things besides."

"Fetch it." As Bartholomew darted away, Copson waved his gun to the rest of the *Purgatory*'s crew. "All of you. A dowry is nothing to die over."

The sailors scrambled below deck. Copson finally lowered the gun and turned toward the stern, studying each passenger's face. "Who's the lucky bride?" he asked, taking slow steps down the line of frightened people as though he hadn't already seen her. They shook their heads and flinched from his gaze. "Don't be shy."

"Sir, please," said the other captain. "There's no need—"

Copson lifted his gun again, his smile gone. "Why are you not below deck with your crew? Go. Now."

Paling, the man ran off. The sound of shifting cargo came from below, and Aurelia's trunks began appearing, carried by frightened sailors from the *Purgatory* to Copson's ship.

Aurelia's pulse thundered, drowning out everything but the captain as he continued perusing the line of people. His steps were slow and sure until he neared the bow where Aurelia stood behind her soldiers. He met her gaze and stopped, and the edge of his mouth pulled into a half grin. "Hello," he said.

She still didn't smile, though everything in her wanted to. "Captain Copson," she said quietly.

"I assume you're the bride."

The soldiers stiffened, and Copson glanced at them as though noticing them for the first time. After a cursory inspection of their faces, weapons, and uniforms, his face fell into amusement.

Then he looked at Aurelia. "Who's the lofty groom who's earned such a dowry?"

"A prince," she said. "Pierre."

Of course, he knew this already. He gave a humorless smile. "How awful for you. That French fop doesn't know his ass from his face."

The soldiers surged forward. Faster than Aurelia thought possible, Copson reached into his coat, drew a second gun, raised it next to the first, and pulled both triggers. She jumped at the sound, and the soldiers fell to the deck, blood spilling from their heads.

Gentlemen screamed and ladies fainted. Aurelia remained still, carefully expressionless, as she wrung her fingers around the compass hidden in her muff. She didn't dare look down.

Completely unruffled, Copson shoved one of the guns back into the holster hidden beneath his coat. "Your name?" he asked, loud enough for the others to overhear. This was calculated—a signal to play along while also telling everyone who she was before he took her away.

He was *taking her away.*

Relief loosened her breath, and she relaxed her hands and held his gaze. "Aurelia Danby."

"Like the Duke and Duchess of Danby?"

"Yes, sir." She spoke softly, her nervousness hiding how eager she was to go.

The edge of his mouth lifted. "I wasn't aware they had a daughter."

"You wouldn't be the first."

He stepped closer, avoiding the dead soldiers at his feet. She sucked in a breath as she was suddenly a foot away from the boy who'd taken her heart ten years ago. She'd wondered if age would fade his beauty, but time hadn't dared to do such a thing. He was older now—twenty-nine—but the years only made him look more distinguished, from his wide shoulders and angled jaw to his sharp cheekbones and his eyes.

Her memories had been so unfaithful to their color.

"I'll make you a deal," he said. "Since I already have your dowry, and it'd be rather rude to send you on to France with nothing to pay off your fiancé, come with me and I'll spare every soul on this ship."

Years had passed since she'd last played any game, but a girl in distress wouldn't so easily give herself to a pirate when a prince waited for her.

"You have my dowry," she ventured slowly, conscious of the sound of her voice and the watching eyes and the blood soaking into the hem of her skirt. Her pulse only quickened under the intensity of Copson's stare. "And you killed my guards. Why take me?"

"Oh, I assure you it has nothing to do with you personally," he said with blithe arrogance. "You're plenty lovely, but I only want to irritate your fiancé. It's been too long since I last bothered the French crown or held a ransom." He leaned in and lowered his voice. "And what's life without a little trouble?"

She swallowed. "Sir, I…"

His eyes squeezed. Behind him, scared passengers watched with pleading looks.

"If I go," she said, "you won't hurt anyone on board." The *Purgatory*'s crew continued moving her belongings to Copson's ship, but they had to be nearing the end.

"I swear on my honor as a gentleman," Copson said.

She schooled her expression to hide her eagerness to be off this ship. "And what will happen to me?"

"You'll live safely with me until your piddling fiancé offers something I want." His eyes glimmered beneath the shadow of his hat, and her heart thundered wildly in response. "And once I have my gold, I'll hand you over, safe and sound and perfectly whole for your intended."

"The navy is coming!" someone yelled from the other ship.

He didn't break Aurelia's gaze as he shouted back, "British or French?"

"British!"

"Perfect," he muttered. "Lady Danby, I will give you ten seconds to decide before I start shooting." He cocked his gun, drawing yelps and cries from the passengers.

"I'll go—" She stepped forward, but her foot slipped, skidding through the soldiers' blood.

Copson caught her arm and hauled her to her feet before she could hit the deck, growling, "Careful, Aurelia, I said I'd get you back whole. Try not to undermine my best intentions."

The heat of his hand seeped through her sleeve. It was different, now that she was older, and his touch left her dizzy and distracted and feeling quite a bit warmer than before.

He didn't let go, but his hold became light enough that she could pull away. When she didn't, he pivoted out of her way.

"This way, my lady," he said in a tone that might've sounded mocking to anyone else.

With another steadying breath, she trod carefully around the blood, pointedly avoiding the gruesome sight. Copson walked with her, his gun still in hand and his fingers wrapped around her arm as though she had little choice. Like she was being kidnapped.

Like she didn't want to fling herself across the gangplank.

"Tell the squealing French pig I stole his bride," Copson said, releasing Aurelia as she climbed onto the plank. He hoisted himself onto the rail. "He'll have her back when it pleases me."

Aurelia clung to the ropes binding the *Purgatory*'s sails and looked into the sea churning below.

Copson stepped closer, looming over her shoulder and effectively cutting her off from the rest of the *Purgatory*. His free hand hovered by her waist, a silent promise to catch her. "Don't look down," he said with that same teasing lilt.

"Too late," she gasped into the wind.

Some of the crew from the *Purgatory* waited on the other side. Among them was Bartholomew, his eyes tight. Swallowing, he rose to the gangplank and held out his hand.

"Take my hand," he said.

Steeling herself, Aurelia met Bartholomew's gaze and rushed to him. He took her fingers in his and tugged her to safety. A second later, Copson dropped to the deck beside her, and the *Purgatory*'s crew scrambled back toward their ship.

"You too, boy," Copson said to Bartholomew. "I'm not signing on any more crew."

Bartholomew made a face. "I wouldn't sign to your crew if you paid in diamonds."

Copson lifted an eyebrow.

"The gun was unnecessary," the boy said under his breath. "Damn near gave me a heart attack."

"Don't whine, Bartholomew," Copson replied lowly, and Aurelia watched in shock as he appeared to grab Bartholomew's head—and roughly ruffled his hair. "I wasn't going to shoot you."

"Don't point your damn gun at me," Bartholomew said. "If mother knew—"

"Tell her. She's far more tolerant than you think." Copson shoved him toward the *Purgatory*. "Get off my ship."

"Not even a thank you," Bartholomew grumbled lowly as he stalked off. "After all I went through to mark her luggage to put it on last and get her on board and convince the captain to leave at this time, not that one, and damn near doing everything short of controlling the weather." His stomped to the plank, crossed, and dropped to the other side.

The pikes withdrew from the *Purgatory*'s hull, and Copson's ship pulled away.

As soon as they were out of earshot, Aurelia released a held breath. "You got my letter."

William smirked. "I got three of them." He started for the stairs leading to the helm. "Welcome aboard the *Ophelia*."

12

The Cruel Captain Copson

"The *Ophelia*? This isn't the *Destiny's Revenge*?"

Aurelia climbed after him to the raised quarterdeck at the back of the ship. Another man at the wheel spared her a glance and nodded, but he said nothing about the presence of the captain and a lady.

"No," William said with a laugh. "She wouldn't make it through the Dover Strait without fanfare." He patted the rail. "The *Ophelia* is much less noticeable."

Behind them, the *Purgatory* grew smaller, but beyond it were two war ships.

"Don't worry about them," he said, following her gaze. "They'll stop at the *Purgatory* to get the story, and we'll be too far gone by the time they realize what happened."

Aurelia glanced at the coast. "And the French?"

"They'll know by tonight and set sail in the morning," he said, sounding completely unconcerned by the prospect. "But only if they're half as organized as they want people to believe."

The man at the helm chuckled. "They still wouldn't be fast enough to catch us."

"This is Thomas," William said. "My cousin, and second captain over the *Ophelia*."

Thomas waved, his sandy hair blowing in the wind. "This is the lass from the tree?"

"The very same," William mused.

"I was in the boat that day," Thomas said. "Good to see you again."

"His brother, George, captains the *Fortuna Royale*," William said, "which is with the *Destiny's Revenge*."

Her heart swelled. She was actually here—with Captain Copson. She'd see the *Fortuna Royale* and the *Destiny's Revenge*.

She wasn't going to France.

William folded his arms and leaned against the rail surrounding the quarterdeck. "When I invited you to write again, I thought it would be casual conversation about your aunt or telling me what a drag life was, or at least a vague update on tea with my parents. Not a plea for help to escape an arranged marriage."

The wind tugged at her dress, pulling the ship farther down the channel and calling her attention toward the ocean beyond. She tore her eyes away from the water and set them on William to find a much better shade of blue. "I would've written something much better. I intended to, but the engagement was rather last minute."

"I assume you sent five letters," he said, "to the five addresses I gave you."

"I wasn't sure if you'd get them in time. I thought you hadn't." Even now, her dreadful morning clung to her like a morose little gremlin, its claws sunk into her back with the pain of hopeless acceptance. But William was here, and with every glance, with every word, those claws retracted, bit by bit.

"I had very little time to make arrangements," he said. "We were about to depart for the Americas when I received the three I have now, and my brother, first mate, and second captains are the only ones who know why we delayed. All the others will only know I wanted to bother the French."

"So you told the truth on the *Purgatory*. You wanted to hurt my fiancé." Cold dripped down her spine when she spoke of the prince, as though she'd spoken some awful bit of heresy in front of a priest. *Fiancé* was not a title he deserved, and it was not one he would have from her lips.

"Oh yes," William said. "Picking you up has been a satisfactory change of plans. But I did lie—I have no intention of handing you back unless you truly want to go." He studied her carefully. "Though judging by your letters, I assume that is not the case."

"It was a political match," she said woodenly.

"Tragic," Thomas said.

Aurelia looked at William. "That boy back there—Bartholomew. He's your brother." The youngest Kingswood son, whom she'd never met.

William folded his arms tighter and crossed his ankles. "Yes, unfortunately. I used to like him, but he's gotten wise as he's grown older. It's rather annoying, though he's perfectly fine to Ralph."

"Ralph is more likable," Thomas said.

William ignored that. "I'd pay Bartholomew well, but he wants to be a *fisherman*." His face scrunched as he said the word. "I expected more from him."

"Piracy isn't for the faint of heart," said Thomas.

"He's not faint of heart, he just *has* a heart. I'd hoped he would've grown out of it by now."

Her gaze turned wary. "You wouldn't have really killed them—everyone on the *Purgatory*."

"You wouldn't have really declined my offer," he countered. "But you worried me for a moment. I thought I'd have to follow through on my threat, and I had nowhere near enough bullets."

Thomas laughed. Aurelia's eyes widened as she sputtered, "But you—the soldiers!"

"Well I've got to shoot *somebody*," William said casually. "You wouldn't have come with me if I hadn't. They wouldn't have let you."

That was true...and the whole ordeal would make a good story.

Aurelia suppressed a shiver that had nothing to do with the breeze. Her hands trembled in her muff as the implications of what she'd done grew starker by the second.

Captain Copson had kidnapped her from the French *and* the English. He'd ruined a royal engagement. The Duke and Duchess of Danby had lost their daughter to a pirate, and a prince had lost his betrothed. Two kings had lost their alliance, which wouldn't only land in small, local papers—it would be in *every* paper.

Aunt Clara would be devastated.

Her breaths quickened. "My aunt," she gasped. "She's already so upset over me leaving, and to think I've been captured by pirates—*the* pirate." She looked at William. "She burns the paper at any mention of you."

He seemed proud to hear this. "Does she really?"

"I thought you would come take me away from home. I didn't realize I'd be..." She looked out over the ship, realizing the folly in her expectation. What business had he of showing up at her front door as William Kingswood? And what would he have said? *Pardon me, but I'm taking Lady Danby far away.*

He surely wouldn't have wasted an offer of marriage solely to release her from duty—not when he had an exciting life and adventures and she was rather useless with her half-forgotten stories, expert fake smiles, and newspapers. She was no match for him.

Of course she'd be kidnapped, and then all would be blamed on Captain Copson.

"She'll be beside herself," Aurelia said in a small voice.

"And I'm sure my parents will hear what I've done and smooth any ruffled feathers if you're all as close as you said," William assured her. "What was it, tea every Tuesday?"

"She didn't even say goodbye." Panic overwhelmed her. If only she could know her aunt would not *hurt*, then she would happily fling herself toward the heart of the ocean and all its wonders. She whimpered too softly for anyone to hear. "This is going to kill her."

William moved, drawing her attention toward the corner of the quarterdeck so she'd turn her back to the crew while she composed herself. Her shoulders heaved, her lungs begging for breath.

"Breathe slower, Aurelia."

She tried, but her dress made it difficult.

His eyes dipped to the turtle at her throat, and he tilted his head. "Did my mother give you that?"

She touched the tiny creature. "For my birthday."

"She used to talk about turtles and resilience." He spoke evenly, his words slow and languid like he had all the time in the world. "I always liked it. I'm fond of green, and I think that pendant was my first introduction to emeralds. She wore it for years."

"I fear I don't deserve it." Her heart had begun to slow—but only just. "She's too kind."

"She is kind." He smiled, and then her erratic pulse didn't know what to do. "And believe me when I say she'll be kind to your aunt. So please don't worry, or this will feel like a very long journey."

She struggled to choose between looking at his eyes and his smile. "How long is it?"

"However long you want it to be." His eyes dropped to her hands and flickered with surprise. "You brought it."

A chain dangled from the muff—the compass. Aurelia freed it and held its silver body in her palm. "In case I pitched myself off the ship and needed to find my way home."

William snorted. "Well, I'm terribly glad to know it would've been helpful."

"Captain." Thomas nodded ahead.

While speaking, they'd left behind the Dover Strait. The channel had widened, the land falling away on either side to the point Aurelia could've sworn she was in the open ocean. Two ships floated in the distance, growing larger as the *Ophelia* cut through the waves. At the top of their main masts flew black flags adorned with a silver anchor crossed with two swords.

Copson's flag. The *Ophelia* raised the same one as they approached.

William pointed over her shoulder. "That gray one on the left—that's the *Fortuna Royale*. It was my father's. And on the right is my flagship, the *Destiny's Revenge*."

The *Destiny's Revenge* was a massive black vessel that looked as if night itself had fashioned a ship for the sole purpose of striking fear into all seafarers. It reminded her of a scary, spiny creature with its decks and sails and protrusions. Three masts towered over the deck, hung with white canvas.

"The one you stole from the English," she said. "The biggest, fastest ship on record."

He chuckled. "That one."

The *Ophelia*'s crew lowered the sails and brought the ship in on the other side of the *Destiny's Revenge*. A gangplank slid into place, and William led her across.

This time, she wasn't so frightened, but it probably had everything to do with her hand in his, which he dropped the moment he helped her onto the deck.

And then a pair of arms wrapped around her. Her feet left the ground, and she was spinning.

"Ralph!" she cried.

He set her on her feet and stood over her, beaming. His golden hair gleamed in the sunlight. "Welcome aboard."

She threw her arms around him, knowing full well it wasn't appropriate. But this was a pirate ship, and he clung to her just as fiercely, lifting and spinning her once more.

Nearby, his brother called orders. Things around them began to shift—sails unfurled and people rushed by, hauling lines and climbing rigging. The other ships did the same, and water splashed over their hulls as they picked up speed.

"I can't tell you how happy I was when he told me we were coming for you," Ralph said in her ear. "I was—I am *beside* myself."

"So am I!" she squealed. She leaned back to see his face, her arms tight around his neck as she took in every subtle change in his angled features, the scruff on his chin, and the muscles that now held her high enough that her feet dangled.

"Ralph, put the lady down."

William appeared beside them, his lips quirked in amusement as Ralph set her on her feet and stepped back, grinning like a fool.

"If you'll join me for a moment," William said and offered his arm to Aurelia. "We have some matters to discuss."

Aurelia squeezed Ralph's wrist one last time, measuring her breaths as she took William's proffered elbow and let him lead her toward the back of the ship.

A positively massive man stood at the helm. An earring swung from one ear, and he looked every bit the classic pirate with the litany of tattoos crawling over his arms and up his neck. He tipped his hat when he saw Aurelia, exposing a bald head.

A thrill tugged her stomach.

William led her through a set of doors under the quarterdeck and drew away as they entered. Aurelia paused, then slowly drifted deeper into the room.

The captain's quarters were much larger and finer than she'd pictured—better fit for a king than a pirate with the stately desk, a long table with chairs, and a couch bolted to the floor before a hearth. A wide swath of windows along the back wall looked out on the glittering water and bathed the room in natural light. His bed stood in one corner, swathed in dark curtains and its linens neatly tucked. Everything was immaculate—not a speck of dust in sight, not a single thing out of place.

Much of the room was decorated in a tasteful shade of emerald.

"You've grown up."

She lowered her gaze to find him watching her from where he stood behind the desk. "Was I not supposed to?"

"I suppose it's only natural," he said lightly. "Though you're different than I was expecting."

"What did you expect?" As the object of his attention, her pulse tripped violently. Surely he hadn't expected the same young girl he'd met only twice before. The thought was more than mildly horrifying.

"I don't know," he said, his expression curious. "But I don't think it was you."

Her skin flushed. "I hope that's not a bad thing. I don't know who else I could be."

"It's not bad at all. It's like meeting someone for the first time." He shuffled an already tidy stack of paper before him. On the corner of the desk, she spotted her letters.

She still could hardly believe it—that her letters had actually made it to the *Destiny's Revenge*, and so had she. Her eyes began to explore again, admiring the ship around her—anything but the boy she'd fallen for, now standing in front of her as a man, watching her so intently.

"There are some things I wanted to discuss with you before I turn you loose on the ship," he said, his voice quiet to not disturb her exploration. "Nothing too torturous, of course."

"Alright." It was too hard to hold his gaze, so she looked at his bed instead. Her cheeks warmed, then the gilded edges of the desk caught her interest.

"First, there are no Kingswoods on this ship. I am Robert Copson, and Ralph is Ralph Barrington. We're not known as brothers here, except by a very select few."

Her eyes flicked up. His gaze was still remarkably direct.

"Other than Ralph, only a few know my true identity—Greyson, who you saw steering the ship, as well as his family, and Thomas and George. Only a dozen of my crew knew me when I sailed with my father, but they never knew me as a Kingswood—only a Smith."

Only a dozen from his father's crew. All the others had signed on several years ago, after the newspapers reported those grisly murders and his stealing the *Destiny's Revenge*.

She cleared her throat. "William C. Smith?"

"Yes," he said with a nod. "The C stands for Copson, if you were curious."

"I was, thank you."

He smiled, but she didn't know why. "Concerning your presence here, the crew doesn't know who you are or what I've done. It's better they don't know of any Danby aboard my ship, so I will insist you have a false name as well."

Her ears rang, but she bottled her excitement so she would appear utterly still and demure. "Rebecca. Rebecca Rowe."

He huffed a quiet laugh. "Eager, are you?"

"I played a lot as a child," she said. "And I often wished I was someone else."

"Then you'll be known as Rebecca—though that's a lot of syllables for some of the lads, so don't be surprised when they shorten it."

"Am I to be Rebecca in private?" she asked. "Are you still Copson in private?"

He stared for a moment, then looked away. "I won't enforce it in private." Clearing his throat, he said, "By the time we reach port and the crew hears I've taken you, you'll have been among them long enough that they won't question your presence, and the *Ophe-*

lia's crew who witnessed today will have either forgotten or assume you're someone else. There are enough ruffians and criminals here that they're doubtful to care, but regardless, I'll not have you stolen or betrayed from my company when I've gone to so much effort to get you here."

He focused on the papers again and held one out. "These are the articles—laws for sailing under my flag. Every soul on these ships has signed them, and they're bound to them as surely as any law on land."

Aurelia scanned the page and the signature at the bottom. Among the articles were terms for payment, expectations of sobriety, and how the crew was to conduct themselves and treat their fellow sailors.

"No harm will come to you while you're here, and no one will touch or harass you," he said. "My crew may conduct themselves as they wish at port, but if they step out of line on my ship or break an article against a fellow sailor on land, they're fined, flogged, or killed."

She nearly dropped the document. "Does that happen often?" she asked quietly.

"Occasionally," he said with a hint of a laugh. "But no, not often."

She was not afraid as she handed the articles back. He didn't give her another to sign for herself.

"Lastly, at least for now, is your role on board," he said. "There's nothing specific I have for you to do, but I only ask that you be useful. Learn some of the jobs and do them when you see a need. Swabbing the deck or running lines or mending sails, cooking food—everyone works together to make this ship run as it does, even myself."

"Alright." She let her smile slip through her composure. Since the beginning of William's letters, she'd wanted this—to know what it was like to be part of a crew. *Copson's* crew.

"You'll be paid," he said. "So you'll have money to spend on land."

She shook her head. "Don't pay me. I'll use my dowry."

"I insist," he said. "Your dowry is yours."

"You took it. Pay me with it."

"Aurelia, I didn't steal it from you. It's still yours."

"I don't want it. I've never even seen any of it before today."

He shifted his weight and braced his hands on the desk. "I'm captain of this ship, and I'll do as I please," he said, his smile softening his words. "You're not paying your way—I brought you here, so I'll pay you for the work you do."

"I asked to come."

His eyes narrowed slightly, but his levity didn't disappear completely. "Most people don't argue with me."

She rolled her lips between her teeth. She was used to the easy, carefree William she knew from his letters—but this was different. Here, he was Copson, who filled the papers with blood. She'd watched him kill two men a mere hour ago. "My apologies."

"Don't fret, Aurelia," he said with a chuckle. "You'll do fine here. And if there's anything I can do to make this journey any easier, please find me."

Her smile returned. "I doubt it'll be anything but marvelous," she said, then glanced down at her dress. "Though...do you have something more practical I might wear? Like pants. And a shirt—like the rest of your crew."

He eyed her dress. "Different," he said, moving from behind his desk. "This is what I mean."

She held his gaze despite how it made her heart tumble. "I'm afraid I don't know what you mean."

He paused next to her. "You're rather cavalier about it all. About everything. Though I suppose I can't really be so surprised."

She thought of the day in the woods and wondered if he thought of it too as he strode to an armoire and pulled out a shirt, a pair of trousers, and a belt. He returned and handed them to her. "Take these until you find a set of your own. I'm sure you'll find something more to your taste when we reach port."

She took the clothes. "Where's that?"

"Settle in, Miss Rowe," he said with a grin. "We're headed to the Caribbean."

13

The Company of Pirates

It was silly to smell a handsome pirate's clothes, but Aurelia did it anyway. Hidden in a small room below deck with two small beds, a trunk, and a porthole, she changed from her traveling gown into William's clothes. The pants were too long, so she rolled up the legs and did the same for the sleeves of the billowy shirt, which she cinched at her waist with the belt.

They smelled like salt and sea and wind.

A beaming smile broke over her lips, truer and lovelier than she'd really felt in years. She laughed quietly, releasing her hair from its pins to braid it, and continued to giggle as she slipped her compass into her waistband.

The door opened. "Ah!" said a feminine voice. "You must be Rebecca."

A young woman stood in the door, wearing something similar but far more flattering to her figure. Her windblown hair was a shade lighter than Aurelia's, and despite her petite stature, nearly everything about her lacked the delicacy Aurelia was familiar with when it came to ladies her age.

Soft skin, thin features, a sallow pallor from sitting inside all day—this girl had none of it. She was corded with muscle, smiled too big, and slouched. There were half a dozen other sins Aunt Clara would've tutted over, and Aurelia loved every single one of them.

The woman's hazel gaze swept over her. "Captain said I'd be getting a bunk mate. I'm Lavinia," she said, holding out a callused hand. Before Aurelia could respond, Lavinia jerked her chin at her outfit. "Copson give you those clothes?"

Aurelia shook her hand. "He did."

Lavinia sucked her teeth and moved to her trunk. "Here—at least put this over it so the wind doesn't turn you into a sail. You're practically swimming in that shirt." She handed over a brown vest that laced down the front like stays.

"I didn't realize there were other women on board," Aurelia said, lacing up the front. "How delightful."

Lavinia's quick laugh reminded Aurelia of a seagull. "Copson has nearly four hundred in his entire company—some of us are bound to be the better sex."

Aurelia's eyes bugged. *Four hundred*? Captain Copson was powerful, but to navigate the world with so many under one man's control...

"It's not that uncommon, really," Lavinia said, folding her arms. "Copson's been around long enough that my ma and pa have been here for ages too. They met when this captain's"—she jabbed a finger at the deck above them—"grandfather took a prison ship headed for some penal colony. He dispatched the guards, but all the prisoners on board were women. Rather than send them on their way, Copson offered to let them sail with him, and since his crew were all men at the time, they nearly all got married—my da and ma included. She was in for stealing some highfalutin' lady's jewels after her first husband died. We're pretty sure she killed him too well to get caught for it, else she woulda been hung, so thankfully it was only jewels."

Aurelia's mind reeled, trying to keep up with Lavinia's rapid storytelling—she spoke like it was a race.

"Rumor has it our captain here was conceived shortly after the prison ship ordeal," Lavinia went on. "Story goes that his father fell

131

for his mother against *his* father's wishes, and it was a whole thing."

Aurelia's eyes widened. Lady Kingswood had been a prisoner? She tried to imagine Cecily as a criminal—but she'd seen the countess wield a sword better than anyone, and suddenly the idea was not so far-fetched. "Incredible," she breathed.

When she'd finished tying the vest, Lavinia gave a satisfied nod and beckoned her to follow her out of the room and up the stairs leading to the main deck, where they almost immediately ran into the captain.

He was with the bald, tattooed man from before—standing this close, he reminded Aurelia of mountains, barrels, and bulls.

"And here I thought you'd give Miss Rowe time to breathe before descending on her," William said to Lavinia.

"And you should know better," Lavinia replied with a wink. "You bring another girl on board, and you bet your ass she's better company than you lot."

William turned to Aurelia. "Be careful. She'll chat your ear off if you let her."

"Hush, she adores me," Lavinia said with a good-natured grin. "And you should thank me for showing her around—you'll owe me a pint for saving you from the embarrassment of forgetting anyone's name should you have done it yourself."

William laughed. "For all the pints you say I owe you, you'll have to be poured out of whatever tavern you choose to patronize with my gold."

Aurelia's stomach prickled. It wasn't jealousy—she was too happy for that. But seeing his familiarity with Lavinia...she wondered if she might eventually have that too.

Though she certainly wouldn't expect it—didn't even know *what* to expect at all, other than that she was here now, and she was just beginning to learn just how much she loved it and just how elated she could feel.

"Sounds like a marvelous time to me," Lavinia said, then looked at the giant bald man. "Da, this is Rebecca. Rebecca, this is Greyson."

Greyson held out a meaty hand. "Welcome aboard, Beck," he said in a deep and gravelly voice.

Aurelia marveled as her hand disappeared completely inside of his. "Nice to meet you, sir."

Greyson smirked at the formality, and she remembered—she didn't have to be Aurelia Danby anymore. She didn't have to be a lady at all.

"Well, I won't keep you—enjoy your tour," William said as he moved toward the quarterdeck stairs with Greyson. Then he called over his shoulder with a sharp smile, "And buy your own pint, Lavi—I know *all* my sailors' names."

Once his back was turned, Aurelia raised a brow at Lavinia. "Lavi?" It sounded almost like *lovey*.

Lavinia made a face and walked on. "Old nickname from *long* ago when he and I were involved before he was captain. Now he only calls me Lavi when he thinks I'm being obnoxious."

Aurelia's stomach pricked again. To think she'd worried William would be courting the ladies who attended balls while he'd really been considering Lavinia. She hadn't even thought to worry about *lady* pirates.

Then she nearly laughed at the thought of what her younger self might've done with that information, and how she might've driven her aunt insane by trying to find a way to become a pirate herself.

Which, in all actuality, is exactly what she'd done.

"We're still good friends," Lavinia said, glancing at William, "but we'd absolutely kill each other if we were any more than that. We're too headstrong, but his brother is *much* more agreeable." Her grin turned wistful. "He's a boatswain too, so his head isn't nearly as strong."

Aurelia remembered the term from one of William's letters—Ralph ran the deck, checked the lines and masts, and managed the crew. She studied the pirates around them and ended up looking toward the helm again, where William was poring over a map with Greyson. As though he felt her gaze, he looked up. Their eyes met.

Blushing, she turned back to Lavinia. "Does the crew think Copson's immortal?"

"They all have their theories. Some assume the truth, or something close to it. Others completely believe the Fountain of Youth bullshit he's been peddling for the last few years. He says a witch—"

"He told me," Aurelia said brightly, pleased to know at least one story. "But she's dead because he forgot to take her with him."

Lavinia rolled her eyes. "It's the stupidest shit I've ever heard, but he gets away with it because he signed on nearly all of his sailors after he got the *Destiny's Revenge*, and they're too fresh to know any better."

Aurelia's stomach was still so in knots from meeting William's gaze that she didn't notice the man walking toward her with a jumble of rigging until Lavinia cried, "Watch it!"

Lavinia grabbed her arm and tugged, but not quickly enough. The man crashed into Aurelia, the ropes went flying, and he fell to the deck. Aurelia's compass fell from her waistband and clattered against the boards, breaking the sliver hinge and sending the lid toward the edge of the ship.

Aurelia gasped and stepped forward, but the man's arm shot out, clapping a hand over the sliver disk before it could fall into the waves.

"Pardon me!" Aurelia said, stopping to help the man to his feet.

He met her gaze, then tore his eyes away. "No, no," he said quietly. "It was my fault."

Aurelia never would've called someone porky—not to their face—but there was something distinctly pig-like about him, from his portly body to his snout nose and the wispy hair over his pink scalp. His dark eyes darted nervously between her and Lavinia and the ropes on the deck. He gathered the rigging while Aurelia scooped up her now broken compass. The needle still worked, but the body was dented and the lid bent.

"I can fix that," the man said.

Before disappointment could settle, she brightened. "Really?"

"Rebecca, this is Offley, our carpenter," Lavinia said.

"I do metalwork too," Offley said, glancing quickly at the compass, the rigging in his hands, Lavinia's shoes. "I do a lot of things."

"Oh, then you must be important," Aurelia said. "I'm terribly sorry for running into you."

Offley stared at her as though she might skin him. Then, seeming to realize she was not terribly threatening, he relaxed a little and held out his hand. "I'll return it as soon as I'm finished. Won't take long."

Aurelia dropped the pieces into his fat palm. "Thank you," she said, and he only nodded once before hustling off.

"He's an odd man," Lavinia said quietly, watching him go. Once he'd disappeared, she grinned at Aurelia. "So *you* got the compass."

Aurelia was suddenly very aware of its absence. "What about it?"

"That's the captain's compass." She jerked her thumb over her shoulder in the direction Offley had run off with it. "I'd wondered what he did with it when he found a new one."

"He told me to use it as a paperweight," she said, because she hadn't kidded herself into believing there was any meaning to it, and didn't want Lavinia to think so either. Clearly, this woman didn't know her history with William, or how little interest there was in it.

Lavinia squawked a laugh. "So you're the inner-circle type. You must know his name then?"

"Which one?" And curse her nerves as she realized too late that she'd only just confirmed Lavinia's suspicions.

"The one that matters." Lavinia winked, linked their arms, and they moved on.

Below the main deck were the living quarters. Most slept in bunks or hammocks strung between posts nearest the bow, while others were allowed cabins near the stern, one of which was Lavinia and Aurelia's.

At the back of the ship on the next level down was the galley where meals were prepared, and even now Aurelia could smell supper. She poked her head into the dim space and admired the stacks of dishes, sacks of flour and rice, and barrels of water. There was even a full oven.

Here she met Hester—Lavinia's mother and the ship's surgeon—who was helping the cook prepare vegetables. She looked remarkably like her daughter, only with wrinkled cheeks and streaks of gray through her hair. She waved her long knife and smiled in greeting, and the expression was wildly unsettling. And though Aurelia had no doubt this woman was genuinely kind, she'd never seen someone make happiness look so off-putting.

Next was the artillery deck where Lavinia proudly declared she was a gunner. Her eyes shone with excitement as she explained how the hull opened for the cannons, and when it came to battle, Lavinia was over six of the teams who manned the ship's hundred cannons.

She'd aimed a grin at Aurelia and added, "I'm a pretty decent shot too."

Guns and *battle*—actual battles! Would she see one? Be part of it? She laid her hand on the cold iron of one of the cannons, giddy because she'd never been so close to something so dangerous.

Her aunt would simply die if she knew.

The lowest level of the ship was the hold, which held so much cargo that it was a wonder the boat didn't sink. Behind the trunks and crates was a small, dingy space enclosed in iron bars.

"The brig," Lavinia told her. "For people who get on our nerves."

Aurelia had never been around so many people from so many walks of life. They were lively and crass, tanned and scarred and utterly offensive in nearly every way. She did her best to remember each name she learned, even though they spanned languages she'd never heard and cultures she'd never experienced.

She was enchanted by every bit of it.

When the tour finished and Lavinia left Aurelia to her own devices, she made her way to the bow on the main deck as the sun dipped toward the ocean, burning the sky with violent shades of orange and red. The colors glinted off the waves, mingling with dark blue water like swirls of paint.

A few people milled about, but they paid her little mind as she stood over the bowsprit jutting from the front of the ship like a spear. She tipped her head back and breathed in the wild, whirling air, savoring freedom and dreams restored. The ones she'd crushed so long ago—and those she'd thrown in the fire that very morning—resurrected with strong, sure wings. She was on a pirate ship, no longer shackled to the whims of proper society, and each time the realization struck anew, her heart expanded and her joy glowed a little brighter.

She lifted her arms, and the wind enveloped every inch of her. It sang in her ears and kissed her cheeks with brine.

A low chuckle nearly sent her tumbling. Her arms pinwheeled as her balance faltered, and she grabbed the rail before she could tip into the sea. Warm hands gripped her elbows to help her steady herself.

"Sorry," William said. "I didn't mean to startle you."

When she gained her footing, he stepped away, leaned one hip against the rail, and folded his arms over his chest. The setting sun lit his blue eyes with flickers of evening flame, and the wind tossed his black hair, teasing her as it ran invisible fingers through the locks.

Years ago, she'd shoved her love for him to the bottom of her heart where she'd hoped she could ignore it. It reappeared now with the resurgence of her wistful fancies, crawling through her chest and up her throat and as vividly alive as it had always been.

Just like earlier, curiosity lingered in his gaze. He nodded to where she'd stood a moment ago. "You've discovered what it feels like to fly."

"It's just like you told me." She turned her gaze toward the horizon. "I feel as though I've never seen the sky till now."

The edge of his mouth lifted. "Just wait for the stars."

Above her, they'd begun to blink into existence against a purple sky. She'd seen stars, of course, but never without a canopy of trees or city light in the distance. "Are they different out here?"

He looked up. "Vastly."

"Do you chart them?"

"I do."

Her eyes bounced between the five stars that had appeared. She saw no map in them, but she imagined lines and words painted over the heavens like the illustrations she'd seen in books. "Will you show me sometime?"

He chuckled. "If you want."

"I want to know everything." Her gaze fell to the ocean. As though to reward her attention, there came a sparkle from beneath the waves before a fish burst through the water and began to soar through the air on shining wings. She gasped and a moment later, two more appeared, then several more, all of them sailing by the ship and then plunging back in.

William peered over the edge. "Odd little things, aren't they?"

"I kept your drawings," she said. "They were in a book, and—" The memory turned to ash, and she quieted as she remembered how quickly they'd burned this morning. Her happiness cooled as she remembered the hollowness that had consumed her when she destroyed the few precious letters she'd kept. "I don't have it anymore."

He looked at her. "A shame. That was some of my best work."

Some of her joy returned at the humor in his voice. She supposed it didn't matter that she'd burned the book—most of what it contained now stood beside her.

She risked a glance at him. His face was still turned to her, but his eyes slanted toward the water where the fish had been. For a single, heart-pounding moment, she studied the stubble that graced his jaw, the slant of his nose and cut of his brows. "A shame indeed," she said. "The real thing is almost as good."

Her stomach flipped as he met her gaze. "So what happened to this book? The one in which you kept my exceptional art."

"I burned it," she admitted. "I kept lots of things in it—bits of stories I liked from the papers and the letters you said I should keep. But then I was off to France, and I thought those simple joys would only be painful." Shyness made her skin prick. "Maybe it was a bit dramatic."

He shook his head. "Prince Pierre is one of the worst people I've ever had the misfortune of meeting. There's nothing dramatic about holding your joy far from his sticky hands."

No one had ever specifically told her she *wasn't* dramatic or silly or ridiculous, and him doing so left her feeling oddly light. "What makes him so odious?"

"Oh, everything. Speaking of any of his redeeming qualities would take no time at all, as he has exactly none."

She shifted her weight. "I would've married him—at least tell me who you rescued me from."

He rested his forearms on the rail and linked his fingers together. Whatever memory came to mind turned his expression cunning, like a cat sizing up a rat. "He sought me at some Caribbean port years ago—said he heard I was a decent cheat at cards and supposed he could beat me. I indulged him, but of course I cheat better than any regular half-brain, and after a few rounds, he was so angry he threw the deck at me." He spun one of his rings around his finger. "If that had been all, I might not've minded, but he continued to drunkenly berate me through the night until I finally put a gun in his face." He smirked. "He didn't like that so much."

"Mercy," she said, her hand at her throat.

"I've been told of his morbid taste for sad, broken women, whether they come to him that way or not." He frowned. "And I remembered you as a small, crying girl in a sopping dress and thought that was one thing Pierre should not have."

Aurelia glanced down to ensure a cannonball had not ripped through her chest. William couldn't have said he remembered her as a sixteen-year-old at a party? No, she was a *small, crying girl*. Like a younger sister, one he encouraged to get into trouble and taught how to hit.

She'd never felt so mortified.

"Your family did you a great disservice," he said. "There was no question of my helping you."

Stars, it hurt. She was a woman now, a whole *woman* standing before him, but he still only saw her as a girl. In spite of it, she managed to force thin words past her humiliation. "Thank you. For bothering the French."

"Thank you for the opportunity. Though concerning our agreement and my debt to you all those years ago, I believe you're no longer in danger from your scary aunt, and I've paid my dues to have my secrets kept." His charming smile reappeared. "If you want more stories, you're here to live them out yourself."

Aurelia opened her mouth to tell him he'd called her bluff that day and she never would've told—that she'd had no one to tell—but Ralph wandered over and spoke before she could.

"Greyson's asked for you, Captain."

William pushed away from the rail with a wink. "Enjoy yourself, Miss Rowe."

Aurelia watched him walk away with bated breath until Ralph took his spot, grinning as he took her in. "You're actually here."

She counted the years as she studied his handsome face. Standing in his presence once again, she felt the same warmth she always had. This was her dear friend—wholly unchanged except in the smallest of ways.

"I loved your letters," she said, not remembering a single one.

He braced one hand against the rail. "Only the best for you."

William's letters came to mind, but she said nothing about them. "I was just thanking Will— Copson. He told me about Prince Pierre."

His eyes began to shine. "Did he tell you about the card game?" She nodded. "I was there. The look on Pierre's face when he lost again and again—and then *again*—I've never seen anyone so pissed. When Copson shot him in the leg—"

Aurelia's eyes bugged. "He *shot* him?"

"Yes," he said, as though it were an obvious part of the story. "Princey howled and cried like nothing you've ever heard while Copson stood over him and laughed."

"He didn't tell me that part."

Ralph leaned closer. "Copson often tells the truth, but usually not all of it."

Didn't she know it. She thought of William's letter about getting the *Destiny's Revenge*, how he'd been so cavalier when the papers had been anything but.

"Why is he like that?" Aurelia asked.

Ralph chuckled. "He's Captain Copson," he said, as though that explained it in full. His teasing smile turned genuine. "It's so unbelievably good to see you."

She reached up to ruffle his hair, just as she'd longed to do after he'd started to wear finer clothes and care more for his appearance. "You don't look nearly as put together as you once did. You look *free*."

"A temporary plight—someday I'll be back to the gentleman you know and love." He pushed his hair back, leaving it in a perfect swoop the wind didn't dare ruffle with the same greediness it had shown with his brother. "After adventure."

"After?" Aurelia snickered. "I suppose you haven't changed in *every* way."

"Neither have you, sweeping onto a pirate ship like a natural." He took in her outfit for only a gentlemanly amount of time, then met her gaze. "All the practice in your aunt's garden paid off. If I didn't know any better, I'd assume you've been here as long as I have."

She scoffed. "I wish I *had*."

"You actually came at the perfect time. The captain's been doggedly pursuing a map, and he finally found it a few months ago."

Her eyes lit. "A treasure map?"

He knew exactly how much this news would delight her. "Yes, to a *legendary* treasure."

She bit her lips to keep from bursting.

"Perfect timing," Ralph said again. "Now that there's gold in sight, you're here for the best part."

"I have a feeling it's all the best part. Better than what I was headed for."

Commands were flung over the ship then, calling for the sails to lower and the anchor to drop, but Ralph remained in his spot, his eyes bright. "Much better than that."

14

Tales of Witches and Treasure Maps

As spring faded into early summer, Aurelia learned to be a pirate.

She learned to mend sails and cook, swab the deck and run lines. In the afternoons, she sat with Ralph and learned to tie knots, cackling over wrong loops and old jokes as the sun burned away the blue, porcelain tint of her skin and left behind a smattering of freckles.

And after a decade of loving William from afar, his presence was nothing short of thrilling. Her breath always caught at the sight of him, but she didn't seek him out, even though he'd told her she could. She didn't know what she'd talk about if she did, because she still wondered what one could say to entertain a legendary pirate.

He ran his ship like clockwork. Everyone had their purpose, and they did their jobs without a single complaint that Aurelia heard. When the work was done, they hung around to play cards or read books—some played music, and they reveled and danced. The days passed quickly, and Aurelia always went to bed excited for sunrise.

One day, William called to her from across the ship. She met him at the bottom of the steps to the quarterdeck, where he handed her a gold spyglass and pointed to the sea.

Far from the ship, something moved through the glimmering waves. She raised the spyglass to her eye and gasped. "Are those whales?"

His unbuttoned coat snapped in the wind. "About five of them."

Massive creatures breached the surface, sucked in a breath, and arched back down, their fluked tails waving a brief goodbye before they disappeared. She looked up at him, breathless with delight. "They're incredible."

He nodded to the instrument in her hands. "Keep the spyglass for as long as you like. I've got another." Then he left her to marvel while he returned to the helm.

Days later, she saw a pod of dolphins, which excited her as much as anything she'd seen and came with extensive giggling. They weren't as impressive as the whales, but as she watched them jump, she decided they were, as William had once told her, very charming.

And try as she might to manage her feelings, her sensibilities were in shambles. If she'd ever been a truly sensible girl, she would never have written to a pirate captain, and she would've married a beastly prince because there was no chance of someone saving her, not ever, because things like that didn't happen outside of storybooks.

But she had been stolen and saved by a liar and a thief. Her world had come to life, thanks to William. He'd always kept it alive, and now he'd pulled her into the adventure she'd always craved.

With impeccable weather and a faithful wind, they made it to the Caribbean in only a few weeks. She was in the crow's nest when she first caught sight of land. A short pirate named Fenner handed her the spyglass to spot the green islands, and told her to call out, "Land ho!" She did—which caught the captain's eye—and then began the terrifying descent back down.

"Nicely done," Ralph said, appearing behind her as her feet hit the deck.

It was a fine thing to be reunited with Ralph—so much so she nearly forgot the pain of his absence. He was easy to be around, and she'd slipped back into their familiar friendship like one might put on a favorite pair of warm socks.

"Thank you," she said, exhilarated from being so high. She perched next to him on a crate near the mast. "So this legendary treasure we're headed for, Captain Robin's treasure—"

At that moment, Lavinia walked by. She halted and turned. "It's Copson's."

"Aurelia hasn't heard the story," Ralph said, nudging Lavinia's boot with his.

"Oh." Lavinia sat on another crate. "It's Copson's treasure," she said to Aurelia, her hazel eyes intent. "With the way the captain's gone on about it, I'm surprised Ralph calls it anything else."

"What use have I to flatter him?" Ralph asked with a rueful grin. "You think he'd care if I did?"

Lavinia shrugged. "He's not immune to flattery."

"You'd know," Ralph said pointedly.

Aurelia's heart jolted and she looked to the lady pirate, wondering not for the first time how deep her relationship had gone with William. They were friends—that much was obvious with their comfortable affection and frequent teasing around deck and at meals. But Lavinia's real attention was saved for Ralph.

Lavinia playfully grabbed Ralph's chin to turn his head away. "He was the only one worth flattering until *you* came along," she said sarcastically, but her eyes gleamed.

They'd make a fine couple, Aurelia thought, and wondered why they hadn't already become one.

Ralph turned back to Aurelia. "The treasure was supposed to be Copson's, but Robin's the one who hid it. Most everyone calls it Robin's, which has only served to taunt Copson for the last century."

Fenner reached the bottom of the mast then, and he looked over at their conversation.

Aurelia had come to know Fenner as the superstitious pirate, and she would never have thought of disparaging his faith in any way, as she was a believer herself—in the Lord and a great many unexplainable things.

However.

Fenner wore seven crucifixes at all times, which he claimed warded off the copious amounts of bad luck they might draw at sea because seven was God's lucky number. He wore one on each ankle and wrist, and another at his throat. The final two swung from his ears, but even surrounded by crosses, he was the most anxious man she'd ever met.

Consequently, he was one of her favorite sailors in Copson's company, and she made a point to sit next to him to hear all the latest things that would bring her terrible fortune.

She waved him over. Ralph and Lavinia exchanged amused glances as the man regarded them with big, dark eyes, smoothed his short gray beard, and seemed to finally decide it was alright to sit with them.

"He's been after the treasure for a *century*?" Aurelia asked. There was a lie in there somewhere, either about the treasure, the time frame, or merely the common fib about Copson's immortality.

"Almost," Ralph said. "Nearly a hundred years ago, Robin and Copson were partners, and they robbed a royal fleet and took off with the treasure. But when it came time to split the gold between their crews, Captain Robin stole it all and sailed away in the middle of the night on his ship, *The Dawn Chorus*. Copson had two ships at the time, and Robin even took one of those too. He hid the treasure, and people have been looking for it ever since. Including…" He glanced over his shoulder. Copson stood at the helm, unaware that he was the topic of conversation.

"Any pirate would sell his soul for a loot as legendary as this," Lavinia said.

"Bad luck to sell a soul," Fenner said gravely, and Aurelia agreed.

A couple other sailors had joined their group, listening intently to Ralph's tale. "Some say that's why the cap's immortal," one of them said. "The Witch of Tortuga had him hunt down Robin over thirty years ago. Copson done killed 'im in cold blood in exchange for immortal life so he could find the treasure, and she's still waiting for her cut of the gold."

Ralph met Aurelia's gaze and lifted one brow before wiping his expression and nodding along. Aurelia giggled.

"No," said another pirate. "He's immortal 'cause he kissed a mermaid and it was his reward for surviving the siren sickness."

Aurelia turned to the pirate who'd spoken—a Persian man with an uncanny knack for catching fish. "A mermaid?"

"Sure," said the pirate. "Everyone knows it."

"First time I've heard it," someone else said, and several others began arguing over a witch that died and one that didn't, or whether the captain drank from immortal waters or killed an important man to live forever.

"Copson got a map," Ralph said over them. "A treasure hunter found it in an antique vase in England and didn't realize what he had. He wouldn't sell it, so Copson took it."

"He shot him, is what I heard," someone said. "Right in the back of the head."

"That's not what I heard," said another.

"You're all so full of shit," Lavinia said with an eye roll. "And no one more so than Fenner."

Fenner frowned at the undue insult, then huffed. "He shouldn't have shot a man in the back or stole a cursed map. Robin's spirit haunts the treasure and anyone who takes it."

"Sounds like a lot of bad luck," Aurelia mused. Fenner nodded, deadly serious. "But maybe the map and the murder cancel each other out?"

"Even if there was a spirit haunting the treasure," Ralph said to

Fenner, "it wouldn't bother Copson. No ghosts ever bother him."

"A fable!" someone declared. "He just hasn't pissed any off."

"It's only 'cause ghosts aren't real," said another, and he was shushed by half a dozen others.

The group continued bickering as they sailed through clear blue waters between reefs and mountainous islands teeming with towering palm trees. Aurelia stared, open-mouthed, at the beauty of it.

When the sun was high and blinding, the ships anchored off a deserted beach. Sailors made their way to the shore in small boats—not the entire company, but a small portion of it.

Aurelia was about to get into one such boat floating at the bottom of a ladder flung over the edge of the *Destiny's Revenge*, but she lingered at the top. She curled her fingers into the straps of the pack slung over her shoulders, which were no longer so bony. Her arms were stronger too, thanks to the duties she'd happily taken on.

Her next adventure—*treasure*—waited for her at the bottom of that ladder. She'd be in those beautiful waters, walk across that beach, and traverse the jungle, and would be forever changed as much as she had by merely stepping onto a pirate ship.

It was a good thing. A big thing, but wonderful in such a way she had to take a moment to savor it.

Copson approached, shoving a piece of aged parchment into his coat. "You have learned to swim, haven't you?" He spoke low to keep the question between them, and there was a note of teasing in his words.

"I've always known how to swim," she replied matter-of-factly. "The issue was not that—you try swimming in a dress and see how it goes."

"Only if you can assure me I'd still be dashing." He nodded to the boat. "Go on then, Miss Rowe. Save me time in having to tell you about it later."

With how little he'd said to her these past weeks, she liked the idea of talking to him—enough that she wondered if she might like it better than the treasure. Nevertheless, she found herself in a boat next to Ralph and bobbing over crystal waves an ocean away from princes and suitors.

She dipped her fingers into the cool water and grinned.

Near the shore, the pirates dropped into the surf and started for the beach, pulling the boats behind them through the knee-deep water. Aurelia flung herself out of the boat too, driving her feet through the waves to keep up. The surf pushed and swirled around her legs like a cat eager for attention, soaking her pants and her boots, and it was messy and undignified and wonderful.

Copson sloshed through the shallows a few feet away, announcing to his gathered crew, "My treasure has been lost for long enough—today we bring it home!"

A cheer went up. Copson drew the parchment from his coat and unfolded it to reveal the faint lines of a map, then started for the jungle with Greyson at his side.

There were maybe sixty pirates altogether, and they tromped through thick undergrowth, hacking leaves with swinging machetes while Aurelia drank in her surroundings. Birds called to each other between the towering trees, singing and squawking warnings as the pirates neared. Creatures howled or skittered through the underbrush. Somewhere nearby was a waterfall or a river, or maybe both, crashing and rushing through the jungle.

Her shirt stuck to her back as they hiked, but she didn't mind the humidity as the pirates' stories and banter made the hours feel short. They moved slowly as Copson and Greyson stopped often to consult the old map and a compass, discussing and pointing to towering landmarks.

By the time the sun set and the last vestiges of evening faded above the trees, the pirates set up camp in a small clearing. Aurelia was happily tired, her legs sore and twitching as she helped Lavinia pitch a tent. They'd only just finished when Ralph sauntered over and settled on a log near a campfire someone had built near them.

"What will you do with your cut of the treasure?" Lavinia asked Ralph as she took a seat to his right while Aurelia sat on his left.

Ralph leaned closer Aurelia. "She always asks me this." He straightened and answered, "Something practical."

Across the clearing, Copson and Greyson stood with their heads bent over the map. Aurelia's eyes locked on the golden parchment, itching to know the secrets it held.

"Saving it still?" Lavinia asked.

"Of course," Ralph said.

"Your nest egg must be impressive."

Ralph swayed as Lavinia bumped him with her shoulder. "Enough for a house, a business, and a wife," he said. His voice was low, his chin pointed toward Aurelia. But she hardly noticed, her gaze locked on the map and the fine hands that held it.

And then it tilted slightly in her direction—just enough to see the vague outline of an island. Startled, she looked up.

Copson watched her from beneath his brows, his blue gaze amused while Greyson continued gesturing to the inked lines and symbols.

"Piracy pays," Lavinia said lightly. "It'll keep paying if you stay."

Ralph laughed. "It should pay for something beyond itself."

Lavinia grunted. "Someday, Ralph. Someday you'll see you *love* this."

Aurelia didn't think Lavinia was talking about piracy, and she might've grinned if she wasn't so focused on the treasure map. She craned her head for a better look.

Copson shifted, folding his arms and letting the parchment hang from his fingers with the drawings facing outward. He didn't look away from his first mate, nodding along with whatever he said, brows pulled together in thought. Aurelia squinted, trying to make out the fine lines—

A cry went up from somewhere to her left. At the edge of the clearing, Offley's tent had collapsed on top of him, and the canvas undulated as the squealing carpenter struggled to find his way out.

Ralph and Lavinia rushed to help him as some of the other pirates laughed and mocked the poor man. Aurelia frowned, then looked back at the captain.

He was gone.

She scanned the clearing. Maybe he'd turned in for the night or wandered off, but the flaps of his empty tent were pulled back, and he was nowhere to be seen with any of the other pirates—

"Here." Golden parchment appeared next to her face, folded into a long rectangle. "Before you strain your neck trying to spy."

Aurelia whipped around. Copson stood behind her, his cool gaze amused, the map extended between them.

Her heart fluttered. "Is this...?"

"The treasure map." His hand bounced, urging her to take it.

A one-hundred-year-old map to a lost treasure. She clenched her jaw against any happy sounds that might burst from her as she took the parchment and slowly unfolded it. A giggle escaped her anyway.

The map was beautifully drawn. There was an ornate compass rose in the upper left corner and a mermaid lounging in the lower right with a wavy music staff emerging from her mouth. Notes dotted the five lines, nearly overlapping in some places to make the bars look more like a scribble than a melody. An octopus's writhing tentacles emerged from tiny waves nearby, reaching for a ship with *The Dawn Chorus* written across its hull as it sailed for the island in the middle of the map. A thin, dotted line wound through mountains and thick jungle, jutting rocks and a river, leading to a large *X* at the heart of the island

and a drawing of a cave. On top of the cave sat a robin, its eyes locked on the singing mermaid.

Aurelia studied it closely. "How'd you get it?" she asked, running her finger over the compass as she thought of the tale the pirates had told on the ship—that Copson had shot a man for the map. Would he tell her a different story?

To her surprise, he said, "The Witch of Tortuga told me where to find it. Did I tell you about her?"

She twisted to look up at him. "Was she the one who told you where to find the Fountain of Youth?"

He clasped his hands behind his back and smirked, watching his crew mill about the clearing. "No, but she inspired that tale. She lives in a haunted forest you can only find your way through if she's interested in letting you in—and back out. Legend says the forest once swallowed an entire regiment of Spanish soldiers in one night, and their screams were heard for miles. Either she ate them or the trees did—no one really knows for certain." He looked down at her. "The locals aren't too keen on her forest, and not many venture in."

Aurelia raised a skeptical brow. "And she let you?"

"Of course," he said with an arrogant grin, and she knew there was a story there too. She thought about asking, but if she started plying him for *all* his stories, she doubted she'd ever stop. So she decided to show restraint and asked instead, "What'd you give her in return?"

"Naturally, I gave her what any witch would want." As he spoke, he nudged aside the part in his shirt, exposing the end of a cruel scar that ran through his chest and disappeared under the linen. "I carved out my infernal heart and gave it to her."

Aurelia stared wide-eyed at the awful mark. Before she could express her horror, he leaned down to whisper, "I asked her nicely."

Her cheeks burning, she folded the map along one of the creases, hiding the mermaid but leaving the ship and half the island. That's when she noticed thin words scrawled along the left side, so tiny they nearly blended in with the intricately drawn border.

"Do manners go far with witches?" she asked.

"Most of them." His gaze moved to his brother who was now re-pitching Offley's tent with Lavinia's help while the carpenter stood by, his head bowed. "How are things with Ralph?"

"As lovely as ever," she said absently. Ralph's casual words from minutes ago pricked at her. All of this—piracy, treasure, witches—how was this not better than a business? She held an actual treasure map, and Ralph only saw it as a necessary means to a boring end.

She finished folding the map and held it aloft, meeting the captain's gaze. His eyes held questions, but he asked only one, and she didn't think it voiced any of the thoughts in his head.

"Already done?" Copson took it but didn't put it away.

"I could never be done," she said with a laugh. "But thank you for showing it to me."

He studied her for a long moment, the look heavy with curiosity. It wasn't the first time he'd looked at her like that, and she hoped whatever he was looking for wouldn't end up shaming her if she was found either too overbearing or lacking in some way. It made her nervous, but she didn't dare wilt.

The map disappeared into his coat. "You need only ask."

Across the way, Ralph and Lavinia had finished with Offley's tent and were now on their way back. Before they were close enough to hear, Aurelia began to say, "Does Ralph really not want to be a pirate?"

But when she turned, William was gone.

15

Robin's Dawn Chorus

Birdsong woke Aurelia early the next morning, loud as a symphony. She stood by the embers of the campfire to listen, even as some of the pirates grumbled and cursed the poor creatures—but they were also the ones who'd stayed up too late sharing ghost stories and lewd tales that made Aurelia blush.

She'd slept well enough, dreaming of witches and haunted forests. She hadn't been scared, though, as even her unconscious mind knew whatever terrors might dwell in the nighttime forest were more afraid of Copson than she was of them because he could wander through a witch's woods and emerge unscathed by *asking nicely*.

A hearty breakfast and a cup of black coffee had her jittering and excited for a day of trudging through the jungle, and before the sun had risen above the mountains, they set off.

This small group of pirates was better armed than a small army. Greyson alone wore enough weapons to arm a militia—in addition to the two long, wicked blades he used to cut through the foliage—and Aurelia amused herself by trying to count them all as she walked behind him.

Greyson peered at her over his shoulder. "A'right, Beck?"

She pointed to his litany of knives. "May I carry one of those?"

"You gonna stab me?"

"I don't think so."

He tossed one of his short swords, grabbed it by the non-lethal edge, and extended the hilt. She took it, and another weapon immediately appeared in his hand.

She weighed the sword, comparing it to the sparring saber she'd held for the last year. The blade was thicker than she was used to, and sharp enough to kill. Ensuring there was space between her and the first mate, she gave it a test swing. It felt natural enough, and she enjoyed the satisfaction of slicing cleanly through the unruly undergrowth.

"Good form," Ralph said from behind her.

"A countess taught me," she said, and chopped away a rogue leaf the length of her leg. The birds sang and sang from the jungle canopy, quieter than they'd been this morning, but still loud enough to make her feel serenaded.

Ahead of Greyson, the captain abruptly stopped and pointed.

A net hung high above, its weathered ropes dripping with long, green strands of lichen. People were trapped inside, their bones brown with rotted flesh, skeleton mouths open in silent screams.

Aurelia stumbled back into Ralph with a strangled gasp. All around, the birds kept singing.

"Booby traps," Ralph said.

She swallowed against a closed throat. It wasn't like it was her first time seeing dead people—she'd even stood in their blood, but they'd still *looked* like people. This was more akin to the terrors she'd read about in her books as a child.

Copson rolled his shoulders. "How fortunate someone already sprung them for us," he mused with not an ounce of remorse or horror. With a wild grin, he continued on.

Aurelia met Ralph's stare, her wide eyes asking, *Is he insane?* But Ralph, too, seemed unruffled.

She clenched her jaw. How many times had her favorite heroes breezed through trials and tests that proved them worthy of their names? These pirates were doing the very same, and she could do it too—Rebecca Rowe could be as fierce a name as Hercules or Psyche or Captain Copson.

Steeling herself, Aurelia passed under the net, breathing through her terror. The back of her neck prickled, and she wrapped her hand tighter around her sword. Then she was past it, as fine as any other who cared little for those long-dead souls who'd risked and paid everything for a legendary treasure.

As they continued on, the ground turned rockier and rose on either side of the path, growing into the towering, smooth gray walls of a narrow slot canyon. Aurelia trailed her fingers over the rock face, through soft moss and thin trickles of water.

Ahead of the company, Copson tread turned a corner and stopped. The mouth of the slot canyon loomed ahead, and the path continued beyond it. He pointed to another cliff face far beyond, through a wide clearing filled with bushes and sparse trees. "There's a doorway over there."

Greyson squinted. "The one we need?"

"Yes...but it's too tempting." The captain's gaze lowered to the ground. "Robin wouldn't make it so easy."

Beside Aurelia, Ralph folded his arms. "He'll find it," he muttered.

"Find what?" Aurelia whispered back.

"The second trap. There's never just one."

"*Flattery*," Lavinia said from his other side, a crossbow propped against her shoulder. "Five pounds says he can hear every word you're saying."

"Greyson," Copson said.

The first mate didn't move. "Aye."

The captain's voice came light and unbothered. "Tell them to still their tongues before I cut them out."

Greyson glanced at the three over his shoulder. Ralph's expression didn't change, Lavinia rolled her eyes, and Aurelia merely waved. The first mate said, "Shut it."

Copson crouched, his long coat pooling on the ground. He surveyed the dirt, then pointed. "There. The ground dips—it'll give way the moment we step on it."

"Good eye," Greyson muttered, almost too quiet to hear, then he stood and wandered back the way they'd come. The crew parted for him without a word. He returned a minute later, every muscle in his massive, tattooed arms pressed starkly against his shirt sleeves as he carried a small boulder to where Copson remained on his haunches.

With a loud grunt, Greyson threw it into the path. The ground gave way, swallowed by a ten-foot hole without even a ledge one might shimmy across. Furious hissing sounded from the bottom of the pit.

"Venomous snakes?" Greyson guessed.

"What other kind would you use?" Copson asked lightly. "Robin really thought of everything. Clever bastard." He prowled along the edge of the pit, his hands clasped behind his back. "If anyone has an idea, do come forward..."

Aurelia studied the walls around them, and the ancient trees growing from the tops of the canyon. Their roots hung over the edges, solidly anchored to the rocks.

While the other pirates muttered about ladders and makeshift bridges, Aurelia glanced at Lavinia. Their gazes met, and Aurelia turned her face up, toward the trees, as though to say, *What do you think?*

Lavinia followed her attention to the towering walls and tree trunks high above. She studied them for a few seconds, then muttered, "That could do." Swinging her crossbow off her shoulder, she called, "Captain."

Copson turned, his eyes alighting on her crossbow. Some silent communication passed between them—understanding Aurelia imagined could only have come from years of knowing someone well. Lavinia didn't have to say anything—he simply gestured to the pit and said, "By all means."

As Lavinia moved to stand beside Copson, she procured from her bag a long, thick bolt with a rope affixed to the end, which she let fall to the ground. She lifted her crossbow, loaded the bolt, and aimed.

With a snap, the bolt went flying and buried deep into an old tree growing above the wall. She lowered the weapon and gave the rope a sharp tug. Her arms bulged, reminiscent of her father who watched from the opposite wall with no expression, his arms folded over his chest.

The bolt remained lodged in the tree. Lavinia spared a glance at Greyson. He nodded once.

"Go on," Copson said without taking his eyes off Lavinia. If he was worried about whether or not her idea would work, he certainly didn't show it.

Aurelia leaned into Ralph and whispered, "What if she doesn't make it?"

"Her idea," he replied. "So she goes first. Careful what you suggest around here."

Squaring her shoulders, Lavinia eyed the pit, then the rope, and released some slack. She double-checked herself, then stepped back. Without a second of hesitation, she sprinted forward and threw her body over the pit. She thrust her legs forward, propelling her to the other side where she landed in the middle of the path with plenty of space to spare.

Spinning back to the pirates, Lavinia flashed a sharp grin and snapped the rope back. Copson caught it. With her hands on her hips, Lavinia said, "Easy."

Copson went next, followed by Ralph. Aurelia stepped aside,

watching the pirates swing across one by one. She committed each step to memory—the way they gripped the rope, ran, swung, landed.

When Greyson offered the rope to Aurelia, she took it despite the trepidation stirring in her gut.

"Run as fast as you can," Greyson said. "Don't doubt or you're dead."

She took the rope and walked to the same spot the others had, her heart pounding furiously. By now, a path had been worn into the ground. She knew what to do—now she only had to follow what everyone else had done.

Across the pit, Copson caught and held her gaze with expectant blue eyes, which certainly didn't help her nerves.

Was she fast enough? Was she strong enough to hold onto the rope? What if the bolt ripped from the tree and threw her into the pit with the snakes? Their hissing had quieted, but she'd caught sight of their long, black bodies and wicked white fangs.

"Don't doubt," she said to herself. "Don't die."

The captain nodded, the gesture so small she nearly didn't catch it were it not for the shadow of his hat moving across his lips.

With one last deep breath, she charged forward. Air rushed past her ears, drowning out the sound of her thundering pulse. The snake pit neared, the hissing grew louder, she lifted her feet—

The rope pulled taut, throwing her over the deep pit. The snakes hissed at her with wide, venomous mouths, snapping their jaws as her shadow soared over them. She crossed the far edge and released the rope, her boots skidding through the dirt as momentum carried her forward and sent her careening toward a boulder hiding in a patch of leafy bushes.

Copson stepped into her path, halting her as she nearly stumbled into him. She was so delighted from the swing—and still giggling with the rush—that she almost didn't notice his hands on her waist.

His eyes were cool and his words nearly inaudible as he said, "Alright, Miss Rowe?"

"Swell, Captain," she answered, breathless and flushed as one of the other pirates snapped the rope back across the pit.

The edge of Copson's mouth twitched, betraying his amusement for half a second before he retreated a step and settled back into flawless nonchalance—the kind that said he'd easily cut out someone's tongue as reward for being mildly annoying.

Aurelia moved to Ralph's side as Offley swung over and nearly missed the ledge. His foot slipped, and he teetered back with a cry. Copson surged forward with two other pirates to grab the carpenter before he could tumble into the pit. They set him to rights, and Offley quickly scurried to the edge of the group.

"Why'd he come?" Aurelia asked Ralph, nodding to Offley.

"He doesn't look it, but he's one of the most valuable men on the ship," Ralph told her quietly as Greyson swung last. "He can build or fix or dismantle anything, so the captain keeps him near just in case, and he's paid better than most." Ralph frowned. "But he's an easy target because...well."

Others were already mocking Offley for his misstep, just as they had with the tent the night before. Aurelia's heart sank, so instead she watched Greyson tie the rope around a thin tree. He moved to the head of the group with Copson, clapping a heavy hand on Lavinia's shoulder when he passed. She smiled up at him.

"There's a pecking order," Ralph said with a note of regret as they headed for the opening in the cliff face that Copson had called a door. "Unfortunately, Offley's put himself at the bottom and never made the right choices to do any better. The captain's tried to help, but there's only so much one can do."

Aurelia caught Offley's shifting gaze and smiled. He blinked and ducked his head.

The path into the cave was smooth, but Copson didn't enter. He eyed the darkness and the bird carved crudely into the rock above them, musing, "Robin always did like games."

"Which one would this be?" Greyson asked gruffly.

Copson held out his hand. "Torch, if you please."

Greyson grabbed a short limb from the ground and cracked it over his leg. One of the others handed him a smelly strip of fabric, which Greyson tied around the end of the stick. A match struck, and the torch went up in flames.

Copson took it and held it aloft in the passage. He took a step—and fell back as a pike sprang from the wall and embedded into the other side. Before he could catch his breath from the surprise, he grinned. "The game is don't get impaled," he said merrily.

Ralph said to his brother, "Captain, maybe someone else should go in—"

"Nonsense," Copson said. "Where's the fun in that?"

Aurelia's pulse thundered as Copson wandered farther into the passage, moving slowly over the ground and ducking as pikes shot from holes in the wall—flying for his head, his knees, his chest. But with the torch in hand, he anticipated every strike and made it to the other end unscathed, having missed one or two by only a hair's breadth.

He turned back to his crew standing at the entrance with twelve iron bars crisscrossing the passage between them. "Come now," he said. "Don't dawdle when we're so close."

Two more torches were lit, and the pirates followed, ducking and climbing over the pikes until they found themselves in a large chamber with a high ceiling.

Gold coins and tiny gems glittered in shallow puddles scattered over the floor. Aurelia marveled but didn't dare touch anything as she remembered Fenner's warnings about cursed treasure. Not that she really believed him, but in case he was right...

The pirates scoured the cave while Copson stood in the middle, his torch held high. Another bird was carved into the far wall, but aside from the scattered bits of treasure piled in the corners, there was little else.

Copson's jaw clenched. "This can't be it. This isn't it."

"Maybe someone beat us here," Ralph said from his right. Aurelia stood behind them and searched for something they might've missed.

"No," Copson said. "If someone had found it, it would be all over the Atlantic. No one took my treasure."

Greyson grunted from where he stood by the wall, surveying the carving. "Think the map was a trick?"

Copson handed the torch to Ralph and unfurled the map. "There's no trick," he said after a moment of study. "No mistake. This is Robin's map."

Aurelia ghosted closer, peering between the brothers at the words she'd seen scrawled along the map's border the night before. "What does it say on the side?"

"Where?" Copson said.

Ralph stepped aside as she pushed closer, her eyes only on the map even as she drew near enough to feel Copson's warm breath stir the loose strands of hair hanging by her face. She pointed to the far-left side of the page. "There."

Copson and Ralph leaned in, squinting.

"That's just the design," Ralph said.

"They're words," Aurelia insisted, and pulled the map from Copson's grip. He let it go without protest, his gaze heavy with shadows and firelight. She turned the parchment and held it nearly to her nose to read the tiny letters. "*The defiant anthem of silent night announces the golden sun...* It's a riddle."

She looked up at the wall. *The golden sun...* Treasure was gold—did the sun mean treasure? She peered at the robin carving and thought of the bird song that had woken her while the others grumbled about the deafening beauty.

A thought struck her. "Ralph, what was the name of Captain Robin's ship?"

"*The Dawn Chorus*," Copson said before Ralph could answer.

She read the riddle again. "The last defiant anthem of night is the dawn chorus," she said, and looked at the captain. "When all the birds sing before sunrise."

Ralph asked no one in particular, "Do most captains write poetry about their ships?"

"You would," Aurelia said with an unladylike snort. She was certain a few of his letters had contained poetry about the sky and sea and whatever else. Out of the corner of her eye, a smirk flashed across Copson's face.

"Silence," she said, pointing to the word. "Can we have silence?"

"Quiet!" Copson barked. Aurelia jumped, and the voices around them ceased. As the echoes faded, she strained to hear the birds outside. She'd listened to them all along their morning trek, but the passage behind them was too long, and the cave was achingly silent.

She turned to the robin carved into the wall. There was no possibility of catching enough birds to sing in a cave, let alone getting them to do something akin to the dawn chorus. The answer was right in front of her, begging her to see it as the captain's gaze bored into her.

Break the silence.

Dawn chorus.

Announce the gold.

Then she spotted it on the map—the mermaid with the music staff near her mouth. She was *singing* to the robin perched on the cave.

All too aware of the way Copson's attention burned into her neck, she prayed all those music lessons would finally prove their usefulness

163

as she ran her finger over the tiny lines and dots, deciphering the scribbled melody. It wasn't a familiar tune, but something more akin to birdsong.

Of course it was. She pulled in a long breath and whistled the flurry of notes, drawing out the last tone for a count of four.

Nothing happened. Ralph began to whisper, "What is—"

Copson shushed him.

Sweating, Aurelia tried again, whistling louder than she had the first time. The last high, piercing note split the stillness of the cave. Something clicked within the wall, and then the rock slid away, pulled on hidden mechanisms. From behind the door, a burst of metallic breath tossed her braid back from her shoulders, and she laughed against the quick roar of wind.

Copson started ahead. As he crossed the threshold, his torch illuminated a monstrous cavern filled with gold. He flashed a manic grin. "Summon all hands."

Aurelia wondered how she'd ever thought the cave's antechamber was impressive with its smattering of coins.

This room was piled high with relics and stacks of precious metals and gems. Stalactites hung from above, a mirror image of the floor below, the rock glistening in the reflection of torches and treasure. As hundreds more pirates arrived and hauled off the fortune, Aurelia roamed the edge of the cave with her hands buried in her empty pockets, marveling at how anyone could have this much wealth. How so much could exist in the first place.

Legendary indeed.

Copson lingered nearby, watching his crew. His arms were folded tightly over his chest, his feet spread like he was bracing himself. Or like he was a king.

She'd solved his riddle and opened the door to his gold, which left her feeling like she'd proved herself as more than a silly, shivering child. It gave her the confidence to wander nearer. "Are you not impressed?" she asked.

"On the contrary," he said. "I am relieved."

She glanced at the others and tried to ignore the warmth radiating off him as she shivered in the damp, chilly air.

"This should have been my great-grandfather's," he told her, pitching his voice low enough that it wouldn't carry. "My grandfather swore he'd find it, and my father searched obsessively for a time. Of the few things that might tempt wicked men toward true immortality, this is certainly one of them." He looked at her, his eyes bright in the dimness. "And to think I might've been thwarted by a vain man's poetry."

She prayed he couldn't see her blush, but she dared not look away. "A couple more minutes and you'd have seen it. You'd have solved the riddle just as well."

He arched one brow.

Flattery, said Lavinia's voice in her head. Aurelia wasn't sure why she bothered flattering this man in the first place. Perhaps it was because she still loved him. Or maybe she believed in him, and he *would* have found this legendary treasure—because he was Captain Copson, and he was legendary too.

Aurelia turned, freeing most of her face from the heat of his gaze. "What will you do with the map?"

"I'll gift it to my father as peace offering, as I expect he'll be miffed that I failed to invite him for this."

Surely the earl was not so severe. "He won't be impressed?"

He chuckled. "Impressed, but terribly jealous. So maybe it's more of a consolation prize." He nodded to the remaining treasure. "Has anything caught your eye?"

"All of it," she said. "It's rather shiny."

"Take something."

"You haven't."

"It's mine anyway." He spoke so blithely, like there was nothing incredible about it at all.

"Fenner said I'll be cursed," she said, her words flat.

Fenner wasn't even in the cavern, having preferred to stay on the ship and log the gold. His report would be compared to that of Ralph's, who counted the money as the gold left the cave, to ensure nothing was lost or stolen on the way.

"Only if I think it appropriate," Copson said with a mischievous smile. "But I swear not to curse you."

Her eye caught on a blue stone at the bottom of a shallow pool filled with coins, but she didn't move to grab it.

"If it'll ease your mind," he said, "I'll take something too." He picked up a gold ring. It wasn't big enough to slip over his finger, so it perched above his knuckle as he held it up for her to see. Then he pulled a long chain from around his neck, slipped it through the ring, and swept his hand toward the remaining mounds of treasure.

Sighing, she dipped toward the blue stone and lifted it from the water. It emerged attached to a gold band that looked small enough to fit her. The gem sparkled in the firelight.

"A sapphire," Copson said. "The ancient Greeks said they bring wisdom to the wearer."

"Do they?" Aunt Clara might've covered Aurelia with the jewel if she'd known—or forbidden them altogether for the assumption a stone could thwart the Lord's divine intention for one to be an idiot.

"The only wisdom I see is in what you buy with it. Or how you wear it."

She looked between the captain and the stone glittering in her palm.

166

The perfect color blue, she thought, and though she'd never dedicated any time to exploring the topic, she said, "It's my favorite gem."

The captain folded his hand around hers, curling her fingers over the ring. "Then it's happily my gift to you as thanks for opening the door. I've never been much good with riddles, so take ten more if you like—I'm ever in your debt."

Then his hand disappeared and he strode off, leaving her shivering and the tiniest bit richer.

16

The Republic of Pirates

The ships sat noticeably lower in the water with treasure aboard, but the captain was eager to remedy this. After spending the night off the island's coast, they sailed into Nassau.

Copson paid his crew well, even granting bonuses for the pleasure at having found the wealth that was rightfully his. As promised, Aurelia was no exception to the payout. While the others collected their salaries from Greyson or Fenner or Ralph, Copson himself handed her a small, heavy bag that chimed with gold.

"Spend it wisely," he told her as many of the crew started for the shore. "And please, Miss Rowe, don't get into too much trouble."

She held the money in her palm like an offering. Even with far more riches to her name stored in the belly of the ship, she'd never held so much money all at once. Aunt Clara would've called it obscene, but Aurelia felt only pride. "I'm afraid I'm not sure what kinds of trouble I should avoid."

"Preferably all of it," Copson replied simply. "Unless it is entertaining—then at least be judicious about what you seek out." His gaze moved to Ralph who was explaining the history of a certain design stamped on a gold coin while Lavinia watched him with a wistful grin. "Go with them and watch them bicker over the meaning of fun."

As the pirates descended on the city and scattered through the streets and taverns to debase themselves in all the ways that suited them, Aurelia stuck close to Ralph and Lavinia with hopes they wouldn't lead her anywhere that would make her blush or rob her of her innocence too quickly.

Too quickly, Aurelia thought, because she was sure it would all be gone at some point. She just wasn't sure she wanted to face all life's truths at once. And since her conversation with the captain, she was nervous Nassau might subject her to just that.

Nassau, Ralph and Lavinia told her, was run entirely by pirates, making it a safe place for Copson and his crew to dock. In fact, Copson had even been invited to help govern the city, which he'd turned down in favor of "pirating, pillaging, and promiscuity," as he so proudly announced to the council of captains who'd offered him the position.

Even in turning it down, Copson was still regarded as highly as the pirates who presided over the city now, which garnered his crew a certain elevated favor. This came as discounts, nicer rooms at the inns, and whatever else the citizens might do to impress Copson and his sailors so they would return with their gold.

By the time Aurelia reached the small city, the streets were abuzz with the news of Robin's treasure, and the gold had already found its way into bars and brothels. Aurelia was not inclined to visit these places, so she looked instead for new clothing. Thanks to Lavinia, she found several things that fit her better than the borrowed garments she'd worn these past weeks. She bought a sword that cost more than the average pirate was willing to pay, after which she found a laundress to wash the clothing previously loaned to her, and purchased a satchel to carry it all.

Lavinia and Ralph spent their gold on various pursuits. Ralph found a diary and a new pot of ink, and Lavinia got a long purple scarf to tie around her waist because she liked it and Aurelia said she should—and because Ralph would appreciate its fine fabric. She didn't say that, though, and enjoyed the simple reward of being right when Ralph noticed and complimented Lavinia's taste.

And Lavinia, for all her teasing and banter, blushed deeply and thanked him.

That evening, they pulled Aurelia into a tavern, where pirates imbibed all around her. She didn't mind so much as a steaming plate of food was set before her. She imbibed herself, even, and tried mead for the first time. After champagnes and bitter wines served at balls and horrid social events, she didn't expect the sweet taste of the honey wine, or that she would find it so delightful. She was a bit peeved she'd never been offered it before.

By the time evening fell, the three made their way back to the *Destiny's Revenge*. While Ralph and Lavinia disappeared to their quarters, Aurelia stayed on the main deck to watch the city. Gunshots, screams, music, and drunken laughter carried over the harbor.

Stars winked overhead, silently judging the debauchery she'd been warned from and was still unsure of. Maybe it was purposeful on Ralph and Lavinia's part—Ralph took pride in being the one to show her these more palatable parts of pirate life, even as Lavinia teased and taunted his goodness, but she stayed by his side and never once tried to lead him from it. They bickered over what they considered fun and interesting, as William had said they would, but Aurelia saw nothing that made her feel less innocent than she'd been this morning.

Her satchel weighed on her shoulder. Reminded of William's clothes inside, she peered over her shoulder at the light glowing faintly from beneath his door. She padded silently over the deck and hesitated for a breath before softly rapping her knuckles against the wood.

"What," came the snapped reply.

Aurelia slowly turned the handle and only swung the door in far enough to let her stand on the threshold.

Lanterns cast the room in shades of orange and yellow, dim enough to leech the brilliant shades of green from the walls and leave them in murky shadow. Clad in a loose black shirt, William glared at a log book on his desk and spun a pen through his fingers. When his gaze lifted, his expression thawed.

"Oh, it's you," he said, his tone lighter. "I assumed you'd stay in the city."

"I didn't mean to interrupt. I only came to return these." She pulled his clothes from her bag.

He stood and strode to her. "You're not interrupting. I'm only updating my books and praying for relief from it. It's honest work, so naturally it's my least favorite." His easy smile appeared, and her toes slid another inch into the room. He took the proffered clothing and smoothed his hand over the clean fabric. "You washed them."

"Had them washed," she clarified, ignoring the way the lanterns lit his dark hair with gold. "I probably would have ruined them."

"I'm afraid there's not much to ruin."

"Oh. Well. I'll know that for next time." She barely stopped herself from sinking into an awkwardly unnecessary curtsy. "I'll leave you to your books."

"Don't bother. Truly, I was doing nothing I wish to return to tonight." He waved her inside and moved to a low cabinet by the fireplace. "Come in, have a drink." He set the folded clothes aside and opened a door to reveal glasses and a half dozen bottles of varying sizes.

Two glasses sat on top of the cabinet, which he filled amber liquid. He tipped one back, swallowing the drink in one gulp, and immediately set to refilling it.

Like the first time she'd been in his quarters, she was taken aback by its opulence. Tonight, it was cozier with the flickering lamps, the bed covers turned down, and save for the log book still on the desk, the room was spotless.

William returned and handed her a crystal glass. "Have you had whiskey before?"

She shook her head. The glass sparkled as she swirled the alcohol inside, intrigued by its burning, woody scent. "Aunt Clara locked her liquor away because she said it was the devil's way of turning young women absurd."

"What about old women?"

She smiled. "They're already plenty absurd."

A laugh puffed through his nose. He clinked his glass against hers. "Sip it. Don't shoot it like I just did."

Raising the glass to her lips, she did as recommended. The small sip melted over her tongue, warm and smoky and tasting vaguely of caramel. She ran her tongue over the inside of her lips to catch the comforting burn.

His eyes dipped to her sword. "Is that new?"

She followed his gaze. "It is."

He held out his free hand. "May I?"

Aurelia slipped the sword from its sheath and set the hilt in his palm. He stepped out onto the empty, moonlit deck and strode a few paces away, swinging the blade with deadly precision, his face drawn in concentration as he ran through the very same movements his mother had taught her. Then he held the sword horizontal and eyed it from point to pommel, his whiskey secure in his left hand.

"You picked a good one," he said. "Well made."

"I asked a lot of questions." She'd actually asked the shop owner so many questions that he was practically sweating by the time she left his store, and he'd nearly forgotten to take her money.

She accidentally brushed William's skin as he handed it back, sending a jolt of heat up her arm. Thankfully, she managed to slip the sword back into its sheath one-handed without shaking, and by the time she met his gaze again, she was certain of her composure and her ability to keep it. Regardless, she moved out of the light spilling from his doorway, lest it reveal her blush.

"You said you learned from a countess," he said quietly as she joined him in the darkness. "Did you mean..." His eyes dropped to the turtle at her throat.

Aurelia touched the pendant. He'd heard what she'd told Ralph the day before—she hadn't realized he'd been listening. "Yes. She's a fantastic teacher."

"And her husband?" A veiled way to ask about his father, in case there were listening ears, even though she was sure they were alone.

"Gave me bad advice so she'd win."

He smirked. "Sounds right."

Aurelia lowered her satchel and sat on one of the crates near the main mast while he remained standing in the middle of the deck. "May I ask you something?"

"Sure."

She hesitated. As much as she knew him through letters and watching him as Captain Copson, she wasn't sure what she was allowed to say, or if some questions might be dangerous. She held her drink in both hands and said quietly, "Lavinia told me a story about the countess... Was she really a prisoner?"

William wandered over and leaned against the mast, close enough that she might touch him if she held out her arm. "Yes," he answered simply. "Though it's not a story she tells often. She wasn't pleased to be on the *Fortuna Royale*, and he wasn't particularly keen on her being there either. They tried to kill each other but enjoyed the experience so much that they married instead."

She swung her feet, lightly kicking her heels against the crate. "So she was a pirate."

"For a time." He stared at her for a long moment. "May I ask you something now?"

"Anything," she said, and regretted both the answer and how quickly she spoke it.

"What do you think of it? Piracy, sailing, being on the *Destiny's Revenge* with the dreadful *Captain Copson*." He said his name with a note of sarcasm, as though he found the infamy ludicrous. Which she knew he didn't because he seemed to enjoy the position far too much.

She sipped her drink and set it down beside her, mulling over the right words to say. He shifted his weight as he waited. "It's probably the most incredible thing I've ever done," she finally said, softly enough to not draw the silent stars' attention, lest they judge her too. "Here I feel like every character I've ever read about and loved. I even found *treasure* yesterday." She planted her hands on the crate and tipped her body forward like she could pour out her enthusiasm before him. "There's nothing like it, and my only disappointment is that I didn't do this sooner."

His teeth flashed in the moonlight. "I'm glad to hear it."

She glanced at his open door and the golden stripe of lantern light over the deck. "Why aren't you on land tonight?"

He peered up at the lowered sails. "For the same reason I'm careful where I sail this ship," he said. "Too much fanfare."

She tilted her head. "Really?"

"Yes," he said with a small laugh. He brought his gaze back to hers. "There are many perks to being me, but it can be suffocating."

"I thought you wanted everyone to know you found your treasure."

"I do, but I'm also tired, and a couple shots of whiskey before bed sound as nice as a hero's welcome." He lifted his glass in a salute. "For that matter, you didn't stay on land either. You seem keen to embrace every experience you can—does a pirate city not fit the bill?"

"It fits," she said, swinging her legs again. "In truth, you frightened me."

A peculiar look crossed his face, his brow furrowing with a hint of apprehension. "Frightened you how?"

She swung her feet faster, staring at the moon now. "What manner of trouble is so terrible that you, of all people, would tell me to avoid it?"

"You already know the trouble."

Her nervous kicking stopped. She looked at him and found laughter shining in his eyes. "I do?"

"You were out in society." After a moment of silence, he seemed to realize this was not enough of an explanation. To affirm it, she raised one brow and shook her head. His smile faded into something more understanding. "Several years ago, you asked me the proper way to strike a man. Why?"

She'd hoped he might simply tell her what he meant, but from his letters and sailing with him these past weeks, she'd learned William was rarely simple or brief when there was a journey to be had. "I told you then."

"Tell me more."

"I hardly remember," she said, which wasn't the truth. She wished she could so easily forget Lawrence Talley's hands on her neck and his tongue in her mouth. It had been her first kiss. The kiss she'd once fancied to give to William.

She plucked her whiskey off the crate and drank more. It burned all the way down.

"He forced himself on you," William said evenly, "didn't he."

Staring into her glass, she nodded.

He was silent for a moment, then said, "I assume there were other suitors? I don't imagine you had any shortage, being who you are."

A Danby. An heiress—virtues she'd learned to despise. "Yes, there were others."

"Proposals?"

"Some." She remembered what it was like at sixteen when she'd told herself William would one day see how desirable she was when men were throwing themselves at her and the ladies were clambering to be her friends. How funny it was to think he'd be so impressed by such a thing when he clearly disliked society as much as she did.

His stare was unwavering. "Why'd you turn them down?"

She wouldn't say the first thing that came to mind—that it was because none of them were him. Other, better answers came in quick succession, a list of sins so unattractive she wanted to choke.

"You already know the trouble." He spoke softly, plainly. "The people in that city aren't so different. Our drunkenness is louder and more violent than that of the high and mighty folks back in England. The prostitutes don't hide like their mistresses do, and the murders come without the trappings of a gentleman's duel." He shrugged and sipped his drink. "It's the same."

Her brows knitted. She struggled to picture a slovenly pirate getting along with—being the *same* as—someone as refined as Lawrence Talley. But she thought of the men she'd entertained—the proud, the greedy, the wrathful, the boring, and any number of sins besides. They were disappointing and awful compared to the boy who'd assuaged her frustration at their inadequacies with his letters.

She met William's gaze. "You're right."

"It's not my favorite thing I've ever been right about," he told her quietly. "I'm rather sorry."

"You shouldn't be. Your letters were a boon," she said. "Especially then."

He continued to watch her without blinking. She might've handed over her little bag of gold and her whole dowry to know what he saw and thought of her. Whatever it was, she had no hope of him revealing it as he said, "I didn't fear for you when I told you to stay out of trouble. I only worried because lascivious heathens are often more shocking in the streets than they are behind closed doors. Otherwise they're everything you're used to—just ugly, smelly, and obvious." He lifted his glass. "But I know you'll throw a perfect punch."

"Yes, and I have a sword now." She patted the hilt.

"A fantastic choice too." He pushed away from the mast and stepped closer, his features edged with silver from the moon. The effect was unfairly beautiful. "I hope you'll forgive me for frightening you. It wasn't my intention."

"You don't frighten me." As soon as the confession left her lips, she felt it was a lie as well. He did frighten her—both as William and Captain Copson. William terrified her for everything he made her feel, and Copson was unsettling for his wild, wicked grins and deadly threats, and especially his cool, swaggering nonchalance. Her safety, however, felt sure with both, so she added, "Not generally. Not like you scare so many others."

"Oh, well I frighten them purposefully, and because it's fun. But you are one of few exceptions to the rule because I've already seen you terrified—by an old woman, no less—and I went to such lengths to fix it." He lifted his drink to his lips, peering at her over the rim. "I do hate to be counterproductive."

There it was again—his memory of her as a shivering, scared child, even after she'd told him of her proposals and dodging men's iniquities. She scowled. If she could go back, she would have written him after her debut if only to prove she'd grown up. But if this conversation hadn't done it, perhaps nothing would. The thought left her feeling hollow.

Gunshots and laughter peeled over the water from Nassau, a constant, dim reminder they weren't in the open ocean even as the ship creaked softly beneath them. But as she drummed up an answer for him—probably another lie, but something smart and grown up nonetheless—a haunting melody rose from the sea.

Aurelia's ears pricked. "Do you hear that?" It was heartbreakingly lovely and unlike anything she'd ever heard. Perhaps it was the alcohol loosening her thoughts, but at that moment, memories of the lake and the forest flew from her mind as she hopped off the crate and wandered toward the edge of the ship.

"The singing?" William followed and looked out to the black expanse of sea. "I usually do when I'm here."

She searched the water and scanned the islands in the distance. "Where does it come from?"

"It's a mermaid." He said it with no humor or malice, not an ounce of sarcasm.

She pulled her gaze to him. "What is it actually?"

He chuckled. "A mermaid, I swear. She's been in love with me for ages, and she sings when she sees my ships in harbor."

Her eyes narrowed. "If you're making fun of me—"

"I'm not making fun of you."

"Because I don't know any better, and it'd be cruel to do that."

"First of all, would that terribly surprise you? Do you know anyone crueler than I?"

"Yes," she said, though a name didn't come to mind.

Another low laugh. "Think what you like. I won't tell you anything other than that voice is a mermaid. Most of the crew will tell you the same."

"Why is she in love with you?" The words made her shiver for how close they were to the very declaration that sat in her chest.

"Why is anyone in love?" He turned his face to her, and she realized how close he stood—near enough to see the stars reflected in his eyes. "I suppose she saw my face and thought me handsome."

Aurelia drained her whiskey. The singing continued.

"What is your opinion of your aunt now?" William asked suddenly. "You tease her without malice, but you also said she didn't say goodbye."

Aurelia watched the moonlight sparkle in her glass as the whiskey bloomed through her. "She's the only mother I know, and she was beside herself with my engagement and hid away for the pain of my departure..." She looked up at him. "I love her dearly, and she loves me too."

"Shame on the Danbys," he grumbled, and the last of his drink disappeared.

Her eyes lingered on the sharp cut of his jaw before he met her gaze again. "Aunt Clara told me her opinion of my family, as did your father," she said. "I appreciate the new name."

William still studied her intently, as though she were the riddle on his map. He still didn't speak about what he saw, and said only, "I'm happy you enjoy it. All of it."

She could stay awake forever if only to keep talking to him, but his *watching* made her nervous in a way even the whiskey could not soothe. She held her glass between them. "Thank you for the drink."

"Thank you for sparing me from drinking alone." His fingers brushed her hand as he took it, and the same thrill as before lit through her chest. He stepped back to let her pass. "Goodnight, Aurelia."

A full smile broke over her lips, loosened by the liquor. "Goodnight, William."

17

The Wickedest, Most Troublesome City in the World

The next morning, Aurelia emerged on deck while the few who stayed on the ship still slept. Across the harbor, the streets had fallen silent, so the argument brought her up short.

"—wasting your time, Ralph." William's sharp words drifted from the quarterdeck, and she shrank into the shadows. "You've had years to act on your feelings, and now I'm watching you pansy around what *you told me* you wanted. Do you actually know?"

"Maybe that is what I want," Ralph bit back. "To *pansy*."

"Don't be smart with me. You have to grow up sometime. You're twenty-six, for God's sake—"

"And you're nearly thirty!" Ralph retorted. "When are you—"

"I chose my path. What are *you* doing?"

Ralph gave a harsh laugh. "I have a path. Just because you don't understand it doesn't mean it's wrong. I came here for you, and I stayed because of her."

Aurelia dared not breathe. So Ralph did notice Lavinia, and it made all the more sense why he hadn't come home or written.

"You've earned your own wealth," William said. "You've got prospects. You've got everything you wanted to give her. Why are you waiting?"

"Tell me, how am I to court a woman on a pirate ship, surrounded by stinking idiots? Invite her straight to bed? I was raised better than that—I was raised to treat my intended with honor, to ask permission to court her first. With all we have at our disposal, *who I am* outside of this ship, how could I give her less?"

"Then get off the ship," William answered, his voice hard. "Stop wasting your time and hers. You're not being as honorable as you think by drawing this out for as long as you have."

Ralph laughed again. "Oh, like you're so honorable?"

"When I'm not, it's because I'm choosing to be so," William said coldly. "I am not so easily fooled to believe otherwise. But this isn't about me—it's about her."

His anger surprised her. Though William and Lavinia were clearly friends, she'd never seen him protective over her. In fact, he'd showed more concern over Aurelia in the short time she'd been here. Maybe he still felt something for his former flame, and the thought sat in her chest like a stone.

"Don't be a fool and lose the chance *you told me* you wanted," William said. "You talk about her like she's the sun, but you do nothing to gain her warmth."

"I am not entitled to it," Ralph hissed, his tone as frosty as his brother's. "I will give her the courtship she deserves when it's time. Until then, I'm content to be as we are."

"You're a prideful fool to think she'd give a damn where you court her. She's not going to wait forever."

"I don't need your lectures or timelines, and I certainly don't need your help. I don't *want* it."

William huffed. "Fine. Then you won't have it. But there are always consequences to complacency. You'd do well to consider them—I truly don't want to see you broken."

"How kind."

A beat of silence. Then a growled, "Get off my deck."

Aurelia scurried away before Ralph could see her. By the time they went to shore later that morning, Ralph showed no sign that he'd argued with his brother. Or taken his advice.

For the entire next week, in fact, Ralph treated Lavinia as he always did, and Aurelia understood William's frustration with his brother for doing nothing to solidify what would be a great match.

She also understood, even from childhood, how staunchly Ralph clung to his convictions. It had annoyed her then and still bothered her now. She might've spoken to him about it, but couldn't think of anything William hadn't already said. So she observed and stayed silent on the topic.

The city remained frantically abuzz at Copson's presence, but while Ralph and Lavinia pulled her into Nassau each day, William rarely left the ship, spending his time ensuring the proper shipments—cannonballs, gunpowder, food, water, tools—made their way aboard.

When they were fully stocked, Copson announced they'd head for Port Royal to appease the crew and their increasing talk of a more sinful city. Two days later, they were there.

Though Nassau was ruled by pirates, Port Royal sounded like the kind of place Aunt Clara might say was lorded over by the devil himself. The sailors spoke of brothels and taverns as though they were all the city had to offer, and they hadn't even fully docked before she saw a man completely sever another's arm and stroll away, leaving his victim screaming in the street with blood pouring from his shoulder.

"S'not so bad," Fenner said morosely from beside her as she watched in shock. "I once saw a Dutchman roast two men alive on a spit for refusing to give him a pig." He heaved a sigh and clutched the crucifix around his neck. "No place worse than Port Royal."

Aurelia remained on the *Destiny's Revenge* with the skeleton crew that day while most of the others ran amuck well into the night. The mermaid had followed Copson to Port Royal, and the creature's nighttime serenade lulled Aurelia to sleep in the midst of contemplating futile ways she might convince Ralph to be less of a gentleman.

On the second day, she took advantage of the quiet to write a letter to her aunt.

Dear Aunt Clara,

You will have read about my kidnapping in the papers by now. Please know I am fine and unharmed. And all things considered, I am happy.

Please don't worry for me.

Love,
Aurelia

She read the letter over. She didn't want her aunt to worry. Neither did she want to sound too content, lest Aunt Clara get upset for a different reason entirely.

Sighing, she folded the parchment.

Aurelia had been on board for two months now, and she'd only sought William once—the night she returned his clothes and drank his whiskey. The thought of it still made her nervous, but her stationary kit was buried in her trunks on the *Ophelia*, and she needed sealing wax, which she knew he had...

She made her way to the main deck and knocked softly on his door. Steps approached, and the door swung open.

"Miss Rowe," William said, seeming surprised to see her. He

scanned the empty deck behind her before his gaze settled on the note she raised between them.

"Do you still have the seal you used for my letters?" she asked.

"Of course," he said without pause. "Come in."

She followed him to his desk where he lit a candle under a wax warmer and retrieved a small metal stamp with a red wooden handle from a drawer. He set it on the edge of the desk.

"Sending a letter?"

"To my aunt. To tell her I'm fine." She held out the folded parchment. "Did you want to read it? In case I said something too obvious?"

He shook his head. "I don't need to read it."

She lowered her hand, her face warming. Of course he wouldn't need to read it. She wasn't a child to be checked, and she silently chided herself for playing into the perception.

"Unless you want me to," he said as her silence stretched. "But you haven't told anyone anything terribly secret in ten years. What's a couple weeks at sea?"

She lifted the stamp and looked at the inverse of the Danby crest, deferring to sarcasm as she silently entreated God to take away her ability to blush. "I wouldn't want to undo a century of Copson infamy by daring to tell her I'm happy."

William chuckled. "That's nothing I couldn't handle with a few well-placed lies."

"Fenner told me about a pirate who roasted people on a spit—perhaps you could draw inspiration from that."

"Ah, you've heard about Roche Braziliano," he said. "Good pirate, awful man—but no one's seen or heard from him for years." He winked.

Aurelia stared intently at the flame and melting wax as her heart attempted to return to a normal rhythm. Her blazing cheeks, however, were hopeless.

He nodded to her letter. "Are you sending it today?"

Her attention remained firmly on the candle. "That was my plan."

"May I join you?"

She looked up. "In Port Royal?"

"Unless you planned to send it from somewhere else."

She touched the edge of the small melting spoon. Wax swirled around the edges. "I'm sure I'll be alright," she said, and set her hand on the sword at her hip. The thought of wandering into Port Royal alone made her sweat, but for all his memories of her as a child, maybe this might convince him she was more than a girl to be worried over.

"I know. I ask as a friend, not a chaperone."

Shyness overshadowed the will to prove herself. An outing with William, more than small talk or sipping drinks on deck. Now she wasn't sure if she wanted to go by herself solely to prove she was capable or to save herself from being a fool in front of him.

A smile teased at the edges of her lips as she remembered being fourteen and accepting his offer to carry her home. At the time, she'd needed a good excuse to skirt impropriety—now she needed no other reason to say yes other than she wanted to. She wanted time with William, even if she had no idea what to do or say once she had it.

But she could be brave. She'd proven that much. "Do you know where the post office is?" she asked.

"As a matter of fact, I do," he said. "I've patronized it once or twice."

She grinned at his implication. The wax had finally melted enough, so she dripped a small circle onto the letter and sealed it with the stamp. "Alright. Come with me if you want."

"Perfect." William blew out the candle. "I swear to be the best guide you've ever had to the worst city you'll ever see." He headed for the door, grabbing his coat and hat on the way.

They descended the gangplank to the dock and started for the city, and the entire time, Aurelia wracked her brain for something to say.

Something to ask him. Something witty and bright and amusing. But nothing came to mind as they moseyed between weather-worn buildings and avoided stumbling drunks—despite it still being morning—and busty ladies who leered at William from open doors.

He walked with his hands clasped behind his back, watching the cobblestones pass beneath his boots. Then, mercifully, he spoke first.

"Did you ever get your books back? The ones you said were taken."

She thought of Aunt Clara's dusty attic and her countless failed attempts to break the lock between her and her books. "No, I didn't. I don't think they're even among my dowry." None of her trunks on the *Purgatory* had looked like the one she'd known to hold her childhood. If it had been among them, she would've been glad to see it.

"Do you still wish you had them?"

"Of course." She smiled at the thought. "They're still precious to me, whether or not they're locked up."

"There's a shop that sells books a couple streets that way." He jerked his head toward a side street. "I'm sure you could find something to your tastes."

The debauchery of the wicked city unfolded around them, but Aurelia focused only on the man beside her and the way he stared resolutely at the ground, as though to bore right through it. She stared at the same bricks he did, wondering yet again what made his stare so intense.

"Why didn't you write back?"

Suddenly, she was pinned by his blue gaze, weathering the full force of his curiosity. She blinked but couldn't bring herself to look away. "I...I don't know."

"Surely you do." The edge of his mouth curved up. "I only received two short notes from you in the lifetime of our arrangement, a brief letter about your plans to travel, and then three rather desperate pleas aside from the two I have yet to collect. I thought I'd get stacks of mail after I invited you to reply."

She ripped her gaze away, looking to the shops passing by with hopes they'd tell her what to say. But she only saw a man's bare backside on one side of the street and another throwing up his liquor on the other.

Paling, she stared at her shoes. "I didn't know you wanted me to."

"Of course I did," he said with a laugh. "Or I wouldn't have sent you addresses by which to reach me. I enjoyed the few words I did manage to get from you."

"I hardly said anything," she said, breathless.

"Which was why I sent you the addr—" He sighed, grinning fully now. "I swear I'm not scolding you. I'm only curious."

"What did you want me to say?"

"Whatever you wanted. You're quite witty, and I quite enjoy it."

"I have nothing witty to tell you why I didn't write." She followed as he gestured for them to turn down another street. "I didn't because..." She fell back into step beside him, and now she was the one who glared at the bricks beneath her feet. "Well, I suppose it's because I did all I could to be sensible in my aunt's eyes—and my parents'."

William waited for her to continue.

"And I hated it," she continued. "I well and truly hated it, but somehow they convinced me it was right. Simply receiving letters from a pirate felt like...like a book I could close. Each one was only a story—I read it, burned it, and I was done. It was as simple as reading the paper, so I could excuse it and still be sensible." She met his gaze. "But to write you back would've been like never closing the book. It'd be like beating it against my head and hoping for something impossible to happen. I'd have stepped into your world in some small way, wished for more, and descended into madness for not having it."

He considered this with pursed lips.

"And I very nearly did write," she said when he still didn't speak.

"Every one of my suitors was a fiend or a bore. Being sensible only made me sad, and I thought if anyone would be receptive to hearing that, it might be you. But no one likes a girl who complains, and besides, I never did anything interesting, so I burned every letter I wrote before I could send it."

"I wouldn't have minded in the least. You should've sent them." He turned his shoulders toward her, sidestepping up the street. "And what's this about impossibilities? All it took was one of your letters asking for my help and I came, didn't I? If sailing was a life you wanted, it was certainly open to you."

She shook her head. "Proper young women don't run away with pirates."

"I think you listened too much to your aunt and thought too greatly of your parents."

"Pardon me," she said, flustered at the accusation. "Who else was I supposed to listen to?"

"Me," he said, laughing again. "You told me from the outset that you were troublesome, and I wouldn't have endorsed it if I couldn't support you fully. Now look where you are." He swept out his hand. "I've brought you to the wickedest, most troublesome city in the world."

A sign for the post office loomed ahead, its metal face riddled with dents and bullet holes. As they neared, a gunshot exploded from somewhere nearby, and the sign flipped upward before falling back into place with a new dent in the o in *Post*. Laughter pealed from somewhere to their right.

"Humor me," William said, "and tell me what you would have written."

And because she had no doubt now that he truly wanted to know, she laughed sharply as familiar ire roared to the surface. "I would have told you polite society is anything but, and the men who courted me were monsters who fully deserved the catty young women they married. I would have asked you how best to make them hate me so they'd never look my way again. I didn't want to be a stupid oaf's miserable wife meant to throw parties and make babies and be a pretty, soft thing while my husband had his mistresses and gambling and masks. I even determined I wanted to be like my aunt so I could be grouchy and unlikeable while I grew old with my fortune, and everyone could pity me while I laughed at them."

His answering guffaw bounced off the buildings around them and drew looks from the people in the street. "You look up to old Lady Wedderburn after all," he said as they reached the post office. He held the door open. "That explains it fully."

Aurelia approached the clerk and slid her letter across the counter. William set two silver pieces beside it, his gold rings glinting.

"I have money," she said to him.

"So do I."

The door opened behind them, and several pairs of boots thudded inside. A man sidled up next to her, but Aurelia paid him no mind—until he snatched her letter off the counter.

She spun, a curse ready on her tongue as she grabbed for the letter. "That's mine!"

He tugged it beyond her reach, scrutinizing the wax seal.

"This is the Danby's crest," the man said, a French accent warping his words. "How did you get it?"

"You're mistaken, sir," William said in a hard voice. Aurelia swiped at the letter again.

The man's eyes widened. "You—you're Aurelia Danby." Others turned, and beneath their coats were the blue uniforms of the French. "She's Aurelia Danby!"

Her blood went cold. Behind her, William cursed as the Frenchman grabbed her arm. A half second later, William's fingers wrapped

189

around her other elbow. He yanked her to him and drew his gun as the Frenchman cried, "I found Lady Danby—!"

The gun exploded into the officer's face, the bullet blowing into his skull and out the other side with a spray of blood and brain.

The man's hand fell away.

Aurelia gasped. William turned, shielding her with his body as the others surged forward, drawing their weapons, but before they could shoot, he shoved Aurelia toward the exit. His gun discharged behind her, the shots coming in quick succession. She was outside before the bodies hit the floor.

William kept shooting until his gun clicked, the bullets spent. Moving with quick, deadly precision, he shoved it back in its holster and reached across his body for the other as he took Aurelia's hand and dashed down the street, shoving past pirates and locals, their faces a mix of confusion and irritation.

French commands and more gunshots pursued them. Bullets whizzed past their heads and cracked into brick walls and cobblestones. William dragged her around a corner and onto another street, then into a shadowed alley where he pinned her against the wall and dipped his face toward hers, angling his head so his hat blocked their faces. To any passersby, they might look like drunken lovers too eager to make it back to an inn.

"Are you alright?" he whispered as shouts grew louder from the way they'd come. One hand gripped her upper arm, the other held her waist.

She nodded, fighting for breath as his chest pressed against hers. "I think so." But she was very much not fine with William nearer than anyone she'd ever liked. She could hardly think past—

"Good," he panted, his breath warm against her neck. His jaw brushed her cheek. "I'm terribly sorry, my lady, but they won't look twice if they think we're otherwise engaged."

She shook her head, but stopped when she felt his stubble graze her face. "It's fine." She was not fine—she was, perhaps, actually quite more than fine.

"Welcome to Port Royal," he said with a chuckle that skated over her skin and left goose flesh in its wake.

The soldiers passed the alley, yelling commands coupled with her name. When they were gone, he slowly pulled away, his eyes bright, and glanced toward the mouth of the alley. "It won't take long for the rest of the French to know we're here. They'll know to look for you with me, and with the *Destiny's Revenge* in port..." He swore. "We need to leave the city."

"The crew," she said weakly. They'd been given three days here, and many wouldn't return to the ship until that time was up. Captain Copson couldn't sail away without them, but it seemed their stay was approaching its end faster than anticipated.

With another muttered curse, he lifted his hands to his forehead, tipping his hat back to dig his fingers into his skull. "Let me think, let me think..."

Aurelia remained against the wall while he paced. With his eyes covered, she let her smile appear. He stopped and let his hands fall to his sides. Her smile vanished a moment before he turned to her, his jaw working.

"I have some friends," he told her, his tone cautious. "But to meet them...you'll have to trust me."

She blinked. "What kind of friends?"

He reached for her hand and pulled her back the way they'd come. "Important ones."

18

The Five Kings of Port Royal

It looked like a normal farmhouse, but William didn't bother to ring the bell or knock before walking inside.

The reek of tobacco and sweat greeted her wrinkled nose. She could hardly see through the hazy gloom, but she glimpsed a mismatch of expensive furnishing, odd knickknacks, bits of gold, and bottles. She squinted toward a set of steps, where heavy, deep voices drifted from above.

"Thursdays are for poker," William said, as though she would know what that meant. He gripped the railing leading to the second floor, and his gaze bored into hers as he said one last time, "Trust me."

What sort of danger was he leading her into? "I do."

He hesitated for a breath before ascending the creaking steps, his coat quietly brushing the narrow walls before he emerged on the top step before a closed door. He pushed it open and stood in the doorway. As the voices quieted, he removed his hat. "You started without me."

A chair scraped against wooden floorboards and a growling voice said, "Get in here, Copson, you wily bastard!"

"Gentlemen." He stepped into a room that looked and smelled like it hadn't been cleaned in weeks, lit by a single lantern in the middle of the table, and a shuttered, grimy window. But the men inside didn't seem to care as they played cards and swirled red or golden drinks in crystal glasses.

Aurelia wandered over the threshold, and as her eyes adjusted, the faces became apparent. She stopped short, her breath freezing in her lungs.

Four infamous pirate captains sat around a circular table scattered with cards and a pile of gold. She'd never seen them, but she knew them from Aunt Clara's papers. And as Copson moved to the only open seat and hung his hat on the arm, they all turned to look at her.

Copson looked at her too, his blue eyes piercing through the dimness.

Trust me, he'd said, before marching her into a den of the most villainous men in the world. *Trust me*, because if he'd told her where he intended to take her, she might've screamed. For excitement or fear or both.

Closest to the window, a stout pirate with a long beard and a patch over his right eye ignored his cards to peer at Aurelia from across the table. Captain Frederick Henry—he was known for exploding captured enemy ships and had once done away with twelve rivals in a single night before sailing away unscathed. Faint ribbons of smoke rose from his entire person to hang around him like fog.

To his right, a well-dressed man grinned at her, gold teeth glinting. From the garish shade of his pink coat and matching vest, she knew this was Sir Hector Hein. He'd been a prominent Spanish naval officer before he led a spectacular mutiny against his captain. Since then, he'd captured plenty of trade ships and demanded their gold, sinking them with their crews when they refused. He was famously flirtatious, and faced with his dangerously alluring smile, Aurelia understood how he got away with it.

Next to him, a man wearing a gold wig tied with a black ribbon studied her with vacant eyes, as though he lacked something very crucial—like a soul. This, without a doubt, was Killian Barstow. He'd gained his fortune by terrorizing the Spanish in the Caribbean after they killed the girl he loved in his youth. Aurelia had always thought this was romantic, even as those who survived him talked of his cold, unfeeling eyes—the ones that watched her now.

Aurelia's gaze moved to the final captain on the far right, and she nearly squeaked as she recognized Davy Silver—the former slave who was such a headache for the Dutch East India Company. He'd always been her second favorite to read about in the papers, and was written about nearly as frequently as Copson. And while the gathered pirates were mostly middle aged, Davy was only in his thirties.

The pink-clad Hein set down his cards. "You've brought a friend," he said, his words lilting with a Spanish accent. "For yourself or to share?"

Aurelia flushed and nearly stepped away, but Copson stopped her with a look that said, *Don't back down*. He grinned as he turned to Hein and said, "For myself, naturally. This is Rebecca Rowe."

She moved deeper into the room, nearer to the pirate kings who ruled the seas and had colored her imagination for years. She schooled her features to appear more daring and braver than she felt.

Hein's tongue flicked over his teeth. "You're rather pretty."

Don't back down, she told herself. *Don't back down*.

The only thing William had prepared her for was lying, as the way here was short and he walked fast. *The best lies are truths*, he'd told her. *But when you must bury the truth, play to expectations. Answer questions before anyone can think to ask. Control their perception, and you control them.*

It's what she thought of as he gave her another meaningful look out of the corner of his eye.

Then he grabbed her hand, sank into his chair—upholstered with plush green velvet—and tugged her onto his lap.

She might've gasped if her lungs had worked. He was suddenly so close and warm, and electricity seemed to thrum under her skin everywhere his body pressed against hers.

Everywhere. He was everywhere.

She fought to maintain her nonchalance, grappling with her own body and mind and heart as they exploded and burst and screamed at her for excitement and fear and *dear God he was holding her.*

"Put your arm around me," he breathed, then slumped back into the cushion, lounging as though he sat on a throne. He pulled her flush, one hand low on her hip and the other resting lazily on the arm of the chair while she draped her arm lightly around his neck.

And just like that, any leering became grossly unwelcome—especially as Copson adjusted his coat to reveal one of the guns hanging at his side. Her blood burned, and Hein looked away.

Henry, however, studied her through his cloud of smoke, his voice gruff as he asked, "Where'd you find her?"

"Pilfered her from another crew," Copson answered easily. "She's naturally wicked, and I couldn't resist." His nose skimmed her neck, and it took everything in her not to gasp or throw up, to appear indifferent, as he tipped his head back and brought his lips to her ear to whisper, "Relax."

Oh, how she wished she could. Surely the others could hear her heart pounding. She couldn't take her eyes off them—her favorite villains all together in one room—or ignore the muscles cording William's shoulders and the ends of his hair brushing her skin. His fingers gently brushed her side, threatening to strangle every ounce of sense from her mind.

But this is not William, she told herself. No, he was Captain Copson, and she was Rebecca Rowe who did not simper or crumble. She knew these pirates and was one of them. And if they thought she was more to Copson than she truly was, then she would act as though it were the most normal, inconsequential thing in the world.

Even though in another life, as another girl, it would have been everything to her.

She breathed evenly, relaxed her shoulders, and said as coolly as Copson himself, "He tried half a dozen ways to convince me to join him before I finally did."

Davy's dark eyes caught her from the next seat over. "Never thought him to be charming."

"Oh, I'm not," Copson said.

"He had good stories to tell," Aurelia said. "And I liked them better than his gold or his name." This was good. This, she could do. Lying was very much like playing pretend, and she liked it as much as she did as a child. It was even more thrilling to fool terrifying men while the most terrifying of them all held her so close.

Yes, this was good. She loved this.

Henry barked a laugh that swirled the smoke around his head. "He's a liar, you know."

She attempted the aloof, calculating kind of look Copson so naturally wore. "Aren't we all, Captain Henry?"

Henry's beard twitched with what she assumed was a smile.

Davy flashed a wicked grin. "She knows us."

"Of course I do," she said. This room encompassed every topic of conversation she'd craved while listening to sniveling socialites discuss the blandest subjects.

Davy jerked his head at Copson. "From what he's told you?"

"I haven't breathed a word of you, Davy," Copson said.

Aurelia released the butterflies spiraling through her middle with a hum of amusement. "He didn't need to."

Hein sipped his wine, silver buttons glinting on the sleeve of his fine coat. "You know he only tells so many stories," he said in a low, seductive tone, "because he likes to hear himself talk."

Aurelia took him in. "A benefit, Sir Hector, since I like it too."

Copson's smile appeared, then vanished just as quickly.

Henry rolled his single eye. "You must not have known him long, else you'd know better than to encourage his ego."

"Why, sir," she said, "just think what he's done to mine." And there was a truth, one she hadn't realized till now. Her confidence was different, boosted, hopeless, and she leaned into him as though she were the sultry, fearless pirate she pretended to be—or perhaps she simply *was*. His hand tightened on her hip, and she added, "We're horrible for each other."

Copson's quiet laugh brushed over her skin, genuine despite their ruse.

Across from them, quiet, soulless Barstow collected the cards on the table and began to shuffle. He cut the deck, shuffled again, and started dealing—to only the four pirate captains.

"Not dealing me in?" Copson tsked. "I'm tempted to be insulted."

Henry's eye blazed. "Better you're insulted than cheating every speck of gold off us."

In a thin, tinny voice, Barstow said, "I don't like playing with you."

Copson's free hand lifted to lazily twine through Aurelia's fingers hanging over his shoulder. His skin was warm and rough, and her heart kicked out of rhythm. "What if I promise not to cheat? I have so much money and nowhere better to lose it."

Henry slapped his hand over his cards and fanned them before his eyes. "No. Not even for all your great-grandaddy's treasure."

So they knew Copson's family secret—at least part of it. They knew he wasn't immortal.

Copson idly spun Aurelia's sapphire ring around her finger. "I'm delighted you've heard the news."

"Everyone's heard," Henry replied. "The whole Caribbean knows. And you didn't even have the good sense to warn us."

"And let you take it? Why would I do that?" Copson's opposite thumb moved in circles against Aurelia's hip. She quietly cleared her throat as her stomach somersaulted, and he stopped.

Henry shot him a look. "Your father searched most of his career for that treasure. Bored us all with his constant griping. I half thought it was a myth and told him so."

"Mmm, and how did that go?"

Hein snorted and Henry grumbled, "Smart-ass kid."

"It went as well as you'd expect," Barstow muttered in his strange voice, tossing a handful of coins in the middle of the table. "Vicious threats, curses, and knives, as was his way."

Aurelia studied the game, rather comfortable now, even as she tried to imagine the quiet, stoic earl as the man Barstow described. She'd never even seen him with a knife, let alone saying anything vicious.

Davy matched Barstow's bet and raised it. "Glad I never met him."

"I think you'd get on famously," Copson said with a threatening grin. "Maybe I'll convince him to come back."

"One of you is plenty," Davy said with a sour look.

Hein folded as Henry matched and Barstow called. They revealed their hands, and with a groan from the other two, Davy pulled the gold toward his growing pile. When he caught her looking at his winnings, Davy asked in a low rumble, "Fancy a hand?"

"So what brings you here, Copson?" Henry asked. "I hear more *of* you than *from* you in recent months." The other pirates mumbled their agreement. "You didn't come to catch up."

Copson rolled Aurelia's ring between his fingers, which he'd somehow slipped off her hand without her noticing. "It seems I've incensed the French."

"You took whatsername—Danby!" Henry lifted a finger as he remembered her name. "You kill her?"

"The Danby girl is on the *Destiny's Revenge*," Copson said with rather convincing disdain, "sulking after her lost prince and bemoaning my kindness in relieving her from his porky clutches."

How strange it was to hear him speak as though she were someone else, and to do it so easily, without a shred of doubt or hesitation. And how exciting to hide in plain sight.

"The French discovered I have their intended princess alive and well in Port Royal," he said on as Davy collected the cards and began to shuffle. "We need to leave, but I can't get out of the bay without my crew, who are God-knows-where in this insidious town. You all have ways to get word through the city faster than I can on my own. If you'd feel so inclined to use them, I'd owe you a great deal."

Davy grunted and cut the deck. "Hand over the Danby girl if she is so miserable."

"I went to great lengths to steal her, and I'm not done shoving it in Pierre's snide little snot nose."

The others snickered. Aurelia, however, rolled her eyes and scowled, playing the part of the jealous lover. "She's nothing but trouble," she said acidly. "I said we should kill her if only for being such a dreadful *bore*."

Copson swept a quick finger down the line of her jaw, leaving her skin blazing in its wake. "Don't be jealous, love. She's too frail and fussy for my tastes."

She was thankful for the dark as she turned a deep shade of red, her heart thrilling at his endearment, his touch. "If I were jealous, *love*, I would've gutted her weeks ago."

His eyes glittered with mirth. "It's only a bit of fun," he said quietly as Davy finished shuffling.

She fought hard not to smile and bared her teeth instead. "I'll put a bullet in your fun if she whines anymore."

"You'd be wise to heed her," Hein said. "A man does well to listen to his lady."

"And you'd know?" Copson drawled. "Have you had any lover more than once?"

Henry made a noise that could've been a laugh or a cough and said, "Davy, deal," before Hein could snap back at the younger captain.

Davy quickly dealt the cards, this time dealing a fifth hand. When Copson reached for it, however, Davy stabbed a knife into the table an inch from the cards. Aurelia hadn't even seen him draw it. "They're for the girl."

"We'll help," Henry said, "if your Miss Rowe can win a hand against us."

Aurelia's stomach plunged. Next to her, Davy winked—so quickly she thought it might've been a trick of the light. None of the others looked his way, so they hadn't seen. Their attention was on Copson whose eyes were tight as he said, "Gentlemen—"

Davy flashed a wicked smile.

"I'll do it," Aurelia said, and reached for her cards. A king and a six.

"This isn't your favor to win," Copson said to her, his tone gentle but firm. "They're being grotesque to rile me."

"I know," she said, glancing at him over her shoulder. "But I won't say no to playing cards with kings."

Henry grumbled, "Do you doubt her?"

Copson hesitated, but then broke into a cunning smirk. "I wouldn't dream of it." He leaned in, his chest pressing against her back and his hand drifting over her stomach as his arm wound tighter around her. "You're one of the best players I've ever seen."

A lie. A bold-faced, blatant lie. She'd never played cards until a few weeks ago, and she had the most dreadful luck and mortifying strategy. He'd actually looked horrified when he watched her play with a group of pirates one night on the *Density's Revenge*, and it had been embarrassing enough that she'd planned to never touch another card again.

Henry glared at him. "Stay out of it, Copson."

Copson leaned back as though he had far more confidence in Aurelia's abilities than she knew he did. "I wouldn't dream of butting in."

"He doesn't need to," Aurelia said, sounding as nonchalant as he did.

"So, Miss Rowe," said Hein, his grin no longer flirtatious, "is poker a favorite of yours?"

"I haven't played in a while," she said, aiming to sow some doubt of the skills Copson had inflated so they wouldn't know what to expect from her. She hardly knew what to expect, if not for Davy and his winks. "I don't play with Copson. He cheats."

At this point in the game, she remembered she was allowed to trade one or both cards with the dealer, so she lowered the six and slid it back to Davy. He gave her a new card, and once she'd peeked at it—out of Copson's sight for the sake of the kings—she nodded to Hein.

The others traded or kept their cards. Then it was time to begin. Sitting to the left of the dealer, Aurelia was the one who'd start the betting. She held out her hand.

Copson's eyes squeezed. "You said you had gold."

"I do, but this is your aid I'm playing for." She wiggled her fingers, thrilled by her own boldness. "Quickly, please."

From a seemingly empty hand, he produced a gold coin and rolled it over his fingers until it hit his thumb. He set it into the center of her palm. When her brows raised, he gave an arrogant smile and said, "You get what you get. This is *my* aid, after all."

"I'll turn *you* in to the French," she mumbled, and slid the coin to the center of the table. "And your whiny French bitch."

The pirates chuckled, met her bet, and raised it considerably. When it came back to her, she looked at Copson.

"My whiny French bitch?" he asked lowly.

"She could afford the bet," Aurelia said. "Can you?"

Hein put a hand to his heart, Davy Silver barked a laugh, and Henry grinned at his cards. Barstow merely watched.

"It'd certainly be nice if you could," Copson said. Nevertheless, he handed her more coins. She raised the bet, and again the pirates matched and raised.

This time, she didn't ask for more gold. Instead, she plucked her ring off Copson's finger. He snatched her hand before she could bet the ring, his objection clear on his face.

"Trust me," Aurelia said pointedly, and pulled free to place the ring on the pile of gold.

Henry sneered. "I've never seen you so docile, Copson."

"And what do you think would happen if I forced my will on her?" he replied, toying with the end of her braid. Heat shot from the base of her head down the length of her spine. "Or ply her with threats?"

"Do it," Hein said. "She has a place on my crew if she wants."

"Keep trying, Hein," Copson muttered as Aurelia laughed to herself. "I've heard your stories, and they're not nearly as good as mine."

Hein chuckled as Barstow called. They showed their cards. Aurelia's king now had a queen, and together they won. She nearly squealed her delight but kept her face serene as she scooped the pile of money toward her, as though winning against famous pirates was a normal occurrence.

"Admirable, Miss Rowe. You're a benefit to your captain." Henry shoved his cards toward the center of the table and faced Copson. "I'll have my crew find what they can of yours and send them home early. And as for the French, I'll put a bullet through any I find."

Barstow nodded once, while Hein added, "Mine as well."

Davy drove his knife into the table, which made Henry frown. "You have my help, Copson." A wild grin appeared. "But you owe me."

"Thank you, gentleman," Copson said, and Aurelia took that as their cue to leave. She stood, slipped the ring back onto her finger, and gathered her gold into her pockets. Copson pushed to his feet beside her and donned his hat. "As always, it's been a pleasure."

"Rowe." Davy rose from the table and came to tower over her. He handed her his knife, its bronze hilt glittering with tiny red gems like drops of blood. "Takes a bold sort of person to come here." He jerked his chin at Copson. "With him, no less. You're welcome back, either with him or as a captain yourself."

She broke into a smile, losing her grip on the cool, calm, collected face of Rebecca Rowe for the first time as she faced him. "Thank you. I...I'm such an admirer of your work. Seven slavers ruined—"

He rewarded her with a booming laugh she felt through the floor-boards. "Eight, now!"

"*Eight*?" Copson scowled. "I'm still at six."

Davy clapped a hand on Copson's shoulder. "Sounds like you have ships to sink."

He shrugged Davy off. "You didn't tell m— Actually, never mind, Davy. Keep your eye on the papers." With that, Copson set his hand on Aurelia's waist and ushered her out. As they exited, a bell rang and a servant scurried past and into the room. There were muttered instructions, then the servant sprinted down the stairs and out the door before Copson and Aurelia reached it.

Aurelia squinted as they emerged outside and pointed their steps toward the docks.

"Whiny," William said, stuffing his hands into the pockets of his coat. "Really?"

She twirled the knife in her fingers, trying to find the words, the feelings, the *breath*. "That was..."

William's expression turned apologetic. "I'm so—"

"*Amazing*." She whirled on him, practically bursting with excitement. She fought to keep her voice low so it wouldn't travel back to the house, and nearly swore with the effort. "You never told me *they* were your friends!"

"I couldn't very well write that in a letter," he said, humor returning to his features, "even if I had anything particularly interesting to say."

"*Interesting*," she parroted. She stepped in front of him and stopped in the middle of the street. "That was Frederick Henry. And Davy Silver! Davy *Silver*, who I've read about nearly as often as I've read about you. And Hector Hein and Killian Barstow—"

"Yes, I know," he chuckled. "God, I know."

"And Robert Copson," she finished, beaming. "You were always my favorite, and perhaps I would've told you that if I'd had the good sense to write back."

His cocky smirk appeared, but there was something truly pleased beneath the expression. "Your favorite, you say." He threw his arm over her shoulders and steered her down the street. "Do tell me more."

She grabbed his wrist, pinning his arm in place as they wound toward the sea, their ears pricked for mutterings of French as she recounted tales of pilfering newspapers from neighbors so she could read about the greatest pirate in the world.

19

The French Offense

By the time the sun dipped low enough to paint the city gold, the entire crew had come back—some of them haggard, drunk, and a little irritated, but there nonetheless.

Copson hadn't stopped moving since returning to the *Destiny's Revenge*, checking rigging and sails, and plotting courses. Now he stood on the dock with Thomas and George while Aurelia waited with Ralph at the helm.

Ralph lifted his face to the wind. "Something's off."

She sniffed, sensing the quiet through the harbor. "How can you tell?"

"My gut." He looked at her. "You'll get a feel for it."

She met his gaze in time for his eyes to raise from her mouth to her eyes. "Will we die?" she asked with a sardonic grin.

"Don't say that loud enough for Fenner to hear, or he'll knock on every inch of wood till the ship goes down."

Lavinia scampered up the steps. "What aren't we telling Fenner?"

"Rebecca is developing a gut feeling and teasing the superstition," Ralph said.

Lavinia raised her brows at Aurelia. "Last time someone pulled that shit, it took Fenner three days to let it go. Captain even docked the wages of the man who set him off, so no one thinks it's funny now."

"It's a little funny," Ralph said.

"Hush." Lavinia's eyes glittered. "Forget about fines—Cap would do worse to you for such a thing. Maybe throw you off altogether."

"He wouldn't dare."

Copson mounted the quarterdeck, sweeping behind the wheel with an intensity that leeched all mirth from the air. His voice boomed over the deck, "Weigh anchor! Hoist the mizzen!" To Lavinia, he said, "Ready the guns."

Ralph and Lavinia rushed off. Aurelia made to follow them, but Copson's voice stopped her.

"Wait." Sails unfurled and snapped in the breeze as he pulled a revolver from the holster beneath his coat and held it out, handle first. "Take it."

Aurelia had never shot a gun, let alone held one. "I have a sword."

He didn't lower the gun. "For my peace of mind."

Thinking of Ralph and the wrongness he'd felt, she took it. The weapon was heavier than she'd expected, and the barrel dipped toward the deck. "I don't know how to use it," she admitted.

"Pull back the hammer, point, and shoot—simple as that." He nodded to her hand. "Don't point it at anyone you have no intention of killing. And don't touch the trigger if you don't mean to pull it."

"Won't you need it?"

He tilted his head. "Concerned for my safety, Miss Rowe?"

"Not at all." And she wasn't, not really. Not when he had a second gun—and even that was probably more for convenience.

Copson grabbed one of the spokes of the wheel, holding it steady as the ship drifted toward the mouth of the harbor. His long coat fluttered in the wind. "Luckily you have such a fine sword, in case I've made a mistake and need protecting."

She glanced at Ralph amidst the rushing crew. Even when everyone else was so clearly uncomfortable, Copson was teasing her. In fact, he didn't look uncomfortable at all, but almost...*anticipating*.

"Let's hope it doesn't get as bad as that," she said, and left the quarterdeck. As she hurried down the steps, she shoved the gun through her belt with the handle against her back. Then she paused.

A sword at her hip. A knife in her boot. A gun at her back. Treasure in her pocket and on her hand.

Aurelia Danby was a pirate.

She smiled to herself. She didn't know when the change had occurred—if it was all at once or a slow transformation over several weeks. But she was different from who she'd been on the *Purgatory* weeks ago—and today she had finally let go and let herself be someone she'd dreamed of being.

An adventurer. A hero.

A *pirate*.

The orange sun hovered over the city behind them, its warmth pushing them from the harbor and toward the purple night rising in the distance. The crew waited silently on deck. More were below, standing behind the one hundred guns protruding from the sides of the *Destiny's Revenge*. The *Ophelia* and *Fortuna Royale* sailed at her flanks, ready for battle with forty guns each.

The water rippled against the *Destiny*'s hull, the wind whispering of things they couldn't yet see. Copson's gun was warm at her back, her sword a comforting weight at her side. All was tranquil, but Aurelia hardly dared to breathe as they approached the edge of the bay.

Ships began to appear. Three from the right, two from the left, all flying French flags. Aurelia stiffened. They were here for her.

Instead of unease, anger took root in her chest. Surprised at its tingling presence, she shook out her arms. She'd played this game a thousand times as a child. She'd faced invisible enemies and their ghostly armies—only now they were here in the flesh, and she nearly laughed at the familiar readiness to vanquish them.

Copson said, eerily calm, "Steady as she goes."

The French rushed forward, closing in on Copson's fleet and narrowing the way to the freedom, their cannons ready and manned by soldiers dressed in blue.

Greyson came to Aurelia's side, guns in hand and axes strapped to his back. "A'right?"

She unsheathed her sword and freed Copson's gun. "Alright."

Ralph came to her other side, holding a cutlass. "You sure? You can go below deck."

"I'm sure," she said with a firm nod.

"You'll kill people," Ralph said, softer now. "Are you okay with that?"

The thought of killing made her fingers twitch. Today she would cross a threshold she'd never thought possible. Surely she was a pirate today, but by tonight she'd also be a murderer.

As a child, she'd planned adventures and pretended to be all manner of heroes, villains, and knights, so she was not surprised or shocked that she had come to this. Rather, she faced it with resignation, an unpleasant but necessary side effect to the life she'd asked for.

"It's either bloody hands or a prince." She squared her shoulders. "And I won't be Pierre's."

Ralph's eyes were reserved, but he nodded. He was good company, she realized—her good, perfect, gentlemanly friend had also killed people. And if he was not spectacularly changed or damaged...well, perhaps she would be okay.

Either bloody hands or a prince.

The French hastened to close the gap at the mouth of the cove, but the *Destiny's Revenge* was faster. Copson's flagship slipped between them, followed closely by the *Ophelia* and *Fortuna Royale*.

The cannons began exploding.

Bang.

Bang.

Bang.

Every shot vibrated through her being, the blasts discharging so violently that she half expected the ship to be torn in two. Cannonballs blew into the nearest French vessels, ripping through the hulls and sending splinters and chunks of wood raining into the water, crippling them as the sea rushed into their innards. Their crews began evacuating, throwing themselves into the water as their ships began to sink, leaving only three to face Copson's fleet.

The cannons kept firing, one after another after another—shooting, then reloading in a perfect cycle so none of Copson's ships were left without firepower at any moment.

Two of the remaining French ships turned to sail on either side of the *Destiny's Revenge* as it left the bay, leaving the third to fall prey to the *Ophelia* and the *Fortuna Royale.* The opposing crews roared at each other, brandishing guns and swords.

A French officer paced over the deck of his ship next to the *Destiny's Revenge.* "Give us Aurelia Danby," he shouted at Copson, "and we will spare the lives of you and your crew!"

"You waste your time," Copson jeered over the cannon fire from the ships behind them. His eyes glittered with malice, and Aurelia's heart thrilled. "But perhaps I'll tell you where I left her if your cretin prince gets on his knees and publicly declares what a sniveling idiot he is—"

"Lady Danby belongs to Prince Pierre!" the officer shouted, red-faced and spitting. "To continue harboring her will cost you your life."

A maniacal laugh pealed from the helm. "Try and take it, clumsy swine. See how far you get."

The Frenchman bit out orders to his crew, and Copson did the same. Hooks shot from the French ships and caught on the *Destiny's* rails. Aurelia tightened her hold on his gun and her sword and headed for the starboard, hacking through each rope with a swing of her blade. As she did, soldiers fell into the waves below with startled screams while others swung in from overhead and dropped to the deck with heavy thuds.

Behind Aurelia, a sword rang from its scabbard. She spun, raising her arm to block the soldier's sword with her own. She shoved him away with a grunt, hooked his pommel with her blade and yanked it from his hand. His face fell into rage, his fingers curled into fists. He yanked a dagger free from his hip and started toward her.

In a single, panicked heartbeat, she raised Copson's gun and shot him in the chest.

Sounds of battle paled into a dim cacophony as he fell to the deck. Aurelia stood over him, suddenly feeling rather cold. She'd seen dead before—had seen a man shot in front of her today. And while she'd never been sensible enough to feel horror as she ought to, this was different. This was jarring.

He was dead because of her. And it had been so easy—horribly easy.

"Rebecca!"

Ralph's cry broke her from her shock, and cannon fire and screams of dying men came back into sharp focus. While she'd been staring at the dead man, four soldiers had surrounded her—including the officer from before.

"You are Aurelia Danby?" he asked.

Contempt swept through her so fiercely that she could have screamed. "Like hell," she spat. The other soldiers glanced at the officer, unsure, so Aurelia doubled down. "I'd rather be *dead* than be that sad, simple strumpet. I couldn't give a shit if she were living or dead, on your boat or mine."

The soldiers gripped their guns and blades, but the officer didn't seem fully convinced. He exchanged a glance with one of his soldiers who, after only a moment of hesitation, lunged for her. Aurelia dodged—right as the officer swept behind her, hooked his foot around her ankle, and jerked it out from under her. She fell to the deck with a cry, and her sword clattered from her grip. She still held the gun, however, and attempted to roll off of it so she could aim, but the officer was faster. He hauled her to her feet and pinned her arms behind her.

"Drop the gun, Lady Danby," he said, his voice gentle and his hold anything but. "We're here to rescue you."

"Rebecca!" Ralph shouted again.

Aurelia struggled in the man's grip, fighting rising panic as the other soldiers hemmed in. They'd take her back—back to France, to a prince, to a cage filled only with dreams she'd never be allowed to pursue. Back to being her royal family's passive, pretty pawn.

She couldn't breathe. She didn't want to, if that was the life they'd take her back to. She cried out in despair and tried to wrestle free. The gun had slipped in her sweaty grip, and now her finger twitched toward the trigger, reaching, straining to wrap around it and *pull*—

From the other end of the ship, Copson met her gaze. In a blink, his fierce grin fell into wrath. A dozen soldiers fought between them, and half as many separated her from Ralph.

Copson couldn't get to her, even as she begged him with her eyes. He raised his gun, shot a nearby soldier, and roared over the ship, "ROWE!"

His thundering bellow tore through the din and jarred her into remembering—she was not Aurelia Danby, and she hadn't been all day. She'd handled worse in the last few hours, and she'd certainly handle this.

They would not take her, because she was not the girl they wanted. She never would be.

She stopped struggling and went utterly still. The suddenness caught the officer off guard, and his arms relaxed the slightest bit. She used the distraction to pull the gun back into place in her palm. "My name is Rebecca Rowe," she said to the men around her, "and Copson himself begged me to join his crew." She gave them an unhinged, slightly insane smile. "Would you like to know why?"

Before they could answer, she twisted her wrist, aimed the gun at what she hoped was the leg of the officer who held her, and pulled the trigger. The man screamed, and as he stumbled back, she slammed her elbow into his face. Bone crunched, and he tumbled backward over the rail.

She ducked to scoop her sword off the deck, then swung it wide as she rose. The first man blocked her, so she shot him in the chest. He fell as she ran through the second, and then Ralph was there, dispatching the third.

"Alright?" he panted, his dark eyes wild and his hair somehow perfect.

All around them, cannons blasted, guns exploded, and bodies fell. But having been so close to capture and thwarting it, Aurelia smiled and nodded once, then threw herself back into the fray. She danced past the dying and the dead, lashing at blue coats as the *Destiny's Revenge* charged ahead. She sparred with sword-wielding men twice her size, besting each one as though it were an afternoon with Countess Kingswood, and she didn't let herself feel sorry for it. She stabbed them in their bellies and slit their throats, ignoring the blood and gore that splattered across the deck and soaked her boots, and pushed on by a single, intoxicating thought.

I will always be free.

There was a cost to what she wanted—becoming a killer like the man she loved, and his family—but she would gladly bear it.

From the helm, Copson held the wheel and aimed his gun, picking off Frenchmen one by one. When he pulled the trigger and no bullet came, Aurelia yelled, "Copson!" and tossed his second gun high.

He whirled to her as the weapon twirled through the air. Then he caught it, flipped it, and began shooting again.

Something flashed out of the corner of Aurelia's eye, and she whipped her head to see a splash of white fins. A second later, a lilting, haunting melody as deep and mysterious as the ocean rose through the air, seeming to come from everywhere all at once.

Everyone paused to listen, both pirates and soldiers, their expressions a mix of confusion and fear.

And then a monster emerged from the sea.

It was the size of a small island—so massive that Aurelia had to turn her head to see it from one end to the other. Slimy orange tentacles rose from the depths, longer than any of the main masts, and coiled around the French vessel to the right of the *Destiny's Revenge*.

Aurelia watched in horrified amazement as the creature's limbs tightened, breaking the ship clean in half. Water rushed into it, and the creature pulled the entire splintering ship beneath the surface in a matter of seconds, as though it were only a toy. Surviving soldiers shrieked and paddled frantically for shore, but they were pulled under too, and they did not return.

"Copson commands the very sea," cried a Frenchman before he pitched himself into the waves.

One of the remaining French ships turned away, while the other, gouged with gaping holes from the *Ophelia* and *Fortuna Royale*'s assault, finally began to sink. The remaining soldiers either surrendered—and were immediately killed—or threw themselves to the mercy of the sea and the monster beneath the surface.

As the *Destiny's Revenge* sailed into open water with its sister ships, a great shout went up from all of Copson's sailors. Aurelia held her bloody sword high and hollered along with them, unleashing her joy in a way she never had before. Arms slipped around her middle and Ralph hoisted her into the air, spinning her and laughing with victory.

At the helm, the captain smiled. The sun finally set behind them, and encroaching night rose to swallow them whole.

20

The Sea Stared Back

Shortly after the battle, the captain's voice rang from the quarterdeck.

"There is no Aurelia Danby on this ship," he said as the *Destiny's Revenge* rushed away from Port Royal. "The French chase a ghost. But had she been here"—his lips curved—"she might've been left to the whims of Port Royal."

It had been nearly two months since Aurelia joined their number. Most had hardly noticed her arrival and never assumed she was anyone other than Rebecca Rowe—they wouldn't care if she was. And now, Copson had made sure they wouldn't look her way if anyone suggested he had Aurelia Danby in his possession.

Over the next few hours, the crew disposed of the dead and dying. They pitched bodies into the sea and scrubbed the deck to relieve it of blood. When it was done, some followed Offley to repair the holes left by cannonballs blasted into the ship, and many went to bed. No one grumbled about leaving Port Royal, but if they did, Aurelia heard none of it.

She was one of the few who remained on the main deck, her body pitched over the rail as she coughed up what little was in her stomach under a dazzling night sky. Ralph stood behind her, holding her hair and rubbing her back.

"This happened to me after my first kill," he said.

She sank to her knees and pressed her cheek to the cool rail, praying for the memory of that first dead man—and the way she'd felt standing over him—to fade. Even though the ships were no longer moving, she savored the chill breeze on her face.

Ralph lowered his face beside hers. "I'm so sorry. I should have insisted you go below deck during the battle."

"Don't you dare," she rasped. "I *chose* to stay. I don't want to be a princess." Her stomach turned. "Would you please get out of my wind?"

"Sorry," he said again, straightening to let the air brush her skin.

He still looked apologetic, so before he could continue on about how he thought she shouldn't do what she wanted, she said, "I'd like to get better at swearing. Perhaps if I did, they'd have believed me sooner, and I wouldn't have had to kill them." Not likely, but perhaps it would placate Ralph.

"You needn't bother," he said. He didn't say it was unladylike, but she could tell from the look in his eye that he was thinking it. In response, she stuck out her tongue. He laughed, then his gaze moved beyond her.

"Tea," said a new voice—William's. "For the nausea."

Ralph reached past her, then handed her a mug.

The scent of lemon and ginger floated to her on a tendril of steam, and she drew in a long, comforting sip that soothed her stomach while the brothers stood by. They stood alike, their feet shoulder width apart and their arms folded. She gripped the warm mug and studied them.

"What?" Ralph said.

She cracked a smile. "You both look so severe."

Ralph relaxed his arms to his sides, looking sheepish, but William didn't bother. She could still hear the way he'd shouted her name over the deck, and how it had spurred her to remember who she wanted to be—who she *was*.

"Thank you for the loan," she said, nodding to where his guns hid beneath his coat. "Your peace of mind paid off."

He smirked. "It usually does."

The door to the lower decks opened, and Lavinia emerged, strolling toward them. William looked at her over his shoulder and warned, "There's blood."

She stopped several yards away.

Aurelia glanced between them. "Where?"

"Your arm," William said.

Sure enough, there was blood splattered over her sleeve. She prodded her flesh and hissed as pain lanced through her bicep.

"Shit," she said, but the word sounded as pithy and weak as if she were dressed in yards of chiffon and crusted with jewels. She looked at Lavinia who'd taken a step back, and pressed her hand over the wound. "Trouble with blood?"

Lavinia shook her head. "I blow holes in ships, not people. S'why I like being below deck while you all slaughter folks up here."

"A fine job today, by the way," William said to her.

"Of course it was. I'd say you owe me a pint, but French are usually easy targets."

"You're *not* trying to get me to buy your alcohol?" William asked with a devilish smirk. "Dear Lavi, did the cannons rattle your brain?"

Aurelia sipped her tea and, before she could stop it, imagined what it'd feel like if he called her *dear*. Then she remembered him saying, *Don't be jealous, love*, and couldn't tell if the jolt in her stomach was pain or happiness.

Lavinia squawked a laugh. "No more than usual—and no more than they've rattled yours." She turned to Ralph. "I need your help with one of the cannons. A rope is caught, and we all want to cut it. Figured you'd probably lose your mind if we did."

"Don't cut the line," he said, nearly jumping in his haste to head to the artillery deck. "I tied them very specifically..."

When they were gone, William faced Aurelia. "Are you feeling better?"

"Yes." She stood and raised the mug. "Thank you for the tea."

He stepped closer and reached for her torn sleeve, lifting one side away to see her wound. "And your arm?"

"Just a scratch," she said, savoring the brush of his fingers. "It's not bleeding anymore."

His hand fell away. "You should still get it mended."

"I will," she said. To hide the infernal redness creeping up her cheeks, she looked after where Ralph and Lavinia had gone. As she did, she was reminded of the conversation she'd overheard between the brothers the other day, and frowned. "I wish he'd court her."

William's brows drew together. "Who, Lavinia?"

"She clearly adores him." She mirrored his expression. "And he likes her too, doesn't he? They're so often together, and... What?"

He gave her an odd look. "So you don't—" He stopped himself, swallowed, then turned to the open ocean. "Ralph and Lavinia," he finally said. "I could see it."

Would he hate seeing his former flame with his brother? If he would, she saw no sign of animosity on his face—only contemplation.

"I can't think of a single thing to say to bring him to his senses," she said. "But then I never could."

"I applaud you for trying. He lacks ambition, and it drives me mad. Always has." He spun one of the rings on his fingers, the gold glinting in the lantern light. "And I must also commend you for battling as fiercely as you did, since Ralph didn't seem inclined to compliment you as he should have."

"It was my fight. My freedom." She stared at the constellations diving slowly into the sea. "Though I should thank you, Captain, for summoning a whole sea monster."

"Oh, come now," he said with a laugh. "That's how all these ridiculous rumors start." As though he didn't love them. As though he didn't gleefully perpetuate those very rumors himself.

She anchored her hands to the rail and leaned back, hoping her next words wouldn't make her out to be a fool. She still wasn't sure if he'd been teasing a couple nights ago, but after today, she was inclined to believe he'd told the truth. "I think I saw her—the mermaid."

"You did... In fact, there she is now."

Aurelia shot forward. She might've mistaken the glimmer of silvery-white for moonlight on the rippling water had he not been pointing to the sparkling tail as it flashed past. A heartbeat later, a woman's beautiful face appeared beneath the surface, her features sharp and smooth. She wore a crown of pale coral and shells atop her strawberry hair that flowed in long, gossamer waves. Below her waist, scales gleamed like mother-of-pearl.

She held a man in her arms, his dead body limp as she twirled him in a slow, macabre dance.

"I believe she's trying to romance me," William said. "Though she hasn't tried this before."

Horror knotted in the pit of her stomach, clashing spectacularly with fascination. "So you weren't lying..." She peered at him out of the corner of her eye. "But you told me you'd never seen a mermaid."

He lifted one shoulder. "It was true at the time."

Now the mermaid's pale face was the only thing visible in the blackness, the corpse gone as she stared at William. Then she slowly rose, broke the surface, and extended her arm, reaching for him.

Her hand was deathly pale, cut with fine scales and tipped with long, pearlescent fingernails. Pink hair swirled around her, and Aurelia thought the girl must be a princess for how lovely she was.

William shifted closer to Aurelia, his voice dropping to a whisper. "Shall we tease the creature?"

Then he leaned in and—ever so lightly—pressed his lips to Aurelia's cheek. She nearly gasped and dropped her tea.

Far below, the mermaid's elbow buckled, and for a long, heartbreaking moment, she only stared, then slowly descended until she vanished completely.

Aurelia pressed her palm over William's kiss, trapping it against her skin. Her cheeks felt like they were glowing, but he only watched the water, smirking and completely unaffected.

She had no time to gather her wits before a small, folded square of parchment appeared between his index and middle fingers. He held it out to her, and she took it with shaking hands.

"What's this?"

"An offer for ransom," he said nonchalantly.

Her eyes cut to him. "A ransom—for me? To send me back?"

"One of the sailors came back with it. Say what you will about the French, but they can work quickly when they want something."

She read the offer, which killed any butterflies left from his kiss. "This is—they're offering you a pardon for taking me."

"So it appears," he said jovially. "And quite a bit of gold."

The note trembled in her hand, and she felt sick again for an entirely different reason. It was an obscene amount of money—more than she thought she was worth, but these were kings who desired an alliance, and a prince who was surely embarrassed. "But you won't... You said you won't make me go back."

"God no." He straightened and plucked the note from her fingers. With a lazy flick of his hand, it soared away from the ship and was swallowed by the sea.

Her heart still hadn't calmed. "Why tell me? And why not agree to it?"

"Since they're spreading word so far and wide, I'd rather the news come from me than someone else, lest you assume I'm actually considering the offer. Of course, they'll try to kill me first to save money and time, but in case that doesn't work, ransom is always a pleasant second option." He poked the worried scrunch between her eyebrows, adding, "Peace, Miss Rowe. I'm not sending you back."

She drew in a long breath. He dropped his hand, and she banished thoughts of it holding her face or cupping her chin or his lips on her cheek.

"The French will keep pursuing you," she said on a shaky voice. "They'll keep pursuing *me*."

"But isn't it terribly fun to have an entire navy after you?" He winked, but sobered a little when she didn't smile. "They won't catch me. And they won't take you, which you proved well enough today. Fantastic shot, by the way—I saw you put a bullet in that officer's leg and found it hard to believe you'd never shot a gun before."

"I had by then," she said absently. "That was actually the second time."

"You smiled like a madwoman." He lowered his voice. "You smiled like I do when I'm trying to frighten people, which took me *years* to perfect."

And as easy as that, she realized he'd disarmed her. Her heart was calmer—as calm as it could be while William Kingswood turned those stunning blue eyes on her.

"I'm not worried about the French," he assured her. "I do like their ships, though, and I almost regret sinking them. I suppose one day I'll take one."

She didn't doubt he found this fun—after all, he'd laughed all through the battle today. He was truly thrilled by danger, and, she supposed, so was she.

Suddenly, French ransoms didn't seem so terrifying.

"Where are yours from?" she asked, nodding to the *Fortuna Royale* in the distance.

"Oh, it's dangerous to ask me about ships," he said. "I've annoyed many with my inexhaustible interest, which I'm told is rather bland."

She leaned her elbows on the rail and rested her chin in her hand. "Tell me."

"The *Fortuna Royale* is English." His words came slow and measured, as though to not appear too eager. "It's not the original ship, but we keep the name for the sake of legend. This one is English as well, and the *Ophelia* is Spanish."

"There's been more than one *Fortuna*?" She'd always assumed the *Fortuna Royale* had survived all these years, but now she realized the ship looked too new to be a century old.

"Several," he said. "At least a dozen."

"A dozen!" And to think they'd all been stolen. Four generations of Copson men had simply *stolen* over a dozen ships, just to make it look like one.

Strands of dark hair fell into his face as he peered down the hull. "It's not so impressive," he said with a reserved, almost uncomfortable smile. "Zheng Yi Sao heads a confederation with well over fifty thousand pirates. And she personally commands two dozen ships."

Aurelia stared at him open-mouthed. She couldn't conceive of such numbers. Could Aurelia ever be so incredible? Maybe if she stayed a pirate, she'd one day have her own fleet...

"Thankfully, she sails the Pacific," William said. "I'd hate to find myself on her bad side."

"Are you on her good side?"

"As far as I know. She sent me a jade pipe two years ago."

An amazed giggle rose in her throat. "I should have demanded more letters. The longer I'm here, the more I realize you withheld."

The tips of his ears darkened. "Tell me something you like before I bore you to tears."

"It doesn't bore me," she said sincerely. "It never has."

"Tell me your favorite story," he said, and maybe it was a trick of the low light, but his face grew darker too.

"I don't know if I could pick," she said. "King Arthur has everything—knights and chivalry and romance. But I'm also partial to Robin Hood."

"Why?"

She looked down, suddenly as sheepish as he'd been. "I don't want to bore you either."

"You won't. Robin Hood is one of my favorites too."

She liked it for the love story, but was too embarrassed to admit that. "Perhaps I like it for the very reasons I boarded your ship." Her cheeks blazed as she realized this answer was probably no better than the alternative—she only heard herself insinuating William was Robin Hood, which undoubtedly made her Maid Marian, a likeness she'd only be too eager to occupy. To save face, she added, "Robin and his merry men had such fun terrorizing people they disliked. Who wouldn't love a story like that? Let alone the thrill of living it."

"Mm, it is rather thrilling, especially when there are few consequences."

"It is," she said with a wistful smile.

"G'night, Captain," a pirate called, waving a lantern as he made for the door to the lower decks.

William looked over his shoulder and nodded in acknowledgment as a few others also bid him goodnight. As it quieted, she could hear the ship creaking, the slight breeze spiraling past the lowered sails, and a faint thud followed by scratching.

William cleared his throat. "I should turn in too. We're off bright and early, wind permitting."

"Sleep well," she said, trying not to let disappointment color her words.

He hesitated, his blue eyes dark in the night, before he nodded his farewell and headed for his quarters. "Take care of that cut," he said.

At his doors, he paused, then added, "I'll see you in the morning."

The door shut quietly, and she exhaled.

The moon rose higher, lighting the waves with bands of silver. The few remaining voices nearby eventually quieted as sailors tiptoed to bed, careful not to disturb the captain in his cabin.

Despite the heaviness in her limbs, Aurelia didn't follow them. Instead, her mind raced through the day, gathering every detail and cherishing each one before setting them, polished and perfect, in the bank of her memory.

William asking to join her in Port Royal and telling her she should have written. His laughter as she damned their mutual acquaintances. She touched her neck as she remembered hiding in the alleyway, his warm breath against her skin. And then there were the pirate kings, who'd liked her and gifted her a dagger, which she now wore at her hip, opposite her sword. A battle. A monster. A mermaid.

She smiled at the night, thankful for so many wondrous and amazing things.

"Is he in love with you?"

The soft, lyrical voice carried to her on a chill, brine-kissed wind. Aurelia whirled, but there was no one there. She scanned the deck, her eyes probing the small pool of light left by a single lantern hanging on the main mast, and then the deeper shadows, searching, searching, until—

Perched on the rail near the bow, a pair of glowing golden eyes pierced the dark. The figure was half hidden behind the foremast, and Aurelia had to step to the side and squint to see the body attached to those eyes.

To see the *tail* attached to that body.

"Stars above," Aurelia whispered as she faced the mermaid. Her iridescent fins hung off the side of the ship, but the mermaid was half turned to face Aurelia. Dripping pink hair clung to her pale skin, but somehow the effect was still astonishingly beautiful on the strange creature.

And her fingers—blood dripped from long, claw-like nails, landing in a small puddle that had gathered beneath her.

The scratching Aurelia had heard earlier—her skin went cold as she realized the mermaid had *climbed* the ship. And had been watching, listening...waiting.

"Is he in love with you?" the mermaid asked again. Her voice was ethereal, the soft tones lilting and flowing like the sweetest music.

"N-no," Aurelia said. "He isn't."

The mermaid's eyes lowered, assessing her in a single, clinical sweep. Aurelia flicked her gaze toward the captain's quarters. Should she call for him? Should she reach for her sword? She couldn't tell if her heart was racing because it wanted to warn her or because she felt like she'd stepped into another of her childhood fantasies.

The mermaid spoke again. "He kissed you."

"Not because he loves me," Aurelia said quickly, and stepped a little closer so she wouldn't have to raise her voice. Only a few yards separated them, Aurelia in the lantern light while the mermaid remained in darkest shadow.

The mermaid cocked her head.

Aurelia wavered, her hand itching for the hilt of her sword as the blood continued to drip, drip, drip from the mermaid's fingers. But how threatening was a mermaid, really, when she had no legs or weapons aside from her long nails and sharp teeth? "He...he was only teasing. Even earlier today, he pretended to kiss me to get other pirates to look away."

"Because you're his?"

Aurelia's breath whooshed from her chest. "No," she said firmly. "Because I asked him to save me, and he did. But he's...he sees me as little more than a little sister." *A small, crying girl in a sopping dress.* It was good to remember that when adventures like the ones she'd had today blurred the lines. "He kissed me because he was teasing," she said again, stopping short of saying the teasing had been meant for the mermaid. "It wasn't love."

"What would make it love?"

Aurelia rubbed her arm. "If he loved me, it would've been different. Like in the storybooks."

"Storybooks?"

"Tales," Aurelia said. "Legends. Stories... Surely you have them."

The mermaid straightened. "We do."

"Do they speak of love?"

The mermaid smiled as though Aurelia were a child. Faced with that grin, Aurelia felt as though she was. "Some do, I suppose."

Aurelia cleared her throat, now the one to ask, "How?"

The mermaid looked out to the sea. "The legend of my kind," she said, "began long ago with a sailor who loved the sea, and a sea goddess who loved the sailor, but she was afraid he would scorn her for being a creature of the deep. So instead of speaking to him as she wished to, she sang to him. By day, her songs warned him of reefs and shallows, and by night she sang lullabies so that he might sleep sweetly."

The mermaid turned to Aurelia, twisting her body and gripping the rail next to her with red hands. "She watched the man each day. Watched in agony as he loved village girls on land, and rejoiced when he never brought any back to his home on the sea. She saw the sailor also yearned for love, one truer than his dalliances with the human women who did not want to travel with him, for they were scared of the sea and of leaving their homes. For years, he looked for someone to love him while the goddess sang her love to him every day.

"Then one night, he cried out his despair, and the goddess came to him. Upon seeing her, he was allured by her beauty." Her eyes swept over Aurelia again, but it wasn't flattering. "He told her how his heart broke for the true love he craved, so the goddess offered him her hand. She said, 'Come, fair sailor, and join me in the deep. For someone who loves the sea so fiercely shall find a worthy home with me.'

" 'But I will die,' the sailor replied. The goddess laughed and said, 'Kiss me, then. Kiss me, and you will not die, but live.' So he did, and he joined her in the sea. He lives with her to this day as her consort, as beautiful and immortal and powerful as she, and his heart is full and loved."

Aurelia swallowed. "That's…" *A fairy tale.* "That's true?"

The mermaid flashed a smile, revealing elongated canines. "It's a very old story, older than you and older than I, but yes, it is true."

Aurelia didn't know what to think other than to believe her.

The mermaid touched her throat, and when her hand came away, she held a small conch threaded on a thin strand of seaweed.

"What's that?" Aurelia asked, because she had a feeling the mermaid wanted her to. But instead of answering, the mermaid held out the shell, letting it dangle and spin. Aurelia crept forward. Her heart pounded as she neared, begging her to step back, step away from those fangs and claws and pointed fins. This close, the mermaid's beauty only became more terrifying.

Aurelia held out her hand, and the mermaid set the shell in her palm.

It was just a shell. Just a necklace.

"Beautiful," Aurelia said anyway, because it was the only normal, bland thing about the mermaid, and somehow the simple trinket seemed even more precious for how terribly unremarkable it was. She tried to give it back, but the mermaid didn't take it.

"You tell me a story," she said. "Your story. With him." She looked to William's doors where the light had faded but had not gone out altogether. He must have left a lantern lit, must still be awake.

Aurelia's shoulders relaxed. She could still call for him if she needed.

She swept her thumb over the shell. In her moment of silence, she'd taken an unconscious step back, edging away from the creature on the rail.

"I met him ten years ago," Aurelia began quietly, and told the mermaid a version of her story that lacked her love for William. A tale that made them sound like acquaintances, friends at best, and she was an unremarkable girl who happened to gain a pirate captain's pity.

And though she told the mermaid this tale, she also told this version to remind herself that she *was* unremarkable. A girl who was kissed without love because she had little to offer by way of interest, and this was okay because she still got to go on an adventure and should not want more than that. It eased the tendrils of hope that had grown over the day—the dangerous, thorny ones that wondered if they might ever be more.

As the mermaid listened, her eyes were cold. Watching the shell Aurelia mindlessly rolled through her fingers or scrutinizing her face with unfeeling calculation. When Aurelia finished, the mermaid held out her hand. "You're right," she said as Aurelia handed the shell back. Her fanged smile reappeared, wicked and cunning. "He couldn't love you."

"As I said," Aurelia replied, and regretted the sharpness in her tone, because the mermaid's claws were too close and still bled.

The mermaid fastened the shell at her throat. "As I said," she repeated, but the voice that came out was Aurelia's.

Aurelia gasped. She reached for her sword, but the mermaid only pushed from the rail and dove into the waves. Aurelia ran to the edge of the ship just in time to see the mermaid's tail glint as she swam away with her corpse, her lips pressed against his.

21

Mermaids and Monsters

Aurelia dreamed of sea creatures and magic shells, and of goddesses with kingdoms in the deep until early morning sunlight woke her. It streamed in through the porthole, promising she hadn't been dragged to the bottom of the sea by a jealous mermaid.

Her sore muscles protested as she stretched, begging her to remain still, but she eased herself up with a heavy sigh, shaking off the dreams and the prior evening that *should* have been a dream.

He couldn't love you.

As she righted, something dribbled down her arm. She peered down at the fresh blood dotting her shirt from the broken scab over the wound on her arm.

Across the room, Lavinia pulled on her boots with a frown. "You should've wrapped it last night."

Aurelia grimaced. "I forgot," she said, and pressed her hand to her neck, blinking rapidly at the sound of her voice—or lack thereof. She cleared her throat and tried again—"I forgot."—and again, her voice did not come, as though it had simply decided not to wake that morning.

That damn mermaid.

"That's not good." Lavinia crossed to Aurelia's bed and pressed her hand to her forehead. "Are you feeling okay?"

Aurelia nodded absently, her mind whirling. Last night, she'd groaned as she fell into bed, and that was the last time she'd heard her own voice, not thinking that the mermaid was *stealing* from her when she pulled her little trick with the shell. And now...

She had to get that shell back.

Before Aurelia could move, Lavinia took her hand and said, "I'll take you to my mother. She'll make you tea for your throat and wrap your arm."

Aurelia couldn't protest as Lavinia towed her toward the crew's quarters where Hester sat among some of the others eating breakfast. Lavinia made Aurelia sit next to her mother, her bloody sleeve facing the older woman.

"We need a fix," Lavinia said.

"Oh, that's not so bad," Hester said, her hazel eyes tracing the gash through the cut in her shirt.

"She lost her voice too," Lavinia said.

"Dear me." Hester placed a warm, callused hand against Aurelia's cheek. "Are you feeling alright?"

Aurelia nodded and pointed to her throat and said, *The mermaid took it*, but the words were lost. Huffing, she tried to stand, but Hester grabbed her in a surprisingly strong grip that rivaled Lavinia's.

"Offley," Hester said. The shifty-eyed carpenter jumped as he heard his name. "Fetch some tea—peppermint or elm, preferably. Chamomile'll do if we don't have the others."

Wrinkling his pig nose, Offley abandoned his breakfast and set off for the back of the ship. Hester set to work, rolling up Aurelia's sleeve and bidding her to hold it there while she reached for her bandages.

Aurelia acquiesced, though she turned to Lavinia and tried to mime writing with a pen, mouthing, *Paper?* A note to William was her first order of business, to tell him what had happened. She needed to find the mermaid. But Lavinia was watching Ralph come down the stairs, fixing his golden, windblown hair.

"This happens," Hester said, grabbing Aurelia's miming hand to hold it still while she cleaned the cut with a stinging ointment. Aurelia flinched, her startled squeak swallowed by silence. "Losing your voice—sometimes the stress of a battle is lost on us in the moment, and we fall apart after, 'specially if you were yelling the whole time."

Mermaid, Aurelia tried to say again, and Hester nodded as though Aurelia had just agreed with her. Aurelia turned to Lavinia again to ask again for paper, but she was still watching Ralph talk with another pirate.

"This cut should heal nicely," Hester said as she unraveled her bandages. "Now your throat—does it feel raw? Dry?"

It was magic, Aurelia tried to say, and realized—even in silence—how ridiculous that sounded. And she planned to take this predicament to William? Her cheeks flamed. What would he say to her getting her voice magicked away by a sea creature?

He couldn't love you.

Offley returned with tea, which he handed to her. She took it with her free hand and flashed a smile in thanks. His eyes widened, and he offered a shy grin in return before taking up his breakfast again. He glanced at Aurelia once more before tearing his eyes away for good.

Ralph sidled past Lavinia, nudging her with his elbow as he did, and dropped into a seat beside Aurelia. "Are you getting cut or fixing one?"

"Fixing," Aurelia breathed.

Ralph's brows pulled together. "Pardon?"

"Fixing," Hester said, wrapping Aurelia's arm now. "Poor thing lost her voice."

"Must've been all the barfing last night," he said rather confidently.

"That happens," Hester said with a sage nod as she tied off the bandage. "When Copson took on all the new crew several years ago, I had to nurse a dozen boys back to health after their first battle."

Lavinia squawked. "Their stomachs couldn't take it. Never seen Ralph so green."

Ralph frowned. "I could take it, it was just...different than I thought it'd be." He looked at Aurelia. "You never really get used to it."

"Killing's in your blood, Ralph," Hester said. "Has been for generations."

His frown turned into a grimace. "It's a temporary means to an end."

Lavinia plopped down beside him and draped her arm over his shoulder. "What better end could you have than a pirate's life for us all?" She winked at Aurelia while Hester rolled her sleeve back into place.

Aurelia didn't wait for Ralph's answer. She tried to stand, intending to flee to find some paper, but Hester hauled her back down, saying, "Drink your tea first."

With a grunt no one heard, she raised the mug to her lips, preparing to gulp down the steaming drink, but the ship gave a violent lurch, and she curled away from the cup as half of the tea sloshed to the floor.

Everyone launched to their feet, their faces turned toward the main deck as screams broke out above. A bell rang, summoning all hands.

"*Guns!*" Lavinia yelled, and many ran after her toward the artillery deck a level below. The others ran for the main deck, Aurelia on their heels as the ship trembled and beams began to splinter. When she emerged, massive orange tentacles were wrapped around the *Destiny's Revenge*, tightening until the wooden rails cracked and buckled.

Pirates ran at the massive creature with swords and axes, cutting chunks from the beast's slimy flesh. Smoking, blasting guns ripped through the peace of the morning. A tentacle swung low, grabbed a sailor, and tossed him through the air. He screamed and smashed into the water near the *Fortuna Royale* as its cannons extended from its hull.

Aurelia pulled her sword and dagger. And then she heard it—singing, off in the distance.

"Net off the port!" Copson roared from the helm. "I want that blasted fish!"

Aurelia dashed to the rail. Not far from the ship, a pretty head lingered just above the waves. The shell hung around her neck, and Aurelia nearly pitched herself overboard—before seeing the monstrous creature writhing beneath the ship.

Her eyes snapped back to the mermaid. Her angry golden gaze locked on Aurelia, and the song changed.

The tentacle came out of nowhere. It wrapped around Aurelia's ankle and tugged her into the air. She screamed, but no sound came.

"Hold on!" Ralph cried from below.

Aurelia desperately swung her sword and dagger at the tentacle and missed entirely. Blood rushed to her head as she dangled and swung, fighting to line up one of her blades with the slippery, writhing tentacle. She tried to scream again, but her voice betrayed her while the mermaid sang and sang, and the creature obeyed.

She smacked into the mast, which knocked both weapons from her hands. They clattered to the deck among the scrambling sailors and came to rest near Greyson who'd dug a bloody gouge into the beast. With a final swing of his ax, he severed a limb. It slid off the ship and sank into the sea where the creature roiled. Still, two more tentacles hugged the ship, a third dangling Aurelia high above, toying with her soundless terror. Gunfire blasted over the mermaid's song as Ralph shot at the tentacle holding Aurelia, not missing a single time.

Aurelia reached for her captured leg, gripping her thigh as though she might climb up to her ankle and claw the tentacle away.

Copson's voice tore through the din. "GET THAT BLOODY FISH ON BOARD!"

The mermaid attempted to dive as the crew tossed a net, but she'd drifted too close to the ship and tangled in the ropes. The crew hauled her, hissing and spotting, toward the *Destiny's Revenge*, but in the absence of her song, the tentacle around Aurelia's leg released, and she fell.

Air whipped past her, snagging her hair and ripping against her skin. She prayed, waiting an agonizingly long heartbeat to hit the deck and break her neck.

But then was Ralph there. She crashed into him, and both fell to the deck. Gasping, Aurelia pushed herself off him. He scrambled to his knees, his hands on her shoulders and eyes roving over her face.

He panted, "Are you hurt?"

She shook her head, massaging her hip. As far as she could tell, nothing was broken beyond what would certainly be a couple bruises, but she trembled horribly.

"Lord, you could've died," Ralph said, then he clutched her tightly, dampening the shock and fear buzzing through her.

As the mermaid was hoisted from the water, the monster released the ship and swam off. The net thudded to the deck. Inside, the mermaid gripped the ropes with one hand and fought to untangle herself, and even from where Aurelia huddled with Ralph, she could hear the frightened gasps coming from within the net.

Aurelia pushed forward, her eyes on the shell around the girl's throat, but Ralph held her back as Copson strode toward the creature, snarling, "I ought to kill you."

The mermaid leaned back as though she might escape his fury, but the net held her in place. "Please—please, I only—"

Copson out his hand to silence her, his features shifting into revulsion. Because as the creature spoke, it wasn't the lilting, beautiful voice from last night—it was Aurelia's.

Under her sparkling crown, the mermaid also wore her pink hair in a similar braid slung over one bare shoulder—the very same Aurelia favored for her own.

Copson turned to Aurelia. "Speak," he said.

The shell! she tried to say. *I need the shell!*

"Never mind my ship," the captain growled at the mermaid. "You stole her *voice*?"

A strange relief that he'd guessed it so easily, that she didn't have to plead or ask or make herself understood. He heard well enough.

"I didn't mean—I only wanted—" The mermaid finally worked free of the net, and now her hands fluttered to the shell around her neck. Tears glittered on her cheeks. "I wanted you—to speak with you."

The captain bent to rip the shell from her throat. It clattered to the deck, and he smashed it under his heel. As it shattered, Aurelia began coughing. Sea water spurted from her mouth, salty against her tongue, and she scrambled back, sputtering and gasping.

"Speak with your own voice, sea witch," Copson ordered. "You won't seduce me with someone else's."

The mermaid hung her head and unfurled her clenched fist to reveal a wad of soggy paper. She flattened it and held it aloft.

It was a page from a storybook with an illustration of a prince and his princess, her back bent as he dipped her in a passionate kiss. When the mermaid spoke again, it was with the ethereal voice Aurelia had heard the night before. "I only wanted a kiss," she told him softly.

Copson took the page and studied it. "Why would I ever touch you?"

"I've sung to you," she said. "I helped you... I thought you might—"

A mocking grin twisted his lips. "Did you think destroying my ship and abusing my crew would make me *want* you?"

"I-I'm sorry. Please. Kiss me just once like that, sir, and I...I promise you'll never see me again."

He dropped the page, his lips twisted in disgust. "Swear on your life."

More tears spilled down her pretty face. She reached for the page, but it was now firmly wedged beneath the captain's boot where it would tear if she pulled it. She clasped her curled fingers against her chest. "I swear on my life."

"You'll leave me alone. My crew as well."

"Captain," Greyson warned, stepping forward.

Copson ignored him. "And you'll provide everything I need to fix my ship."

"Yes," the mermaid said through gentle tears. Aurelia grimaced. "I'm sorry."

He loomed over the mermaid, his eyes shadowed under his hat. "Mark me, fish," he said coldly. "If I see you again, I'll put a harpoon through your heart."

"Copson," Greyson grumbled.

The captain stared at the creature. "We have an agreement."

Her face became anguished. "I—"

"Captain!" Greyson lurched, his arm outstretched as though to haul Copson away, but it was too late. The captain sank to one knee, took her face in his hands, and crushed his lips to hers. His hand rested against the bare skin of the small of her back, tipping her like the woman in the picture. Her arms wound around his shoulders, nails glittering as she pulled him close.

Aurelia shrank into Ralph, her heart beating oddly as William kissed a face she would consider far more beautiful than her own. He lingered in the embrace, his lips still, hands stationary.

Aurelia hated mermaids.

Then Copson broke away and said, "Never return, or I will kill you."

The mermaid cried out as he pried himself from her grip. Other sailors came to grab her wrists and slide her toward the rail, dodging her snapping teeth. They tossed her over the edge.

Copson scrubbed his lips with his sleeve. "Get us going," he said, and the crew burst into motion. He looked at Aurelia. "You're okay?"

"I'm fine," she said, her hand at her throat as her voice came strong and perfect. "I'm sorry. I didn't know she'd take my voice…"

"You've nothing to be sorry for," he said succinctly. "All this was my bloody fault."

His kiss the night before—there was regret in his eyes now, and with it came the mermaid's voice telling her once again, *He couldn't love you*.

William started for the quarterdeck. Ralph helped Aurelia to her feet, made sure she was steady, and headed off to assess the damage to the ship.

While she picked up her sword and dagger, Greyson chided Copson at the helm. "You shouldn't have done it. Siren sickness—"

Copson waved him off. "That's a myth."

The first mate frowned. "It's not, Cap."

"If you're so superstitious, what do you suggest I do?"

"Pray," Greyson said. "Pray and lock yourself away before you go pitching yourself into the sea for that wicked thing to have you forever."

Offley and Fenner appeared at Aurelia's side. She asked quietly, "What does he mean by siren sickness?"

"Kissing mermaids is bad luck," Fenner said.

Offley's gaze bounced between her and the deck. "There are stories about men being overcome with madness and throwing themselves into the ocean to be with the creatures they kissed. Some say these unfortunate souls turn into sea foam—others say they grow tails, and that's how the maids find their mates."

"She's only a fish," she said, but her words were hollow, wrung with hope she didn't really feel.

Offley shrugged. Fenner looked at her and said, "That's probably what they all say."

22

The Sea Calls the Siren Sick

They didn't come upon any more sea monsters or merfolk after the attack, but the crew watched their captain throughout the rest of the day. Greyson shadowed him, his eyes shrewd and displeased. At any given hour, Aurelia could hear Copson saying, "I'm not sick, I won't be sick, siren sickness is a *myth*," in increasingly frustrated tones.

Eventually night fell, the sails lifted, and the crew turned in. Greyson finally relented and left Copson's side, and Aurelia returned to her cabin. But as she readied for bed and reached to extinguish the light, unease sent a shiver down her back.

Across the room, Lavinia was already asleep. Aurelia checked for her sword and dagger, which were in their scabbards by her head. The ship rocked gently in the waves, and all was quiet and calm.

Except for her gut.

Ralph had accused her the day before of not having the sense, and if this was it, she wouldn't ignore it. She stood, tugged on her boots, strapped on her weapons, and grabbed the lantern.

All was dark and quiet beyond her door. The crew's quarters were filled with gently swinging hammocks and soft snores. She spent only a moment looking at them before she headed for the stairs.

The stars and moon bathed the misty main deck in a pale glow, and water lapped gently against the hull. The *Fortuna Royale* and the *Ophelia* slept soundly on either side of the *Destiny's Revenge*, and nothing was amiss.

Light poured from the crack beneath the captain's door, but that wasn't necessarily different. Still, she bit her lip, considering. Then she mustered her courage, tiptoed to the door, and knocked.

"Who is it?" called a strained voice.

"Miss Rowe."

Footsteps, then the door wrenched open and a hand flashed into the dark to pull her inside.

"Thank God," William said, striding for the couch as she froze, dumbfounded, by the door as it closed behind her. Every lantern was lit, as was his fire, and the room blazed with light and heat. She nearly blew out her lantern until William held out his hand. Strands of black hair were matted to his pale, sweaty face, and his damp shirt clung to his torso beneath the gun holster still strapped to his chest as he said, "Don't. Please. I need light."

She tried not to let her gaze linger on his body as she edged toward the couch and set her lantern on the low table between him and the fire. "What's wrong?" she asked hesitantly.

He sucked in a loud breath and sank onto the cushion. "I'm about to be very ill."

She took a step back. "Um—"

"Not like that," he said quickly. "Siren sickness."

"You said it was a myth."

"I say a lot of things." He placed his head into his hands and curled his fingers into his hair. "I didn't want them to know. I didn't want Greyson to worry."

Aurelia knelt, tilting her head to see his face between his arms.

"I've been resisting the urge to throw myself into the sea all day, but it's so much harder when the sun is down. Heat and light buy time and stave off the effects, but the madness comes when night falls. The change begins, and my only hope is to light a fire and pray I don't succumb for long." He spoke quickly, his words running together. "In total darkness, the sickness takes hours to get over if one doesn't reach the water, but I hope I've already cut the sickness short with—" His head swiveled toward the door.

Above the crackling fire, she heard the delicate harmony of otherworldly voices. A chill shot down her spine. "William?"

He looked at her, his eyes crazed. "They're coming for me."

Her hand drifted for her sword. "What should I do?"

"Sit with me. Distract me." He leaned closer, gripping the cushion. A faint patch of blue-black scales webbed over the back of his hands. Her breath caught at the sight.

"Aurelia, you mustn't believe a word I say tonight—if the sickness overtakes me—" He gave a violent shudder. "I will do anything, say anything, to get to the water. And if I do it, if I reach the sea, I'm done for. I'll become one of them." He shook his head. "I don't want to be one of them."

"You've been sick before?"

He didn't answer immediately. "I have no memory of it," he finally said. "My father's old crew said I became someone else—some*thing* else. They tied me to a mast to keep me from throwing myself over." His eyes snapped back to the door and the siren song beyond. "They're all dead."

She sat on the couch beside him. "Can you fight it?"

He shook his head, then nodded, then his head was moving in diagonals before he shoved it back into his hands. His nails had lengthened, darkening at the edges. "Even with the fire, it's like there's a monster in my skin and it's so damn *hard* to— God, I'm fighting like hell." His blue eyes sought her. "If I can't do it, you must get Greyson. I don't want—" He flinched and groaned. "Speak to me. Tell me anything, I beg you."

Her words spilled out in a rush. "I've been hearing about a pirate's intuition since I got on board, though I didn't understand until tonight when I...I felt something was wrong. I also wonder how you're such a cheat at cards, because I can't figure out how you could possibly do it."

"I pay attention," he said with a strangled laugh. "To the deck. I count cards. Never let me shuffle."

She nodded too quickly. "I also wonder why you didn't tell me you shot Pierre. Everyone says you did."

His eyes were pained, his face gleaming with sweat. "Impulsivity is often not the virtue I like to think it is, even if I don't particularly regret it." An almost-smile flashed over his face before it was replaced by a grimace.

Aurelia kept talking. "This morning when I lost my voice, everyone told me something different about what caused it."

He rocked back, his eyes shut tight. "I'd have told you it was because of something your aunt might say about the devil."

"I might've been inclined to believe you, had I not watched that awful creature take it." She laughed weakly like it was funny and not as embarrassing as it felt.

The dark scales on his hands caught the light as he flexed his fingers. "Don't believe me—please, Aurelia, don't believe a word I say."

"Tonight?" she asked quietly. "Or always?"

His eyes snapped open, and he threw his arm toward the door. "Greyson," he choked. "Now. Quickly."

She pushed off the couch and sprinted across the room. But as her fingers closed around the doorknob, William's palm slammed against the door, holding it shut.

He stood behind her, no longer panting or wrung with nervous energy. He was oddly still, save for his slow breath passing lightly over her ear. "Don't go," he said in a voice like warm honey and chocolate. "How I do love your company, Lady Danby."

She flipped around. His irises had turned the deepest black—even the veins in his eyes had turned the color of charcoal, and black scales marked his neck. He grinned at her, revealing longer, sharper canines as he caged her between his arms.

William had lost the battle with the sickness. Now she faced the monster.

Her back pressed into the wood, as though she might force herself through it as he leaned close—so, *so* close. She could see his pulse fluttering in his throat, feel the heat radiating off his body, those powerful muscles honed by years of sailing. How easily this monster could overpower her, she realized. How cruel he might be with those claws and teeth.

"I-I'm going to get Greyson," she said. "Like you told me."

"No, stay with me." His finger trailed down her cheek, dragging a long, dagger-sharp nail against her skin. Her breath faltered as it passed over her jugular.

She reached for the doorknob. "William—"

He snatched her hand and pressed it to his clammy cheek, his nose at her wrist, sharp teeth so close to the delicate flesh. He closed his eyes and inhaled. "Beautiful," he breathed, and his eyes opened, black as pitch. "So very lovely."

She stopped breathing altogether. *Don't believe a word I say.*

"I'm getting Greyson," she said. She tugged at her arm, but his hand was like a manacle, unforgiving as steel. "And everything will be okay. He can keep you safe."

"Swim with me in the moonlit sea," he murmured. "Do you know how freedom feels slipping over your flesh?" He leaned closer, his voice a whisper. "Like love and starlight."

Oh Lord. The monster was *seducing* her into letting him get to the sea. As though he knew her deepest desires. As though he desired the same.

Wicked. The monster was wicked.

But if Aurelia had learned anything these past months, it was that she, too, could be wicked.

She looked into the obsidian eyes that hadn't been merciful enough to leave even a hint of blue. With a thundering heart and quaking knees, she matched his smile and dropped her tone to match his. "Do you know what sounds like an even better idea?" she asked in a soft, sultry croon. His breath hitched. She stared at him through half-lidded eyes as she said, "Fetching your first mate."

He yanked her hand above her head and pinned it against the door, digging her bones into the wood as he brought his face close. "Join me where I want to go," he said roughly. "Come with me to the water, held in love and dipped in starlight."

And then his lips were at her throat.

She gasped. In that moment, she wanted to follow him. Anywhere he would ask her to go, she'd happily take his hand and join him, just as he'd asked. Even to the depths of the sea—

Don't believe a word I say.

She wanted it. She wanted William. But not like this. Not this half-dream—not whoever this was who wore his face and spoke with a voice like his, even as her heart thundered for so many years of wanting, *dreaming* of him seeing her as desirable.

With great effort, she planted her free hand over one of the guns on his chest and shoved him away, releasing the weapon at the same time. She cocked it and aimed at him. "No," she snapped. "You won't do this to me."

His black eyes moved between her face and the gun. "Do what, lovely one?"

The gun trembled in her grip. "You're not well, William. I'm going to get your first mate, and you'll stay here until we help you."

"I feel wonderful," he said, creeping toward her. "I feel fantastic."

He grabbed the barrel and pushed it down to her side, whispering and sweating. He slowly reached around her, as though to grip her hip, but the touch didn't come. "I feel...sweltering."

He pushed her back, but no door stopped her. She stumbled onto the misty deck, surrounded by a hauntingly beautiful symphony of voices rising from the sea.

His teeth flashed in the darkness as he prowled after her. "Positively *scorching*. Such that I think only a swim would ease the heat in my bones. And to be in the water with you..." His eyes dropped to her lips.

She lifted the gun as he moved forward, and this time it did not tremble. "I will shoot you."

His smile made her blood go cold. "No, you won't."

She squeezed the trigger. With a loud *crack*, a bullet embedded in the plank an inch from his boot. "I'll do it," she said.

Whether it was because of the sickness or purely William's own ability, he moved faster than she could react. His arm swung, knocking the gun from her grip before he threw his arms around her and tugged her toward the edge of the ship as easily as if he were leading her in a dance, even as she thrashed.

"Greyson!" she gasped, breathless in William's tight hold.

"Let the ocean lay claim to us both," he said in that lilting, lovely voice. He dipped her, bending her back so far over the railing that a slight shift in weight would send them both falling. The sea below churned with songs and scales. Pale hands rose from the water, begging them toward the deep with sharp claws and webbed fingers. "We shall make a home in the waters and live forever."

"William, please! Let me speak with you first." She clung to the railing, anchoring herself to the ship and its captain. Her braid swung through the open air. It was a long, long way to the water...

"Speak, lovely," he said into her neck.

She locked her feet around a baluster and shoved him. For a split second, her balance tipped toward the water, but as William stumbled back, she gripped the rail and swung herself up and away from the edge. She'd hardly gained her footing before his arms locked around her once more.

She went limp, slipping from his grip to the deck. She swung her leg and kicked his feet out from under him, stood, then leveled her sword at him, praying someone had heard the gunshot and would come to investigate. She tossed a quick glance at the door to the lower decks, but it remained shut.

He grinned at her. "What must I do." The mermaids grew louder as he rose to his feet. "What must I say."

"Nothing. You won't leave this ship without me." She approached, her sword between them, driving him toward the center of the deck. "And I am not leaving."

"You're frightening," he said with a wicked smile. "But I'm frightening too."

He charged, ducking below her sword and sliding for her legs. She danced out of his way, but not fast enough as he hooked his arm behind her knees and pulled her down. He lunged for her sword and knocked it from her hand, sending it skittering over the deck.

"*Greyson!*" This time, her scream pealed through the night, carrying over the siren song.

She reached for her dagger and William's second gun at the same time before twisting to elbow him in the head. He rolled and sprang to his feet, looking angry now.

"Your mother taught me," she said breathlessly, backing away. "Don't forget that."

Out of the corner of her eye, wet hands gripped the balustrades, followed by impossibly beautiful faces and bodies that ended in shimmering tails. Though she still doubted her skill with a gun, she aimed at one of the merfolk and pulled the trigger. The creature fell back into the sea, so she shot the one next to it too. She surged forward, shooting twice more, and then threw herself into William.

They tumbled to the deck. "Wake up!" she cried, meeting his dark glare with one of her own as she straddled his stomach and pinned his arms with her knees.

He hissed. "*Let me go.*"

"This is your fault for kissing a mermaid, you fool!" Had she not been holding a gun and a dagger, she would have slapped him. Instead, she held the dagger to his throat, and lifted the gun to shoot the creatures climbing the ship as they crooned with terrible, beautiful voices. She screamed as she shot, drowning out the song and the man she loved as he writhed and cursed beneath her.

William worked an arm free and clawed at her leg. His eyes remained hateful and black, but his nails weren't so long anymore, and they didn't break through the fabric of her pants.

The merfolk kept singing. She kept yelling.

Greyson burst from the lower deck, brandishing a torch. He bludgeoned the merfolk nearest him, beating them off the side of the ship. At the sight of him nearing, many hissed and dove.

Still, the song continued.

Aurelia knocked William's hand away from her leg with the butt of his gun before aiming it at his face. He stared at her with wide eyes—at the edges were threads of blue. "Stay down or I'll put a bullet in you."

She launched herself toward the bow, shooting until no bullets were left. She dropped the gun, retrieved her sword, and started swinging for the infernal creatures, hollering the same foul curses William had shouted at her moments ago.

While Greyson fought on the starboard, Aurelia took to the port, hacking at hands and faces and tails—anything that shimmered or gleamed or sang. And as she went, the song quieted.

Shots rang out behind her, and she spun.

William standing in the center of the deck, his discarded gun—the first she'd taken—in hand as he picked off the remaining merfolk.

Then the song stopped altogether. Silence fell, leaving only the sound of the water lapping against the ship.

In the light of Greyson's torch, William's eyes were clear blue again, and the scales were gone. He pulled his sweat-drenched shirt away from his skin, holstered his gun, and grumbled, "Damn bloody fish."

23

Ghost Ships in the Night

Greyson crossed the deck and gripped the captain's shoulder. "You a'right?"

William looked past him at Aurelia. She glared back. "I'm fine," he answered gruffly. "Utterly perfect."

A soft song lifted from the water. William cocked his gun and strode to the rail, peered over the side, and aimed. "What do you want?" he demanded.

"I brought what I promised," came the mermaid's soft voice. Aurelia crept toward the edge until she saw the pale pink hair illuminated in the moonlight.

The mermaid lifted a delicate arm and pointed. From mist and shadow, a bow emerged, followed by an aged, sun-bleached hull covered in barnacles and green, flowing things. The small vessel drifted silently closer.

"It would have been nice to have you," the mermaid said.

A gunshot tore through the night. The bullet hit the water, but the mermaid was gone. William grumbled a curse.

"Captain," Greyson said. "Go to bed."

William set off toward the bell near the door to the lower decks. "I need all hands. I need that ship to fix what that infernal fish did with her monster. Put your sword away, Aurelia."

"I'd rather not," she said. "Thank you."

Greyson glanced at her as the bell's shrill cry pierced the stillness. "You need bed," he said to William. "Leave the ship for the morning."

"It is the morning," William replied on his way back to them. "I won't let it sail away without getting what I need." He glanced at the door. "What's taking so long? Where's Offley?"

"Will." Greyson's voice fell like a boulder. "You can't carry on like this. Let us take care of it."

"I'm fine—for God's sake, Aurelia, put your sword away!"

She shoved it into its scabbard.

William started to pace, but a few steps in, he stumbled. Greyson caught his arm.

"Sleep, boy," Greyson commanded, as sharp as she'd ever heard him. "I'll summon Offley and get crew on that ship if you're so damned determined."

William allowed himself to be hauled to his cabin and said nothing more as Greyson shoved him inside and shut the door.

The first crew members appeared on deck, rubbing sleep from their eyes. Greyson spared them a look, but made his way to Aurelia first.

"I'm going to kill him," she grumbled.

"Get in line." Greyson put his massive body between her and the crew. "You a'right?"

"Utterly perfect," she spat. "I was on my way to get you—he *told* me to—and then he—"

"Did he hurt you?"

"No." She sucked back angry tears and scrubbed her hand under her nose. "Bastard tried to take me with him. I nearly shot him."

His hand landed on her shoulder, and her legs nearly buckled beneath the weight of his arm. "Good."

The light beneath the captain's door had gone out. "Will he be okay?" she asked quietly.

"Yeah. Just needs a good sleep."

"He won't remember this tomorrow?"

He shook his head. "Probably not a thing but the ghost ship. But I wouldn't know for certain."

Aurelia sighed and let her shoulders fall. "Were you there the last time he had siren sickness?"

"Nah. I was on another ship with my family, but I heard the stories. He always claimed the tale was slander. And after what that crew did to him later, I decided to believe him over them."

She shuddered. "What'd they do?"

"That's not for me to tell," he said, "'Sides, I don't speak of the dead."

She blanched. William had alluded to something similar not even an hour ago—*They're all dead.*

Greyson faced the gathering crew. "Most'a you I'm sending back to bed," he said. "Put that ship on pikes, and we'll scavenge it in the morning. Offley, take a few over and take stock of what you need."

Aurelia lingered off to the side, but grabbed a lantern when she saw Ralph and Lavinia head for the other ship with Offley. Fenner watched from the bow of the *Destiny's Revenge*, his own lantern illuminating his lips as he prayed and clutched the cross at his neck.

They waited for the pikes to drive into the other hull before lowering the gangplank and crossing.

Lavinia sidled up next to Aurelia on the ghost ship's deck. "What happened?" she asked quietly enough to keep the others from overhearing.

"Malevolent mermaids." The words came harsher than she intended. "We handled them."

She furrowed her brows. "You and Copson?"

Aurelia nodded absently, eyeing the splintered wood beneath their boots. If William had never told Greyson the truth about his run-ins with siren sickness, he'd probably never told Lavinia about it either. "The mermaid came back for him, and I helped him keep his promise—that he'd kill her if she returned." Lies. As smooth and easy as William himself might tell them. "She had some friends who didn't like that very much, so it was more of a hassle than we expected."

"I woke my father as soon as I made out you were yelling for him," Lavinia said.

Frustration burned, but Aurelia could no longer tell for whom. The captain was fine, and that was well and good. But while Lavinia had heard Aurelia's cries for help, the rest of the crew—where were they? "Glad everyone slept so fine through it," she said bitterly.

Lavinia grabbed Aurelia's arm. "If it was really so dire, the captain would've rung the bell."

"Dire," Aurelia grumbled. "The gunshots didn't summon you?"

Lavinia looked confused. "Why would gunshots worry us?"

Right. Pirates. They were probably used to gunshots in the middle of the night. Used to hearing mermaids sing. And of course they would ignore it, because no one wanted to be lured to watery grave. And the bell...

Aurelia should've thought to ring it.

Lavinia spoke so assuredly that Aurelia almost felt bad for misleading her about Copson's role in the night's horrors. "No one bests the captain," she said. "There are wicked things in this ocean that won't dare touch a Copson—nearly a hundred years of agreements, trades, and deals with people and things you could never imagine." Her face softened. "And you were safe—he's handled much worse than a couple mermaids."

Rather than contradict her, Aurelia simply walked away. Surely William had handled much, much worse, but when he'd been part of her deadly problem, it was much, much different. But she wouldn't say that to Lavinia.

Aurelia had never disliked William before now and wasn't sure why she defended him. Maybe she was only so foolishly loyal because his face and his smiles made her stupid.

Offley scoured the main deck. He stopped to scuff his boot into the wood to dislodge a few splinters. His lips thinned, and he moved on.

Aurelia found the entrance to the lower deck and scrambled down the steps into the gloomy, empty darkness. She craved a boon from her anger, but found no ghosts, corpses, or curses to scare her. Any sense of foreboding remained hidden in shadowed corners, too afraid to approach.

"Anything down there?" Ralph called from above.

"No," she said. *Unfortunately.*

Another set of footsteps pounded down the stairs, and Offley appeared. "This will do," he said, looking around. "This will do very well."

She half expected him to fall through the floor or for something to go terribly wrong, but nothing did.

Some ghost ship.

She scolded herself for expecting something terrible for a man who'd done nothing to her or anybody else. Then she cursed William too, for leaving her so irritated.

"I haven't forgotten your compass."

Aurelia looked at Offley, and he didn't hurry to look away. "Oh," she said. "I nearly forgot—thank you."

"I needed a couple things from port to finish it."

"Sounds fine." Aurelia would do anything to take her mind off the captain, and talking to Offley would be as good a distraction as any from her churning thoughts. So she asked, "How long have you been a carpenter?"

Offley assessed the ship around them. "You really wanna know?"

Over the past weeks, she'd watched so many people mock and belittle him, and despite how frosty William made her feel now, she didn't want the carpenter to feel her coldness. "Of course."

"I was a carpenter in a small village outside Liverpool," he said.

She watched him inspect the space, marking the bits of wood and nails he wanted to bring back to the *Destiny's Revenge*. "I assume you were good at your job."

In the low light, his cheeks turned red, but he didn't deny her compliment. "I was." He stated it like fact—and for the first time, he grinned, showing small, sharp teeth. "I was very good. But then...well, my wife left me. Ran off with the blacksmith and told the town I was unfaithful and cruel to her. They said the most wicked things about me and what I did. I told them it wasn't true, but she took my money and fled, and they ran me out of town."

The base of her spine prickled. "That's awful."

"I wandered through Liverpool for a week, and that's when Greyson found me." He looked at his feet and gave a self-deprecating laugh. "He offered me a job to sail as a carpenter. Didn't realize who it was for till I reached the *Destiny's Revenge* and signed the articles." He turned his face in the direction of the ship, even though there were no portholes through which to see it. "Copson was younger than I thought he'd be," he said quietly. "I was drunk when we met, and I half thought I'd died and gone to hell."

In her mind, she saw black eyes and pointed teeth. "Why's that?"

"He looked like the devil." He marked another beam. "Had just stolen the ship, and he had no good humor those first months."

She remembered what Greyson had said about William's father's crew, and how they were dead. "Do you know why?"

"Never asked. Never wanted to know. Did my job like I was paid to do." He held her gaze, all his shyness gone. In fact, there was confidence, and perhaps even a little wonder.

She was glad for it, even as another shiver ran over her flesh. Perhaps there were ghosts on this ship after all, and the longer they lingered, the more curious the souls became. Offley's lamp sent the shadows flickering behind him.

"I think I have all I need," Offley said. "Best be gettin' back."

Aurelia nodded and turned for the stairs.

"You're kind," Offley said, and she paused. "You're generous to have wanted to know anything about a sorry sop like me."

She smiled back at him, holding still on the step even as something in her urged her upward. "Not at all—you're a pleasure."

When they returned to the *Destiny's Revenge*, Greyson was sharpening an ax before Copson's quarters, where he looked content to stay for the rest of the night. A rather relieved-looking Fenner fell into step beside Aurelia as the rest of them moved toward bed.

"Did anything happen?" he asked quietly.

"Nothing to worry about," she said, softening her tone to ease his concern. "We're getting all we need to fix the *Destiny*."

"It's bad to take from a ship that sails itself," he muttered. "Let alone making it part of *this* ship."

"What kind of bad luck do you think this will bring?" Aurelia asked, half to lighten her own mood and half from true superstition after all she'd witnessed over the past two days.

"Storms, mutiny, curses—who's to say." He turned a hard gaze on her. "You think me mad, but I tell ya, a ghost ship always comes with terrible things aboard."

Aurelia stopped halfway down the steps. "I don't think you're mad, Fenner."

He rapped his knuckles against the wooden wall. "Watch the skies," he said, his voice low. "Watch yourself. Bad luck always comes for a lady on board, and I dread it finding you." With a firm nod, he walked off, leaving Aurelia standing outside her door.

Maybe it was the nighttime chill or Fenner's words—but foreboding dragged a cold finger down her neck.

24

The Stars That Guide

Sleep did little for Aurelia's roiling emotions.

Last night had been some kind of cruel, cosmic teasing—offering what she so desperately wanted in a twisted, wicked way she hated. And she was the only one to remember it, like a bad dream that left real bruises.

Lovely one.

He'd warned her. He'd told her he would say or do anything to get to the water. She'd been prepared for bargaining and threats, not...

Phantom lips pressed against her neck. She clapped a warm hand over the spot and shivered.

When she emerged on deck—closer to noon than she would have liked—stacks of wood had been piled near the bow. The ghost ship was still held on pikes, with the *Ophelia* and *Fortuna Royale* hemming it in. All three crews hustled to and from the ship, and Offley stood in the middle of it all, giving directions.

Fenner watched by the rail, his face pale and arms crossed tightly over his chest. Seeing Aurelia, he gave a firm nod.

Though she didn't intend to look for William, she found him. He blended in with everyone else, his white sleeves speckled with dirt and dust, and strands of dark hair hanging in his face as he sawed a beam in half on the ghost ship. He stacked the halves, hoisted them onto his shoulder, and carried them to the *Ophelia*.

How I do love your company, Lady Danby...

"I can't tell if that look on your face says you want to kill him or bed him."

Aurelia jumped. Fenner had moved off, and now Lavinia stood beside her, following Aurelia's gaze and saying with a wolfish grin, "I understand the appeal of both, is all, and I wouldn't judge you in the slightest either way."

Aurelia folded her arms. On the *Ophelia*, William looked up, but she tore her eyes away and determined he was the last thing she wanted to talk about. "Do you speak to Ralph that way?"

Thankfully, Lavinia took the topic shift in stride. "Corrupting Ralph is a slow, delicate process. I wouldn't want to spook him."

A smile tugged at Aurelia's lips. "You're good for him."

Lavinia blushed.

William mounted the gangplank between the ghost ship and the *Destiny's Revenge*, headed in their direction. As soon as she saw him coming, Aurelia found Fenner busying himself with the neat piles of supplies, and entreated him to give her something to do.

For the rest of the morning, she flitted from Fenner to Offley, searching for things to keep her head down and her hands busy with excuses to not look at William or cross paths with him. Offley was happy to give her tasks or talk to her, and she made sure to look entirely enthralled at everything he said or gave her to do as discomfort burned in her middle.

She assumed it was William's fault, and so she ate lunch after he did and refused to meet his gaze. Every time he started in her direction, she fled to some other side of the deck or traipsed across the gangplank to peruse the ghost ship.

Don't believe a word I say...my lovely one.

By midafternoon, the ghost ship sailed away, drastically lighter after the crews had picked it clean of usable materials. Around this time,

William called to Aurelia, but she pretended not to hear. She watched out of the corner of her eye as Ralph approached him, muttered a few quick words, then took off at a sprint toward the rail. William followed close behind.

Aurelia whipped around as they flung themselves overboard, crowing all the way to the water. Lavinia followed moments later, along with a few others, and laughter echoed from below.

All was normal. Everyone was fine, except for Aurelia who felt an awful tug to follow them. But then she remembered William's long nails and scaly hands, his whispered *beautiful—*

"A'right?" Greyson asked from beside her.

She swallowed. "Fine."

"He wants to talk to you."

Speak, lovely... "I've been very busy. I woke up late."

"Captain said to let you sleep."

Aurelia grunted.

Greyson looked at her. "He's better, Beck."

"I know," she said, and went to her quarters before she could pitch herself off the ship.

Hester found her in the galley that evening, and with a warm smile and not a shred of dishonesty in her eyes, she asked Aurelia for help folding a sail on the main deck. Beneath a starlit sky, she followed Hester all the way to the quarterdeck where a small table had been set up with a single lantern weighing down a stack of parchment.

William waited there with his arms crossed and a small, telescoping spyglass in his hand.

Aurelia stopped several feet away. "There's no sail."

"Who works out here when it's black as pitch?" Hester asked with a snarky grin and a loving touch to Aurelia's elbow.

"Thank you, Hester," William said as the woman cackled and walked off.

For the first time today, Aurelia let herself hold his gaze, ensuring his eyes were actually blue. No dread pooled in her gut like it had while she worked with Offley, but even so, she struggled to scrub siren-William from her mind.

"You've been avoiding me," he said, not unkindly. "You had me half convinced I was a ghost for all my attempts to catch your attention today."

Her jaw worked. "I didn't know what to say."

"That's fine. I do." He moved the lantern and spread the parchment before them, revealing hand-drawn star charts. "As I wracked my brain this afternoon for some way to redeem what I imagine was an arguably disastrous night, I remembered you'd asked if I mapped stars, and I said I'd show you." He handed her one. "This is above us now."

"You don't have to do this," she whispered. She thought about leaving, just simply walking away, but she knew she'd never escape his determination to have this conversation.

He only gestured to the sky. She slowly approached and took the map. Lifting it, she compared the drawing to the sky but saw none of the patterns in the stars scattered above her. William watched in silence, offering no direction. After a few moments of searching and turning the map this way and that, she finally picked out a constellation she recognized, due to the bright star on the edge—but instead of telling him, she lowered her arms.

William was not looking at the stars. His eyes bored into her, intent and seeking. "The crew, I've discovered, is under the impression we were caught in a rather intense fight defending the ship last night—on the same side, no less." He tilted his head. "You didn't tell anyone what really happened."

She nodded curtly.

"Why?"

There were a few others on deck, and the quiet strains of a violin drifted from the *Fortuna Royale* floating off the port side. On the starboard, behind Aurelia, the *Ophelia* was dark and silent.

"You tried so hard to hide it yesterday," she said, "so I suppose it felt like the right thing to do for a friend—as we are friends, I think. Air your own indiscretions as you see fit."

He sighed. "I must apologize. You stumbled in on my condition without warning, and I asked you to stay. I don't remember much after that, but from the state I was in when I started coming back to myself, I assume I put you through something awfully unfair."

She toyed with the corner of the map. "What state was that?"

"Well, you were on top of me, shouting profanities and shooting mermaids." He gave a wry smile. "I believe you threatened me—I remember feeling threatened. I also woke with a lump on my head."

"I'm not sorry for that."

"You shouldn't be. I'm grateful you went to such lengths to save me, despite how I must have treated you."

"Love and starlight." She watched him carefully for any hint of recognition. Nothing lit behind his eyes, and it both stung and relieved her. She wished he would tell her what it meant—if it meant anything at all—so she might confirm that they were just fevered words to beguile and torture her. She'd been beguiled by impossible things her whole life only to be tortured by wicked reality. Knowing for certain that this would be no different would make it easier to let go and move on.

She turned toward the stern, avoiding his gaze. "You called me lovely."

"Did I?"

"And you told me not to believe anything you said." If only she'd had the presence of mind to say absolutely anything else.

His voice dropped. "Are you worried I don't find you lovely?"

"No," she lied. Her thoughts were still so muddled with his declarations and sentiments, sick and crazed as they were. They twisted her insides with how much she wished they were true.

"Outside of whatever else I said, I didn't lie about that," William said gently. "I do think you're lovely. I told you so on the *Purgatory* and will gladly assure you of the truth of it once more."

Her cheeks flushed. How ridiculous she was to still want him so badly—worse, even, than before. How painful this would become if she couldn't manage herself.

"What other sins must I beg forgiveness for?" he asked.

The kiss to her throat. The seductive whispers. The fight. The begging. "Nothing."

"You still won't look at me." He said it like it didn't bother him, but when he spoke again, his voice came slightly strained. "I loathe any destruction I may have caused and desperately wish to remedy it."

She set the map on the table and faced him fully. "You already have my forgiveness." Her forgiveness had never been a problem—only her ridiculous heart and her spinning mind.

He studied her. "Did I frighten you?" She ducked her head, and he rushed on, "You must tell me something. I'll let you keep avoiding me if it pleases you, but I confess I'd hate it. Because we are friends, aren't we? You said as much, and now I'm feeling rather covetous."

A friend was a fine thing to be to William, she thought. And siren sickness aside, he was a *good* friend—one who saved her from a prince and showed her the world and all the marvelous things in it. She could continue happily being his friend, but she'd just happen to love him too, like she always had, and she would tell herself it wouldn't hurt worse than it already did.

"We are friends," she muttered. "But you shouldn't covet. It'll turn your complexion the most awful shade of green."

"Fresh air and sunlight must negate the effects, since I fear it's far too late for me. I'm covetous by nature." He turned his face to the sky. "I told you before I don't wish to frighten you. And whatever you witnessed last night—what Greyson described—it's fully gone."

"You did frighten me," she admitted, and his chin dropped to bring his gaze back to hers. "But I'm not afraid of you. I'm never afraid of you."

"Then today—"

"You weren't cruel to me, if you absolutely must know. You became someone else, like you said you would, and we squabbled over your need for water and how to get it. Never kiss a mermaid again, or I'll do more than shoot your boat."

His head whipped toward the main deck. "You shot my—?"

"You deserved it."

William looked at her out of the corner of his eye.

"You deserved it," she said again, her voice harder, daring him to disagree.

"I don't doubt it." His smile came slowly. "You have my word—I'll never kiss another. It hasn't been fun for me either time. But were it not for you, I wouldn't be here."

Her tone thawed. "Have you apologized to Greyson?"

He chuckled, and his shoulders relaxed. "Profusely. Though he scolded me far worse and with far more profanity, which I bore without complaint. He admonished me thoroughly on your behalf as well."

Aurelia reached for the map, feeling her anger and discontent drain away. "Did he compliment my abilities too?" she asked dryly.

"Yes, but he didn't have to. I was myself long enough to see them."

She stabbed her finger at the constellation she'd seen minutes ago, and the blazing star that called her attention to it. "That star there."

"That's Vega," he said. "Congratulations, you found one of the brightest stars in the sky."

She watched it twinkle. "I'm quite deft with using my eyes."

"Very fine eyes indeed," he said with his usual dry humor. "What else can you find?"

She lifted the chart again, searching. Then she pointed to another star as she found it on the map and said, "This is easy."

"It took me years to learn and draw these maps, but yes, I suppose you're a natural."

It felt so much better to be at peace again. The words running through her head had quieted with the assurance of William's easy friendship.

"Aurelia?"

Her heart skipped at his tone. It caressed her name like it was something delicate and precious. The deck was now empty behind them, though music still drifted from the *Fortuna Royale*. "Yes?"

He held her gaze. "Thank you. Truly. You saved me."

Behind her, a lantern flared to life on the *Ophelia*. He'd saved her first, more than once, but all she said was, "It's the least I could do."

25

Evil in the Dark

Aurelia Danby was a liar.

Days passed, and loving William hurt worse than it ever had. The ache of it persisted, even as William was the same laughing, teasing, amiable man he'd always been. Nothing changed between them as they settled into a friendship that felt exactly as it had since Port Royal, but Aurelia still grappled with her heart, which grew claws and shredded her chest with wicked taunts and the memory of his smile and the sound of him calling her beautiful.

He couldn't love you.

While they sailed through islands and coastal waters, Aurelia occupied her time by helping Offley repair splintered railings and creaky steps. She liked that she got him to laugh sometimes, and that his eyes didn't seem so shifty. As she was near him more, the crew mocked him less.

She supposed that was something to be happy about. Her heart didn't mind it so much, even as her gut continued to twist, reminding her of dread and danger and William Kingswood who didn't love her and never would.

Small, crying girl...

Aurelia found her glimmers of happiness during the evenings after everyone had finished their work and eaten and turned their minds to enjoyment. Tonight, as darkness began to creep up the horizon, the ships anchored and music struck up from the *Fortuna Royale* first, played by half a dozen pirates. Minutes later, those on the *Ophelia* began their own revelry, the sound of it blending perfectly with the tune coming from their sister ship.

The melody carried over the water, clear and resonant. Anchored between the two, the crew of the *Destiny's Revenge* scrambled for their own instruments. Horns, lyres, and fiddles appeared, and a few drums made their way to the bow as the deck cleared and sailors began to dance. Ralph was among them, grinning wide. Then he danced his way to Aurelia to grab her hand and pull her into the fray.

The heavy pain that had haunted her these past days lifted from her chest as she matched his steps. Giggles erupted from her middle, which turned to uproarious laughter every time she missed a step—though she always quickly returned to prancing around the deck with the others in time with the lively music.

Soon enough, the last rays of light disappeared from the sky, leaving only a smattering of stars and a bright moon. Lanterns flared to life around the deck, hanging on hooks and nails or balanced on crates, their flames dancing as merrily as the sailors.

With nearly thirty women in Copson's company and plenty of pirates to go around, Aurelia switched partners often. The pirates' hands were weathered and rough, but polite. Greyson was surprisingly spry for a man so large, and Offley stared at her almost reverently as he led her over the deck. Then Ralph was with her again, his cheeks flushed and eyes sparkling with mirth and ale.

For hours she danced, stopping only for a drag of golden mead as the bottle passed between hands. Even the captain joined in, stomping around with as much hilarity as the rest.

Eventually, Hester climbed to the quarterdeck with two of the fiddlers. She caught the eyes of the musicians on the other ships, and they also moved to their respective quarterdecks. For a few moments, there was no music. Then the fiddlers lifted their bows, and Hester began to sing.

Aurelia hadn't expected the lady convict's voice to sound so lovely, but it settled over the three ships like fairy dust—a lilting song about young love, wondering, and forever.

The women chose partners—those who were married danced with their husbands, and others had chosen their lovers. Lavinia approached Ralph and pulled him into a slow sway, even as he glanced at Aurelia over his shoulder. She waved him on with a smile.

Watching a lovely dance like this one might have hurt and reminded her of watching another dance eight years ago in her aunt's house. But Aurelia looked on with heavy eyes and a heart made lighter by just enough alcohol to thoroughly enjoy herself and ignore the creeping, dreadful agony that waited—

"May I?"

Her heart lodged in her throat as William appeared beside her, offering his hand. She stared at it for a second too long, wondering how much more she could lie to herself.

Dancing with him would make it easier to be his friend. His nearness would make her content.

Clinging to these desperate falsehoods, she set her hand in his.

He led her toward the others, then turned to her. His cool blue eyes pulled her in as he placed his opposite hand on her waist. It was warm, even through the fabric of her shirt. Or maybe she was warm—getting warmer—as he looked at her.

And kept looking. He watched her like he saw her every thought—like they were playing cards and he knew exactly what she held.

She placed her hand on his strong shoulder, struggling to keep her breathing even as she reminded herself that she liked being his friend. That being friends was incredible. They began to move in leisurely circles to the sound of Hester's voice and violins crooning a melody too sweet, too romantic, for a pirate ship.

He smirked. "You look as though I killed your dog. Do you find my dancing odious?"

"Not at all," she said breathlessly. "The lantern light must make me look disagreeable."

His hand slid from her waist to the small of her back, pulling her slightly closer. "I never said you look disagreeable."

If she'd been breathing, she might've choked.

They spun slowly, and as her back turned to one of the other ships, William nodded in its direction. "Have I told you the story of the *Ophelia*?"

She shook her head.

"Surely I must have," he mused. "Ah, you heard about it that day at the lake when I bragged to my cousins about its acquisition."

"Then I know of it." Her voice was thin, suppressed by her thundering pulse.

"Since I captained it home, my father let me name it. I didn't take such a responsibility lightly."

"Naturally, you shouldn't."

"As I was writing you that first ghastly letter, it came to me. *Ophelia*. Named for the girl who fell from a tree and drowned in a brook." He grinned. "It seemed fitting, and I couldn't think of one I liked better."

He would be the death of her. "Do you say things like this to most ladies?"

"How do you mean?"

He was so cool and composed. Never ruffled. Never bothered. Never tripping over himself like she did. "Telling them they inspired the names of your ships."

"No, I can't say I've told them any such stories. But none of them have required my rescue in such dramatic fashion, Lady Danby."

She glanced to the others around them, but turned back at the sound of his quiet laughter.

"No one can hear us," he said.

"That's what you thought ten years ago, on the lake." Her voice came stronger now that he wasn't telling her silly things about his silly ships.

He laughed again. "Touché. Though as far as other ladies, I'm sure they'd inspire a name or two for doing anything half as memorable as that."

"Then I won't think much of your telling me."

He leaned in, narrowing the already dwindling space between them. She watched his lips as he said quietly, "On the contrary, you should think the world of it."

Her throat closed. She swallowed and looked at the stars over his shoulder. "Are you teasing me?"

His grin turned roguish. "You're very easy to tease."

Despair weighed heavy in her middle. Her fingers tightened in his. She couldn't do this—she couldn't bear to be teased. "Please, don't—"

Applause interrupted her, and a rush of air chilled her skin as he stepped away. New, merrier songs began to play, and he winked and was gone.

Feeling unmoored, Aurelia stumbled to the edge of the ship and braced herself against the rail. She prayed for a breeze to come and relieve the heat rising to her cheeks, but the Lord apparently did not feel so merciful tonight.

Ralph came to her side. "Still enjoying yourself?"

She forced a smile, unsure if it was convincing. "The dancing has me flushed."

"I'd thought to dance with you again, if you're up for it."

She was shaking her head before he could finish speaking. "I think

I'm quite tired. Hopefully no one will miss me if I turn in."

"I'll miss you," he said with a friendly smile. "But turn in. Get your rest." He gently pushed her toward the stairs, his hand skimming the spot on her waist where his brother's had just been.

"Goodnight, Ralph," she said, then hurried to her quarters and shut the door.

She stood in the pale, sickly moonlight streaming through the porthole, her mind spinning and her skin tingling while muffled music drifted from above.

"Don't tease me," she begged the moon as though it might deliver her message to William. "Please, *please* don't tease me."

Being friends was almost harder than being nothing at all. And for the first time, she considered what it might be like to confess to him, if only that it might finally set her free. If William knew of her feelings, even if he never returned them, then at least he would not tease her so—

There was a soft knock on the door. "Miss Rowe?"

Her heart jolted. Only one person called her that, but it was not William who stood on the other side.

"I'm sorry," Offley whispered when she opened the door.

"For what?" she asked.

He pitched forward to crush his mouth to hers, his fingers digging into her waist as he pushed her back into the room.

With a choked cry, Aurelia pulled away, curled her fingers into a fist, and punched him square in the face. He fell back with a loud grunt, and she scrambled for the knife she kept around her bedpost. She tore it free from its sheath and threw herself toward the door, dodging the man as he came for her. But his arm came up and connected with her middle so hard that it knocked the breath from her.

He shoved her against the wall, his hands back at her waist and one thumb wedged in the band of her trousers. She raised the knife, but he grabbed her wrist and hit it against the wall, forcing her to drop the blade as she cried out in pain.

Her sword was only two feet away, but under his grip, she had no hope of grabbing it. Even if she could, the room was too small, and she'd never fought in such close quarters.

"I want you," he said, his drunken breath putrid and hot against her neck. "I need you."

She screamed for help. His hand clamped over her mouth and she bit into his palm. With a grunt, he shoved her head back. Bright spots burst across her vision as her skull connected with the metal edge of the porthole.

Offley cursed. "I'm so sorry!" His bitten hand moved to her arm and squeezed it hard enough to bruise. "I don't want to hurt you."

"Please don't," she begged, thrashing and finding no purchase against his heavy body. "Leave me alone!"

"I can't," he said, his voice thick with tears. Chapped lips pressed to her neck, and she cried out in disgust. "You're the only one who's been kind. You smile at me and talk to me, and no one else will. No one else will."

Her insides twisted, and she was nearly sick. She wished she would be, if only to make him stop. "Go *away*!"

"The captain will have my head," he mumbled, and his breath hitched as though he were crying. "But I s'pose it's worth it to be loved by you." His hand at her waist slipped lower, and he shoved her toward the bed.

Aurelia wailed as the door burst open.

"I heard a scream—*shit*." Ralph cut off, then charged forward to slug Offley in the jaw.

The carpenter staggered toward the porthole. Ralph followed, kneeing the man in the groin as Aurelia pushed off the bed and careened into the hall. Lavinia was there, holding a lantern. She reached out, but Aurelia slipped by, thinking only that she had to get *away*. Something dripped down the back of her neck as she ran for the steps—and collided with William.

He stumbled with the force of her hit, but his arms cinched around her, keeping them both from falling over.

For a brief moment, she felt as though she were tumbling through murky water with no way to the surface. And though she knew she was not drowning in any true sense, she clung to him as though she were.

"What's going on?" William's face was drawn in alarm. He pulled his hand away from her arm and looked at the red staining his palm. His voice chilled. "Whose blood—?"

A scream ripped through the hall, and Ralph emerged from her room, dragging Offley with his arms pinned behind him. His face was bloodied, one eye swelling shut. William tensed, and upon seeing his captain's murderous glare, the carpenter cried out and struggled against Ralph's grip. But the boatswain shoved him forward, closer to the steps leading down to the lower decks. As they neared, William turned to put his body between Aurelia and Offley.

The silence stretched, prickling and charged, as the captain stepped away from Aurelia and stared down the carpenter. He spoke with lethal quiet. "You touched her?"

Offley sputtered, and Ralph answered with a hard, "Yes."

William's gaze fell to a silver chain glinting around Offley's neck. His eyes narrowed, and he hooked a finger through the chain to pull it free. At the end hung the compass he'd given Aurelia, fixed and polished. With a vicious tug, William snapped the chain, leaving a bloody groove in Offley's neck. "You'd better start praying," he growled. "For God will have to save you, as I certainly won't."

Ralph pushed a pale, blubbering Offley down the steps. William made to follow, but Lavinia blocked his path.

"Go," she said. "Ralph's got it."

William cursed. "*Ralph's got it*," he repeated derisively. "Offley broke an article—it's my concern."

"So kill him tomorrow. Tonight, take care of your crew."

"He *is* my crew."

He moved again, but Lavinia planted her hand on his chest. "And you'll deal with him *when it's time*." She jerked her chin at Aurelia, who trembled as shock and fear threatened to make her ill. "Go get Hester."

William bristled. "Lavinia—"

"Will." Her voice dropped so low it was nearly silent, her eyes boring into his. "Mind the people you like, and leave us to the ones you don't. Go."

They squared off for several seconds, and Aurelia finally understood why Lavinia said she would've killed him if they were ever more than friends.

Lavinia seemed to win their silent challenge as William looked away first. "Come," he said quietly to Aurelia, setting his hand on her back to leading her up the steps to the main deck.

Light, music, and dancing wavered before her as she let herself be steered into his quarters and toward his couch where she sat and pulled her knees to her chest. He knelt before the hearth to coax the flames higher, then set a pot of water over it. He slowly rose and stepped out of sight.

A minute later, he crouched before her, the compass in hand, wiping it clean with a rag that smelled strongly of alcohol. He held it out. "It's yours if you still want it."

For a moment, she only stared. Then she slowly extended her hand.

He set it in her palm and wound the chain around it. "From me to you," he muttered. "Scrubbed clean of anyone else."

From me to you. As it should have been. She wrapped her fingers around the cold silver.

"I'll find Hester," he said, and left, shutting the door behind him.

Aurelia watched the fire crackle, her thoughts quiet, mind numb. There were feelings there—terror and agony—but they held back, waiting and lurking in shadows, wearing Lawrence Talley's face and speaking with Offley's voice. She shoved the compass into her pocket, pressed her face into her arms, and breathed deeply.

When the door opened again, Hester walked in. At the sight of Aurelia curled up on the cushion, she sighed, "Oh, pet." There came the sound of splashing water, and then Hester was beside her with a wet cloth in hand. She swept it over Aurelia's mouth and arm, and it came away red with Offley's blood.

Aurelia squeezed her eyes shut and whimpered.

"Oh, dearest," Hester said. "You're safe now."

The cloth moved to her neck. Hester's hands were cool as she prodded along Aurelia's hair for the gash. "It's not deep," she said. "I shouldn't need to stitch it. You might have a bit of a bump in the morning, but it'll be alright."

Aurelia's head swam and her eyes flashed with spots of color as fear escalated and faded and seared once more. She gritted her teeth and breathed.

The door opened again, but this time it was Ralph and Lavinia.

"Ma," Lavinia said.

"She's okay," Hester said, dabbing away the last of the blood. "Just shaken."

Aurelia knew she was much worse than okay, but she only buried her face into her knees and held back the burning tears.

"I don't know what came over him," Lavinia whispered. "I didn't think Offley could ever..."

"Sometimes you never think they're capable until they do it," Hester said flatly. "There's always been something terrible in that man.

He's got eyes like a shark."

"He's in the brig," Ralph said to Aurelia, his voice shaking with anger. "Locked away—Greyson and Will are with him now."

William.

Her heart cracked. In her mind, she saw Lawrence Talley leering and Offley crying, and there was William, saving her again, and again, and again—from the lake, the prince, the mermaid, the carpenter.

She opened her eyes and stared into the fire to burn away the lines of his face, but the feelings persisted, tearing at her, punishing her for being less than the formidable Rebecca Rowe she pretended to be.

Because that's what she did. She pretended, and she always had. She pretended to be anyone other than who she was—Aurelia Danby, the discontented heiress who let others dictate her life until she finally found the courage to run toward what she wanted. Aboard the pirate ship, she pretended to be fierce and unbothered and unbreakable. She pretended she might be satisfied by adventure alone, and anything less than love.

But she could not pretend anymore—not as wicked pains tore from her heart and seethed through her. And tears—those were tears pressing behind her eyes, but still she pretended they were not there, and she wouldn't let them fall as Ralph, Lavinia, and Hester muttered quietly to each other.

It was time to face all she'd been running from these past weeks—hell, even the past *years.* There was nowhere else to hide from all she'd shoved down within herself, and no way to pretend that she was not being torn apart.

She jumped as William swept through the door. He moved to the liquor cabinet on the other side of the room and began pouring a drink without sparing a look at any of them.

Ralph's frown deepened. "I'm sorry," he said to his brother. "I should've...I could've—"

"You did enough," William said curtly, coming to stand by the hearth with a glass in hand. "What's done is done." Then he looked at Aurelia.

She held his gaze and curled in tighter on herself as the terror, the hurt, the anger finally pushed free and rolled down her face as tears—there would be no more avoiding the torrent. She took a great, shuddering breath and held it, feeling as wild and unpredictable as the flames in the grate.

William looked at Ralph. "Get some air. Lavinia, help yourself to another cabin if you want."

"I'll be okay, but..." Lavinia glanced at Aurelia.

William followed her gaze. "You may stay here as long as you wish," he told Aurelia.

Tears dripped off her chin and sobs gathered in her chest as Lavinia and Ralph moved to leave, but as Ralph passed his brother, he muttered, nearly too quiet to hear, "Make him regret it."

William said nothing. As they left, he said to Hester, "Will you tend to Offley?"

Hester patted Aurelia's hand. "Are you sure?"

"Don't patch him up too well," he said icily. "I'd hate to undo all your hard work in the morning."

The surgeon left the room, and the door was hardly shut before William met Aurelia's gaze and nodded once.

Great, heart-wrenching sobs burst from her chest.

"Do you want to be alone?" he asked over the sound of her weeping. "I'll leave and you can lock the door."

She shook her head and hugged her legs closer.

He pulled the pot off the fire. "Do you want tea?"

Again, she shook her head.

"What do you need?"

You. She wanted to pretend she didn't need him, but she couldn't anymore, so she sobbed harder and held herself tighter to keep from begging him to come closer and make her forget Offley's lips and breath and fingers and—

She convulsed. Breath sawed down her throat, coming in ragged gasps that tore and choked and were entirely unsatisfying. She scrubbed her sleeve over her lips to wipe away what Hester had already removed.

"Aurelia," he said on a tender breath. He came to sit beside her. "Slow breaths, or you'll make yourself sick."

He sat close, but he didn't touch her, and she wondered how one could possibly be so close and yet so utterly far away as to inspire the most unbearable agony unlike any she'd felt before. Being locked away with only one letter each month seemed like paradise next to this.

"Breathe or talk to me," he bade her quietly. "Please, before you retch on my floor."

"He said he was sorry," she said, forcing the words. "Said I was kind to him... I didn't think being kind would make him think he could—"

"It shouldn't have happened." He set his glass on the table before the hearth, and she noticed his red, split knuckles. They hadn't looked like that an hour ago. "My crew knows my laws."

"He said it was worth it." She met his gaze. The fire had imprinted in her retinas, leaving dark spots of green in the shape of angry tongues of flame, but they didn't obscure the way his eyes burned. "He said—" Another sob broke from her chest.

"Aurelia," he whispered.

"He touched me," she wept. *And it wasn't you*.

It wasn't you.

Offley had taken something that hurt worse than what Lawrence Talley had done. Because William was here now, and he was not the one trying to kiss her.

He was not trying to hold her.

He wasn't trying to make her his.

And sitting next to him as he watched her cry made the truth as unavoidably bright and blindingly painful as being thrown into an inferno.

She was a stupid girl falling for a boy who would never be hers, who would never want her, but who would only bear witness to her tears and shame. He would help her but never love her, and the anguish released in torrents of broken breaths and weeping. Yet she remained here because she still wanted to believe she was wrong and not every dream had to die for her to be happy.

And there he sat, watching and waiting, believing she cried for a different man. Believing she cried over minutes rather than years.

William heaved a sigh. "Do you trust me?"

She blinked away her tears.

"Do you?" he asked again, his gaze boring into hers.

She muttered words straight from her traitorous heart, "More than anyone."

"Tell me immediately if that changes." One arm swept behind her knees to pull them over his lap, and he folded her into his embrace. He didn't tell her she was alright or that everything was fine. He only held her, wrapping her in silent warmth, and she tucked in her elbows and listened to his quick heartbeat and breathed in the salt and breeze scent of him.

This would be some kind of agony later, but for now it was too wanted—too needed—to pull away from. It chased away the bad memories and pulled her thoughts into line where she could manage them one by one while he glared into the fire.

And for a long time, they sat there, quiet and warm and safe. And when her tears had dried, she asked quietly, "Will you kill him?"

"Do you want me to?"

It was a terrifying question. Would he actually kill a member of his crew for her? Would he judge her if she responded either way? "Would you do it if I asked?"

"I'd do a lot of things for you," he said, speaking as casually as he always did, as though his eyes didn't still burn. "What do you want?"

You. Her stomach rolled as the word nearly left her lips. They stared at each other for a long moment, his face unreadable. There was no cool calmness, no humor.

She almost said it then—*I only want you*—even opened her mouth to set the words free, but then he sighed again and looked away.

What good would it have done to tell him anyway? He'd only pity her, or send her away to spare them the awkwardness.

She curled into him, huddled against the dark reality that threatened to swallow her whole. Her pretty adventure with treasure and zany pirates was now wrought with pain and villains who were scarier than she'd realized.

When she began to tremble once more, William's arms tightened, and then he slowly nudged her off and stood. He was gone for a minute or two, rummaging through a cabinet until she heard a quiet, "Aha."

He returned and sank into the opposite corner of the couch, clutching a small book bound in green, the words *Robin Hood* written in gold down the spine. He opened the cover and flipped a few pages until he reached the beginning, then cleared his throat.

But instead of reading, he met her gaze over the top of the book. "Come over here," he said. "It has pictures."

Was he teasing her again? "I'm not a child, William."

"I'm very well aware of that, Aurelia. But suit yourself—*I* like the pictures." He turned the book to show her one of the pages. "They're even painted."

"What are you doing?" she whispered. His holding her, his reading to her—she didn't understand, and his face was so closed off that she hadn't a hope of seeing what he actually thought.

The book fell into his lap, his thumb marking the first page. "You are beside yourself, for good reason, and I have nothing pleasant to offer you because *my* mind is full of murderous thoughts and wicked misdeeds. But you like *Robin Hood*, and I have it, so this is the best I can think to do for both of us." He waved the book. "And it has pictures, which are actually very good—and I would know because I've seen a lot of very bad art."

She managed to crack a smile, even as she noted the tension in his body. His eyes weren't fully present, and they were dark with something she didn't wish to see unleashed.

It was her first time seeing his rage, if that's what it was.

He held out his hand, beckoning her closer. "Come here."

"This feels ridiculous," she said.

"So what if it is?" His voice betrayed only a small measure of the anger she saw in him. "Does that make it inherently wrong or bad?"

I don't want to be ridiculous to you, she thought, holding utterly still under the weight of his gaze. "It makes it ridiculous," she said with a harshness borne from those who'd long ago accused her of the very same—and the fear that they were right.

"Then come be ridiculous with me so neither of us has to wallow in odious contemplations," he commanded. "Or I will read *Robin Hood* alone and you may sit there and enjoy none of it while I hoard all the fun for myself."

"That would be gluttonous," she muttered gloomily. "And Aunt Clara says gluttony makes you terribly fat so the devil will have to roll you into hell."

The edge of his mouth twitched, but his smirk didn't appear. "Then you'd be most gracious to spare me the embarrassment."

She slid across the cushions until she was at his side. He settled his arm around her and pulled her close until she'd nestled comfortably into to his side with her head on his shoulder.

Then he began to read, and she found he was right about the pictures being lovely.

Eventually the sound of his voice lulled her to sleep. At some point, she was carried to a bed that smelled like him where she was tucked in and left in peace.

26

The Cat Bites Nine Times

Aurelia slept in William's bed with her head on his pillow, and while she did, she dreamed of him.

His eyes—the loveliest shade of blue she'd ever seen—watched her sleep, and he skimmed her cheek with the backs of his fingers. But when she woke, her head throbbing, he wasn't there.

The fire had burned low, and his cabin was dark, the night beyond the windows black and starless. She quietly rolled out of William's bed and crept toward the door without sparing a glance at him sleeping on the couch.

She would not greet the day from his bed. She'd leave it to the night when dreams were more compelling.

The ship was quiet, and Lavinia remained asleep as Aurelia slipped into their cabin and locked the door. Even in the darkness, Aurelia could see Lavinia had set the room to rights. The knife was still on the floor, and Aurelia kicked it under her bed before changing into a fresh set of clothes.

Then she pitched herself into bed and let sleep suck her back in.

When she opened her eyes, bold morning light filled the room. Lavinia was gone, and no one had bothered to wake Aurelia.

The ship was not moving.

She hurriedly strapped on her boots and left—only to climb the stairs and stop in the doorway.

The three ships were anchored next to each other, their sails lowered. All was quiet, but every pirate stood in complete silence. They lined the decks and hung from the rigging with their attention turned to the *Destiny's Revenge*, where high up on the quarterdeck, Copson pulled on a pair of black gloves.

Ralph, Greyson, Hester, and Lavinia stood on the steps below him, their somber gazes turned to the main mast where Offley was strapped to the wood, his shirt torn and back exposed, his face battered and bruised.

Even the wind held its breath—the air didn't move, and neither did the sea. There weren't even clouds in the sky, as though everything had stopped to watch.

"My deepest apologies for rousing you all so early after last night's festivities." Copson's voice carried over all three ships, not losing a bit of its power or resonance with the distance. "But as you all deserved the revelry, you also bear witness to what happens when drunkenness overtakes one's better judgment and leads to the gravest sins. Luckily, Offley has offered to serve as an example of what happens when you break my articles, which you've all signed with full understanding of the consequences."

He braced himself against the rail over the main deck, leaning forward as his tone took on a more sinister bite, "Last night, Offley thought to force a woman before he was caught by Ralph Barrington, Lavinia Greyson, and myself. Under my flag, rape is worthy of death. Thankfully Offley was stopped, but since he thought my wrath to be *worth it* for a forced night, he shall have every bit of it and be flogged until dead. If anyone sees reason to let him live, speak now."

A stricken cry came from the man tied to the mast, but no one protested. Aurelia braced herself against the wall, suddenly cold. Days ago, Offley had told her about being run out of his village for being cruel to his wife. He'd lied when he said it wasn't true.

Copson descended the steps, grabbing a heavy cat-o-nine tails from his first mate as he passed. Shards of broken bone and glass were tied or embedded in the whip's brutal ends. It unfurled and landed with a *smack* next to his boots, those wicked tips clattering against the wood.

Without preamble, Copson swung the cat-o-nine above his head and snapped it back down.

Offley's guttural scream turned Aurelia's stomach as blood welled on his back in nine smooth lines. The second blow came, crossing the first in the opposite direction.

"I'm sorry!" Offley screamed. "I swear! I'll never do it again— *Mercy!*"

Another lash. Aurelia winced.

"*Please have mercy!*"

Copson whipped him again, and blood oozed down Offley's back to stain the top of his pants. The fifth came, and Offley wrenched a horrible screech through the air.

Do you want me to?

She'd never answered William's question. She wished she had. The whip struck again, and she flinched as though it were her skin being shredded. The rest of the crew merely frowned or looked on with somber indifference. Lavinia stared at her boots.

I'd do a lot of things for you.

Seven strikes, and Offley grunted, crying now and whimpering how sorry he was. He'd said the same last night, and though she still didn't believe him, she dreaded being the reason William exacted such violent revenge.

Did he think this was what she wanted?

The eighth strike came, and Aurelia pushed through the crew, clawing toward her captain.

Nine, and she finally broke through the pirates. But before she could reach him, a heavy pair of hands caught her shoulders and forced her to a halt. She tried to twist free of Greyson's unrelenting hold as the captain lifted his hand, curling the whip over his head.

Trapped against the first mate, she reached out and cried, "Stop!"

At the sound of her voice, Copson faltered, and the whip flew off course. As it fell to the deck, one of the tails struck her hand, leaving a welt across the back of her fingers.

Greyson tugged her backward as the captain spun, his eyes bright with fury. A few pirates backed away, but she held Copson's stare.

He growled, "You dare—"

"I never answered when you asked," she said, trying to conflate this man with the one who'd held her last night. "Not this. I don't want this."

His jaw worked. Conflict smoldered in his gaze for only a second before his expression shuttered into contempt. He stalked toward her. "You cross me, madam. The time for dissent has passed."

"You *asked* me."

Her determination only seemed to incense him further. His nostrils flared, and his grip tightened around the whip. Then his attention shifted briefly to Greyson above her. For the space of a heartbeat, she could've sworn he looked almost...haunted. But when he brought his gaze back to her, there was only indignation. "Barrington!" Copson barked.

Ralph descended the steps and stopped beside Greyson. "Captain."

"Take her away," he said. "Lock her up—I don't care what you do. Get her off my deck."

She prepared to argue, but Ralph grabbed her wrist and pulled her toward her quarters, his steps so quick she nearly tripped. Once they reached her room, he pulled her inside and closed the door.

"You shouldn't have done that," he said, his face drawn.

"He's going to kill Offley," she said, swinging her hand toward the upper deck. "He's killing that man for *me*."

284

"As he should!" Ralph pushed away from the door to stand over her. "You didn't see what I saw last night. What we all saw, and I—" He choked on his words and cleared his throat. "Don't think he made this decision lightly. If he doesn't do this now, others will think he'll go easy on them when they do the same."

"What about that seemed *easy* to you?!"

"None of it! You think it's so great for him? He fought to get to where he is, and this is part of it. Being Robert Copson isn't as simple as going by a different name, and he does what he has to do to be respected, to avoid mutiny, to keep over four hundred men and women at peace on these ships. This is bigger than you. It has nothing to do with you, in fact, and you've only just embarrassed him."

She reeled back as though he'd slapped her. "He asked me what I wanted."

"And what did you say?"

She looked away. "I didn't have an answer." How could she have known what to say when she was reeling and hurt?

"Then his decision weighs on his conscience alone—his and Greyson's and mine. This morning we told him it was right—we all agreed. You're not responsible for Offley's death. The second he touched you, the articles demanded his punishment, and Will's only following through as he should."

Offley's death. Aurelia's chin trembled.

Ralph cocked his head. "What is it?"

"I...I'm confused."

He stepped closer. He'd seen her cry before, for everything from skinned knees and mean tutors to general melancholy and disappointments. "Why?"

"It's different than I thought it would be," she said. "For all the people I've seen die—William shot two soldiers in front of me the day he took me away, and I hardly cared. But now..." She sucked in a breath. "Offley...I know him. He has a name. I sat with him, and he taught me carpentry, but...but he hurt me. He hurt me, but I-I don't— I don't know how to want him dead."

Ralph frowned. "Try as we might, sometimes we can't avoid these things."

The adventure wasn't always pleasant, and fantasy never told the whole truth. She knew that. She'd lived it. And maybe she'd believed that William stealing her away on the *Destiny's Revenge* was so fantastic that everything would be entirely fine and wonderful. She'd wanted to believe it would be, because for a moment, it was.

"I think I always knew," she went on, staring at his chest. "Every time I was around Offley, I felt sick to my stomach. I knew, in my gut...but I thought it was because of William."

"William?" His brow furrowed. "Why?"

She clamped her lips shut, realizing her misstep a moment too late.

"What do you mean?" Ralph pressed. "Did Will do something?"

She shook her head.

"Aurelia." Anxiety warped her name. "What did Will do?"

"Nothing." She said it too quickly, and Ralph tensed. His eyes narrowed as he caught every emotion, every worry, every thought that passed over her face—and misunderstood all of them. "Truly nothing. I've been confused since that night we fought the mermaids and—"

"Was he sick?" Ralph asked, breathing faster. "I wondered if he was—if he lied to everyone to be a hero. You were so angry that night, and it didn't make sense. But if Will was sick—"

"Yes, he was sick," she said. Curse Ralph for being so damn perceptive. "And I fought him. But he didn't hurt me. He...it's fine, Ralph."

"You lie as much as he does." Ralph was very close to her now, his nose mere inches from hers.

"Ralph," she pleaded. "It's not what you think."

"Was he cruel? Did he say something to you?"

"Not in the way you think!" She reached for his arm. "Stop it. Please, stop it." She couldn't tell him. If he knew how she felt, the shame of all she'd hidden from him—

He blinked, frowned. Took a half step back. "Not in the way I think...?" He tilted his head, considering, calculating. Ralph had always been so smart. "Are you...are you in love with him?"

Her body went cold, and then very, very hot. Blood rose to her cheeks, giving her away as surely as screaming. So she turned her back to him, as though that would make it any less obvious.

"You are, aren't you?" The words were quiet and heavy with an emotion she hated. It sounded like her very own heartbreak speaking back to her, and she ducked her head as though she could drown it out by pretending she wasn't there. He touched her shoulder. "Aurelia."

She shrugged him off. "So what if I am? There's nothing I can do. It's only like having a rash."

It was like having a hole blown through her, but she wasn't about to get into medical semantics with Ralph.

"Have you loved him this whole time?"

At the sound of his brokenness, she slowly turned back to him. He wore the same expression she'd masked on herself for years, like he also had a rash that was really a hole blown through him.

Now she was the one to look at him oddly, piecing together something she should have seen long ago.

"Did you ever consider me?" he asked. "Even once?"

Her jaw hung. "Ralph...I didn't know."

Dejection smoldered in his gaze. "He hasn't even been around. You met him once? Twice? Was it the letters to keep you silent?" Ralph had never been an angry person—he was always so controlled and gentlemanly. And while she found William's bursts of colorful emotion unsurprising and manageable, she didn't know how to handle good, gentle Ralph when he was upset. "I was there every week. I spoke with you, listened to you—I *knew* you! All while Will was selling his soul for a boat and a bloody name."

His words stoked her anger. If he was going to blame her for love, she had plenty to bring to the table—Ralph wasn't the only one who could be angry in this friendship.

"You never came *back*," she retorted. "Perhaps then I would have considered you if only you'd kept your promise. Did you think I wouldn't notice? Did you think I wouldn't miss you? And did you think I wouldn't resent you for never returning like you *said you would*?"

His eyes darkened. "You don't understand—"

"Maybe I do love him because of his letters, but they were all I had while I sat there waiting for you to come home—"

"I couldn't make you a pirate!" he burst out, then immediately quieted as he fought to calm himself. "You were precious to me—you *are* precious to me. And I wanted to earn enough to afford a good life and then come home and court you and give you everything you deserved, and it wasn't this." He gestured to the ship around them. "I wanted to provide for you without making you give up a good life."

"You wanted a wife and a house and a business, Ralph, but I could never have been that woman for you! And you would've known that if you'd come home. I would have told you—I would have told you everything! And I might've asked you to protect me instead of asking William to tell me how to do it myself when every man who called on me was so damn *awful*!" Her voice went shrill on the word, and Ralph flinched. "I love sailing. I *love* being free. And you're my best friend, or you were—you should've known me well enough to know I'd want this."

"Is it freedom?" Ralph demanded icily. "Or are you in love with whatever silly dream you've concocted of my brother where he's the king of the sea and brings you along for adventures?"

"Ralph—"

"And would you really hate that life so much if it was with me? Would you even consider it?"

"No, I would never consider it. Not after being here. I can't be the perfect wife who follows every rule and does no wrong. I'd be no good at it, and I'd despise every second. I told William that, and he laughed. He *agreed*."

Ralph rolled his eyes. "Because he's the epitome of wisdom."

"He's like me," she said, her voice a near whine as she fought to make him understand. "He doesn't fit that life in the same ways that I don't. And I don't care if you hate it, but he was there when you weren't."

"My God, Aurelia!" he snapped with a hard expression that looked so much like his brother's. "It's my fault—it's *all* my fault. Is that what you want? I'm sorry I wasn't there. I'm sorry I didn't write to you every damn day. I didn't realize you wanted novels from me."

"Don't be cruel," she hissed.

"Don't be ridiculous."

She flinched. Ten years of being his friend, and he'd never dared say that to her. He knew how those words had followed her, cursed her throughout her life. He knew the pain wrought on their behalf, even if they were true.

But he'd never had the audacity to actually say it.

"Ass," was her only response, but as he turned for the door, she let slip a small request that managed to bypass her thorny resentment. "Please don't tell him."

"I'm not enough of an *ass* to do that," he said. "Stay here until someone comes for you."

The door slammed behind him.

27

The Storm Surges the Sea

Lavinia entered the cabin with a small bowl of stew. "I thought you might be hungry."

It had been hours since Aurelia fought with Ralph, and as her thoughts had churned, the windless, motionless sea began to do the same. The bright welt on the back of her hand shined starkly against her skin as she reached for the food. "How badly have I ruined things?"

Lavinia sat beside her, pale and sagging. "With Copson? I don't know. He didn't kill Offley, but...barely." She scrubbed her hands over her face. "He's a horror to look at. Ma's tended to him all day."

Copson hadn't killed him. Was it because of her? Or had he intended Offley to die slowly? She studied the weary lines on Lavinia's face. "Are you okay?"

"It's not the first flogging I've seen, and it won't be the last." Lavinia frowned. "I always hated this side of him, you know. When I thought I loved him, it was seeing him like this that made me change my mind. He's good, but...he's a Copson." She looked at Aurelia like she was implying more than she let on.

"I know," Aurelia said quietly, stirring the broth. "I know he's a Copson." But that didn't scare her. It never had.

"What'd you say to Ralph?"

Her stomach rolling with dread, Aurelia set the bowl down without taking a bite. "I broke his heart without realizing I could." She shook her head. "I thought he loved *you*. I wanted him to love you."

Lavinia laughed without humor. "Ralph doesn't love me," she said, and there was sadness in her voice. The same that was in Ralph's. The same she felt herself. "He's loved you since boyhood."

That made her feel even more dreadful. "We want such vastly different things. I thought he knew me better. I thought I knew him better, but now we're..." She sighed. "I'm afraid of losing my friend. Both of my friends."

Lavinia laid her hand over Aurelia's. "Ralph will forgive you. He's not one to hold grudges."

"And...William?"

Lavinia pursed her lips. "I am less familiar with his forgiveness, as I've not often seen it."

Despite Aurelia's hunger, the bread and stew became even more uninviting as her insides twisted.

"But I don't know," Lavinia went on quickly. "I won't pretend to know your friendship with the captain—Will doesn't tell me shit. Doesn't tell anyone anything and then dashes everyone's expectations by doing something completely within character. But I'm just his crew now, and we all see a different man than perhaps you or Ralph get to see."

"I should talk to him." Aurelia got up, fully aware she might regret this. But she was feeling greedy, and if she'd already ruined one brother's opinion of her, maybe doing the same with the other would finally fix her ridiculous heart—and it would be a good thing, because nothing else had managed to finish the job.

"Maybe you should wait?" Lavinia called after her. "He's still—oh, fine. Your funeral."

Storm clouds rumbled in the distance as she reached the main deck. Frothing waves rocked the ship, and rain obscured the horizon. She opened the doors to William's quarters and stepped inside.

He looked up from his desk as she came in, his windblown hair gilded in lantern light that did little to warm the room. Lightning pierced the dark clouds through the window behind him.

"You want to do this now?" he asked. His eyes were the same dark, stormy blue they'd been this morning.

Aurelia's cheeks flamed in the heat of his anger and her own. She shut the door and started across the room. "I'm not waiting any longer."

"Then by all means." He stood in a smooth movement. "Let's talk."

She stopped in the middle of his quarters. "Why are you so—"

His voice rose over hers, stealing the words from her tongue as it thundered through the room. "Your blatant defiance this morning was applying and utterly disgraceful. You forget this is *my* ship, and you are no guest, you are no princess, you're not even a Danby. You are a member of my crew and nothing more, and you publicly undermined me in front of every one of my *four hundred* sailors. And after all I've done to maintain the order among my company, I will not let someone like you destroy it."

Just his crew. Nothing more. Not his friend or neighbor or anything greater than an employee.

"You *asked me* what I wanted," she bit back. "I didn't realize you'd rescind that right when the sun rose. Or do you not discern any difference between friend and crew?"

His eyes narrowed. "Would you like to hear a story?" His tone was cold, and for a fleeting moment she considered leaving as he moved around the desk and stalked toward her. "You probably already know part of it, what with how devoted you were to my name in the papers." He towered over her, but she didn't back away. "Six years ago, my father retired and made me Captain Copson. But I was young and brash and had little understanding of how to demand respect through anything other than my name. It made me weak and a fool, and my crew revolted and mutinied. They dragged me from bed one night, cut me from shoulder to stomach, and dumped me overboard, intending for me to die at sea."

Her eyes dropped to his chest where she'd seen his scar—the one he'd teased her with when he'd said he cut his heart out in exchange for Robin's treasure map. Cold dread washed through her, but she still managed to meet his gaze again.

"But I washed up on a beach and lived, injured, for an entire week before Greyson found me. The crew had split, and the mutinous ones had taken the *Fortuna Royale* while Greyson and the few loyal sailors had the *Ophelia*. They reinstated me as captain, but I wanted my ship and my position back, and I knew that if I didn't make my mutinous crew regret what they'd done, I didn't deserve my name.

"So we found the *Fortuna* at port and boarded it in the middle of the night. My small crew overpowered them, then we sailed both ships out to sea. I was merciful to the complacent ones—just a single bullet between the eyes. But for those who'd planned the mutiny, I cut them open as they'd cut me. They were still alive when I shackled them to the dead and threw them all overboard."

She remembered that newspaper. Running down the lane to get it. His mother crying, his father so severe. Wondering how he could do such a thing.

"*I* did it," he said, stabbing a finger at his chest. "I alone sent those men, my *father's friends*, to their grave. But it wasn't enough for me. With only half a crew, I stole the best ship from the most powerful navy in the world so *no one* would question me or my place as Captain Copson ever again. Then I signed on nearly four hundred sailors who'd heard the stories and wanted to sail under my flag, and they all know what I do to those who cross me."

He bent closer. "And then I sent you a letter, some piddly little thing to a bored, friendless, *pitiful* child who wanted a life like mine and blackmailed me to get it." His words dripped with venom, each one meant to spear her through the middle and poison her slowly.

He was successful. She felt battered and bruised in ways that had nothing to do with the attack the night before. But she refused to back down or look away as he exuded every bit of the cruel captain she'd read about—and now seen.

And hurt she may be, but she wasn't afraid, even though it probably made her irrational. But that was nothing new for her.

"It was my right to carry out Offley's punishment according to the articles *he signed* with all the others," William said. "He knew—they *all* know the price of breaking my laws. There is no ignorant, boyish hope that I'll have respect without demanding it, and if I let myself believe otherwise for even a moment, they will kill me. And I refuse to lose my life, my position, my ships, or my reputation."

It explained his haunted look from earlier, but it didn't excuse him for being repugnant. "That doesn't change the fact that you never gave me a chance to answer you when you asked what I wanted," she said. "I hardly had a moment to think straight before you decided to viciously torture him—"

"*He would have had you, Aurelia!*" he shouted, his face contorting with rage. "He made you bleed, and had Ralph not been there, Offley would have carried through, and I could've done *nothing* about it. I don't care what sad story he told you to make you feel bad for him—it doesn't change what he did to you, or what he would've done. I called for his death because I wanted it—because *Ralph* wanted it—and I was justified. Offley was willing to die for what he did. He knew I would kill him, and he said it was *worth it*."

"Then why didn't you?" she demanded.

"Because of you," he hissed. "Again, always, because of *you*. And because I offered you a choice." He paced away. When he turned to her again, he wore a deep scowl that turned her stomach. "I didn't beat him to death, but I certainly left him in enough pain to make him wish I had. I did as I swore and remained a man of my word to you and my crew. Then if anyone ever says I'm ever merciful, let them also say it is rare."

Aurelia squared her shoulders even as she crumbled inside. "What do you want from me? To say I'm sorry?"

"I don't want your apology," he said. A wave hit the ship, agitated by the coming storm, and she stumbled while he remained perfectly balanced. "Don't cross me. Don't betray me. And don't make me despise you."

After the siren sickness, William's teasing, and Offley's attack and watching him be flogged, she finally decided this was not the adventure she wanted anymore. So after she righted herself, she quietly said, "I think I'd like to go home."

"No."

Her eyes snapped to his, her skin crawling with the threat of no escape. "Why?"

"No one leaves without my say."

"I didn't sign your articles!" She flung her arm toward his desk where he kept the signatures. "Will you fine me? Flog me if I try to go?"

His eyes flashed. "Are you not having fun on your grand pirate adventure? And here I thought I was doing a fine job keeping you entertained."

Her anger burned against his sarcasm. "Let me go."

"We're half a world away from your home. I'm not turning three ships off course solely because you're upset at how I run my crew."

Her voice lowered. "I'm not your crew. I'm not a pirate."

"You are now," he said coldly.

The urge to get away, to leave him and spare herself, churned so violently she could've hit him. "Leave me at the nearest port, and I'll find my own way back."

He barked a laugh. "Absolutely not."

Just then, there was no one she hated more than William Kingswood. "I'll leave at the next dock."

"Leaving the ship at port is a privilege I don't feel inclined to grant you at present." His terrible words lilted as though he enjoyed stringing her along, hurting her as she'd hurt him and Ralph. "And even if you did manage to slip away, I'd find you. No one abandons my crew, not even you."

Thunder crashed outside just as the door burst open and Greyson's voice called, "Storm's nearly upon us."

William didn't look away from Aurelia. "I'll be there."

The door shut, and for a moment they stood in silent stillness. Then William moved past her, shrugged into his coat, and stuffed his tricorn hat on.

"It's not so bad, Aurelia. In a few days you'll forget you ever wanted to return to your aunt or your line of suitors or your prince." When she didn't answer, he came to stand before her again. "I've given you everything you've asked for. All I ask in return is that you understand your place on this ship and respect mine."

"I do respect it." She nearly spat the words.

"Then show it."

Her hand flew for his face, but he caught her wrist before she could strike him. His eyes moved to the dark welt marring the backs of her fingers.

"I'm sorry you're hurt," he said, and they were the first words that didn't feel like daggers. "Let us not repeat today's events. I much prefer being your friend." He released her and headed for the doors. "I'll see you on deck."

The bell rang, summoning all hands. Infuriated, she marched to his desk, ripped the silver compass from her pocket, and threw it into a random drawer. He could keep his awful adventures and foul piracy.

She finally wanted nothing more to do with him.

She stalked toward her quarters, pulled on her coat and hat, and headed back to the main deck where the rain had picked up and lightning forked overhead. William stood at the helm, shouting orders through the whipping wind.

The *Fortuna Royale* and *Ophelia* had moved far off so as to not get buffeted into one another. She could barely see their ghostly silhouettes through the heavy sheets of rain. Massive waves churned toward them. One of the sails snapped and billowed as sailors fought to lower it while the rest were already down and stored. The main mast groaned.

"Get that sail down!" Copson yelled from the helm.

Aurelia joined the scrambling crew tying off ropes and clinging to lines.

The captain spun the wheel, its spindles blurring as he wrestled the pitching ship into the oncoming waves. "Lower the damn sail!" he roared again, his voice cutting through the downpour.

"Rebecca!" Ralph was next to her, straining as he tugged a line to the main sail. His boots slipped over boards slick with sea foam. "Tell the captain the line is stuck—we can't get it down!" His eyes snapped to the mast as someone scrambled up it with a knife between their teeth, and he yelled, "Don't cut the line!"

Aurelia sprinted for the helm, careful to keep her balance as the ship tipped and rocked. She threw herself up the steps to the quarterdeck, squinting against the rain pelting her face. "The line is caught!" she shouted through the din. "They're getting the sail down as fast as they can!"

"I'm so sorry for all I said," William called back. "I can explain—"

She clung to the railing as the ship bucked. "This might not be the best time."

"Say you'll forgive me, and I'll save it for later."

"I'll forgive you later," she said, and turned away.

"Aurelia, please—"

A wave barreled toward them like an angry god. The *Destiny's Revenge* took it head on, and pirates scrambled for purchase as the main deck flooded with foamy water. As the ship fell down the other side of the wave, the wind blew sharper, knocking Aurelia's hat from her head and filling the caught sail. The ship jerked to the side, and Aurelia slid on the rain-slick step. She pitched into the rail, tried to catch it, but the polished wood slipped from her fingers.

The ocean opened up beneath her, the foaming, turbulent waters ready to welcome her to her death.

"*Aurelia!*"

William's scream pierced through the storm as she hurtled toward the sea. Though the world tumbled around her, oscillating violently between ship and sea and raging sky, she caught sight of a rope ladder affixed to the sides of the ship. She threw out her hand, desperately praying for purchase as the black ocean rushed closer. Her fingers snagged on a rung, and she held tight, smacking into the hull as her descent abruptly ended and knocked the air from her lungs.

She couldn't summon breath to scream or whimper, and managed only a sip of air before forcing herself to climb, her body barking in pain.

William's face appeared above, chanting her name like a prayer, his arm stretched over the rail. When she neared the top, he grabbed her wrist.

But with no one at the helm and the other pirates scrambling to get the sail down, the ship began to turn off course. Instead of slicing through the waves, the *Destiny's Revenge* bounced between them, threatening to tip and be swallowed whole.

Even then, William did not let go. He tugged her toward the deck, but her foot slipped off the ladder. She gasped as she jerked downward, held only by her captain.

"The ship," she gasped. She scrambled for purchase as, over her shoulder, another wave loomed like a mountain, dark and terrifying as it prepared to devour her and the *Destiny's Revenge*. "Save the crew!"

"I won't let go." He turned his face toward the deck. "*Help!*"

The wave was upon them faster than she could've anticipated. It was so large and seemed to move so slowly, but then it was upon them, crashing into the ship and ripping her from William. She dragged along the hull, screaming as she was carried away by the ocean's cold, clawing, greedy depths.

She heard him shout her name as the *Destiny's Revenge* moved farther away, and she cried out in response. Before the waves could suck her under, a figure leaped off the ship and dove into the water.

Moments later, William was with her, pushing a small circular buoy into her hands. "I've got you," he said, gripping her tightly. "Hold on to me. I've got you."

She opened her mouth to respond, but water rushed in as another wave threatened to swallow them. The current wrenched her down, tearing her away from the buoy, but William tugged her back to the surface.

The ships faded into the distance behind sheets of silver rain, leaving William and Aurelia in the middle of roiling waters desperate to kill them. Lightning forked through the sky and turned the world blinding white.

"Hold on to me," William said, his face inches from hers as he took her hand through the buoy.

He kept her afloat as the storm raged, and he never let go.

28

Marooned (But Apparently Not Technically)

Aurelia thought the ocean had some nerve to tickle her awake with soft, lapping waves. She opened her eyes and, squinting against the sunlight, took stock of her surroundings.

Blue sky. Morning sun. Sand beneath her and water pushing her farther into it as though the sea had given up trying to steal her life and now wanted nothing more to do with her.

A shadow fell over her face. She blinked at William hovering over her, his black hair sandy and dripping. His coat and hat were gone, and his shirt hung open, exposing the edge of the scar arcing over his chest.

"Oh thank God!" he said, and scooped her into his arms.

With a low curse, Aurelia planted her hands against his shoulders and shoved him away. Then she got to her feet and stalked off.

They were on an island, and the beach stretched for a mile or two before curving sharply to the right. Beyond the beach was thick vegetation—green trees and scraggly bushes, but little else. Her coat was gone too, shrugged off in the ocean to keep it from pulling her under. Her shirt and pants dripped into her soggy boots, and she imagined her pale hair was horribly disheveled.

William's footsteps followed. "Where are you going?"

"You—you!" She turned and stabbed a finger at him, walking backward. Her voice was rough and broken, made raw from shouting through the storm and coughing up seawater. "You have some nerve, *Copson*, yelling at me and then marooning me with you on some godforsaken island!"

"Excuse me?" He followed at the same pace, maintaining the distance between them as she tried to increase it. "I saved your life! And I didn't maroon you. We're not marooned."

She threw her arms out, gesturing to their surroundings. "Then where are we?"

"Lost," he said. "But I didn't put you here—you're not marooned."

She rolled her eyes with a loud groan and stomped away.

"God, Aurelia, are you truly so upset with me, or did all your fairy tales make you so dramatic?"

"I'm not dramatic!" She stumbled, lost her balance, and careened into the sand. Then William was there, reaching for her, but she slapped his hands away and stood. Her ankle protested and pulled her back down.

"What's wrong with you?" he demanded.

"My ankle," she snapped.

"No, I mean your—whatever this is." He waved his hand before her face, and she grimaced. "That storm should have killed us and you should be crowing to be alive. Instead, you're cross with me."

Ire burned in her belly. Instead of answering, she got up and limped toward the trees.

"Aurelia," he growled. "Have it out with me."

She spun to him. "No." She started for the trees again, unspent tears from the night before beginning to race down her cheeks.

"You are the most maddening—" He caught her hand and tugged, forcing her to face him. As his eyes fell on her tears, the irritation dissipated from his face to leave only worry and confusion. "Why are you crying?"

"Because you called me your crew!" She yanked herself free from his grip. "And you won't let me leave even though I'm miserable. You make me miserable!"

He met her gaze, and there was no hostility to his words as he asked, "You want to know why I won't let you go?"

She rolled her eyes again. "Your *articles*."

"You didn't sign the articles."

"That's what I said!"

William took a slow step toward her. "I said I won't let you leave, Aurelia, because I don't want you to."

She scrubbed the tears from her cheeks. "So you can tease me with ships named for me and remind me that I was once a child who you had the misfortune of having to save, and then I *blackmailed* you because I only wanted stories after they took mine! I'm ridiculous to you, and I'm sure to lose me would make life very boring indeed."

He scrutinized her with narrowed eyes. "You think I'm using you for entertainment? After everything I've done for you, you have the nerve to think so ill of me? If you think one bad night of being awful negates months of friendship—"

"You don't understand, it's not just *one bad night*, William! And if you cared for me, you'd let me go—"

"Then go! I'll let you go!"

"—instead of dangling your heart before me and watching in amusement while I helplessly pine for you!"

"You can go—" He froze, his eyes wide. "Pine for me?"

"Yes! You, William, it's always been *you*." Her hands lifted—to knot in her hair or throttle him, she wasn't sure. She curled her fingers into fists...and deflated. Her arms fell to her sides. Now that she'd finally spoken the awful truth, her words turned helpless and pitiful. "Since the day you pulled me from that blasted lake and took me home and lied to my aunt, you're all I've wanted." Her eyes dropped to the sand.

"For years, you were the only one who didn't make me feel inadequate. When everyone demanded I be less, you told me to be as curious and troublesome and impolite as I was, and I didn't feel so odd or alone. But you were so far away, and then you were a captain and I was hardly more than a girl. And I have done everything in my power to forget you, but you won't be forgotten, and it is *excruciating* to be near you and love you as much as I do with no boon."

"Aurelia—"

"You are torture!" she cried, finally daring to meet his stunned gaze. "And I'm a fool because I can't stay away from you like I should because every time you look at me, every time you smile or call me lovely or seek me out for conversation or stars or dancing, it makes me feel like I am *flying*. I'm so helplessly, hopelessly yours, and it terrifies me that I'll never be anything else."

He said nothing, his expression frozen in shock. Her cheeks flamed, but rather than stand here and wait for his answer, she turned to leave again.

"Aurelia." He grabbed her wrist, pulled her back—

And kissed her.

She gasped at his sudden nearness, her body going rigid with alarm as his arm snaked around her waist. But then the hand around her wrist abandoned its place to cradle her cheek, his long fingers sliding into her hair.

Her heart pounded feverishly as his lips pressed to hers, lingering, waiting. When she didn't pull away, he tilted her head and gently nipped at her bottom lip. She opened to him, and he deepened the kiss.

He tasted like the ocean and broken rules, like she'd always imagined he would. Kissing him felt like giving up, like giving in, and going mad for something deadly and dangerous and completely, utterly lovely.

When he took a breath, she nearly didn't speak. She wanted him to come back, to keep kissing her and letting her live in this dream—but before he could return, she whispered, "Please don't tease me." He paused, and more tears slid down her face because if this wasn't real, she'd very much rather have drowned. "Please, William, don't tease me again."

"I'm not teasing you," he said just as quietly. "I'll let you go, Aurelia, I swear I will, but you have to know you were never just my crew."

"But you said—"

"You were *never* just my crew," he said again. "You never signed the articles, and I never asked you to because from the moment I saw you on that ship bound for France, I wondered if you'd make me a lovesick fool. Then you came to my quarters and drank my whiskey in Nassau, and I knew you would. And then we were in Port Royal, and you were charming and funny and brilliant. You slipped into my life, delighted and unafraid, as though you'd always belonged there—and I was done for."

The warmth of his palm bled into her skin, and the length of his strong body pressed against hers. And his words—so many of them, so suddenly. She stared into those blue eyes she'd loved for ten years and tried to speak, but shock rendered her mute as the world spun around her.

His thumb swept over her cheek, wiping away her tears. "I would've made my feelings known had it not been for Ralph. He's been in love with you for ages, and I've only encouraged him to pursue you. But he didn't—he never even tried, and these past weeks I wanted to be near you and tease you and flirt with you because he *wasn't*. And maybe that makes me terrible..." His voice trailed off. A shadow fell over his eyes and he stepped back, leaving her cold and trembling as he sighed and shoved his hands through his hair. "God, *Ralph*."

"Ralph," was all she could manage to say.

His gaze dropped from her eyes to her lips. "What happened between you two yesterday?"

Trepidation wrapped her stomach in a vice. She and Ralph had hurt each other, and if Ralph's pain made William walk away from her now, it would destroy her entirely. "We fought," she said. "Over you and over his feelings—but I knew nothing about them. I didn't know he felt that way about me."

"Could you love him?" He didn't look scared now. No, he was a concerned older brother—a good brother. Because he was a Kingswood, and they were all so damn *good*.

"No," she said. "No, I can't, because I already—" She broke off as her throat closed against everything she'd never wanted to admit to him, even though she'd flung the words at him only moments ago. And now he stood there, hearing it, knowing everything, and *staring* so intently.

Staring like he had since the moment he saw her on the *Purgatory*.

"It's not Ralph," she rasped. "It was never Ralph."

A muscle fluttered in his jaw as he watched another tear roll down her face, then he stepped closer and pulled her into his arms once more. He muttered huskily, "I love you too, Aurelia Danby," and kissed her like she'd always hoped he would—like he loved her.

He loved her.

Suddenly, after a decade, she was no longer pining, for one could not pine for what they had been given. She'd never even needed fairy godmothers or wishes or magic—she'd merely had to ask for what she wanted.

So she did. She pulled away and breathed, "Say it again."

"I love you, Aurelia." He rested his forehead against hers and sighed heavily. "God, I was going to go about this differently... I was going to tell you how I felt—I intended to, that night we danced, and I'd have done the honorable thing and asked Ralph if I might pursue you.

Instead, I blathered about my damn ship and walked away." He gave a self-deprecating laugh. "After you left, I decided to find you and confess, but instead I found..."

She knew what he'd found. And here, in William's arms again—as she'd been that night after Offley's attack—she felt safe and secure in a way she'd only ever felt with him.

"I couldn't tell you then—not that night or this week. Not when you were in pain at the hands of another man. And holding you, having you near me... It was the only thing that kept me sane."

She let out a broken laugh—to think if they'd both simply been honest that night... Well, perhaps he was as ridiculous as she was.

He did not mirror her smile though, or echo her laugh. "When I woke to find you gone...I lost control." The words heavy with pain and regret. His hands tightened against her waist. "No one defies me, Aurelia, but Offley—that sniveling, weak little man—he, of all people, tested me and hurt you, and I became the worst version of myself to correct it. I was already in agony from waiting for my brother to choose you when all I wanted to do was pull you aside and kiss you senseless." He ran his hand down her cheek, caressing her jaw and running his thumb along the edge of her mouth, his eyes burning with longing. "And I was furious someone touched you and it wasn't me."

Butterflies ran themselves wild through her middle as she remembered the feeling of curling into him and listening to his heart. She splayed her fingers over his chest, feeling its quick, steady beat beneath her palm.

"I lost control," he said again, his voice a mere breath. "I wanted to kill him for what he did to you, and to prove to my crew that I wouldn't be tested again. I yelled at you when I should have explained. And when you said you wished to leave, the thought of letting you go felt like it would destroy me completely." He tilted her face up toward his. "Forgive me, Aurelia, for how I've behaved. For the way I spoke to you and the horrible things I said."

"I forgive you," she said in a small voice, dizzy from the wonderful weight of all he'd confessed. "And...I didn't mean to hurt you. I'm sorry I did."

He gave a watery chuckle. "I have no quarrel with you." He brought his face closer, whispering now, begging. "Just say you'll stay with me. Please."

"William..." She shook her head to clear it. For a breath, he looked uneasy until she said, "I only wanted to leave because I've had enough of loving you unrequited."

"Your feelings are not unrequited. I'm yours, Aurelia. Helplessly. *Hopelessly*. I don't want anything or anyone but you. And had I been home instead of gallivanting through the seas, had I even fully known who I was writing to, I would have made you mine ages ago."

Aurelia laughed again, more tears slipping free. To be so close to him and held so tightly, and to hear all these words she'd always wanted but never thought she'd have—her heart cracked and burst, bleeding and blooming all at once. "You still can."

"Then I'll tell Ralph when we return to the *Destiny*," he said. "And I'll take you home, where I'll court you properly in front of everyone, if that is what you wish. We'll go to stuffy balls and dine with your aunt and have tea. And when no one's looking, I'll steal a kiss." He kissed her now, and definitely not in a way one would steal a small kiss. "I'll be a proper suitor and defend your honor from anyone who objects to you having been stolen by a pirate." His smile flashed, radiant and hers alone. "And I'll make you my bride, and we'll make all society horrifically jealous for how happy we are before we return to the sea and our wild adventures."

Those had once been her very dreams, but they didn't matter so much anymore—she was perfectly content to be here, to be his, with no rules or titles or propriety.

She raised her hands to his face, reverently caressing the lines of his jaw and cheeks and the corners of his lips. How long she'd imagined what it'd be like to run her fingers over the planes of his face, and now he responded to her touch. And his hair, always windblown and wild and now dripping with diamond-fine drops in the sun—she sank her hands into the soft strands.

"That all sounds lovely," she said, smiling. "But for now, all I want is this." She pulled him down and kissed him.

He gripped her hip with one hand, the small of her back with the other. She arched into him, drawing a low sound from his throat. Hearing it—the proof of his desiring her as much as she craved him—her shyness fell away and she clung to him, revealing every want, every need, everything she'd ever felt for him in the way she kissed him.

To her delight, he responded in kind and stole every sensible thought. And for the first time in a long while, she let them go without protest.

29

Love and Starlight

William said smoke could work wonders for lost pirates.

He taught her to build a fire pit and start the kindling with a piece of flint he kept on him at all times. He blew air over the embers to encourage them into dancing flames, and within minutes, a white plume hung above them.

Next, they wandered into the trees where they found curled leaves filled with fresh water from the tempest the night before. Then he handed her a knife—one of many he carried—and showed her how to fashion a spear from a long stick. Once she had one, he led her to the water and showed her how to catch fish and crabs.

She failed her first attempts, laughing as the creatures escaped her until William came to watch over her shoulder, holding her still with a firm hand against her belly, her back pressed against his front. She lofted the spear, holding her breath and waiting despite the rising warmth in her middle.

A fish approached their feet, and when it was close enough, he whispered over her skin, "Now," and Aurelia threw the spear.

Blood and sand bloomed through the water. She hefted the stick and stared in wonder as a silvery fish flopped on the end. Bursting into excited laughter, she threw her arms around his shoulders, proclaiming she'd done it.

With their faces so close and lit with so much glee, they ended up snogging again—as they did several times that day—and got nothing else done for as long as they pleased.

That evening, they returned to the fire with several fish and crabs, and sat on a sun-bleached log, roasting their catch and throwing the leftover bones into the flames while the sun slowly lowered into the water.

Aurelia spat a pin bone from her tongue. "How'd you know how to do all this?"

"Paranoia, mostly," William said, watching the stars emerge. "I learned through desperation after my crew mutinied. Then after my rescue, I studied survival obsessively—I read books and listened to stories and filled journals with all I learned."

She twirled her roasting stick. The fish at the end was nearly a skeleton, its charred flesh the only thing holding it there. Quietly, she said, "I'm sorry for what they did to you."

He lifted a shoulder. "I suppose I won in the end. I'm still Copson, and they're..." *Dead*. The word hung between them, heavy and silent. His gaze bored into the horizon. "Only Greyson really knows how much the mutiny continues to haunt me. I was so embarrassed and ashamed...and the fear of it happening again never really went away." He glanced at her. "But the letters—I enjoyed writing them."

"Even though I blackmailed you?" she asked, lifting a brow.

"That wasn't wholly fair of me to say last night...even though you did blackmail me that day in the forest." He gave her a look, then smirked. "But by a few years in, I knew you weren't malicious. You were desperate, and you didn't fit the life you'd been born into. So even if you'd threatened me into writing to you, I couldn't fault you for the reason. I'd have done the same.

"And as much as you needed those letters, I needed them too. During the darkest times, especially in the months after the mutiny, writing to you reminded me my life was an adventure. And despite all the hardships I endured, there was someone who thought it was amazing—a gift, even. So instead of resenting the life I'd wanted, you forced me to see all I loved about it."

The sun dipped nearly entirely into the waves, and the top turned bright green for a fleeting moment before falling in completely.

"You've thanked me for writing," he said, "but it's really I who should thank you for making me do it. Our silly little deal gave me perspective, and I'm convinced it's what made me a good captain." He smiled. "One who's worthy of being your favorite."

She nudged his knee with hers. "Your life is an adventure. I'm ever so grateful you let me join it."

"You've been part of it for a long time. And you belong as much as I do."

She leaned back to look at the sky. "And to think, I still have so much left to do and see."

He craned his head and brushed his lips over her throat. "Name the adventure, and I'll take you to it."

"This one has been grand so far," she said, giggling as she tried to lean away only for William to pull her back and pepper more tickling kisses over her neck. "I think I'll tell everyone you marooned me to keep me from running off with Hector Hein."

He released her and pulled away to stare into her eyes. "I suppose marooning myself with you isn't too far out of the realm of possibility. I was patient for five years."

"Patient? What do you mean?"

He laughed once. "When I gave you my addresses and invited you to write back, surely you didn't think it was for nothing."

Her brows drew together in question.

"I saw you in London the day you debuted." He said it as though remarking on something as mundane as trees or stale biscuits.

Aurelia's breath hitched. "When?"

"I brought Ralph to see you—which was really the only reason we came back at all. We were outside the palace, and I saw you in your carriage, staring out the window, right at me, and appearing so completely miserable at an event you should've loved. And while my brother talked about something inconsequential and bland, I could only think you were beautiful, and I wanted to know why you looked so dreadfully bored."

She remembered that carriage—the great black one she'd nearly flung herself into. To think he'd been there—right there—looking back at her and thinking she was beautiful.

"So within an hour of returning home," he went on, "I wrote down every address I had and delivered the letter to your aunt's house. I wanted to know what had become of the girl who threatened me in the woods—I was curious to know what you'd say."

She gaped. "You should've said something."

He kissed the tip of her nose. "You should've written me back."

She should have, because now she was certain he would have taken her away much, much sooner if she'd only reciprocated. But, "Five years," she breathed. "You waited for me to write back for five years—why? Why keep writing? Why not stop when I never responded?" She was grateful he hadn't stopped, but it had been so long...

"Because I cared," he said simply. "And you asked me how to wallop rude men, which only told me you had no one looking out for you. But I'd saved you from a lake, told you how to fight, and entertained you with adventures. And I'd taken Ralph. So I suppose I felt responsible, and I'd be damned if you didn't have, at the very least, a handsome neighbor to rely on." He shrugged. "I cared."

Her heart swelled. "That's it?"

"I wish I had a more interesting reason to give you, but yes, that's it." He smiled. "The letters gave me something too, Aurelia. As I said, they weren't just for you. It was also nice to be known—to not be just

Will or just Copson. And I supposed that if you'd wanted me to stop writing, you'd have told me. Until you did, I took advantage of being as honest as I liked without fear of reproach."

"I wish I'd written," she whispered.

"Well, we have plenty of time to talk now," he said, and grinned. "You won't get away with avoiding it—not like you did for so many years, and the day after my dreadful illness."

Aurelia pursed her lips as she thought of his siren sickness. If they were being honest now... "I only avoided you that day because you tried to seduce me."

He made a sound in his throat. "What?"

"After the mermaid. When you were sick." William went very still, and she could no longer hear him breathing. But she had already started, and the memories weren't so painful anymore—in fact, they hardly hurt at all, and now that she'd kissed him and held him and heard him confess his love for her...well, it was actually rather funny. "You pushed me against a door and kissed my neck."

He shoved his face into his hands with a groan. "Oh, God."

"That's why I couldn't talk to you," she said, torturing him now and not feeling so bad about that either, because he'd done the same to her with his infernal teasing and flirting. "You tried to convince me to come to the ocean with you in rather passionate terms—"

"I'm *so sorry*," he said, dragging his hands down past his mouth. "I'd have been mortified if you'd told me. I *am* mortified."

She noted the redness creeping up his neck. "You told me not to believe you, and I was crushed that *none* of your wanting me would be true."

"Oh, it was true, but the siren sickness twisted it beyond reason."

"Hm." She looked at the ocean again. "Hopefully not too far beyond reason. I'd like to be pushed against a door again."

"*Again.*" He picked up his knife and lobbed it into the sand. "You know, I worried that I might've revealed my feelings and that maybe you ignored me that day because you didn't want me to love you—you certainly wouldn't be the first. Then I thought it was because I drew you into a fight. I chose to believe the latter and make up for it with something akin to the former." He made a face. "And then I thought I was blatantly romancing you under those stars, but you said we were friends, and I told myself to love it because it was more than I deserved even if it was so much less than what I wanted."

"I wouldn't be the first...?" Her heart twinged. "Why wouldn't I want you to love me? Why wouldn't anyone?"

There was a glimmer of uncertainty in his eyes. "I am complicated and distasteful for many, and unapproachable to nearly everyone decent."

She sneered. "You're not distasteful."

He gave her a look. "I've killed men for you—in front of you—several times. I've marched you into pirate dens, pulled you into battle, nearly got myself turned into a fish, flogged a man, and yelled at you—and it's hardly been two months."

She chewed her lip. When he put it like that... "Then what happened with Lavinia?" It was a question that had lingered in the back of her mind these past weeks. It had never been her place to pry, but now... "She doesn't seem to think you're distasteful."

"Lavinia." There was affection in the way he said her name. "She's one of the few who truly knows me, but we ended after she begged me to walk away from being Copson. After the mutiny, she was scared the infamy would eventually get me killed, so she wanted me to *just be Will*. I couldn't, and I didn't want to, and when she saw who I became to preserve my name and reputation, she decided it was too much. It was fair, and I never blamed her for it. We both wanted things the other couldn't live with. Being friends with her—or even just captain and crew—is easier."

She mulled over this new story. She tested the weight of it, added it to her trove of tales, and decided, "You still don't scare me. None of that ever has...or ever will."

"And in that, you are the first." He hooked his finger under her chin and tipped her face toward his. "There were other women," he admitted quietly, "other attempts at finding love, but you are the only one who hasn't run from me, cursed me, or cowered, even when you've seen me be cruel and hateful. Even then, your biggest complaint was that you thought I did not *love you*." His thumb trailed over her bottom lip and sent butterflies careening through her middle. "Since the first time you said I did not frighten you, I've told you I love you a hundred ways without ever saying the words. But you also scared the competency right out of me, so I panicked and reduced it all to banter."

"I *scared* you?" she snickered. "You. Copson."

"Let it boost your ego, you unexpected, curious woman," he said, and silenced her laughter with a kiss.

The sky grew darker, and they fed the fire to make it taller, brighter, and warmer as a cool breeze rolled off the lapping waves. Nearly all the color had left the horizon when William said, "I want to make a request. But I must insist you don't have to agree to it. It's troublesome and impulsive and breaks more than a few rules."

"What is it?" she asked.

The fire reflected in one of his eyes as he peered at her, leaving the other cool and blue in the night. "I warn you—it's a lot of rules."

She might've teased him about both of their general disregard for rules had he not looked so serious. "Alright."

"You didn't seem to have qualms when I spoke of marriage earlier."

Her smile broke through. "I have no qualms."

"So you'll marry me when we get home."

Everything in her sparkled. "Of course."

William looked at her for a long time. "Will you marry me tonight?"

Her heart faltered, and she might've fallen had she not already been sitting. But she merely tilted her head.

He eyed the fire. "For all my talk about going home with you, I'd weigh an equal possibility of being here a rather long while. If that's the case, I don't want to waste time—not when I've already wasted so much of it concerning you." His eyes came back to her, his gaze resolute. "I want you, Aurelia. In every way, and as my wife, if you'll have me. But I'll understand if you want to wait. Say no, and I will accept it just as readily."

Her mind was utterly quiet. There was only his question—his proposal—and her lifelong desires rising to answer.

Marrying William tonight didn't seem any more dangerous than pirate's treasure, poker games, or sea monsters. It was more real than fairy princesses and fainting damsels, and excited her just as much. "Who will marry us?"

He looked to the stars. "God, I suppose. A covenant made before him is hardly less than what a priest would do for us."

She reached for his hand, bringing his attention back to her. "Are you sure?"

"I already declared my intention to make you my wife. The venue matters little to me, and I'm okay with now if you are."

She touched his cheek. This face, this man—all she'd dreamed of in the palm of her hand. "Now sounds like a fine time."

He kissed her palm before he stood and pulled her to her feet. "You'll be a Kingswood, not a Copson. Is that enough for you?"

She blinked, and he must have mistaken her confused expression as he said, "Though Copson is a name I'm proud of, it's a cruel, bloodstained thing. And as much as I know you love your stories and the character I've played in them, I would much rather you wear my family name and not our infamy."

She smiled to herself and turned his hand, studying its calluses and cuts. *What's in a name*, she thought.

"A Kingswood saved me," she muttered, running her fingers over his, "and kept me from years of boredom by filling my head with adventure. A Kingswood rescued me from a marriage I didn't want and showed me the world." She met his gaze. "And through it all, you, William, saved me from being the forgotten, unwanted Danby. You gave me a new name and now offer me another I have loved for a long time." She pressed her palm to his chest where his shirt hung open to expose the long, crude scar. "I *want* to be a Kingswood."

"You saved me too, Aurelia. More than once." He grasped the thin chain he wore around his neck, lifted it over his head, and caught the dangling gold ring, which he slid free and held between them like an offering.

And there on the beach they were married, their sacred vows hidden beneath the sound of waves and the gentle breeze. Aurelia looked into his eyes, into a heart and soul sworn to her. She smiled around his name as she made it her own, and a tender kiss sealed their vows.

They hardly had the will to stop there, however, as talk of marriage and seduction and doors had emboldened them. Perhaps it was Aurelia who pushed it further, or maybe it was William. Very likely it was that both of them were made silly and absurd by the other's hands and lips and breath.

Their troublesome natures and morbid curiosity made quick work of their clothes. For a brief moment, Aurelia was nervous until she learned the luxury of the way his eyes trailed over her skin, followed closely by his hands. He was reverent and unhurried, as though to memorize every inch of her. She did the same, exploring his tan planes of corded muscle and shaking for the exhilarating newness and sheer audacity of it all.

He kissed her too, and kissed her well, his lips exploring her face and skin and body with the same care. She supposed he made up for her never having being kissed well before, and for once she was glad to have waited so long, if only to have it like this.

To have *him* like this.

They smiled until it hurt to be so happy, and on a beach hidden away from the rest of the world, a bride and groom became husband and wife as William made her his.

The summer night deepened and the stars shifted in a dazzling display of darkest blue and glittering silver. Lying side by side on top of their discarded clothes, William and Aurelia dozed and talked of nothing important, happy and content to be as they were. All the while, she gently traced the edge of his scar. Her finger lingered over his sternum where his heart—which finally belonged to her—beat steadily beneath her touch.

She didn't have to pretend anymore. She was not a princess or a damsel in distress, nor was she saving herself through frightful and exciting adventures. This was the adventure, and she was finally the very character she'd always wanted to be.

30

Saviors in the Morning

Aurelia had learned a great many things since leaving home—like how to keep her balance on a rocking ship and tie several kinds of knots. Three days into living with William on a deserted island, she'd learned that she liked living with William and would happily keep doing it regardless of the setting.

Each morning, he grabbed their spears and Aurelia's hand, and they headed for the shallows to find enough food to sate them. They built a small shelter and explored the forest for fresh water, interesting creatures, and trees to climb. The fire remained lit and smoky, and they constantly scanned the horizon for signs of rescue.

All the while, they talked of anything they could think of, sharing all they loved and liked. William ranked his ships for her, unprompted but excited to share nonetheless. He unabashedly told her about the smallest details of each, and even though she understood little, his excitement was *very* endearing. In turn, Aurelia shared her favorite tales and how she'd wanted to be a knight until Aunt Clara told her girls couldn't be knights—but that didn't stop Aurelia from beheading her garden gnomes.

William enjoyed her stories as much as she liked his, so she told him about everything, even her dreadful suitors. After the mention of them, however, her mind began to wander. If impossibilities and what-ifs were now solidly part of reality, her imagination could hardly resist the urge to explore.

"What," William said as the morning sun crept closer toward noon. He stood by a natural platform next to a massive outcropping of lava rock they'd climbed twice—once to watch the sunset and again to leap off the top. He relieved his spear of the fish dangling off the end and left it next to three others they'd caught. "You've looked pensive since last night."

"I had an idea," Aurelia said slowly, her spear lifted and eyes on the water. She'd rolled her pants up to her knees, but the bottoms were still soaked. "Well...perhaps more of a daydream than an idea, really, or maybe a musing."

He returned to her side. "Of what?" When she didn't immediately divulge, he said, "You may as well tell me—I've got nothing better to do than pester you until you do."

She rolled her lips between her teeth in thought. "A ruse," she finally said.

"Oh?"

"I was thinking about after. When we leave the island. I wondered what becomes of Aurelia Danby now that I'm a Kingswood." She looked up. He leaned on his spear, his expression intrigued as the surf swirled between them. "Do we go back to England and announce you found and married me while abroad? What's the story of how you, as William, got me away from you as Copson?"

"Oh, well I've already thought of—"

"And then I remembered the prince," she barreled on, her annoyance rising. "And the kings. And my parents. And how they don't know I'm married, and I doubt they'd really care, short of losing their arrangement." She shoved the tip of her spear into the sand, twisting it sharply to dig it deeper. "And I thought, how dare they try to ruin my life and expect all to go well for them. And now that I'm with you...well, I think of what you might do if you were me, and revenge sounds quite fitting...if not a bit fun."

He smiled maliciously.

"I think about what it might be like to waltz into the prince's home like the sad, obedient girl he was expecting, and how it might feel to quietly learn all his secrets and steal everything from him. I think about making the kings and my family regret ever forcing me to marry... I think about ruining them all, and how satisfying it might be to pretend to be what they want, only to make them pay."

"And where would I fit into all this?" William asked, though she could see him already considering, calculating...planning.

She lifted a shoulder. "Pretending to be a gardener?"

He shook his head, his eyes darkening. "What if I also want to embarrass them for all they've done to you?"

Her heart fluttered. "You could shoot Pierre again."

"That sounds like a fine time, but I've already done it, and I'd hate to be so one-note. You deserve better. Wickeder."

"What would you want to do?" Knowing he'd commit atrocities for her made her feel deliciously warm inside.

William thought about it. "I'm assuming if you were to go to the prince, the wedding would go on as scheduled." When Aurelia grimaced, he added, "We couldn't have that. But he's also a royal snob, so he'd drag out the affair—I'd give him no less than a month to bring the whole thing together. He'd need to tell everyone about it, if only to hear himself talk."

"I wouldn't want to be there for a *month*." But as soon as the words left her mouth, it occurred to her that it might take time to properly ruin a fool. "What would you do with a month?"

"I'd need a properly outrageous way of getting you back. Nothing's worse than a pirate beating a prince." His teeth flashed. "I'd probably do something ostentatious, like buying the city or making myself governor of Calais. So when I waltz in to take you back, Pierre would have no means of keeping you, and you'd have no way of saying no." He spoke with his typical easy confidence, leaving no doubt that he'd be able to pull it off.

She leaned on her spear. "Rebecca Rowe might take issue with you stealing another girl. We've got to keep our stories straight."

He gave a sultry smirk. "I didn't realize you were the jealous type."

She remembered William spinning a beautiful woman in green across Aunt Clara's ballroom. "I think you'll find I'm rather drastic in my jealousy and would do anything to have you to myself."

Quietly, he asked, "Including murder?"

Fish swirled around their feet, but neither tried to catch them. The silence stretched, and the look in his eyes made her heart flip. Trouble—it was trouble in his gaze, and a thrill tingled along her spine because she knew he would never discourage her from the same. She was just as bad as he was in nearly every way.

Oh, how dearly she loved him, and she'd surely never stop.

"It's all such an awful idea," she said. "Why do you humor me so?"

"You've always seemed rather susceptible to perishing from boredom," he said wanly. "So it's become a habit of mine to amuse you over the past decade."

"Oh, it's *my* boredom you're so worried about." She moved up the surf to toss her spear into the dry sand. "Never your own. You, who called kidnapping me a *satisfactory change of plans* so you could pick a fight with the French because it's *exciting*."

Humor danced in his eyes. "But who made me do it?"

She plodded toward him through the water. "I didn't make you do anything."

As she drew closer, he backed away from his spear. "On the contrary," he said, "I've also made it a habit of swooping in when you're so helpless—"

"Helpless!"

322

William took off. She ran after him, shouting, "I saved you from mermaids and lied to your crew and defended your ship and found your treasure and won the pirate kings' help to escape the French! *Helpless my ass, William!*"

He slowed, gasping with laughter. Aurelia leaped at him and sent them both tumbling into the waves.

"You win—you *win*!" William turned out of her grip and tugged her from the surf, both of them soaked and chuckling.

As Aurelia straightened, a speck against on the horizon caught her eye. For all her staring at the sea for a sign of rescue, she hardly believed her eyes and blinked several times to clear them, assuring herself that what she saw was true before she grabbed his arm and pointed.

"What is it?" He looked into the distance, and his eyes widened. "A ship?"

"It's a ship!" Aurelia took off, sprinting across the sand toward their pile of wood. "We need more smoke!"

Crowing, William ran after her and helped dump everything into the flames. Like zealous worshipers, they danced and jumped around the fire, waving their hands and screaming as the ship grew larger. She grabbed a branch that hadn't started fully burning and ran toward the outcropping. At the top, she waved the torch over her head. William joined her on the rock, and both of them shouted across the water.

Over the next few minutes, the ship sailed closer until she could make out its silhouette. It was black as night and looked like a spiny creature born from the dreadful depths of the sea. At the top of the main mast flew a black flag, and Aurelia was sure it featured a silver anchor crossed with two swords.

"It's the *Destiny*!" she squealed. "It's your ship!"

"We're going home!" He picked her up and spun her. "We're going *home*!"

The ship anchored off shore, and a small boat lowered into the water. Even from so far out, they recognized Greyson's hulking figure. At the sight of him, William dove from the rock and popped up from between the waves, his fists raised in triumph as his first mate neared. Aurelia climbed down, and by the time she made it to the sand and waded into the shallows, the boat was close enough to climb into.

William clung to the side, beaming as he shoved the boat back toward the waves. "Thank God for you, Greyson."

"Glad we finally found you," the first mate said, his face steely as ever. "Thought we'd lost you until we saw the smoke."

"You could never lose me," William said with his cocky smile. He hauled himself in, dripping all over the planks and the small seat he shared with Aurelia.

Greyson stared as he rowed, then his eyes dipped to the ring on her finger. "What happened in that storm?"

"She fell," William said. "I jumped." Greyson raised his eyebrows. The captain held his gaze before finally saying, "We married."

Greyson's grin was wolfy and slightly intimidating, despite its genuineness. As much as Aurelia appreciated it, she wouldn't have minded its absence.

"I'll still be known as Rebecca Rowe," she said, spinning the gold band on her finger. Since pirates believed all fingers were intended for either carrying gold or wearing it, few would care for the meaning, nor would they spend time wondering. "We decided the crew may assume what they like about us."

"They already do," Greyson said.

Aurelia blanched. "Surely I wasn't so obvious."

"Nah." He jerked his chin at William. "He hasn't looked at his compass half as much as he's looked at you since you've come aboard."

"My compass isn't half as clever," William said in the same tone. "Where are the *Fortuna* and *Ophelia*?"

"We split to look for you," Greyson said. "Meetin' in port tonight."

The cheering started before they reached the *Destiny's Revenge*, and only grew louder when they climbed aboard. William didn't seem at all surprised or put off by the attention and grinned broadly as he faced several hundred pirates.

"I'm finally home, friends," he said, his voice booming over the ship. They cheered again. "A man knows his crew is the best when they find him after three days. Truly, no captain is better off or better loved than I, and I will see you all greatly rewarded for your loyalty." The proclamation caused even more of a stir. "You have my eternal gratitude—not only for saving me, but also my dear friend, Miss Rowe." His hand settled on the small of her back—natural, unassuming, and unoffensive as they looked from each other to the crew, searching for the same person. "Though it's only been a few months, her presence would be sorely missed."

And there he was—Ralph emerged from the gathered crew, and Aurelia's heart tumbled at the pain written over his face. Pain and relief.

She was so focused on the sight of him and recalling the words they'd last spoken to each other that she hardly noticed when the captain stopped speaking and the crew began milling about. The slightest pressure of William's hand broke her from her reverie as he nudged her toward Ralph. She moved away just as several sailors descended on their captain, and stopped in front of her friend.

"I'm sorry for all I said," Ralph said quickly, and gulped, his dark eyes searching her face. "I've dreaded that you were dead, and the last thing I would've said to you was meant to hurt you. You're not ridiculous, and I never should've said it. I shouldn't have said any of it as I did, and I'm so sorry."

"Oh, Ralph..." She threw her arms around him. "I'm sorry too."

He buried his face in her shoulder. "Lord, if I'd lost you..."

"We have much to discuss," she said, stepping back. "We—"

"Ralph." William came to stand at Aurelia's side. His hand skimmed her waist before falling away.

Ralph pulled his brother into a crushing hug. "You bastard. How was I supposed to tell the earl and countess you killed yourself *and* her?"

"You could always write to them," William replied, pulling away. "Then wait several years to show up, like I do." He glanced at Aurelia before looking to Ralph again. "May I speak with you?"

Ralph nodded slowly and followed William to the captain's quarters. Before William closed the door, he caught Aurelia's gaze. Touching the turtle at her throat, she silently wished him luck. He took a deep breath, nodded once, and shut the door.

Aurelia stood at the bow, dressed in clean pants and a shirt with stays that laced down her front. The sides had small bands where she'd strapped Davy Silver's knife and the one William had given her on the island.

Every so often, she glanced at the captain's quarters, but she heard no yelling or curses. It was around midday now, and sailors hung around with instruments, cards, or books. Earlier on, Fenner had told her Offley had been transferred to the *Fortuna Royale*. The carpenter could hardly walk, and would undoubtedly be left at the next port.

Lavinia hadn't taken long to find her after that. She hugged Aurelia fiercely and peppered her with questions about being marooned with the captain. After seeing Aurelia's bright blush, she'd declared, "You've been tumbled!" When Aurelia nearly passed out from horror, Lavinia smirked and added, "Several times, by the looks of it."

Hester hadn't been much better. She'd immediately asked, "Did the captain finally make an honest woman of you?" And then she'd cackled while Aurelia swore and turned on her heel to go hide.

Neither of them had bothered her since, but she flinched every time she heard one of them laugh, thinking they'd come to incite her blush again. But it wasn't Lavinia or Hester who approached her, but Ralph.

He appeared at her side so silently and suddenly that she nearly jumped. "Lord," he said with a laugh. "It's just me."

Thankfully, he didn't look unhappy or tortured or hurt. "On edge?" he asked, matching her stance and leaning against the rail. "Hopefully not because of me. I only came to share good news."

Her heart thundered. "Really?"

He turned his attention to the horizon. "My older brother took a wife," he said solicitously. "A lovely girl with dowry like you wouldn't believe, but that's apparently not of much consequence to him."

She gripped the rail. "You're okay with it, then?"

He gave her a kind smile. "I'm happy. Truly. A little miffed, since he always warned me I wasted time. I see now that he was right, which is really the only annoying thing about it."

Aurelia frowned. "Ralph, what I feel for him... It's been so long, and I—"

"You don't have to explain," he said. "I love you, Aurelia, and I won't begrudge you any happiness. After you fell...well, these past days I've been thinking a lot." He scrubbed his hand through his hair. "As a boy, I think I was glad to share my secret with someone, and you were a better friend than my brothers. You still are in a lot of ways, and I suppose I thought loving you was the natural next step without realizing what that really meant. After he told me all that's happened, and seeing how much he cares for you..." His eyes were bright when he looked at her. "You deserve someone who loves you that much. Clearly I missed something."

"I do adore you, Ralph," she muttered. "You must know that."

"I know. And I don't mind that you love him, especially when I never told you how I felt. Or thought I felt..." He smirked. "I did slug him, though."

Aurelia balked. "Ralph!"

"Because he's an ass for going behind my back this whole time. Had he said something sooner, I might not have minded. He actually offered to let me hit him twice—once for being a terrible brother and again for nearly dying, but I was satisfied with the one."

"You— Are you two...?" Aurelia swallowed. She'd heard them fight in Nassau too, but that hadn't come to blows. "Are you two quite fine?"

"We're...yes, we're fine." His brow furrowed. "Are you worried because I hit him?"

"Yes?" She said it like a question, unsure of the dynamics of men and contention between them.

"We're brothers. We fight," he said, as though that would explain everything. Aurelia shook her head. "Lord, we're not—it's fine. Everything is fine, except for his face."

She peered over her shoulder at William on the quarterdeck with Greyson and two others. He was clean now, freshly shaven, and wore entirely black, from his hat to his boots. As though he felt her gaze, his eyes flicked to her, and she frowned as she saw the red mark below his eye. But then he grinned, making her blood warm.

"I've never seen you so happy," Ralph said. "He's a lucky bastard."

"Don't tell him that." She turned back to the bow. "It'll go straight to his head."

"Oh, he already knows and it already has. He's more incorrigible than ever. I've never seen *him* so happy either, and I think you'll both be deplorable for weeks."

Lavinia made her way over. "Have you two made up?"

"Yes," Ralph said.

She didn't slow as she said, "Good," and walked right up to him, knotted her hand in the front of his shirt, and pulled him down to kiss her. His eyes flew wide, but then she pulled away, winked, and strutted off.

Ralph stood frozen beside Aurelia, his cheeks a deep shade of pink. On the quarterdeck, William's back was turned, but his shoulders quaked with laughter.

31

Rowe of Ruses

Hours later, they docked in a small pirate city called Saint Mary's Bay, where the *Fortuna Royale* and *Ophelia* were already anchored. The crews let up a loud cheer when they saw their captain had returned, and he made the same speech he'd given earlier, promising them a handsome bonus. And like before, the crews loved to hear it.

It was right after sunset, and gilded orange clouds reflected over dark water to make the sea look as though it glittered with embers. As the sailors dispersed into the city for the night, William found Aurelia leaning against the main mast.

"I don't know about you," he said as he swaggered closer with a coat and hat in hand, "but I wouldn't mind a hot meal and a pint of something terribly cheap."

She raised her brows. "I thought you avoided cities because of the fanfare."

It was the most they'd spoken to each other since their rescue. What with the storm and spending three days away, William had much to address as captain, and the hours had crawled.

He looked toward the city and the writhing mass of sailors slinking over the docks. "It's a good day for fanfare," he said, shoving his hat on and shrugging into his coat. "We have things to celebrate."

"Celebrate indeed," she said, and ran her finger beneath the red mark on his cheek. It was already turning into nasty bruise. "This looks painful."

"Oh, Ralph doesn't hit nearly as hard as he thinks he does." Amusement lit his face as he offered his arm and led her toward the gangplank. "But don't tell him that. I deserve much worse and don't feel inclined to collect."

The city was much smaller than Port Royal, and the addition of four hundred pirates made it seem like a bustling metropolis with lines of thirsty clientele snaking away from taverns and "No Vacancy" signs being hung in windows. Peeling laughter, shouts, and gunshots carried up into the night. Surrounded by careless men and criminals, Aurelia couldn't help but feel an odd sense of home among it all.

"One of the best parts of being a pirate," he said as they walked, "is that when you acquire something worthy of flaunting, one of the greatest pleasures is showing off."

Just as in Nassau and Port Royal, mutterings of Copson's presence flittered through open doors and down alleyways, and those who recognized him pointed and stared, though he paid them no mind.

"You didn't flaunt Robin's treasure," she said, sidestepping a young man who went sprawling at her feet after another punched him in the jaw. "You celebrated by updating your books."

"I've flaunted enough treasure." He leaned close to say, "I wanted to flaunt *you*, my dear Miss Rowe."

Somewhere nearby, a gun went off, followed by a shriek. "Surely no one knows of me in only a matter of months," Aurelia said.

"The kings met you, so people will know," William said. "And they'll know you have me too."

"Ah, so you want me to flaunt *you*."

They entered a hazy tavern packed with all manner of folks enjoying their evening with food and drink. Her mouth began to water at the smell of roasted meat and baked bread. As he breezed past the chattering patrons who were beginning to realize who had just bypassed the quite lengthy line of customers out the front, he wrapped his hand around her waist and pulled her nearer.

"Don't you want to?" he whispered as they approached a corner booth. Those occupying it grabbed their plates and cups and quickly vacated. "Try it, love, it's horrendously fun."

She slid onto the bench beside him. Then, in front of everyone staring at the notorious captain in their midst, she took his face in her hands and crushed her mouth to his.

He chuckled quietly and raised one hand to her face. Then Aurelia knew she'd set a new rumor into motion—or confirmed one—as he'd most likely intended.

She let him go and leaned back, her heart aflutter. "Terribly fun."

In nearly no time at all, a barmaid appeared to deliver ale and two steaming plates of pork with a roll and plantains. The girl paused at the table, studying the couple with wide, wonder-filled eyes.

Aurelia offered a smile—which fell into open-mouthed shock when the barmaid said, "You're Rebecca Rowe."

Copson smirked into his ale.

"Yes," Aurelia said, reveling in the novelty of being recognized as someone other than herself.

The barmaid grinned, exposing large, square teeth. "My brother heard'a you. Said you're something fierce. Said you challenged the pirate kings to poker and won." She quickly glanced at Copson. "I've told some others about it, but they don't believe me."

"They'll believe it," Aurelia said as evenly as she could. "I'm not going anywhere."

"I like the tales about you." The girl drifted back toward the kitchen as someone began shouting from the back. "You'll make some of the best stories, I'm sure." Then she spun on her heel and fled through a door, calling to whoever had summoned her.

"*I'm sure*," Copson drawled, swirling his ale. Elation broke over her face, and he laughed at its appearance.

They were approached three more times throughout their meal, by pirates and civilians alike. One came to express his admiration for the captain and ask for a position among his crew. The second came for a similar purpose, and the third drunkenly stumbled into the table and declared he would duel the captain for his ships—Copson had released a single guffaw and aimed his gun so quickly that the man stumbled back and crashed to the floor.

After that, Copson left the gun on the edge of the table, which Aurelia realized was a signal as anyone else who attempted to approach them was turned away by one of Copson's crew.

Then drinks began to appear, delivered by the blushing barmaid who told them each was sent by some patron seeking to gain the captain's favor until he kindly told her to stop bringing them.

"Fanfare," he said to her, eyeing the line of glasses and taking none of them.

"Perhaps I'm too new to this to mind," she said, reaching for one, "but I haven't found it suffocating at all." She took a sip and didn't love the taste, so she set it down.

"Then I'll indulge you until you agree with me," he said, and handed her another drink she liked much more.

Another man sidled up to the table then, surrounded by three of Copson's crew. He was young, pale, and his weather-worn coat hung open to reveal a crisp French uniform beneath.

Aurelia's stomach jolted, and her gaze snapped to the other patrons before she could stop herself. She saw no other soldiers and pulled her attention back, forced her shoulders to relax, and took a languid sip of her drink even as her pulse sprinted.

Copson eyed the solider. "What."

He removed his hat and scrubbed a nervous hand through his brown hair. "I don't mean to interrupt, but—"

"The last time a Frenchman approached me in this tavern," Copson said, "he left with a limp."

Aurelia's surprise nearly reached her face. This was where he'd played cards with Pierre? The thought of it amused her enough to take the edge off her fear, but she still palmed her dagger under the table.

The man fisted his hat, his eyes darting to the pirates flanking him. "Sir—"

Copson tossed an arm over Aurelia's shoulders. "Have you met Rebecca Rowe? She has even less patience for the French than I have."

Pressed into his side, she settled into the confidence of her false name as Copson declared it over her like an iron mask. As Rebecca Rowe, the French did not scare her nearly as much.

The soldier looked at her. "I've heard your name. You killed my superior."

She schooled her expression into cool indifference. "Shame."

"I have his job now." A shadow of a smile appeared and quickly vanished.

"Your superior," she started. "Was he the one who would have dragged me back to his ship for the belief I was someone I'm not?"

The man glanced between her and Copson, then swallowed. "I won't make the same mistake."

She gave a humorless, close-lipped smile.

The soldier removed a slip of paper from his coat pocket and slid it across the table. The point of Aurelia's knife stabbed it into the wood, and then she lifted her blade to offer the skewered note to Copson.

He plucked it off the knife and unfolded it, but his expression revealed nothing as he scanned the words.

"Since you've not accepted the previous offer," the soldier said, "we're prepared to double the initial ransom for Aurelia Danby."

Double. Aurelia looked at the note, appearing nonchalant even as her insides twisted at the obscene amount of money.

"Is this offer only for me?" Copson asked.

"It's for anyone who can return the girl, but the ransom was to be extended to you first."

Even though he'd never consider it, Aurelia felt cold. An offer like this was enough to tempt anyone else to find and return her to the French. But it was a mercy that so few people knew her true identity. Her secret had been kept so well that there was little chance anyone would assume she was anyone but who she claimed to be.

"What makes you think I still have her?" Copson asked.

"I don't know that you do," the man said. "But manage her return, and all will be forgiven. And rewarded."

"And the English? Do they not wish to tempt me?"

"They're prepared to pay half the ransom," the soldier said. "Both the girl's family and the prince are desperate to have her back."

"Everyone is desperate," Copson scoffed. He folded the note and tossed it onto the table. "Be gone. You bore me."

With a respectful nod, the soldier left.

"You've indulged me," Aurelia said as soon as he was gone. "I've had enough fanfare."

Copson watched the patrons, no doubt aware of every gaze that trailed in their direction. "You're sure?"

"Quite."

He left a few coins on the table, took Aurelia's hand, and led her from the booth. On their way out of the tavern, he whispered awful jokes into her ear to make her smile and appear unbothered, and she was grateful for it.

Even so, the ransom still simmered in Aurelia's mind when they returned to the ship. She was so deep in thought that she nearly headed for her cabin and only stopped when William tugged lightly on her hand.

"Your things aren't down there," he said, and nodded to his quarters. "I had them moved."

Of course. She frowned, regretful that she was so captivated by un-worthy thoughts of a prince she hated. He didn't say anything about it, however, as he led her inside. The trunk she'd been living out of had been set next to his armoire. Lanterns were already lit, casting the stately emerald room in a comforting golden glow, and she wondered if someone had been watching for them to return to prepare all this.

William wrapped his arms around her waist and pulled her back against him, his coat and hat now gone. "Welcome home," he mur-mured.

Surrounded by a pirate king's luxury, to have him deem it as her *home*, she tried to summon joy, happiness, any sense of gladness she'd had only an hour ago. But it did not come, because a scrap of paper promising money and forgiveness stood in its way.

"Has the ransom disturbed you this much," William asked when she didn't answer, "or is it something else?"

"I am nothing to them," she huffed. "Pierre doesn't really want me. Neither do my parents or the kings. They only want some idiotic notion of an alliance at the cost of my life."

"Ignore them."

"They offered you double," she said, watching the stars glitter over the sea through the large windows behind his desk.

"It doesn't tempt me more than it ever has."

She leaned her head back against his chest, her shoulders sagging. "They'll offer the ransom to others when you don't turn me over. It'll tempt *them*, and I'll spend the rest of my life being chased."

Even under the assumption that Captain Copson might have ru-ined her and taken her virtue, there was no fiercer foe than embarrassed royalty with armies at their disposal. What Aurelia wanted wouldn't matter to them when reputations were at risk.

William huffed a dry laugh. "And do you think they could steal you away? Never mind that you've so thoroughly convinced everyone in the Caribbean you're someone else. Do you think they'd even *try*?"

She didn't answer.

"Do you think I'd let them near you?" he breathed over her ear, and she shivered as his hands slid over her hips. "Do you think they could take you? Or that I wouldn't hunt them if they did?" As he spoke, his lips trailed from her ear to her jaw to her neck. "No one steals from me, Aurelia. So put it from your mind. Short of handing you over, Pierre has no hope."

Putting it from her mind wasn't as easy as he made it sound, whether or not he was the most fearsome pirate in the Atlantic. And while seducing her was a wonderful distraction, it didn't fix her worries. William frowned as she pulled away.

"Hand me over," she said, ignoring the delicious way her skin tingled along her neck. "Give me to Pierre."

He blinked. "I *beg* your pardon?"

"Like we talked about," she said, "on the beach."

His eyes tightened. "Aurelia, that wasn't...we weren't being serious."

"You said I could have any adventure I wanted, and it'll fix our problem with the French." When he only watched her with silent apprehension, she said, "I don't want to run or hide. I want them to leave me alone and never dare to even speak my name. And if you hand me over—"

"It was an intriguing idea, but in practice, it's another thing entirely. You are my *wife*, not some pawn to hand to another man—to Pierre, of all people—just to get some kings to look the other way."

Some kings. As though they were nothing. A non-issue. No more a threat than a cloudy sky. His nonchalance only emboldened her.

"I'm not a pawn," she said. "You made me a queen. And you'll get a pardon and money—why not outwit them and take everything?"

He shook his head. "A scheme like this requires more than barely an hour of dreaming on a beach."

"We'll have several weeks to plan on the way there."

"Ralph will never go for it. He'll kill us both."

"Ralph's too nice to kill us," she countered. "You can't tell me your brother is really what's keeping you from agreeing."

"You're right," he said. "I simply don't want to do it. I don't want to hand you over. If you get hurt—"

"They can't hurt me. I can do this, William. I *want* to do this." She took his hand and lifted it to her lips. "Let me wreck them," she whispered over his knuckles. "Let me ruin them and free us both."

It was the kind of thing a villain might say. As a child, she'd seldom imagined herself as such, but even a hero could only be pushed so far.

He hesitated. "When?"

"As soon as we can," she said, like she was the captain and not him.

"Thomas and George will argue about leaving so soon. They'll be less than enthused to tell their crews."

"Your crews love you. You're the immortal Captain Copson who finds treasure and charms witches and commands sea monsters. Your oddities and vague intentions are expected, and they'll go without question."

After a moment of weighing her words, he sighed. "Fine. I'll bow to your whims, since it seems I can't help it. But." He held up a finger and set it on the tip of her nose. "Since I'm agreeing, I want tonight. I'd intended to bring you home—this home—and make a big deal of it. So I'd love not to hear Pierre's name again, or a word of ruses or the French until the sun rises." His finger dropped to her lips. "Let me have tonight."

"No ruses, no French," she said with a grin. "Whatever you want."

"Just you," he said quietly, lowering his hand. "For three days, I've thought of bringing you back here as my wife. To welcome you to my home and refuge, which is made wholly better with you in it."

"This is my place now," she said evenly. Declaring it. The words harkened back to the last time they'd spoken in this room, but they weren't barbed, despite how they'd been spoken the first time.

William's blue eyes were sincere. "You are my equal, Aurelia. In all things. No matter what name you wear, stop me, interrupt me, tell me I'm a villain. Cross me if you believe you should. Do what you wish—you are the only one who may." He leaned in to brush his lips against hers. "But do be kind, love. Your wounds will strike deeper than anyone else's."

She settled her arms around his neck. "I only intend to love you, probably too much and potentially to my detriment."

He pulled back to look at her. "Your detriment? Forgive me for comparing, but you tortured me today, distracting me while I had work to do." He strummed his fingers over the ties lacing her front. "You, done up in all these knots and ties, and I could only think you were testing me."

She lifted an eyebrow. "Like you don't know your way around a knot." In fact, she'd chosen a very specific knot, hoping to make him wonder.

"I know my way, but my God, it's so tiny I'll need a lock pick."

She squealed as he buried his face in her neck, nipping at her ear. As she tried to twist out of his grip, her eyes caught on the black-swathed bed in the corner. The sight of it nearly made her sigh. While she'd enjoyed sleeping on the beach, she looked forward to a real mattress.

William followed her gaze. A lock of hair had fallen into his face, making him look recklessly handsome as he murmured, "Later," and claimed her lips with his.

One hand cradled the back of her head, the other on her hip as he kissed her deeply and took slow steps toward the couch by the hearth. When the backs of her knees met the cushion, William leaned into her, and she sank onto the seat.

He followed, gently pushing her onto her back and breathing, "Aurelia Kingswood, I haven't stopped thinking of the last time I held you here—and all the ways I'd still like to."

"You make me ridiculous," she whispered back, knowing to call herself such a thing with him was not an insult. "Senseless. Irrational."

His gaze dipped to the tie at the top of her stays, and he idly hooked his finger through the string next to the knot. "I like you that way." He met her gaze, and she saw every promise and plan he had for the night. "And I'll happily descend into foolishness at your side, so long as it pleases you."

She flushed, aware of every line of his body and how little space there was between them. "We talked about a door."

He kissed her, slow and taunting, then pulled back, his eyes blazing. "Patience, my love. I've got all night." Then with a smirk and a gentle tug, the knot pulled free.

32

Love He Hates, Hatred He Loves

Aurelia woke to the sound of the door latching, but she didn't open her eyes. Tangled in soft, emerald sheets, she drew in a deep, sleepy breath and sighed into her pillow. She would stay here forever, just like this, if she could.

The mattress dipped, and a calloused hand skimmed the bare skin between her shoulders. She opened one eye.

William sat beside her, lit by morning sun streaming through the windows. He held out a steaming mug. "I brought tea."

Aurelia sat up, holding the sheet against herself as she accepted the cup and leaned into his shoulder. She inhaled his sea-and-air scent, savoring him and his presence as he wound his arm around her and settled his hand on her lower back.

Six weeks had passed, and this morning they would board the *Ophelia* and take it into Calais. The smaller ship had docked for the night and already returned, judging by the neat stack of mail in his lap. On top of was a letter bearing the name *William C. Smith* written in her handwriting—her fourth plea for rescue from the prince, which he'd already opened.

Last night, several of the pirates had been eager to send off letters and money, and William sent a small pile of correspondence with everyone else's—including a letter to the prince saying he'd accepted the terms for Aurelia's surrender.

Getting him to accept the prince's ransom had been no small feat, as he'd given her conditions. He taught her to plan and cheat and steal as well as he could, set lies on her tongue, and spent hours teaching her sleight of hand until she was nearly as good as he was and could steal the rings off his fingers without him noticing. He'd even hidden her compass in an inner pocket of his coat, and she'd stolen that back too.

If she could master swiping trinkets off a paranoid pirate, she could do the same to a prideful prince, and chances were lower that she'd land herself in jail. William could get her out if that happened, of course, but it would come with a fair bit of swearing.

Anticipation weighed on her this morning. It wasn't heavy like dread or trepidation, but it sang along every nerve. Clinging to William made her blood sing for a different reason, and she nestled into his embrace for as long as she could have it.

"I'll miss the *Destiny*," she said.

He gave a low laugh. "Only our ship?"

"I'll miss you," she said, quiet enough for him to hear the weight of just how much she would. When she kissed him to prove it, he groaned.

"God," he said against her lips. "I'm a fool for letting you go."

"You'd be a fool not to with a pardon and riches on the line." She leaned away. "Besides, you won't be far."

"I'll be everything short of living in his house." He took her chin in his fingers. "But if anything happens, get out. Fight, kill as many as you have to—I don't care."

Aurelia didn't like the idea of killing, but she was capable enough. "I'll be fine."

"If I have reason to believe you're in trouble, I'm taking you back." He said it like a threat, though it was one she'd heard a hundred times already. "And I'll murder whoever stands in the way of me getting to you."

"Oh, how you make my toes curl," she said with a note of whimsy.

William crushed her to his chest. She allowed herself a pause to enjoy the last few moments of his embrace before saying, "I'm ready if you are."

He released her and stood, flashing a lazy smile. "Let's ruin a prince."

By late morning, they were in Calais, hidden inside a carriage trundling toward the outskirts of the city. Aurelia had dressed her hair in an elegant twist and donned a light blue gown, while William sat across from her looking every bit like a swashbuckling pirate in his long black coat and tricorn hat.

They rode in silence until the city fell away, their eyes lingering on each other or the windows. Open fields sprawled on one side of the road, and on the other was a copse of trees with long branches that hung low. Sunlight streamed through colorful, early-autumn leaves and cast dancing shadows over the carriage.

They couldn't be far from where they'd meet the prince, and despite her readiness, Aurelia grew more nervous the longer they traveled. William, too, seemed oddly reserved.

She slipped off her wedding ring and held it between them. "Get your pardon," she said, meeting his gaze. "Collect your reward."

He didn't take it immediately, his gaze and demeanor hesitant. "You're sure about this." She nodded. "It's not too late. We can still turn back."

It was a careful offer—not a request or even a suggestion. Just a mere reminder that the option was there. But the money exchanged today represented her life and her heart, and if it should belong to anyone, it was herself. And William.

"I want to do this," she replied evenly. "I'll be fine."

William plucked the ring from her hand. It disappeared into his coat.

A shout came from outside, and the carriage halted abruptly. William set his hand on the door latch, then leaned in to crushed his lips to hers in a short, rough kiss.

"I love you desperately," he said. "And I shall miss you terribly."

He got out of the carriage. For a moment, he stood in the road, looking at what had stopped them. Then he faced the door and extended his hand.

It was time.

With deep breath, she set her fingers in William's and let him pull her from the carriage. Greyson and Hester sat in the driver's seat, and flanking the vehicle were Ralph and Lavinia astride a pair of horses. They wore long, heavy coats concealing a multitude of guns, just in case the prince chose not to honor the agreement of Aurelia's surrender—which she pretended to know nothing about as she strode forward with her hand curled tightly into the inside of William's elbow. He held her fingers there, as though to keep her from fleeing.

Another man stood in the middle of the road wearing a rich shade of plum. Behind him was a small army, all of them dressed in blue.

Aurelia stiffened. "What is this?" she asked, her voice thin and trembling. For now, she was not a Kingswood. She was the sweet, harmless Danby girl who was ridiculous enough to believe a pirate king could ever love her. There were stars in her eyes, and every ounce of her foolish trust had been invested into a liar and a thief.

"Don't be afraid," William said with an awful little smile. He tugged her along until she fell back into step with him. "He likes that."

The man in purple looked to be around thirty with long blond hair tied with a fat bow at the nape of his neck. His face was thin with a pointed chin and gray eyes. And despite having heels on his shoes, he still wasn't as tall as William.

"Thank you for returning my bride," the prince said in a heavy French accent.

"I didn't do it for free," William said coldly, stopping several feet away. "I'm assuming you agreed to my terms, Pierre?"

"What are you doing?" Aurelia demanded in a breathy voice, like she was horrified.

The corner of William's lips lifted, and his gaze held not one measure of chagrin or sadness—only unbothered arrogance. "Sorry, love."

"No!" She attempted to rip herself from his grip. "Please, you said you wouldn't make me go back. You *can't*."

William's strong arm snaked around her waist and hauled her back to his side. He cupped her chin, his fingers skimming over her hammering pulse. "Don't fret, love." She curled her fingers into his coat, like she could anchor herself to him forever as he turned back to the prince and said, "Well?"

Pierre's smile had disappeared. He swallowed and slowly lowered himself to the dusty road where, on his knees, he quietly admitted, "Captain Copson, you have bested—"

"Louder," William commanded.

The prince cleared his throat and started again, raising his voice for everyone to hear. "Captain Copson, you have bested me in all things, and I deserve every humiliation you've wrought."

Behind them, Lavinia snorted. William wore a devilish grin. "And?"

"*And*," Pierre said, his voice thick, "it is only because of your generosity that you have brought my fiancée home to me. And I will be," he gulped, "forever in your debt. Whatever you ask for, you will receive. You are pardoned by the crown now and forevermore."

"Wonderful," William said. "I suppose you've earned your bride."

As Pierre rose, a solider broke from the ranks and strode toward her.

Aurelia lurched, frantically clinging to William and pleading, "No, Copson, no, *please*, no!"

The moment the soldier took her arm, she started screaming. William let her go, his eyes vacant of any tenderness or affection.

And then he *pushed* her away, as though she were nothing. As though she were not the very weapon they would use to shame kings and armies and Aurelia's wicked parents. Aurelia screamed for William as though she wished to stay with him. She hollered like she couldn't bear to be parted from him, knowing the prince would love every second of her pain.

Because he was a devil and a child and a fiend who enjoyed his women broken.

"She was fun for a while," William said to Pierre. "She's a pretty little thing."

Aurelia crashed to the ground as her legs buckled, but the guard was there, holding her arms to keep her from running off. "Copson," she gasped. "Please don't do this."

William didn't spare her a glance. "I dislike you terribly, Pierre, so I hope you'll allow me this one last wound." He spoke smoothly, his eyes lacking anything but mirthful vengeance. "When I took her from you, I only meant to amuse myself at your expense. But encouraging and indulging her affections became a much more interesting game—especially knowing that now, every time she looks at you, you'll know she wishes it was me. Your name is not the one she will sigh in the night, and when she looks at her children, she'll wish they were mine. And every time you see your pretty, broken wife and her anguish at your inadequacies, you will remember—again and again—that you are a fool who could not best me."

Pierre said nothing as Aurelia wept. The tears were almost too easy to call to the surface, and their genuineness surprised her. They were not because she was leaving William, though that was reason enough to cry. No, the tears were because she mourned. She'd been a girl exchanged between countries for an alliance with no consideration to her heart. Now that she'd been loved so fully, this charade revealed just how little she'd been loved before.

What fertile ground for vengeance to thrive.

William strolled closer and crouched before her. With one finger, he lifted her chin, forcing her to meet his gaze. He studied her tears, surely knowing they were more real than they should have been.

"You said you loved me," she said weakly, in an effort to explain what he was seeing without revealing their game. "You loved me, and they don't, and you promised to keep me. You *promised*—" Her voice broke on a sob. "They never loved me like you did."

"You poor, silly girl." His smile was cold, and his voice turned to ice. "That was the point."

She'd never seen this side of William, and it left her awestruck and hollow. "You said—"

"Remember who I am. Who you've known I was this whole time. I'm a pirate—*the* pirate." He leaned in, like he was about to kiss her, his blue eyes blazing. "I'm a liar."

His words sounded so real that they twisted her insides. All the while, he merely watched, clean and unruffled while she sat in the dust with tears streaking her face and her hair falling from its coil.

What an incredible liar he was.

Her shoulders heaved with another sob. His image blurred, and she blinked away the tears. They ran down her face to where his finger touched her skin, and they slipped into his palm. Like he was collecting them.

"Please—" she started, but William cut her off.

"Say my name," he said in a voice like a lover's, his words like silk. "One last time. Say it, and I'll take you back."

Her breath stilled. His expression remained serene, but his eyes were intent. Behind him, Lavinia's hand disappeared into her coat. The prince shifted at Aurelia's back, and his little army gripped their swords tighter.

It was another offer, like in the carriage. Not a suggestion. Not a request. If Aurelia wanted to change her mind, she could, and they'd fight their way out.

"Say it," William said with a taunting edge. "Just as you have so many times—like you love the taste of it. Like it's precious to you, *Aurelia*."

He said her name in the same way he told her he loved her—softly and truly. So cruel...he might have been so cruel had she not heard his true intent beneath the layers of lies.

More tears spilled down her face. The kings and her family might not love her. Neither did the prince. But William did, and so did his family of pirates.

She never looked away from him and his blithe arrogance as she whispered the wrong name. "Copson."

He chuckled lowly and flicked his finger off her chin. "Foolish girl."

"Copson," the prince said as Aurelia sobbed. "Please."

William's lips twitched, and something troubled and truly hateful flickered over his face, nearly too quick to catch before his easy grin returned. "If I left something for you to break, Pierre, this wouldn't be nearly as satisfying." He stood. "But alas, I have what I want."

"Your payment will be at the harbor," Pierre said flatly, eager to have him gone. "No one will give you trouble."

"Fantastic. I truly hope to never see you again." William turned for his carriage.

At the sight of his retreating figure, Aurelia shouted and shrieked like a woman possessed, begging and cursing in equal measure, saying everything but his name. But for all her bawling and hysterics, William never looked back. His carriage turned around and took off, the shades drawn.

The soldier pulled Aurelia to her feet and half carried her to the royal carriage. He lifted her inside and hesitated after taking his hands away, prepared for her to run.

She only pulled her feet up onto the seat and curled into the corner, quietly sobbing.

"*Je vais m'occuper d'elle*," the prince said, limping to his own seat. *I will take care of her.*

The soldier shut the door. As the carriage started moving, Pierre slipped a silk handkerchief from his coat and handed it to her. The smell of his flowery perfume permeated the small space. "Do you speak French?" he asked.

She shook her head. She did speak French, in fact, but she didn't want him to know it.

He nodded once. "You are safe now."

Aurelia held his gaze through swollen eyes. An odd little grin spread over his face, and he looked down to hide it.

It didn't take long to arrive to his country estate, which was ostentatious and roomy and held far too many servants. Maids swept Aurelia into a suite where they bathed her and brushed her hair and told her how pretty she was. They gave her new gowns and hung diamonds from her ears, then held a mirror before her with hopes it would cheer her.

She did not satisfy them with smiles or answer their questions. She thanked them for none of their attempted sympathies as they said *that must have been so frightening* and *thank God he brought you back*.

When they finally left her, she dried her tears, sagged into a chair, and looked out the window toward the sea beyond the horizon. She touched the turtle pendant at her throat, sighed, and said to herself, "Now we begin."

33

A House of Mirth

Of all the characters Aurelia had pretended to be in her lifetime, this was the one she knew best and liked least.

Aurelia Danby.

Her old name fit like child's clothing, itchy and small, and she remembered what it was to be caged, her dreams dead and gone and ripped from her as violently as one might lose an arm or a leg or a head. She was a princess locked in a castle, the ghost of Rebecca Rowe, a helpless young woman with too much money and tragically little sense.

Since the prince was known for liking sad, broken women, she embodied this wretched girl from the moment she entered his home. During the first week, she sulked, wandering the garden or sitting quietly with whatever books she could find in English. She spoke little and stared out windows while she waited and listened and watched.

And while he reveled in her misery, he was fantastically blind to the fact that she was studying him.

If one might tell another's character, they had to look no further than their friends—and Pierre's made her feel like breaking into hives. This ever-present group of ladies and gentlemen lived at the estate, and wherever Aurelia went, there they were, pointing and whispering behind their fans. They wore heaps of white powder on their cheeks and garish clothes they'd been sewn into, but had the nerve to look at

Aurelia as though she was the one dressed as a clown. Believing she knew no French, they teased her stature, her speech, and the color of her cheeks. They called her "pirate wench" and flashed yellow teeth through snickers and snorts.

Pierre was not so blatant—at first. But thanks to his friends, it only took a matter of days for Aurelia to discover why he'd gone to such lengths to have her.

It was childish, really—Pierre's fascination with pirates nearly rivaled Aurelia's own. But while she loved adventure and intrigue, his interest was rooted in horrific pride and deep insecurity, which wasn't surprising for being the fourth son of a king. As the least significant person in his family, he craved fame, and with the rise of piracy and its prominence in the papers, his name next to Copson's was exactly what he wanted, and Aurelia was his ticket to get it.

"I am a hero!" he drunkenly declared one night at dinner as he stood on his chair and planted a boot on the table, raising his wine in salute while all his friends cheered. "And that dirty pirate is a fiend. He may hate me as much as he wishes, but he will never best me, and everyone shall know it!"

Since his friends were leeches who liked his money and luxury, they only massaged his ego because there was much to gain from it.

"You saved the pirate wench!" one declared. "All hail your money and royal blood!"

Pierre chortled and preened as they mocked Aurelia when they thought she could not understand. Then he gifted her a ring. It was the largest diamond she'd ever seen, and he even got down on one knee to slip it onto her empty finger where it glittered like a pretentious little paperweight. All his friends with their painted, powdered faces applauded and fawned and pretended to cry with happiness.

She channeled her disgust into the appearance of misery that she might wear like an ugly frock, and he loved it because it reminded him that he was famous.

Aurelia only allowed this mask to slip at night when she wandered the halls. Guards patrolled the bottom level of the home, leaving her to haunt the higher corridors. On one of these nights at the start of the second week in his home, she passed Pierre's room to hear the sound of him quite engaged with one of the ladies who lived in his house.

And judging by all she heard the following three nights, it was a common occurrence between the prince and most of his lady friends.

She was delighted, then, that he was occupied while she found her way into his study and picked the locks on his desk, and she felt no remorse at all as she pulled out all his financial statements and began poring over them, looking for secrets William had taught her how to find.

She missed him terribly—her heart stabbed at the memory of sitting beside him as he showed her his log books and explained all the ways one might discover hidden payments and debts of those who were up to no good.

Then her heart thrilled shortly after as she found several incriminating expenses and evidence of extensive gambling. Over the next few nights, she set to copying them and filing them back into place as though they'd never been touched. Then she hid the copies within several-page love letters written in French that were signed *Marie*, as there were several Maries serving in the prince's house, and the letters wouldn't be traced back to Aurelia if they were found. She and printed the name *Guillaume C. Lefebvre* on the front along with William's address in Calais and hid the envelopes among the outgoing mail.

Days passed, and the prince's behavior grew steadily worse. He had newspapers brought from England, which he and his friends left out for her to see the headlines about Captain Copson and his antics in North Africa. The pirate was a favorite topic among Pierre's household, but while they laughed behind her back at their snide little jokes, Aurelia sat quietly with a book of fairy tales and learned their schedules.

And then Pierre threw a ball.

Like everything he did, it was a disgusting affair. His house filled with disgusting people who drank disgusting amounts of alcohol and ate disgusting quantities of food. Everyone came in costume, though Pierre took it as an opportunity to dress entirely in gold—even going so far as to paint his skin—while outfitting her in a silver gown that washed her out and made her look on the verge of death.

His friends dressed as fancy pirates with tiny ships set in their blue-powdered hair, and they drunkenly joked about piracy to anyone who would listen.

It seemed everyone in Calais had come to gawk as Pierre put Aurelia on display, even announcing her as his famed pirate bride whom he'd saved in such spectacular fashion with all his money and power—and saying nothing of getting on his knees in the dirt while Copson humiliated him. His guests *ooh*ed and *ahh*ed and congratulated him.

Aurelia gripped her champagne flute hard enough to break the stem.

Her first taste of revenge came soon enough. Halfway through the party, when most of the guests had arrived, a young woman swept through the door.

This would not have been strange, if she were dressed like everyone else. But she wore homespun clothing and holding the hand of a four-year-old boy. Upon seeing Pierre, the woman began profusely thanking him and pushing the child his way while the horrified and considerably drunk prince backed away in a panic and summoned guards to remove the woman and the child.

As it turned out, the woman was a former maid, and the child was his bastard. Somehow when invitations for the ball had gone out, one had also gone to her with a note saying the prince would provide for her son.

There was no saying who had written it—or who'd even known of the child after all Pierre had done to hide his indiscretion. But the staff knew everything, and Aurelia sent the invitation—and a sack of money she'd stolen—after overhearing the maids gossip about how much they pitied her for marrying a man such as him.

This first child's arrival might have been bad enough, but then a second woman came not twenty minutes later with a little girl. The prince paled and hid her away as well, but not quickly enough to avoid two more mothers who showed up with more illegitimate children in tow.

By then, the whole party knew Pierre had sired multiple children who had now paraded before his betrothed. Unbeknownst to everyone—including Pierre—these women and their children had been given large sums of the prince's money for their trouble, and they would continue to receive money long after tonight. Enough to support them for the rest of their lives.

Only Aurelia knew, and she delighted in it. Regardless, she used their presence as an excuse to leave early—she'd never liked parties anyway.

On her way out, a tall, hooded man bumped into her. There was a glint of laughing blue eyes beneath his green hood and the brush of a warm hand against hers. He flashed a cunning smile and slipped a letter into her pocket before vanishing into the crowd.

The envelope was sealed with the Danby crest, and when she opened it in her room, it read in in familiar looping, slightly jagged script,

All arrangements have been made. How sweet it shall be to see you in two weeks' time.

Burn after reading

Thus began her third week in Pierre's insufferable presence.

The morning after the ball, a butler leaned close to the prince's ear at breakfast, his face drawn with worry as he said, "Your Highness, it appears one of the smaller paintings in the gallery has gone missing. The one with the dancing lady you purchased last summer."

The prince's eyes widened. "I paid dearly for that. Tell me it's not *gone*."

Aurelia stared into her eggs and pretended to be sad. She knew the one he spoke of—it was a lovely piece of art. It was also very expensive, and a very unfortunate loss indeed. Especially since one of the ladies, Lady Almary, had recently discovered—through an anonymous note Aurelia had slid under her door—that the prince said she was his least favorite lover because of her awkward body and exuberant puffing during their extracurricular activities.

The day Lady Almary found out (due to an anonymous note Aurelia had slid under her door) she'd been so angry her face had turned a violent shade of red, visible even beneath the layers of powder. She'd made her anger everyone's problem, and then—wouldn't you believe it—it was the *same* day the painting went missing and wads of money were discovered in her jewelry box.

Lady Almary was removed from the house shortly after the butler told the prince. Pierre didn't help matters by saying she was, in fact, his favorite lover in front of his other lovers who then lost their taste for him. This misery compounded as all his friends began blaming each other for inviting so many scorned mothers to the ball so that they might not be implicated for the transgression and be turned out as well, and they achieved a satisfactory level chaos before noon.

Of course, everything was said in French, so they assumed Aurelia was ignorant to it.

The next thing to go missing was a priceless vase one of the lords often joked about stealing. The prince didn't remove him, but there was tension that night at dinner. Some of the ladies had also misplaced many pieces of priceless jewelry, although they didn't know it yet because they were still rather angry with the drama surrounding Lady Almary and Pierre's bastard children.

Meanwhile, Aurelia kept reading and sulking and staring forlornly out windows as the wedding approached. She even read while she walked the halls, and used it as an excuse to clumsily bump into Pierre's friends and sneak trinkets from pockets and watches off wrists.

During the fourth week, Pierre came to some sense, but not about anything that would help him socially or financially. As his lovers abandoned their nighttime trysts, the prince seemed to realize the only woman he hadn't bothered seeking would be his wife in a week. And then came his pathetic attempt to woo her.

He limped into Aurelia's room one night with a posture that reminded her of a nervous cat. It was bold of him to enter alone, but as it was his house and everyone in it was so abhorrently casual with such things, Aurelia was not surprised.

Her book remained open on her lap, exposing a black-and-white drawing of a wolf leering at a child.

Pierre's eyes went to it before he attempted a grin that looked more patronizing than he probably intended. "You find comfort in your little stories?"

"I do," she answered simply.

He settled in a plush chair next to hers, his unbound blond hair turning yellow in the firelight where it cascaded over his green velvet robe. Then he reached into his pocket and produced a small letter with a broken seal.

Copson's name was scrawled across the back in her pretty handwriting, addressed to the harbor they'd sailed into. In it, she'd written that she loved him and believed they could still be together. She'd written like a besotted, foolish girl in love—a pining lady with no malice and no thoughts in her head but him.

The letter was never meant to reach William. She'd wanted Pierre to find it, because it would be undoubtedly irritating for him to learn his soon-to-be wife was still yearning for her pirate love after he'd so brutally scorned her.

Aurelia frowned, and he had the decency to look genuinely pitying. "Even if it had managed to leave the house," he said gently, "it never would have made it to him. He is in Africa, and he will not come back for you."

Pierre tossed the silly letter into the hearth, and Aurelia called tears to her eyes as she watched it burn.

"He loves me," she whispered.

He seemed to realize then that a hungry gaze was not seductive in this setting, and it turned into something akin to sympathy. "He does not," he said softly, and she couldn't despise him for it. He thought it was true.

"He told me he does," Aurelia said, stronger now. "I know he does."

"This marriage was arranged for me as well," he told her softly, "and I have chosen to see the best in it. So should you, and spare yourself the pain of wanting."

"Spare myself," she repeated. "How can I not want him?"

To his credit, he blushed. "Well...I am here. And I am not so bad." He smiled, and she thanked the Lord his teeth were not despicable like his friends'.

Her tears dissipated. "Are you propositioning me?" Now her voice came high and girly, like she was unaware of a man's advances and was delighted to have guessed the situation correctly.

Pierre's smile widened. "I suppose. Since we are to be married in a few days' time—"

"Not as though the lack of marriage has bothered you," Aurelia said, her eyes wide and innocent. "I thought you might've come to me sooner, but I wonder if you haven't because you're afraid."

His expression shuttered. "How do you mean?"

She gripped the edges of her book and looked down at the fluffy wolf and the silly little child. "Well, Copson was right, wasn't he? Every time I look at you, I wish you were him. And...every time you look at me, surely you must know that."

Pierre's nostrils flared, and his voice changed, becoming harder. "So desperate for the man who betrayed you?"

It might've behooved her to quiver and cower, but while she knew Pierre was a bad man, she was also sure he was a coward. And if it turned out that he was not, then there were several things in her vicinity she could use to fight him—her book, the fire poker, a letter opener on the desk. And what with his limp, she supposed he wouldn't be difficult to outrun.

"You haven't allowed me an opportunity to see anyone else worth wanting," she said, "especially when you go to such lengths to remind me of him."

"I see," Pierre licked his lips, "that I must beg your forgiveness."

"You have plenty of time to earn it before you marry me," Aurelia said, flapping the book's covers like a little bird's wings in her lap. "And then perhaps I'll consider you."

"I see," he said again. Then he stood, bowed, and bid her goodnight.

When the door snicked shut, Aurelia waited a few seconds before she giggled to herself and turned the page.

Pierre began behaving differently the next morning. There were no more jokes or teasing, no papers left out with headlines meant to remind her of her pain. She received flowers and cordial conversation, and stacks of English books were delivered to her door.

And when courtiers arrived to show her all the royal jewels she might wear to the wedding, she was so overwhelmed by the options that she asked the servants to leave them in her room until she made up her mind. The prince was okay with this because she was simple and sad and read so many fairy tales. And he wanted her now, more than he did before, and was willing to behave to get her.

It distracted him well enough that he didn't think to consider she was robbing him blind. And for all his foolishness, his gluttony, pride, immorality, and idiocy—and all number of sins besides—Aurelia considered his severe limp and rejoiced at how much he deserved it. And if the Lord would punish her for this thought, she was willing to accept the consequences.

Whatever she deserved wouldn't be as horrid as a bullet to the leg.

34

The Unfortunate Death of Aurelia Danby

No one knew Aurelia existed until Captain Copson made her relevant.

It was a truth that had not been so stark until the beautiful, cloudless morning of the royal wedding. She was the woman stolen by a pirate, and fascination pulled the public from their homes to crowd the streets, waving flags and buying sweet buns and spiced drinks to celebrate their soon-to-be princess.

People from all over France came to Calais to see her, and soldiers held back happy crowds as she passed in a gilded carriage drawn by a team of six white horses.

She checked her bejeweled watch and glanced at a smirking Lavinia, who'd arrived this morning disguised as an attendant among a team of ladies charged with fussing and preparing Aurelia for her wedding.

"You look dreadful," she said, and Aurelia agreed.

It was strange to be dressed as the storybook princess she'd once wanted to be, decked in a heavy gold gown and dripping with diamonds, her blonde hair done in curls and pinned into a complicated coiffure held behind an awe-inspiring tiara. Of all the hours she'd spent acting out this very scenario as a child, she'd never once considered she might be bored.

She suppressed a yawn. Four weeks she'd spent in Pierre's house with his flock of flouncing subjects, and she'd counted every hour, each minute, until this very day. Her time here was dwindling, and the end couldn't come fast enough.

She arrived at the church to the sound of deafening applause. The carriage door opened to reveal Ralph dressed as a footman in spectacular white livery trimmed in blue and gold. He winked at her as he took her hand and helped her out of the carriage.

Aurelia mounted the church steps between neat lines of guards, knowing she should smile and wave and doing neither.

Inside the church, she nearly didn't recognize her father. She'd barely seen him as a child, and her memories of him were very nearly faceless, having worn away at the edges. The man preparing to walk her down the aisle had light hair that turned silver at the temples, and a round, red face that spoke of too many drinks and revelry for too many years. His bright, expensive clothes stretched over a belly that made the same statement as his face.

She assumed he only recognized her because she looked like a bride.

"Your mother and I were beside ourselves to hear of your return," the Duke of Danby said.

She smiled but did not dignify him with an answer.

Pierre stood at the altar, looking every bit like a thrilled groom and smiling like he hadn't been snogging one of the maids in the corridor this morning. Aurelia had graciously said nothing of it, and he hadn't noticed when she'd slipped his golden watch from his pocket an hour later.

Trumpets hailed her arrival, and once again, she was struck by the sense she'd stepped into a fairy tale—just not the one she wanted.

She lightly held the duke's arm, meeting the prince's gaze to keep herself from checking her timepiece again.

When they ascended the steps to the altar ages later, the trumpets quieted, and the duke handed her to the prince. Pierre's fingers were clammy, soft, and weak.

She shivered, her hand limp as a dead fish in Pierre's.

Her parents sat in the front row, her mother dressed like a tropical bird and smiling proudly at the daughter she didn't know. The king and queen of France sat on the other side, looking bored. Guests Aurelia didn't recognize dabbed their eyes, happy to witness this attempted robbery of her freedom, agency, and dreams.

As soon as the sanctuary fell silent, the priest turned around, revealing a clean-shaven, wise face and a ridiculous number of crucifixes—one hung from his neck, two from his ears, two on his wrists, and, if she had to guess, there were two more around his ankles.

She swallowed her smile as Fenner's voice carried through the church, and counted the stones beneath her feet to keep her composure.

The minutes ticked by, and more passed than she would have liked. She was beginning to itch when the massive doors swung open on squealing hinges and thudded against the walls. Fenner's sermon cut off, and the guards remained still as a final guest strolled down the aisle in a long black coat and tricorn hat.

"Apologies for my tardiness," Copson announced. A gun dangled from his hand, and Aurelia's heart swelled at the sight of him. "I do like to be on time, but it seems my invitation was lost."

Gasps erupted from the crowd. They scrambled back in their pews, edging away from the notorious, immortal captain. Pierre's eyes grew wide as Copson swaggered toward the altar.

"Unless you didn't send an invitation at all," Copson said, his voice ringing through the high ceilings and filling the sanctuary, "which would be very rude, considering I delivered you a bride. Not that I planned to attend, but an invitation is common *decency*."

He stopped a few rows away from the front, swinging his gun in twitching fingers. When no one spoke, he turned in a full circle, observing the guests. "I've never been to a royal wedding, but it doesn't seem very exciting. You all look so somber." He gestured to a lady with his gun. "Don't frown on my account."

The woman's eyes fluttered before she slumped, unconscious, onto her neighbor. Pierre's sweaty hand tightened around Aurelia's, and she realized she'd unconsciously shifted her weight toward the pirate.

"We had an agreement," the prince said in a shaky voice. "I have no business with you."

Copson raised his brows. "Oh, I didn't come for you—I didn't even think of you, actually. I've come for her." He looked at Aurelia, and his tone turned mocking. "Hello, Aurelia. How nice it is to see you again."

Hello, William, she yearned to say. *I've missed you dearly.*

Pierre's voice rang through the church. "Guards!" Sweat bloomed over his brow, clumping the white powder. "Shoot him!"

Aurelia's heart stuttered as the guards raised their weapons and aimed—not at Copson, but at the prince.

Pierre's grip on her hand loosened, and she stumbled away, out of the range of so many guns.

When William left her, he hadn't told her how he'd get her back—only that he would, on her wedding day. But this...she looked around the church, at all those soldiers, all those barrels pointed at Pierre, and no one was surprised aside from the unarmed congregation—and Aurelia.

Copson wore a lethal grin. "*Ohh*, now that's rather interesting."

"What have you done?" the prince demanded, his words weak with terror.

"Nothing at all, your highness," Copson said magnanimously. "I certainly didn't spend the last few weeks finding the guards to be posted at your wedding and pay them off while painstakingly installing my own men all over your city to act as your military so I could very publicly steal Lady Danby all over again to your embarrassment and my infamy. Only a madman would attempt such a feat." His smile turned maniacal. "I did nothing of the sort."

The prince fumed. The crowd murmured. The king and queen cowered in their seats.

Aurelia relaxed. A madman indeed.

"After I sailed away with your money and my pardon," Copson said, "I felt rather bored. It was too easy, you see. Everyone got what they wanted—the prince marries the girl, makes her a princess, and everyone rejoices that the savage pirate found it in his black heart to let you both have your happy ending."

He looked at Aurelia again, his blue gaze piercing. "But I wasn't interested in a story ending well," he said. "So I changed my mind."

Her pulse quickened as her heart sighed. She wanted to lose herself in his eyes—now that they were focused on her after four long weeks, she felt like she could breathe.

"You've involved yourself far too much, *pirate*," Pierre spat. "Have you not taken enough from me? From us?"

"Of course, I could let you get married and *then* take her." Copson carelessly waved his gun as he spoke, and the congregants flinched as the barrel swung in their direction. "But I assume this affair will be dreadfully long, and unfortunately I am on a schedule—and my patience is already spectacularly thin today."

The prince stomped his foot. "No! You gave her to me. You are done with her. She is mine—*mine!*"

Aurelia flushed. Copson's lips pulled into a scowl, and he drifted forward, his eyes shadowed under his hat. By the time he reached the steps to the altar, however, the expression was hidden behind a mocking smile. "Yours," he said, and ice hung from the word. "Perhaps we let the lady choose. After all, I charmed her once, and she seemed to enjoy it." His gaze slid to her. "Perhaps you'll enjoy it again, *my lady*."

She called tears to her eyes, whispering, "Copson, please." *Please take me home...*

His lips split into a wicked smile and his words carried a taunt. "Oh, think of all the fun we might have together. You warmed to me before." He turned on his heel, facing the Danbys in the first row. They cowered as he aimed his gun at the duke's face.

"Perhaps that's your fault," he said, pulling back the hammer with his thumb until it clicked. "After you abandoned her and sold her off to an idiot who would've surely given her some terribly itchy disease. She hardly needed any convincing to sail away with me the first time. *Me*, Danby!"

His tone had grown colder—truly cold, in a way that was not congruent with the game he played. He was still the evil pirate captain, but some of William Kingswood leaked into his mask, revealing the anger of the boy who'd always cared for her when everyone else forgot she existed. Aurelia ought to have stopped him...but she didn't want to.

The duke cried, "Kill him!"

"Someone!" pleaded the duchess, cowering beside her husband, but everyone had been scared into silence. The guards kept their guns trained on the prince.

"How hopeless you must make her," Copson seethed at the Danbys, his voice filling the sanctuary, "to make a murdering pirate seem like a better choice than this withered royal oaf who has most undoubtedly found such sick delight in her misery."

The prince sputtered. "I would never—" He cut off as Copson's gun turned on him.

"*Shut up*," Copson spat.

It was too much—too close to the truth. He tread dangerously toward revealing his heart, if he hadn't already. So Aurelia finally spoke up, her voice thin as she said, "A better choice? You threatened to kill everyone on that ship if I hadn't gone with you." She drew a shaky breath. "You didn't convince me—you forced me."

Copson's gaze swept down the length of her body. There was madness in his eyes now, hiding his heart safely behind insanity. "They're similar enough, and pleasantly effective. I always get what I want, so perhaps I'll try it again."

The guns shifted then, aiming at the congregants now. Aurelia's gasp was lost beneath the screams that ripped through the church.

"Come with me, Aurelia," Copson said over their cries, "or paint this church with blood. Your choice."

"It's not a *choice*," she hissed, though her heart sang.

"You won't take her!" Pierre cried, drawing his sword. It was ceremonial and awkwardly balanced with the amount of decoration on it. He certainly didn't know how to wield it, judging by...well, everything.

Copson sneered. "God, you're irritating." He pulled the trigger, and blood exploded from the prince's arm.

Pierre's sword clattered to the floor as he screamed and fell to his knees, clapping his hand over the grisly wound. Cries and shouts carried through the church, but no one moved to help him. The king and queen had sunk from their seats and now cowered behind a pew. Fenner was gone entirely.

Then Copson was at Aurelia's side, his hand wrapped tightly around her arm, and his eyes reckless and blue and as lovely as they'd always been. "Ship's waiting," he said, then he steered her down the aisle, past terrified guests who watched in disbelief while Pierre's howling rang through the church. The guards never lowered their weapons.

At the front doors, a sea of spectators greeted her appearance with a roar. Copson held her at the top of the steps, letting the crowd see her, see that *he* had her. She tried to pull away, but he tugged her down the stairs and shoved her into the carriage as joyful cries turned to screaming.

The crowd began to roil, but no one could reach the carriage as it was surrounded by soldiers who seemed to pay no mind to the infamous captain with their prince's bride. Like they'd been paid off.

The door slammed shut, and Copson sank into the seat across from her, still fully in view of the crowds through the wide windows.

"Still open to murder?" he asked.

She pushed back into the cushion. "Yes."

He lifted his gun. As he cocked it, she cried, "*No, please!*"

The gun went off, and blood sprayed over the window. Aurelia Danby jerked and slumped in her seat.

For a heartbeat, everything fell silent enough for the crowd to hear Copson bark, "Drive!" The carriage took off, surrounded by men who seemed oblivious to the murderer and the dead almost-princess in their midst.

The screams began, but Copson only smiled.

35

The Rise of Rebecca Rowe

Death was a marvelously useful way to thwart kings, which was why Aurelia had chosen to fake her own as the grand finale to her ruse.

Pig blood dripped from the small vessel set over her seat, which Ralph and Lavinia had quickly installed as everyone was too distracted watching Aurelia walk up the steps to be married. Now chaos erupted outside as people saw the dark streams of blood on the window and the pirate inside with a lump that looked like a corpse. The carriage wound through the crowd with men dressed in blue marching before and behind, undeterred by shrieks and fainting ladies and screaming men.

William's hands braced Aurelia's waist, helping her turn her body as she stayed low and out of sight.

"You told me shooting Pierre was too *one-note*," Aurelia said by way of greeting.

"I didn't think you'd object." He pulled a knife and cut through the buttons of her dress in a swift stroke. She shoved the sleeves to her wrists and freed herself from the mounds of silk and petticoats until she was only in her stays and shift. A satchel was tied around her waist under her dress, and now she loosened it and let it drop to the floor. Precious metals and jewels clanked inside.

William pulled away the golden dress and handed over folded pants and a shirt. On top of the shirt was his knife, which she used to saw through the front of her stays, careful not to cut herself as the carriage bumped and jostled. "I don't object. I just—ugh!" She grunted at the knife and the awkward angle.

William took it from her hand, sliced down the front of the undergarment, and tore it open. Then he pulled it away to add to the heap of wedding garb. "If you say I shouldn't have done it," he said, "I'll be very cross with you. And I don't want to be cross when I've just gotten you back."

"I won't say it." Aurelia awkwardly slipped into her pants and shirt from the carriage floor before tugging the final bits of flowy undergarments through the neck, which she placed into his waiting hand. "But what about your pardon?"

"Revenge is non-negotiable, and I can live without pardons. Besides, I've got the money." He took her hand and slipped off the prince's diamond. "And the girl." Her gold wedding band slid into place.

She grabbed the boots next to her and slipped them on. As she did, William pulled the diamonds from her ears and neck. She worked the tiara free from her hair and dumped it into the satchel, and William's hands came beside hers, gently combing away jeweled pins.

Then she set to work braiding her hair as it usually was. By the time she reached the end, William held out a small leather tie. She plucked it from his fingers, and as soon as she'd tied off her braid, he hooked his finger under her chin and tipped her face up.

"I missed you," he said. He pecked her lips and sat back, spreading his arms over the back of the bench seat. "And I'm never doing that again."

Still hiding on the floor, she patted the satchel with a grin. "Not even for a bag of priceless royal jewels? They gave me a choice of what I could wear today, and I stole every single piece they showed me."

His gaze went to the crowds who screamed with excitement and then horror as they saw the blood they assumed was Aurelia's dripping into mounds of gold silk. "Not for anything, Aurelia."

She took his hand. "It was only a game."

"And as much as I enjoy games, I did not like this one."

She studied his face, the dark circles beneath his eyes, and the stubble shadowing his jaw and cheeks. "William, are you cross with me?"

He shook his head. "No, love, not with you."

"I'm perfectly alright. Truly I am."

He appeared cavalier for anyone who might catch a glimpse of him through the windows. His voice, however, was anything but—it was that of a man tortured. "Truly I am not. No ruse has ever hurt before—none have required me to be so vile. And were it not enough that I said all those awful things all those weeks ago and watched Pierre drag you away, I went to that infernal party." His face scrunched into disdain. "I saw how they mocked you. Made a spectacle of you. Pierre deserved more than a shot to the arm. All of them deserve so much more for how they treated you in front of everyone. In front of *me*."

She said lightly, "I got my revenge." The full extent of which wouldn't be known for weeks, as she'd prepared the prince's suffering to continue long after she was gone.

"I courted the notion of stealing you back," he said, as though she hadn't spoken. "Lavinia had to stop me nearly every day, and I had to apologize more times than I can count for being an ass." The anger returned to his eyes, molten and gleaming. "Today I was supposed to walk into that church and take you away. But then I saw you standing there, wearing *his* jewels, *his* gown, *his* perfume, dressed like a pretty sacrifice to appease your family, and I would have happily burned everything down just to spite them. You're not meant to be stifled and trussed."

"Well...I am dead now," she said. "So I'm free to do as I please." The thought made her feel like soaring, like screaming and laughing manically simply because she could. Because she was *free*.

He scrubbed a hand over his face. "My God, Aurelia. You shouldn't have to die. I hate myself for putting you there. Of all the vile, wicked things a husband can do—"

"I had it handled," she said. "And I could've left at any time."

William rolled his lips between his teeth. "And far be it from me to keep anything from you, but in the future I will deny you. I'll deny you my cruelty and abandonment. I'll deny putting you anywhere you'll be treated as a toy." His eyes narrowed. "Are you *smiling*?"

She very nearly laughed. "I love you too, William. More than anything in this world. And now that I've won my freedom and proven myself to be formidable in all things piratey and awful, I am content."

His voice rose slightly. "As though nothing in the past few months has proven you're a pirate? This had to be the test, and not one of the hundred other incredible things you've done."

"I'm sorry this hurt you," she said.

"*I'm* hurt? Aurelia..." He gave an incredulous laugh. "You are utterly maddening sometimes. Did you not hear a thing I just said?"

Now that they neared the docks, she heaved herself onto the seat beside him, her voice as cold as his. "You're a liar, William. A foul, dirty liar. You lied from the moment we met when you told me your father was immortal or that you'd hurt me if I told. You lied when you said I was just a member of your crew and when you told the prince you were done with me."

He scowled. "Thank you?"

She grabbed his jaw. "But do you think I don't know you? You believe you hurt me, but you didn't. You haven't, because from your letters and your love, *I know you*, and I never once doubted you. You leaving me in that house was not cruelty—you prepared me to wreck Pierre, and I did. I'm still wrecking him, and I've loved it." She leaned in, her gaze boring into his. "My heart is entirely full, and I absolve you of any guilt over the game I asked you to play. I'll never ask it of you again. I won't want to."

The carriage halted. Beyond the window was a harbor filled with ships. "Good, because I'm never letting you go," he muttered. He eyed the door and nodded to it. "We should probably get out before the carriage explodes."

Her eyes bulged. "Has it been strapped with explosives this whole time?"

William looked worryingly unconcerned. "I had it done last night."

With a low curse, Aurelia grabbed her satchel, opened the door, and threw herself out while William burst with laughter behind her. "You know me," he reminded her.

Only one ship in the harbor teemed with people. It was the prince's own, a sleek, burgundy vessel populated with blue coats who hollered and scrambled as they unfurled the sails and weighed anchor.

Those who'd marched with the carriage now flowed around her as she and Copson trailed up the gangplank. Aurelia recognized many of them, but others were French who'd no doubt signed on to Copson's crew. He'd need them, now that it appeared he was stealing another ship for his fleet.

In the distance, the *Destiny's Revenge* hurtled down the English Channel toward the Dover Strait. Aurelia watched the massive ship grow nearer as she followed Copson toward the helm.

"Why's the *Destiny* here? You don't take it through the strait."

"Because we're flaunting," he said. "The French and English will have no excuse to ignore us or what we've done today."

At that moment, the wedding carriage exploded on the docks, erasing any evidence that she hadn't died at all. But she didn't even flinch, giddy as she followed William up the steps to the quarterdeck where Ralph stood at the helm, grinning and still dressed in French livery, though he'd abandoned his coat.

"Welcome back, Rowe," he said.

She gave a toothy smile. "Barrington."

Ralph called orders to the crew, which were repeated in French by someone nearby. The sails unfurled, and the ship pulled away from the docks.

It wasn't until they'd left the harbor and were gaining speed that a grumpy-looking Bartholomew mounted the steps, his black hair blowing in the wind. Now that she knew who he was, Aurelia saw the resemblance to his brothers—he'd taken the darkest features of both.

"Cut it a little close, didn't you?" he snapped at the captain. "You said you'd be here ten minutes earlier."

Copson frowned. "Mind your tone," he said lowly.

Bartholomew rolled his eyes, and then his gaze landed on Aurelia. At first, he didn't seem to recognize her, and alarm lit his expression as he glanced at the captain. "Pardon—"

Aurelia nodded in greeting and said, "Good to see you, Bartholomew."

He looked at her again, and after a second, his anxiety vanished as realization settled in. "Oh. You."

"Captain promised him a fishing ship in return for his help pulling the new crew together," Ralph said to Aurelia.

"*Temporary* help," Bartholomew insisted, still fixed under Copson's judgmental gaze and seeming not to care. "I refuse to be stuck here forever."

"Bart, this is Rebecca Rowe," Ralph said.

"Rebecca?" Bartholomew's face scrunched. "I thought your name was—"

"Aurelia Danby is dead," Copson said loudly enough for the crew to hear as they sailed into the channel. "Miss Rowe killed her."

"Rebecca," Ralph said with a shake of his head. "You really should get your jealousy under control."

Aurelia flipped her braid over her shoulder. "And you should keep your opinions to yourself."

"I quite like her jealousy," Copson said mildly.

Ralph smirked. "You deserve each other."

Bartholomew looked between the three of them, confusion written over his face. He mumbled, "I hate it here," and left the quarterdeck.

"He'll come around," Ralph said to his older brother.

The captain watched Bartholomew go. "He unsettles me."

Ralph laughed once. "Because he doesn't fear you?"

Copson's attention snapped to Ralph, and his words came lower, sharper. "Say that any louder, Ralph, and I'll keelhaul you."

"Sounds like an exquisite time." Ralph spun the wheel, bringing the ship alongside the *Destiny's Revenge*. They soared through the channel side by side, the prince's stolen ship easily keeping pace. A flag raised up the main mast, featuring an anchor with two crossed swords.

Though William's face was serene, his eyes were keen as he looked over his newest ship. Aurelia wondered what he saw and intended to ask him later when she'd have an hour or two to listen.

Night fell by the time they anchored well off the coast of England next to the *Ophelia* and the *Fortuna Royale*. William and Aurelia returned to the *Destiny's Revenge*, and they'd hardly crossed the threshold to their quarters when he kicked the door closed, grabbed her waist, and pulled her into a ruthless kiss.

His hands were in her hair, untying her braid. She knocked his hat off, and he slipped out of his coat and tossed it on the couch as they stumbled through the room, not breaking until she laughed and pulled away to shrug off her heavy satchel.

William watched her with dark eyes, his chest heaving. The moment she was free of the bag, he tugged her back.

"Wait!" she squealed. "Don't you want to see what I stole?"

His hold tightened. "No."

"William!" she laughed, dodging his kiss.

He caught her face in his hands. "Aurelia, I've spent every moment of the last month acutely aware of your absence." He pressed his forehead to hers, and she shivered as his words whispered over her skin. "I didn't think it possible to miss someone so much...now please don't make me beg."

After so long apart, she decided the jewels weren't that important at all. The satchel fell to the floor as she surrendered to him. He tugged her toward the bed, both of them kicking off their boots and peeling off their clothes until nothing separated them—not fabric or distance or time. They didn't speak, for they'd done enough of that on the other ship while something else simmered silently between them, stoked by heated glances and the occasional touch until it grew to stifling, pressing need.

So they thoroughly lost themselves in one another until the early hours of the morning.

When they were spent and satisfied, Aurelia laid on her side, facing him while she stared at a new painting hanging on the wall. It was small, with a beautiful, dancing lady. Hidden away, she knew, was also an antique vase that cost a fortune.

"You know, I've never taken revenge on someone," she said. "Not really."

He trailed his fingers through her unbound hair. "And how was it?"

The corner of her mouth lifted. "You were the voice in my head telling me to give in to my more creative ideas." She pulled her gaze from the painting to look at him. "They won't have discovered everything I did to them for at least three months."

The stolen items, the rumors, and the stories that would eventually be leaked to the public—her revenge would last, and it would be divine.

A laugh rumbled through him. "Bravo, love. You're almost as terrible as I am."

She blinked. "William."

He propped his head on his hand, which did impressive things for his bicep. "It's nothing to be ashamed of. I'm sinfully proud of you—it's just that I have several more years at this."

She narrowed her eyes, ignoring the swath of his hard chest, the long scar, and the muscular planes of his abdomen that disappeared beneath the green sheets. "I am your *wife* and therefore equal in all things, and that includes—biblically—your reputation."

"I don't think that's true," he said with the carefree, dazzling smile that made her melt. "But you're coming mighty close. I don't think Copson will be a name that inspires fear for one formidable pirate much longer, but two."

She sat up. "Am I to be a Copson, then?"

His eyes followed her, but he remained where he was. "After these past weeks, I want everyone to know Rebecca Rowe is more than my love—you are my bride, as cruel and bloodthirsty as myself. And they'll be terrified by us both, together, forever. Take my name if you want, or don't—everyone will know who we are either way."

She loved the thought of being known as both a dreadful pirate and the infamous captain's bride...but she also loved being Rebecca Rowe, and she'd keep the name for now. After all, she already had the surname that truly mattered.

Aurelia leaned down to run her finger along his jaw, drawing close enough see the rings of darker blue around his irises. "What about your immortality? Would you go on without me?"

"I suppose we'll have to return to the Fountain of Youth if it'll annoy you to die without me."

"You forgot where it was," she said. "And the witch died."

"Luckily I know where to find another—I think you'll like Tortuga." With a single, quick kiss, he pushed himself up to lean against the pillows and pulled her onto his chest. "We'll make you immortal too, and our children can change the story as they wish when we retire to some ostentatious estate bought with schemes and lies and piles of filthy gold."

Our children. She'd have children with William, and now that she was free, she could think about them, want them, plan for them. They'd be raised in two worlds, as William had been, but they would be safe with pirates for parents—and grandparents, uncles, aunts, and cousins. They wouldn't be neglected or forgotten.

She wanted that life. Oh, how she craved it. And she would have it, in time.

"Schemes," she said as his fingers trailed idle circles over her lower back. "What do you have in mind?"

"Well," he said, skimming her waist, "we have to go set the story straight with the few people we like, as they'll undoubtedly be reading the papers."

She sighed, content to be here in his arms, back on the ship she adored with the man she loved. "Our family?" she whispered, and bit her lower lip as delight sparkled through her.

He chuckled and kissed her brow as her heavy eyes slipped shut. "Yes, Lady Kingswood. Our family."

36

The Lies the Papers Told

No one on the *Destiny's Revenge* commented on Aurelia's absence or sudden return, which meant all had gone exactly according to plan. They assumed she'd been working for Copson and causing trouble in Calais after he'd finally turned over a noblewoman they'd heard little of and had never actually seen on board. Few cared if she'd ever existed at all, or if she merely hid among them—besides, there were enough pirates escaping awful pasts to care if a sad little rich girl was doing the same.

They only knew Rebecca Rowe.

At port, they spread word that Copson had recruited her in the spring after repeated attempts to get her to join his crew, since she was well liked and a formidable pirate. They said she fought valiantly against the French when they attacked Copson's fleet in the Caribbean, and the crew had also discovered she'd battled Copson himself when he went mad with siren sickness.

And no one bested the immortal captain—no one but the woman he was said to love.

There was no moment anyone could point to as the one the notorious pirate fell in love with her. There was conjecture it was when she solved the final riddle to find Robin's legendary treasure, or it might've been the day she was rumored to have won a game of poker against Copson and four infamous pirate kings he was known to associate with.

Many from Copson's crew shared a story about a mermaid who'd stolen Rebecca's voice to seduce the captain, and they said that's when they first suspected Copson's feelings. If anyone had any doubts, they vanished when the captain supposedly killed a man who touched her, and then he saved her after she went overboard in a storm. The couple survived to tell the tale—and began living together.

And then Rebecca Rowe killed Aurelia Danby in a fit of jealous rage after Copson stole her—again—from her royal wedding. The French said it was Copson who'd killed her, but the English liked the money from the captain's stories and happily took the tales the pirates spread, which was that Copson's lover had pulled the trigger.

After all, a woman pirate killing a lady was far more palatable, which made Copson still interesting as a murderer, but not a lady-killer. And with a fearsome woman at his side, he became much more romantic to the newspapers' readers, and sales increased as ladies of all social stations began to giggle and wonder what it must be like to love such a wicked man.

People might not have talked about the murder so much or so quickly had the captain not sailed the *Destiny's Revenge* through the Dover Strait. Witnesses in both Dover and Calais recognized the storied ship, and it immediately piqued interest—especially as Prince Pierre's ship quickly left the harbor in Calais. At first, people thought there would be a battle, but only after the ships had sailed away did they realize Copson had stolen it altogether, and had done so rather easily after infiltrating the military in Calais while everyone thought he was in Africa.

Days later, his crew spread word that he and his lover—or wife, depending on who told the story—had renamed the prince's ship. No one could say which of them had chosen the name, but the public agreed it was the most horrific, blatantly offensive thing they'd ever heard.

The *Aurelia*.

As though it wasn't enough for them to steal and murder, they also reminded the public of the horrendous thing they'd done and paraded it through the Atlantic, mocking the French, English, and everyone who'd heard reports of Aurelia Danby's abduction and prayed for her safe return.

It was tasteless. Horrible. And it sold thousands of papers.

There were other reports, which were not as widely read or cared much about since they were about the French king's fourth son. Royal diamonds and jewels and small, priceless items had been taken from his home in what seemed like a grand robbery. That might have been bad enough, but copies of the prince's financial records were also made public, revealing extensive gambling debts, embezzlement from the crown, and other misdeeds. One of the most embarrassing was a record of treatment after Captain Copson shot the prince in the Caribbean.

After hearing of this, along with how he'd paraded former mistresses and his illegitimate children in front of his now-dead fiancée at a party, the public couldn't help but wonder if maybe he'd deserved to be shot in the church.

Such was the state of Pierre's home—and the people who lived there—that blame for these mortifying revelations spread among his friends and lovers in spectacular fashion. Each of the prince's friends blamed the others for a multitude of reasons until they fled to new cities where they could start over in peace.

They would have no peace, however, as details of their secrets spread through French papers to humiliate them no matter where they went. And no one was more humiliated than the prince who'd wrecked his own home and twice lost his bride to a vindictive pirate.

Meanwhile, the Danbys hid in their home and did not attend any parties for the shame of their peers discovering the depth of their neglect toward a daughter few knew existed. The papers mentioned them specifically as the parents of the girl who'd been stolen, and the family name began to appear next to the prince's as his gross affairs were made public.

"Poor girl is better off dead," many said, "than with a family who loves her so little."

Word also spread about Copson scolding them on that dreadful wedding day, and with the knowledge of how much the pirate seemed to hate the family, no one wished to do business with them, lest the captain discover it and ruin them too.

But their anxiety was in vain, as Captain Copson and Rebecca Rowe cared little for the gossip and vanity of society. Their only interests were in what they might take from those who ruled proper society, and the ensuing entertainment.

After the death of Aurelia Danby, no one knew for certain where the pirates sailed. Many suggested they went to North Africa, or that they were pilfering the West Indies. Perhaps they stayed in Europe, or followed Atlantic trade routes to rob cargo ships and other pirates.

But as things of this nature often were, the fantasy was more exciting than the truth.

37

A Clever Devil Indeed

The carriage trundled down a country road lined with trees that had lost nearly all their leaves. Inside, autumn light cast long shadows over four handsomely dressed Kingswoods sitting in silence.

William and Aurelia sat on one bench, his arm thrown over the back of the seat and his eyes locked on the window to avoid his youngest brother's stare from where he sat across from him. Aurelia bit her lips to keep from smiling as William's arm tensed then relaxed...then tensed again with discomfort at being stuck in so small a space with Bartholomew.

Despite having been around for nearly a week, Aurelia was surprised to learn Bartholomew had not been told about his brother's marriage—until this morning, when she'd insisted William tell him. This was also when she'd learned most men did not talk or share details of mostly anything unless under duress.

So William had acquiesced when they'd all stepped off the *Ophelia*, saying only, "We're married," as he passed Bartholomew on the way to the carriage.

Bartholomew had replied with a bored, "Okay."

Aurelia didn't understand how so little could be shared when they'd had so much time to talk. William had spent most days on his newest ship—on which Bartholomew resided—overseeing its crew's initiation to the company at large and being considerably intimidating. But despite the brothers taking no time for any kind of reunion, there was no love lost, nor did the three of them think much of it.

With the revelation of personal news, however, came questions only Bartholomew would ask—solely to irritate his eldest brother while he was captive in the full carriage.

"So she's my sister?"

"Yes, that's how marriage works," William said.

Bartholomew glanced at Aurelia then back to his brother. "But why'd she marry *you*?"

Next to Bartholomew, Ralph pinched the bridge of his nose. "Bart, stop asking questions."

"I'm trying to understand." Bartholomew leaned toward Aurelia. "You've met other people, right?"

William kicked his youngest brother's boot. "Don't be rude."

"I thought I made a fine choice," Aurelia said, trying to conceal her amusement.

Bartholomew dropped his voice to a whisper. "Was there no one else?"

"Yes," she said. "We married on a deserted island."

"Oh." He sat back and looked at his oldest brother. "That makes sense. I guess something is better than nothing."

William shifted, squirming under Bartholomew's scrutiny. "You're a pest."

"Don't tell me the illustrious Captain Copson can't handle a man ten years his junior."

Ralph said, "Bart, *shut up*."

"I bought you a ship," William said, glowering. "What more do you want from me?"

Bartholomew narrowed his eyes. "*Did* you buy it?"

"*Yes*," William ground out.

"With dirty money."

Ralph and William heaved a collective sigh and covered their eyes. Bartholomew grinned and winked at Aurelia.

The carriage turned, and Aurelia craned her neck to peer out the window. Everything in her wanted to throw the door open and sprint ahead as the house loomed ahead of them. To her surprise, tears pricked her eyes. She sniffed them back as they pulled around the drive and stopped in front of Aunt Clara's home.

The coachman opened the carriage door and helped Aurelia out. William followed, saying to his brothers, "We'll see you at the house." Then he shut the door and waved the driver on.

Aurelia shuddered at the sight of the front door. Her beloved aunt would have read the papers by now and would know Aurelia was reported dead. For a week, Aurelia had dreaded what this news would be doing to her. She couldn't even send a letter as they waited for the dust to settle. Even then, the news was still at a fever pitch with new articles and details written every day—not all of them true, but many accurate enough.

William took her hand. "All will be well."

She was reminded of another day, many years ago, when she'd last stood on this doorstep with him and he assured her of the same. They would tell Aunt Clara a fantastic story—and as he said, all would be well.

William lifted the heavy brass knocker and let it drop. A moment later, the door swung open. The footman looked at William first, but when his gaze moved to Aurelia, his jaw fell. Tears his filled eyes, and he pressed his wrist under his nose as he began to cry.

"Please, please come in!" he begged, swinging the door wide.

They walked in, and the sniffling footman shut the door.

She could hardly believe it had only been four months since she was last here. She'd lived an entire lifetime in a single summer, and though the walls of her aunt's home were the same, and the art was just as ugly, it felt different. But only Aurelia had changed.

"It's not as bad as I remember," William said, his eyes roving the foyer. He brought his gaze to hers and gave an encouraging nod.

The footman edged toward the parlor, gesturing for Aurelia to enter. She glided toward the yellow room and gently pulled her hand from William's as she nudged the door open.

Her aunt sat in a wing-backed chair facing the window, her tuft of silver hair visible above the faded gold upholstery. As Aurelia moved silently over the plush carpet, she saw her aunt had traded her gray gowns for black.

On the table beside her was a paper from several days ago, its head-line printed in large bold letters across the front.

REBECCA ROWE MURDERS AURELIA DANBY

Aurelia slowly moved around the table and said quietly, so as to not startle her aunt, "You shouldn't believe what the papers say. They're awfully full of lies."

Aunt Clara looked up. First she shrank back, but then her eyes welled and her lips parted. With a heart-wrenching wail, she surged to her feet and gathered Aurelia into a tight embrace.

"I'm alive," Aurelia said, clinging to her aunt. "I'm alive."

The old woman sobbed, taking no notice of William, the footman, butler, or the half dozen servants who entered the room. "You died! All the papers—everyone said you were killed by that dreadful pirate!" Aunt Clara leaned away, dabbing her eyes with an old handkerchief. "And you were taken, oh my child, you were stolen so horribly."

Aurelia smiled. "I'm perfectly well."

Aunt Clara's hands fluttered over Aurelia's face, as though she could hardly believe her niece was not a ghost. "How are you alive?"

"Copson brought me home," she said. "I daresay he and his crew took great care of me," her smile widened, "and I had the most wonderful time."

"Oh," Aunt Clara breathed, taking in Aurelia's tanned face and full, pink cheeks. She gripped her shoulders, feeling the strength that hadn't been there before. "My dear...you've had adventures." Her attention moved then to their audience of sniffling servants. A shadow seemed to lift from the household and she called for tea, sending them scrambling to the kitchens.

And then her gaze fell on William Kingswood.

Before she could say anything, he bowed. "Lady Wedderburn," he said with his most charming smile. "A pleasure to see you again."

"Lord Kingswood." Aunt Clara's hand dropped to Aurelia's. Her thumb searched for a ring, which she quickly found, and her gaze snapped to her niece. "Are you—?" She looked at William. "Have you—?"

William and Aurelia nodded at the same time. With a huff, Aunt Clara flapped her hands at both of them. "Sit, sit."

Aurelia settled on the old couch across from her aunt's chair. William sat beside her and took her hand.

"Do the Kingswoods know?" Aunt Clara asked, eyeing their clasped hands.

"They will," William said. "We came to ask for your blessing first."

Aunt Clara's eyes widened. "*My* blessing?"

"The Danbys don't know I'm alive," Aurelia said. "And we don't care so much for their approval, but we would like yours."

The servants returned then, marching through the room one by one to set the small table with tiny plates and sandwiches and a pot of tea. Their interruption gave Aunt Clara time to compose herself.

When it was only the three of them once again, Aunt Clara's tears had dried, and she started with, "The letters?"

Aurelia didn't bother to suppress her grin. "He told me stories."

She raised her brows. "All those years—only stories?"

"He travels," she said. "And he told me all about his adventures."

Aunt Clara narrowed her eyes at William. "How did you find her after that pirate took her?"

"I recognized her at port several months ago." The lie rolled off his tongue so casually that even Aurelia was tempted to believed him. "It was good to see a familiar face abroad, and I practically begged her to sit with me for a while and share how she'd ended up at sea." He looked at Aurelia. "We found we have much in common, and I couldn't tear myself away. But then she was gone again, and everything happened rather quickly after that." He glanced back to her aunt. "When I heard about her return to the prince, I found Captain Copson and begged him to bring her back."

Aunt Clara pressed a hand over her heart. "You know him?"

"I've met him," William said reservedly. "He's a terrifying man, but he took pity on me when he saw I was so besotted, and he owed me for giving him a map. He brought her back—rather dramatically—and I couldn't bear to lose her again, so I asked for her hand."

Aunt Clara studied them for long enough that apprehension began to bloom in Aurelia's chest. Did her aunt know they were lying? Beside her, William remained utterly calm and stroked the back of her hand.

Then Aunt Clara heaved a sigh and said, "It seems I've lost a bet to the countess."

William snorted quietly as Aurelia said, "Pardon?"

"Well, as you can imagine, I was quite distraught over news of your kidnapping," Aunt Clara said, picking a piece of lint off her skirt and flicking it away. "The countess was a comfort to me."

William gave Aurelia a look that said, *I told you.*

"You don't gamble," Aurelia said, horrified that this was how Cecily Kingswood had comforted her aunt and wondering how on earth Aunt Clara would've agreed to such a thing.

Aunt Clara laughed once. "You don't know a thing about me, child. A woman as wealthy as I am deserves a petty bet here and there, and Cecily is sharp and hard to beat."

"But the devil, Aunt Clara!"

Aunt Clara sniffed. "You can't lose a thing with the Lord on your side, Aurelia. It would do you good to know that."

"It's true," William said with a devilish smirk. "Lady Wedderburn, do you play cards?"

"No cards," Aurelia snapped at him.

"The countess said she'd write to William and ask him to look for you after I read what that awful pirate had done," Aunt Clara said, snapping a fan open to breeze away her displeasure at the topic of pirates. "It calmed my nerves to know that she had."

"She did," William said. But as Aunt Clara closed her eyes to pray her thanks, he looked at Aurelia and gave the tiniest shake of his head.

Aunt Clara opened her eyes. "The countess also didn't believe in your despairing of love, and what with you choking over the mere mention of her eldest son"—William's brows rose—"she assumed you'd get on with him quite well should he actually find you. She wagered there would be a love match, and it was the perfect distraction for my anxious mind. It was a comfort to think you might fall in love rather than be terrified. The earl, as well, said William would find you easily, though I was sure it would be Ralph you came back with—and that, dear, is the bet I lost." She turned her beady eyes to William. "I hope this is the most of your dealings with pirates. I don't want my niece in danger if you intend to travel."

William shook his head, looking rather serious. "My lady, I assure you no pirate is a threat to her. She is utterly safe."

Aurelia grinned to herself, thinking it was much safer to be the most threatening people at sea, but Aunt Clara didn't need so many details.

Aunt Clara nodded, satisfied. "Then you have my blessing." She closed her fan and pointed it. "But I insist on regular visits or letters. You are as dear to me as a daughter, Aurelia, and while your mother may scorn such a blessing, I certainly do not. I will not live another week like this thinking you are dead." She lowered the fan. "I am very pleased you are married. Especially to a sensible, respectable young man."

"The most sensible," Aurelia said.

"Very respectable," William agreed.

"You will still be part of my life," Aunt Clara said with finality, "or I will die."

"And you won't tell anyone you saw me?" Aurelia was suddenly shy. She didn't want to ask her aunt to lie for her, even through a lie of omission. But for all the things that surprised her about Aunt Clara, she hoped she might grant this one request. "I'm not overly eager to prove the rumors wrong. We wish to live a quiet life, and all that's happened is anything but."

Aunt Clara pursed her lips, then shook her head. "I won't if you don't wish me to."

"Thank you," William said. "And I assure you'll hear from us monthly, at the very least."

Aunt Clara gave a firm nod and reached for the teapot in the middle of the table. "The tea grows cold. Will you stay a while?"

Aurelia looked at William. "May we?"

He inclined his head. "For as long as you like."

Aunt Clara poured the tea, her eyes on the steaming drink but her eyebrows raised high enough to give the impression of attentiveness. "Now, tell me about these grand adventures."

38

The Kingswood of Consequence

After nearly two hours with her aunt, Aurelia and William left the estate and began the walk down the lane. William's arm hung around her shoulders, and she held on to his waist, leaning into him as the chilly breeze teased her hair and pulled at her hat and skirts with gentle insistence.

"Are you nervous?" she asked, stepping on a particularly crunchy leaf as it scuttled across the road.

Until now, William had spoken of seeing his family again as though it hadn't been five years, with no reservation or even terrible excitement. But then his breathing had changed after they left Aunt Clara's.

"Perhaps a little," he said, bowing his head to watch Aurelia hunt for more leaves to pulverize beneath her boots. "But only because my mother will tell me it's been too long, and my father will know everything I have to say before I say it." Another breath, and his tone became reserved. "Abroad, I am a king. At home, I'm just Will. No one impressive, having done nothing my parents didn't do first. It's not a bad thing...but it can be rather jarring."

She took his hand hanging over her shoulder and threaded their fingers together. "Now I'm here to take all the attention. I'm terribly sorry for that."

He squeezed her hand. "You're not sorry for anything."

They rounded the bend, and the grand white house appeared before them.

"No welcome party," William mused. "You'd think they'd be waiting at the door."

"Your brothers must be too fascinating to forsake."

"Neither of them is more fascinating than I," he said dryly, mounting the steps. He pushed through the massive front door.

The foyer was empty, but fragrant from a vase full of autumn flowers. William crossed the entryway to peer down the corridor. As the smiling footman appeared and greeted them, William handed over his coat and said, "My family?"

"In the parlor—"

The earl's voice boomed down the hall. "*William Kingswood.*"

William tensed.

"Tell me the perfectly reasonable explanation for why the papers say you *killed the neighbor.*"

Aurelia remained out of sight in the foyer, unbuttoning her coat while the footman waited to take it from her.

"Killed the neighbor?" William frowned and spun to Aurelia as his father's steps neared. "I didn't kill her. She's right—"

"*Aurelia Danby,*" the earl hissed. Aurelia had never heard her name spoken so viciously.

"Yes, that neighbor." William held out his hand. "Aurelia, my love, would you please come here before he throttles me?"

As soon as she was free from her coat, she drifted to his side.

The earl moved down the hall like a shadow, his scarred face drawn in a glower dark enough to give her pause. But as soon as he recognized her, his expression softened.

The countess emerged from the parlor. "Alexander, don't—" Seeing Aurelia and William, her hand flew to her mouth. She flew toward them, passing her husband to throw her arms around Aurelia in a crushing hug.

"Wait, did you really think I—?" William cut off as his brothers entered the corridor. "You didn't tell them she's alive? You've been home for nearly three hours!"

Ralph leaned against the door frame while Bartholomew shoved his hands in his pockets and shrugged, saying, "I have a life to talk about outside of yours."

"I wanted to see what they'd do," Ralph said, nodding to their parents.

"God, I'll—" The threat cut short as the earl grasped William's arm and tugged him into an embrace. Then he stepped back and placed a hand on the countess's arm to beckon her to his side.

The earl said to William, "After I read the papers, I expected you to send word about it, as you're usually so quick to do when your antics are particularly worrisome, but when you didn't show up or write—"

William laughed incredulously. "She's Rebecca Rowe. Haven't you seen that name in the papers?" He glared at his brothers. "Seriously, *nothing*?"

Ralph and Bartholomew shook their heads.

"It's a rarity to see you squirm," Ralph said.

"We rather enjoy it," Bartholomew added.

William reached for Aurelia's hand. "She's my wife," he said, his voice thick with happiness. "We had to get the kings to leave her alone."

Both the earl and countess stared at Aurelia, who beamed proudly. Then the countess said, "Oh, I knew it had to be a ruse. No son of mine would lack so much cleverness to kill a girl he ought to love."

"Faking a murder is a little excessive," Bartholomew muttered. "You could've just come back and announced you were married, and no one would've argued it. But I suppose no one is more dramatic than Will."

Ralph barked a laugh. "Wait till you get to know Aurelia."

"That *drama* pays your wages," Aurelia said. "Several times over."

The countess reached for Aurelia's hand. "I was devastated to hear about your engagement, but then we read that Will picked you up." She looked at her son, her dark gaze filled with pride. "I knew you'd keep her safe. And she'd be happy."

The mischief in the earl's eyes looked so much like William's. "You made quite the scene across the channel."

Bartholomew grumbled, "Don't encourage him."

"And you're *married*." The countess released Aurelia's hand and drew William into an embrace, tears running down her pretty cheeks. "You brought me a daughter."

Eyes pricking, Aurelia looked to the earl and found strength in his severe features.

"Do the Danbys know you're alive?" he asked, moving around his wife to stand before Aurelia.

"No, sir," she said firmly. "And they won't."

She half expected him to frown and tell her the Danbys would be glad to know she was alive—that telling them would be the kind thing to do.

But Alexander Kingswood did no such thing. His eyes glittered with vengeance, and his lips slowly curved into the worst, wickedest grin she'd ever seen. And then he laughed—a deep, booming sound that echoed down the hall. It lasted only a moment before he offered his arm to lead her toward the parlor, followed by William and the countess.

"Troublesome young woman," the earl said. "You'll make a fine Kingswood."

Ralph and Bartholomew had already taken one of the sofas, so William threw himself into a plush chair and closed his eyes, his long limbs sprawling and his voice tinged with sleepiness as he said, "You might've warned me, Mother, for I hear you suspected this."

The countess sank primly onto a chair. "Some things you must puzzle out for yourself, Will. Though perhaps I'd have hinted at it if you came home more—"

"Yes, yes," William said, waving his hand. "I'm preoccupied to a fault." His eyes opened then, watching Aurelia settle into the seat next to him. She removed her hat and smoothed her skirt, grinning like a fool to be among her family—all of them fine people and marvelous pirates. He smiled at her before his eyes slipped shut again.

"You have quite the story," the countess said. "Tell us everything."

"From the beginning," the earl added. "The *very* beginning."

Now that they were home, William kept every promise he'd made on the island. He courted Aurelia properly—despite her insistence he didn't have to—inviting her to tea each day even though they lived in the same room and dined at the same table. The earl and countess joined them most days, as did Ralph and Bartholomew, and the family spoke openly of piracy as though it were as common as the weather, and it was not strange or terrifying.

Aurelia visited her aunt as well, and William always joined her. Most times, he sat quietly and listened, but Aunt Clara enjoyed his wit, and Aurelia heard her chuckle more in a handful of weeks than she had in the previous seventeen years.

Autumn faded into colder, shorter days, and William took Aurelia to a winter fair in London for skating and warm drinks. Even with so many people around, he stole a kiss, and neither of them cared if they were caught or scorned for their impropriety. He didn't even need to defend her honor against anyone objecting to her abduction, because even though everyone had heard of Aurelia Danby by now, no one had known her well enough to remember her face, and so they didn't recognize her with her proud, healthy stature, sun-kissed cheeks, and the happy gleam in her eyes.

The few who did wonder quickly dismissed their conjecture as she was introduced as Lady Kingswood, the young Lord Kingswood's wife who *might* resemble a pale and pouting wallflower they'd once seen sulking at the edges of a ball. All the while, Aurelia flaunted her ring, her husband, and her Kingswood name as though it made her a queen.

And because the countess insisted they make their marriage legal, they married again in the small chapel on the Kingswoods' country estate in a simple ceremony presided over by a priest and witnessed by the Kingswoods, Aunt Clara, Greyson and Hester, and Lavinia, who looked rather at home on Ralph's arm. Once again, Aurelia and William vowed their lives and love to one another, and she finally gave him a ring—a simple gold band like hers. Snow began to gently fall outside the chapel windows as William pulled her close and tipped her chin to kiss her in a moment she thought was rather magical.

There was no announcement in the paper, and their marriage certificate listed her name as Aurelia C. Smith.

They stayed through Christmas and the New Year, and the night before they were to return to the *Destiny's Revenge*—where they would most definitely have a third wedding—they attended a stuffy ball at Aunt Clara's.

Dressed in a deep blue gown with sparkling jewels in her hair and around her neck, Aurelia entered the house on William's arm. She looked to the balcony over the foyer as though she might see her sixteen-year-old self standing above them, eagerly waiting with a letter. There was no one there, of course, but the thrill of a dream come true moved her toward laughter or tears—she couldn't tell which it would be—as he led her into the ballroom and to the center of floor.

"Ready?" he asked.

She grinned. "I've been ready for a long time."

His answering smile was radiant. And here in his arms, surrounded by family and friends, she finally had all she ever wanted. It had not come the way she thought it would, but for all she'd dreamed and wondered and prayed, it was here now.

The string quartet struck up a waltz, and William swept her away. She firmly believed then that reality was much better than the stories, and she'd just as certainly live happily ever after.

Epilogue

THE QUEEN OF PORT ROYAL

William Kingswood sat at a table in the corner of a smoky room in
a small house on the outskirts of Port Royal. Next to him, Frederick
Henry leisurely grumbled his way through some story he'd told a hundred times since Will was a kid, so he knew all the right places to nod
and grunt and laugh based solely on the one-eyed pirate's inflection.

Soulless Killian didn't bother to listen as he played cards with the
turquoise-clad Hein, who also ignored Frederick's story. It was only
because Will was the youngest of them that he, specifically, was sub-
jected to the repetitive storytelling.

His false name, Robert Copson, was nothing impressive here—it
was merely a crown passed from father to son. These three older pirates
were practically his uncles, and since they could humble him in any
number of ways with embarrassing stories from his own childhood, he
was left to indulge Frederick. So he kept his mouth shut and nodded
and grunted and laughed as though he were listening and not watching Aurelia play cards with Davy Silver across the room.

"Do it again," Aurelia said, and watched with narrowed gray eyes
as Davy thoroughly shuffled the deck, cut it twice, and shuffled again.
Then he started laying the cards, one by one, on the table before her,
their faces and suits clear through the gloom.

Ace. King. Queen. Jack. Ten. All hearts.

Will tipped his head to shadow his smirk beneath his hat so Frederick wouldn't see it and know he wasn't paying attention. Aurelia leaned back in the green velvet chair with a heavy sigh, her brows pinched. Davy grinned, still placing the cards on the table in order.

"I don't understand," she said. "You shuffled it."

"Into order," he said, his deep voice filling the corner of the dimly lit room.

"But how?"

"Practice," he told her, sweeping the cards into a pile and shuffling again. After a minute, he dealt her a hand.

"Well now I don't want to play with you," she said. "How do I know you didn't just give me a terrible hand?"

He released a single booming laugh. "You don't."

She grumbled a curse and picked up her hand. Then she squinted at him from across the table. He smiled back. "If you're taking me for an idiot..." she said.

"You'll what?"

She settled deeper into her chair and tossed a few coins into the center of the table.

"Shame about the Danby girl," Davy said, betting his own coins.

Will turned his head at this, Frederick's ego be damned. Next to him, the older pirates looked up too.

Like uncles they may be, but they knew nothing about the Kingswoods—neither did they know the truth about Rebecca Rowe and who she really was. Of course, they knew there were false names at play—they weren't idiots. But to say it so specifically...Davy was testing her.

"Eh." Aurelia met his bet and raised.

Will glanced at the older gentlemen out of the corner of his eye. Hein stroked his chin with a smile while Killian stared at Davy and Aurelia. Frederick grinned at Will.

Will rolled his eyes. *Bastard*. Thankfully, Aurelia was no half-rate liar. She was nearly as good as he was, but that wouldn't matter if the kings had already decided the truth about her.

Though even if they knew the truth, they'd most certainly keep it to themselves.

"Must've really disliked the lass," Davy said to Aurelia.

She shrugged, unbothered, as he saw her raise and showed his cards. Aurelia slapped hers on the table and glared. "Stop it, Silver."

"Don't let her win, Davy," Will said. He moseyed to her side where he settled a firm hand on her shoulder. "She's already so terribly spoiled."

"Like you'd say no to a couple extra gold pieces, Copson," the pirate said, lounging in his chair. "You'll need the bonus."

Will arched one brow. "Meaning?"

Davy picked up a glass of whiskey and swirled it. "You spoil your girl—you'll spoil your child even worse."

Aurelia frowned at Will. He met her gaze. Had he said something he shouldn't have? Had she? His eyes dipped to her stomach where a small swell pressed against her shirt.

Will trusted the men in this room perhaps better than anyone beyond his own family. There was surely no harm in them knowing, so he smiled, confirming what Davy had already seen.

"You said it wasn't noticeable," Aurelia said.

"It wasn't this morning," Will said. "But I suppose you do look a little...swollen."

"Swollen!"

He tilted his head, adoring the pink flush in her cheeks. "Glowing?"

Aurelia pushed to her feet. "I better be glowing. I'm *only* ever glowing."

He didn't back away, swallowing his laughter as she peered up at him. "Well, right now you're glaring, which is much less—"

"Cop*son*," Davy Silver said, setting his glass on the table with a thud. "Best watch yourself with your lady in her condition."

Will pulled her to his side. "You're always glowing," he said to her, his voice gentle. "Nothing short of entirely lovely."

It had only been a few weeks since the night Aurelia had told him he'd be a father. She'd written him a letter to tell him, which he'd kept on his desk, visible among neat stacks of documents.

He was ridiculously happy. Most of his favorite memories involved sailing with his family, and now that he would have a child of his own, he imagined teaching his son or daughter to love adventure as much as he and Aurelia did.

"What's this about glowing?" Frederick Henry wandered over, a glass of brandy in his hand. Surrounded in his ever-present cloud of smoke, he looked at Aurelia, then turned his one-eyed gaze to Will's hand resting on her stomach. "Don't you dare make me feel old."

"But age suits you so well," Will replied evenly. "I hadn't planned to make you feel anything, but it appears Mr. Silver pays too close attention to my dear Miss Rowe."

Henry's frown had progressed deeper into his face. "I remember the day your father and mother told us about you," he said. "I was more surprised it took them so long—they were all over each other in Tortuga."

"Everyone was," Hector said. "Ah, to be young."

"I'd desperately love not knowing any of this," Will said, and looked at his wife. "I believe it's a fine time to take our leave."

"If you insist," she said.

Fearing Hein would make some mention of the time he'd been close with Will's mother—an uncomfortable subject that left Will feeling rather green, which Hein found very funny—they bid their farewells and left.

"You could've told me you all were so close," Aurelia said as they walked. Her compass—which had once been his—appeared in her hand, swinging on its chain. "All those months ago."

"Didn't I?" She gave him a dirty look, and he smiled. "I told you we were friends."

"But you acted like we were in some kind of danger."

"They don't trust newcomers," Will said. "Taking you there *was* dangerous, but more for me than you. Even then, they're just a bunch of pissy old men with too much gold."

She raised an eyebrow. "And the poker game I won for help finding your crew. You knew Davy counted cards."

He smirked. "Of course I knew." Despite the other captains trying to annoy him that day, he'd seen Davy winking at Aurelia. "What of it?"

"Your ruse seems like it was rather...unnecessary." There was no bite to her words—in fact, she was grinning.

It was because of that grin that he took her elbow and pivoted, backing her against a wall and caging her with his arms. "Don't tell me you didn't *enjoy* our little game."

There was that beautiful blush. Nearly a year married, and he loved that he could still fluster her. "It's not about enjoying it," she said.

"What is it about?" He ran one knuckle down her cheek, watching her gray eyes widen as her thoughts spun loose. "The flirting? Hein wouldn't have left you alone had I not said we were lovers. He does have *some* manners, but only if the conditions are right." He brushed a piece of hair out of her face. "Or did you want a filthy old man ogling you?"

He hadn't wanted Hein ogling her. He'd been so dreadfully annoyed the moment the pirate had opened his mouth. Annoyed and perhaps a little...possessive.

"You sat me on your lap," she said, her gaze flicking between his eyes and his lips. "You were so *close*, and I thought it was because you had to be."

"*That* was because I wanted you," he murmured. "And I wanted to know what it would feel like if you were mine."

Her blush deepened. He, however, couldn't help the small twinge of regret. He'd pulled her into that ruse knowing full well that his brother might kill him for it if he found out. Will had betrayed Ralph that day, but...well, it was only a *small* bit of regret. Ralph would never have had Aurelia anyway, because her heart had already belonged to Will.

That was a much bigger regret—that he hadn't even considered Aurelia until he saw her on the *Purgatory*. He'd always dismissed her as a little girl to be pitied until her debut when he'd started to think of her more, but not in any true romantic sense. She'd been an enigma, a curiosity, like a beautiful clock one might pause to consider, then forget about until it chimed while it waited, waited, waited for someone to look its way.

He'd been a fool.

"As for the poker game," Will said, "you seemed happy to play, whether it was rigged or not. I wasn't going to dissuade you. You wouldn't have wanted me to."

"Don't you just know me so well," she grumbled, but the delighted sparkle in her eye betrayed her.

"Tell me you wish me to apologize for that day," he said, "and I'll get on my knees and beg your forgiveness." He kissed the corner of her mouth, and her breaths turned shallow. She wouldn't want his apology, despite his willingness to give it. He'd nearly apologized that day before she'd all but erupted with glee after they left the house. It had been so damn endearing that he hadn't dared speak the words and taint her joy.

Thankfully, she'd since proven just how much she *hadn't* minded his actions, though he'd since discovered how thoroughly he enjoyed taunting her.

She laughed and turned her head to peck a kiss to his lips before she twisted away and traipsed down the street, the compass swinging from her fingers. "You're a tease," she called over her shoulder.

Smiling, he jogged the few steps to catch up with her and, like he had last summer, threw his arm over her shoulders. "You're doomed to my teasing for the rest of your immortal days, Rowe." He kissed her hair and was happy that he could.

He'd never known contentment like this—had never thought he would. But as he trailed through Port Royal with the girl he'd met in the woods, the woman who'd wanted to know him when others had decided he was too dangerous, too cruel, too vengeful, his contentment was nearly overwhelming.

There were many stories he still hadn't told her—names she didn't know and places she'd not yet seen. But in time...yes, in time she'd know everything, and he was not afraid for her to know those tales—she'd already heard the worst of them, and for all the wicked things he'd done, she still loved him.

Will was far more than fortunate—no matter how much he had in his coffers, no matter his name, he knew, without a doubt, that he was the richest man in the world.

Acknowledgements

This book has been ten years in the making. From the day I sat down and wrote about a girl named Rebecca being stolen by the handsome Captain Copson, I knew I wanted to one day finish a classic pirate romance filled with clichés and adventure. It wasn't until 2023, when I finally let go of a broken dream, that this story finally found its heart.

My first thanks goes to God. Thank you for my life, my gifts, the good and the bad, and this book. I told you I wanted to quit writing, that I'd take the L and move on, but then you took my devastation and remade it into this story. It changed everything.

Elizabeth Young. Gilly. Gillzabeth. Thank you for championing silly Aurelia from the start, catching my literature references, and seeing the humor in remembering girlhood. This book was made better for your confidence in it. Thank you for talking me down off ledges, listening to me complain about Ralph, and for texting me all your favorite lines.

Danielle Harrington—my birthday twin, writer and editor extraordinaire, and stakes queen. Thank you for loving on my books and for all your encouragement. You've inspired me in so many ways, and I'm so grateful that I've gotten to witness your journey (and now be part of it). You're just incredible.

K'lai and Abigail—thank you for Thursday nights and getting excited about lusty, busty pirates. You're both inspiring and encouraging, and I'm so thankful for our weekly chats. You keep me going. For that matter, thank you to the rest of the Wednesdays—Ellery, Rebecca, Becca, and Jess. All of you ladies have been such an amazing part of my writing journey and I love you all dearly.

Kellin—thank you for beta reading and proofing. I appreciate your eye for romance and for am so thankful you loved this book as much as you did! You helped me be so much more confident in it, and I'm so grateful that you read it.

Faith, thank you for all the hard work you put into formatting this book for me over your summer!

And to Jared—you're the best husband in the world. Thank you for supporting me in my dreams.

And thank you, reader, if you've made it this far, for picking up my book. I've thought of you every step of the way. I hope you come back for more!

Made in the USA
Middletown, DE
09 September 2024

60658193R00243